PRAISE FOR *THE DEAD KEY*

"Fast paced, faultlessly written, and engaging, this is a page turner with a very surprising and plausible twist. There are not enough superlatives to describe this engrossing novel."

—*Publishers Weekly*

EARLY PRAISE FOR *THE BURIED BOOK*

"An evocative, deeply-felt story of innocence lost that glows with the slow burn of suspense."

—Lou Berney, Edgar-award-winning author of *The Long and Faraway Gone*

"A beguiling family drama that sucks you in and never lets go."
—Simon Wood, author of *The One That Got Away*

"With a remarkable protagonist, a fully-rendered setting, and plenty of surprises, D.M. Pulley weaves an enthralling mystery while also showing the power of a child's love for his mother."
—Ann Howard Creel, bestselling author of *While You Were Mine*

THE
BURIED
BOOK

OTHER BOOKS BY D.M. PULLEY

The Dead Key

THE
BURIED
BOOK

A Novel

D.M. PULLEY

LAKE UNION
PUBLISHING

Published by Lake Union Publishing, Seattle

www.apub.com

Amazon, the Amazon logo, and Lake Union Publishing are trademarks of Amazon.com, Inc., or its affiliates.

ISBN-13: 9781503936720
ISBN-10: 1503936724

Cover design by Kimberly Glyder

Printed in the United States of America

For Jack

CHAPTER 1

Let's start from the beginning, shall we?
Please state your name and age for the record.

"Jasper."

"Hmm," he mumbled.

"Jasper, wake up." His mother shook his shoulder. "You need to get up, baby. Get dressed."

"What?" Jasper Leary opened his eyes. It was still dark outside his window. "What's wrong?"

"We're goin' up to the farm. Won't that be fun, baby?" She flipped on the bedside lamp, blinding him for a moment.

Jasper sat up and blinked at the windup clock on the bedside table. It wasn't even 6:00 a.m.

"C'mon, sweetie," she called from the hallway. "Let's go! The day won't wait."

He was only nine years old, but Jasper could tell by the awkward lilt in her voice that she was trying to sound cheerful. Frowning, he pulled on his clothes. He double-checked the calendar on the way out the door. It was Tuesday, August 12, 1952. His mother should have been heading to work down at the dairy that morning. She put on a strained smile for him as he stumbled out the back door of their apartment building and into their '47 Chevy.

Be happy, he told himself, trying to shake the feeling that something was wrong. The tires squealed slightly as they pulled out of the parking lot. She hardly ever took off work just to be with him. *Maybe it will be fun, like she said.* He threw her an uneasy grin, but she kept her eyes on the road. Her lips pressed together in a thin line. Her brow furrowed just enough to give away an emotion somewhere between upset and anger. An emotion he wasn't supposed to see.

Jasper had a bad habit of noticing things he wasn't supposed to. *You're too smart for your own good,* she liked to say. If he asked her why she was pretending to be happy, she might give him a worried smile and tousle his hair. Or she might smack the smart right out of his mouth. *Children should be seen and not heard.* Especially when his mother was upset.

Out the rear window, the smokestacks and stone towers of Detroit disappeared over the horizon. Jasper rested his chin on the edge of the passenger door and watched the rows of houses rush past his window as the sun rose behind their roofs. Tract homes gave way to walls of grain as they headed north. As his mother's silence grew louder, Jasper couldn't help but worry it was all his fault.

They'd almost reached Burtchville before he dared ask, "Why are we going to Uncle Leo's?" He did his best to keep any trace of a whine out of his voice, but he couldn't quite muster "happy."

She sighed and pulled the little metal flask out from the bottom of her purse.

Jasper took a quick inventory of the last few days, searching for what he might've done or not done to upset her. He couldn't think of one chore he'd missed. There wasn't any schoolwork to neglect. He'd spent most of his days in the park down the street. The rest of the time he helped out in Carbo's Bakery downstairs. Mrs. Carbo insisted he stay and have dinner when his mother worked late and his father was pulling second shift at the auto plant. He'd had dinner with the Carbo family a lot lately, but he couldn't remember complaining.

The shadow of a barn passed over him.

His mother tipped her head back and took a long drink from the flask. Her eyes didn't blink as they stared down the long drive down Route 25 to Harris Road. He wanted to tell her he was sorry for whatever he'd done.

She finally glanced down at him. "Wipe that look off your face. You love the farm. Don't you, baby?"

Jasper forced a nod. He did love the farm. It was an exotic world of giant animals and loud machinery.

"Cheer up then, silly."

Outside his window, the small shops and cafés of Burtchville came and went along with the boats dotting Lake Huron. He craned his neck as it all blew past, trying not to notice her taking another drink.

As they turned from the two-lane highway down the bumpy dirt road that led to his uncle's farm, something on the horizon caught his eye.

"Look, Mom! A fire!"

Her eyes followed his finger pointing to smoke rising behind the thick trees on the east side of Route 25, and she nearly ran the car into a ditch. The brakes screeched. "Dammit, Jasper! You can't holler like that when someone's driving!"

"I—I didn't."

She slapped at the hand still pointing up at the sky. "Just someone burning a fallow field." But she stared at it a second too long, then took another pull from the flask.

The veins stood up angrily on the backs of her hands as she squeezed the wheel. The car lurched forward again. They rattled through the holes in the road while Jasper kept an eye on the plume of smoke. He wanted to ask what a fallow field was but thought better of it.

A mile later, they slowed down at a slight break in the plantings outside his window. There was no sign or address or any indication anyone lived there at all besides a rusty mailbox hidden in a thatch of long grass. His mother steered the car down a two-track driveway through the wildflowers and trees for a quarter mile before a wood cabin and a faded red barn appeared on either side of a small clearing.

The cabin was more of a pirate's fort than a house. Two crooked but clean windows looked out onto a narrow covered porch. The roof was a patchwork of new and old wood shingles. Its mismatched siding was covered in fresh whitewash, and the stone chimney was smoking, even in the August heat.

His mother cut the engine, and Jasper bolted from the car. A hand-dug outhouse sat twenty feet behind the cabin. The first thing Jasper liked to do when he arrived at Uncle Leo's was take a piss in that tiny shed just like a real cowboy. He sprinted to his sanctuary and slammed the door shut.

She didn't call after him.

He unbuttoned his pants and plopped down onto the small round hole cut through a worn pine board. He didn't really have to go. Half a Sears, Roebuck and Co. catalog sat next to him. He ripped off a sheet and squinted in the slivers of light streaming through the door to see a picture of the latest model sewing machine. *Did Mr. Sears and Mr. Roebuck know their pretty pages would end up at the bottom of an outhouse?* he wondered and set the sheet down.

At low volume, Jasper narrated in his best radio-show voice. "The Lone Ranger moseyed over to the ol' outhouse to answer a call o' nature. Little did our hero suspect that trouble was brewing in town. That no-good cow rustler Butch Cavendish was sneaking up on Doc Rockford's ranch—"

A loud slam interrupted his play. Adults were shouting.

"It can't be helped. It's just for a little while!"

It was his mother. Jasper stood with his trousers around his knees. He cracked open the door and could see her pacing in front of her car in a state. He pulled up his pants.

"You can't just leave!" a man's voice bellowed back.

"I wouldn't ask if I didn't have to. It's serious, Leonard. I have to get away for a while. It's just for a few days. Okay?"

"Away from what? Althea, what the hell are you mixed up in now?" The tall shadow of his uncle grabbed her by the shoulder. "Jesus. You been drinkin'?"

"Just look after him, okay!" she shouted. "He's a good boy. He'll work hard. I promise. He just can't come . . . I have to go." She jerked away from the hand on her arm and headed toward the trunk of the car. The lid cranked open, and Jasper could see her pull a suitcase out and set it down at his uncle's feet.

Jasper's stomach fell. She hadn't said anything about a suitcase. She hadn't said anything about leaving either.

He threw the door open and ran toward her. "Mom! Mom!"

She stopped at the driver's door and stiffened. He picked up speed and sprinted full tilt into her waist.

"Mom! Don't go!"

She pried his hands off her middle. Gripping them too hard, she squatted down. "Jasper, sweetie, Mommy has to go. There are things she has to do that you can't help with. I'll be back soon."

"No!" He shook his head violently. "I'll be good. I promise. I won't be smart. I'll be quiet. I'll do whatever you say."

She grabbed his chin and held it firm. "I know, sweetie. You're a good boy. You be good for Uncle Leo."

Tears poured down his face despite his best efforts. "No. I'll be good for you."

Her red eyes filled up too, and a tiny hope lifted his heart. She wouldn't leave him. She loved him. He collapsed against her, coiling his arms around her, desperate to hold on. But she untangled herself and cleared her throat. "Just stop it. You knock that off . . . or I'll give you something to cry about. Understand?"

He sank his teeth into his bottom lip and nodded, but the tears wouldn't stop.

Squeezing his shoulders, she held his small frame away from hers. "You mind your uncle. You be a help to him. Make Mommy proud."

The ground sank beneath him as she let go.

"So when you comin' back?" Uncle Leo asked, placing his heavy palm on Jasper's shoulder.

"It'll just be for a few days. Maybe a week or two. I don't know. As soon as I can, alright?" Her eyes searched the field as though someone were out there. The plume of black smoke from the burning field hung over the horizon. Her lips clamped together. She wouldn't look at him. His insides were screaming, but she wouldn't listen. She was already gone.

"Forgive me for askin', but ain't you still married? What about your husband?"

"What about him?"

"Wendell know about this?"

"He knows he can't take care of Jasper on his own. The man's helpless. Can't even boil water. Besides, he's workin'." She shook her head. The truth was Jasper's father had stormed out after a fight the night before last and hadn't come home yet. "This isn't about him, okay?"

"Well, what's it about then? Althea, what are you runnin' from?"

She just hung her head and climbed into the car. Through the open window, she whispered so Jasper might not hear, "Just keep him safe, okay? Promise me you'll keep him safe. Don't let anything happen to him."

Jasper didn't know what he'd done, but it must have been something awful. She wouldn't even look at him. A sob swelled up, choking the air out of his throat until he couldn't breathe.

Uncle Leo's voice sounded like it was coming from another room. "What the hell are you talkin' about? Of course. He'll be fine. Won't you, son?"

As the man thumped his shoulder with his giant hand, Jasper's throat closed tighter. Maybe he'd stop breathing altogether. Maybe then she wouldn't go.

But she did.

Everything grew dim as the Chevy disappeared up the two-track drive.

"Jesus, Althea," a voice muttered somewhere far away. "I swear to God, some cows should just be shot."

CHAPTER 2

Where did you grow up?

Jasper sank onto his cousin's bed, with his suitcase heavy on his lap, and stared at the floor. She was gone. To keep himself from falling through the floorboards, he replayed the argument between his uncle and mother over and over. *It'll just be for a few days. Maybe a week or two. I don't know . . .*

"Hey, you just going to sit there all day?" His cousin Wayne poked his head into the tiny alcove that was his room. He was twelve years old, and Jasper could hear the teasing in his voice already. The older boy pulled the suitcase onto the dresser and yanked him off the bed. "What's with the long face? Ain't you glad to see me?"

Wayne dragged him through the curtain that separated the boy's bedroom from the rest of the cabin. A wood-fired stove, hanging pots, a baker's rack, an icebox, a washtub, two rocking chairs, and a narrow bookshelf were all crammed along four crooked walls. A large kitchen table sat in the middle. Uncle Leo and Aunt Velma's tiny bedroom was tucked away in the back corner behind a closed door. Behind the curtain, Wayne's feather bed was pushed against the east window. Jasper felt claustrophobic in the cramped space. He could barely breathe.

"How long you stayin'?"

"Not too long. Maybe a week?" Jasper tried to sound happy about it. He couldn't look Wayne in the eye knowing his own were red with tears. She hadn't told him about the suitcase, Jasper thought bitterly. It was as bad as lying.

"Hey, you wanna go see somethin' gruesome?" Wayne nudged him in the shoulder. "Come on! I'll show ya."

Jasper followed Wayne out the door and across the yard. The sun blazed high in the sky above them, but he felt cold. His eyes fixed on the spot in the driveway where the taillights of the car had pulled out of sight. Uncle Leo was nowhere to be seen. Wayne tugged his arm to keep him moving.

He pulled Jasper through the open door of the two-story barn, past the cow stalls and the goats, to the pigpen in the far corner. Bright stripes of sunlight fell onto the dirt floor through the open gaps in the wood siding. The smells of manure, sweat, and hay mixed with the flies buzzing through the air. A big black one landed on Jasper's arm. He didn't bother to swat it away.

"Come look," Wayne whispered, squatting down over a dark spot in the straw thatch outside the door to the pigpen.

Jasper obeyed and sat down on his haunches next to his cousin. There on the ground lay a wet mass of slime, gray noodles, and blood. There was a halo of matted fur beneath it.

"What *is* that?" Jasper asked, squinting at the pile. It looked as though an alien life-form had slithered out of a meteor.

Wayne picked up a stick and poked at the slime. "A rat. See the tail? Lucifer must've got him."

Jasper found his own stick and began prodding the gray noodles that he now understood were entrails. "Lucifer did this?"

"Not like the devil, dummy. He's a barn cat. Watch out for him. He's the meanest one you'll ever meet." Wayne rolled up his sleeve to show Jasper three pink scars running down his forearm. "This is what happened when I tried to pet him once. You only try to pet Lucifer once, that's what Pop says."

Jasper nodded and looked back down at the disemboweled rat. "Where did the head go?"

"That's how you know it was Lucifer. He never leaves the heads. I don't know what the heck he does with 'em."

"Are you two going to just stand there starin' at the dirt or give me a hand?" Uncle Leo climbed the fence from the outer pigpen and clomped through the mud over to them.

Both boys stood up.

"Good. Wayne, go and grab me that curved knife over there."

Wayne's eyes lit up. "We cuttin' the nuts off that pig today?"

Uncle Leo chuckled. "Don't let him hear you be so excited about it. Put yourself in his shoes."

Jasper just stood there dumb while Wayne ran to the far wall for a knife that looked like a giant hook. *Did he say, "cuttin' the nuts off"?*

His uncle tapped his shoulder. "Wake up, Jasper. I need a few lengths of rope. That wall over there. Alright?"

The boy nodded and walked over to the side wall and pulled two circles of braided horse hair down from a nail. When he returned, Uncle Leo was giving a demonstration to his son on how the knife in his hand worked. "You gotta split, then sever 'em. Got it?"

Wayne nodded and asked, "Won't he bleed out?"

Bleed out? Jasper handed the rope to his uncle.

"Nah. No major arteries to worry about down there. Thanks, Jasper. Now, boys, when you're castrating your stock, you must proceed with extreme caution. That boar Sheldon worked last year nearly killed him. You get knocked down in a pigpen, it's your ass. Got it? This is serious business."

Wayne was nodding as if he understood.

"Jasper, you look confused, son."

"I—I'm sorry, but what are we doing?"

"We're gonna cut the nuts off Roy over there." Wayne grinned and slapped him on the back like he'd just caught a whopper of a fish.

"Easy, Wayne." Uncle Leo gave his head a small shake and turned to Jasper. "What your overly enthusiastic cousin over there is tryin' to say is that we have to castrate that pig."

Jasper felt sick. "Why?"

"'Cause if we don't, he's liable to go wild and hurt the other pigs," Wayne explained as though this were common knowledge.

"Nuts make you wild?" Jasper frowned and fought the urge to grab his own.

"Not wild. Aggressive. Bullish. We want happy pigs in this pen." Uncle Leo was trying to reassure him, but it still didn't make sense.

Why would a pig be happy without his nuts? Jasper wanted to ask but held his tongue.

"Besides," Uncle Leo continued, "one boar is enough to keep the whole county in piglets for years, and that boar belongs to Arthur Hoyt over the hill there. So, we ready?"

Jasper was not, but he stood his ground and followed his uncle's orders.

"You gotta grab and cut quick, or the pig will eat you alive. And it *will* eat you if it gets a chance." Uncle Leo laughed like this was a joke as he led a medium-sized pig into the holding stall and shut the door.

Wayne nodded at Jasper. "That's why you never let yourself fall down in a pigpen. Right, Pop?"

Jasper barely heard his uncle's answer. Poor Roy was being hog-tied on his back to a fence post. Without a moment's hesitation, Uncle Leo grabbed what the good Lord had given the pig and split it in two. Roy let out a tortured squeal. Jasper lurched back at the sound and felt himself turn green.

"Don't worry, kid." Wayne chucked his shoulder. "Pop's done this a hundred times. Right, Pop?"

"Every summer." Uncle Leo nodded. "Wayne, have the salt ready."

"Got it." Wayne slapped a cardboard box onto the fence post.

"What's the salt for?" Jasper whispered.

The question was lost in a high-pitched squall as his uncle sliced off the pig's testicles in one clean swipe. Everything Jasper had eaten the night before rose up in his throat, and his own tiny balls shrank into his stomach.

"Okay, boys. Back up!" his uncle barked.

Wayne grabbed Jasper by the arm and pulled him back several feet. What happened next happened too fast for Jasper to fully comprehend. Uncle Leo dumped half the box of salt on the open wound. Roy let out a shriek twice as loud as when he'd lost his nuts. Uncle Leo released the ropes and hopped the fence in one motion. The nutless pig took off bucking and squealing around the pen.

"Once you're done, you better clear out of there, 'cause he'll be madder than a nest of hornets." Uncle Leo dusted himself off. He rinsed the bloody knife in a bucket of water before hanging it back up on the wall.

Jasper gaped at poor Roy as he circled the pen, kicking and screaming. "Is he gonna . . . be alright?"

"Of course. He'll be fine by supper. Speaking of supper, here." Uncle Leo held a bloody handkerchief out to Jasper. It contained something the size of a grapefruit. "Go run these back to your aunt in the kitchen."

Jasper's jaw dropped at what his uncle was implying.

"This here's a farm, boy, not a zoo. We don't let nothin' go to waste. Not like in your big, fancy city. Now, here." Uncle Leo grabbed Jasper's hand and made him take the bloody rag and everything it held. It was still warm. His uncle clapped him on the back. "You keep your ears open and your mouth shut, we just might make a farmer out of you."

Jasper forced a smile.

CHAPTER 3

Would you say you had a happy home life as a child?

"Where the hell've you been?" Jasper heard his father yelling on the other side of his bedroom door.

"Don't you use that tone with me!" his mother barked back. "I had to pull an extra shift."

"I called down to the dairy, Althea. Now, you better tell me where you been!"

"I wasn't at the goddamned office, now was I!" The door to a cupboard slapped open. Something wet splashed into a glass. "Do we have to discuss this every time? You know Galatas is constantly sending me out on errands. I had to go to the warehouse."

"Why is that? Why's he got so many errands for you, huh?"

His mother sighed. "Because I do a good job. Why is that so hard for you to believe?"

"I'll tell you why! I don't like the way that man looks at you!"

"Don't be ridiculous."

"I don't trust him, Althea! The way I heard it, he's runnin' more than numbers out of that joint."

"Jesus, Wendell! There you go listenin' to gossip again. Tell those boys down at the plant to mind their own damned business! Ain't nothin' coming out of the warehouse but butter and cream. Alright?"

There was a heavy pause. The next time his father spoke, he sounded beaten. "How many nights is Jasper gonna be left alone like this?"

"He wasn't alone . . . He was downstairs with Mrs. Carbo." A glass hit the counter. "I hate it when you do this. You know I'd rather be here with him, but what am I supposed to say to my boss?"

"You should've said no."

"I can't just say no to Galatas, and you know it! Besides . . . we need the money."

His father let out a long hiss of air, and his voice grew almost too quiet to hear. "This isn't just about money. I can't—I can't live like this." A moment later, the front door opened and then clicked shut.

The sound of it hollowed Jasper out. He tried to shout after him, *Dad! Don't go!*

The next thing he knew, he was falling down a long dark tunnel. *DAD!*

Jasper startled awake. It took him several breaths with his heart hammering his ribs to recognize where he'd landed. He was in Wayne's small bed behind the thin curtain. He exhaled in relief. Then he realized his pajamas were wet.

No! He leapt out of bed, banging his elbow on the small chest of drawers under the window. He stifled a yelp and checked Wayne's face. The older boy snored and rolled over. The only other sound was the wind whistling through the trees outside. On the other side of the wavy window glass, the eastern sky was just starting to glow at the edges. Everyone would be awake soon.

Jasper felt the sheet and blanket where he'd lain. There was only one small wet spot. He put his pillow over it. He'd try to clean it later when no one was watching. He stripped off his pajamas and wiped down his legs with them. He couldn't let Wayne know what he'd done.

He'd rather die than have his cousin think he was some baby. He balled up the pajamas and searched for a place to hide them. There was barely space to turn around in his cousin's makeshift bedroom. It was the length of the bed and only wide enough for the mattress and the small chest of drawers that held Wayne's clothes. Jasper's suitcase sat on top.

A rooster crowed from the henhouse. Jasper was out of time. He threw the ball of urine-soaked pajamas under the bed and pulled his last pair of clean pants out of his bag. He quietly closed the lid of the suitcase and bit back tears. It had been ages since he'd had an accident. He glared down at the pathetic organ that had betrayed him. The image of Roy's balls split open flashed in his head, and he nearly doubled over.

Jasper was saying a silent prayer that he would not ever have another accident again in his life when a knock rattled the cabin door.

"Leo? Leo, you in there?" a voice bellowed. The knock turned into a pound.

"Hold your horses," his uncle barked back. There was a creak and the sound of shuffling feet. On the other side of the curtain, the front door opened. "Mornin', Wendell. You leave your manners at home?"

The angry thud of his father's footsteps shook the floorboards. "Cut the crap, Leo. Where is she?"

"Easy, Wen. We'd better go outside."

The door to the cabin thumped shut. Jasper stood half naked behind the curtain, holding his pants and staring after the two men. His dad wasn't even looking for him, but his heart fluttered anyway. *He's come to take me home.* Jasper had never been so homesick in his life. He threw on his trousers and crept out into the kitchen. Out the front window, the two men stood in the yard by a beat-up truck. Jasper scowled at the strange vehicle. His parents only owned one car, and she'd taken it. His father was dressed in blue coveralls for work.

Uncle Leo looked sort of silly standing there in his union suit, but that didn't stop him from being indignant. "What the hell are you doin' here at this hour?"

"She's gone, Leo. She hasn't been home in three days."

The spring in Jasper's heart went slack as his father's words sank in. *She's gone.* He cupped his ear to the bug screen to hear better.

"Yep. I figured as much."

"What do you mean you figured as much? This ain't funny. She hasn't been to work. That boss of hers, Galatas, has been by lookin' for her, calling the house at all hours. Even showed up on my doorstep with his fat red face, making threats. If she doesn't come in today, she's canned." His father ran a hand through his thinning gray hair.

"I wish I could help, I really do." Leo held up his hands. "Last I saw her was three days ago myself. She brought Jasper here and left just like that. Didn't ask, just did it."

His father went quiet as the words sank in, then said, "Did she say where she was headed?"

"Nope. Wouldn't say. She didn't know when she'd be back either. Kept sayin' how I had to keep the boy safe. As if somebody might come snatch him. Woman's got a damned screw loose, but that's Althea, isn't it?"

His father shook his head. "I don't believe it. She wouldn't do that. Althea wouldn't do that to Jasper. She'd die first."

Leo shook his head. "Well, she must be dead then."

In the dull light of morning, he could see his father cover his eyes with his hand. His shoulders shook. He'd never seen his father cry before, and the sight sent a bolt of panic through him. *She must be dead then.*

Jasper sank down onto the floor. *She can't be dead. She's coming back in a few days. She promised.*

"He's inside. You want to see 'im."

"Not like this. I can't let him see me like this. I can't—I can't stay. I gotta get to work. You tell him I'll be back tomorrow. I promise. Saturday. Okay?"

"Alright. You get on then."

"Thank you, Leo. I'll pay back this debt. I will. You have my word."

Jasper didn't hear what was said next. His ears couldn't take it. He buried his face in his knees and clutched the sides of his head. His father didn't want to see him. He wasn't taking him home. Tears streamed down his face.

"He'll be back, kid." His cousin squatted down next to him and patted his shoulder. Jasper had no idea how long Wayne had been standing there and didn't really care. He shot up and slammed out the front door. His father's truck had pulled away up the long dirt drive, leaving a cloud of dust hanging in his wake. Jasper ran after it. He could still hear the sound of tires on gravel up ahead. He wasn't that far behind. Maybe if his dad saw him in the rearview mirror he would stop. Maybe he would take him back home.

Jasper ran for all he was worth. Glancing over his shoulder, he half expected to see Wayne or Leo hot on his tail, ready to take him down. There was no one. They'd let him go. They didn't want him either. His uncle would never say it, but Jasper could see it in his worried eyes every time they all sat down for dinner and divvied up the meat. He was a burden. Another mouth to feed.

The sound of tires grew fainter as he turned the corner up onto Harris Road. A half mile or more ahead, he could see the red outline of the truck. He kept running, knowing he'd never catch him now. His father probably couldn't even see him through the cloud of dirt out his rear window.

Jasper's feet slowed to a stumbling walk as he lost his wind. Even the trail of dust had died down by then. There was nothing but corn. The burning in his lungs was his only consolation. He turned and looked how far he'd gone down the road from his uncle's driveway. He hated that road. He'd watched it for three days, jumping up at the sound of every passing car, thinking it was her.

He couldn't go back and just wait, he decided. His mother was missing, and he was going to find her. He spun back to the road ahead and started walking toward town. Maybe he'd hitch a ride back to Detroit or ride the boxcars like a real hobo. If Little Orphan Annie could solve a crime, he could find his mother.

He stuffed his hands in his pockets and kicked at the larger stones as he went, bashing his toes against them through his dirt-covered socks. His uncle was wrong. His mother wasn't dead. She wasn't even sick. He knew that was how people died, because that's what had happened to the old man who lived down the hall, the one who would always ask him if he liked baseball. He would cough and cough all night, shaking the walls of Jasper's bedroom until, one night, he just stopped. He'd been very old and wrinkled. His mother wasn't hardly old at all. She did complain about getting gray hairs. Those were all his fault, she said. But she didn't have white hair. It was still mostly black. Her face was still smooth and beautiful, with only the smallest crinkles around her eyes when she smiled. He loved it when she smiled.

A stray tear fell down his cheek. He wiped it away.

She can't be dead, he decided. *Not unless someone killed her.*

He stopped walking. His uncle's voice repeated in the back of his head, *Althea, what are you runnin' from?*

"Jas—per!" He heard his name being called from a half mile away. It was his uncle.

The boy turned to the tall rows of corn and ran into the field.

CHAPTER 4

Tell me about your mother.
What kind of woman was she?

The rustle of the corn drowned out the sound of his uncle's voice as Jasper ran through the field. Leathery green leaves clawed his face and shoulders as he pushed his way down the unbending furrow between the rows. Stalks towered over his head, blocking out the sky. The hot air was thick with dirt and pollen. It was like breathing mud. He was drowning in corn. He didn't even know where he was going.

Jasper stopped and forced himself to take ten deep breaths, just like his mother had taught him to do when he'd wake up screaming with nightmares. *Just breathe, baby. Everything will be okay*, she'd say. But it wasn't okay. He couldn't breathe. *One, two, three . . . four . . . five . . .*

Jasper grabbed a thick cornstalk to steady himself. Uncle Leo had told him once that if he listened *real hard*, he could hear the corn grow. It sounded exactly like the kind of stupid nonsense grown-ups liked to tell little kids. But Jasper listened for the corn despite himself . . . *six . . . seven . . . eight . . .* All he could hear was the faint buzz of hidden insects and the hiss of his own ragged breath. He strained again before giving up . . . *nine* . . . *ten*.

No one could hear corn grow. Jasper whacked his forearm against a cornstalk, hoping it would break in half. It just swayed back and forth like it was laughing at him. His uncle had lied. His mother had lied too. *She isn't coming back soon.*

A white cloud passed over his head through the long stems. He was smaller than an ant in the grass. He was Jack looking for his beanstalk. Any second a giant would shake the ground, stomp over, and pluck little Jasper off his lawn.

"Fee . . . Fi . . . Fo . . . Fum," he whispered. *It wouldn't be so bad to be eaten,* he thought and began walking again. The world would go red, then black, and then there would be nothing. He would be okay with that. His skin was itchy with pollen and sticky with sweat. He scratched at a mosquito bite until it bled. *Feeling nothing would feel better than this.*

Jasper's feet had found their way to the end of the cornfield. He'd never seen this part of the farm before. It was a foreign country. He wouldn't have been surprised if some person in odd-looking clothes approached him, speaking a language he didn't understand. But there was no one.

Instead of corn, neat rows of short leafy greens stretched before him for over five hundred feet before turning into tall brown wheat near the horizon. A hundred feet to the left, there was a split-rail fence and then more corn. Three hundred feet to the right, there stood a field of bushy-looking grass that rose up to his chest. At the far end, he could just make out something tall and bulky hidden behind a stand of trees. He puzzled at it.

Jasper picked his way through the leafy greens he suspected were sugar beets and into the thick, bushy grass. *Oats,* he thought. These were probably oats. Uncle Leo always answered his questions about the different crops. He didn't say much else, but his uncle never tired of talking about farming. Leo even let Jasper steer the tractor a few times. He'd stand between his uncle's knees while his enormous work boots operated the metal levers.

Uncle Leo isn't so bad, Jasper told himself. Even if he wanted to shoot his own sister for being a bad cow, he never would. Even as he thought it, he couldn't help but worry.

She must be dead then.

She can't be dead, Jasper argued with himself. He ran his hand over the tops of the long grass. The blades tickled across his palm until he squished a handful in his fist. *The idea that someone might've killed her is just silly.* He could hear her voice saying the word *silly.*

Your head's just inventing more nightmares, Jasper. It can't ever seem to keep still, can it? Stop worrying over every little thing

Jasper looked down at his muddy socks. He hadn't bothered to put on shoes. One of his toes was poking out of a new hole he'd just made in the left one. She'd be furious if she could see him standing there in the middle of a field, upsetting everybody. She'd told him to be good. Jasper looked back over his shoulder at the empty rows of corn behind him. He'd probably get a beating for running off. He probably deserved it. He thought about turning back for a split second but thought better of it. If he was going to catch a whupping either way, he might as well put it off for a while. He wanted to see what was out there hiding behind those trees. Jasper kept heading through the field toward the horizon.

She just went out shopping. That's all. She's just over the bridge in Windsor, buying more of those flowery teacups she loves. Dad's always complaining she cares more about those silly knickknacks than . . .

Bare splintered wood emerged from behind the branches like a shipwreck on the shores of Lake Huron. As he rounded past the trees, the shipwreck became a house. Or what was left of a house.

An overgrown path at the edge of the field led to the falling-down front porch. Half the house was charred away. Black and gray ash had devoured the siding and roof shingles. The windows were cracked and clouded in soot. The roof had caved in along the west eave, making the house as crooked as a bent old man. The front door hung halfway open from a broken hinge, beckoning him inside.

Jasper circled the wreckage of the lonely building. He scanned the surrounding fields and overgrown front yard. The road that had once led to the house had been plowed over and planted. They had just left it to crumble. They hadn't even bothered to tear it down.

It was twice as big as Uncle Leo's cabin. The first floor contained twelve windows and a front and back porch. The second floor was tucked up under the roof with only one window peeking out from each end. It was more of an attic, really, before the roof had caved in.

The handrail for the front porch steps toppled over into the weeds when Jasper gave it a tug. A small creature scurried out from under the deck and into the field on the opposite side. *Badger?* He shivered wondering what else might be living under there. He pounded his foot on the first step and jumped back, waiting. A bird flew out from its nest up under the porch roof. That was it.

Jasper tested the first step with his weight and then the next and next until he was tiptoeing across the porch toward the open front door. A bouquet of dead flowers hung from a wire above the door knocker. They fell apart at his touch. The door hung crooked from its one good hinge. The heavy wood wouldn't budge.

"Hello?" he called out, poking his head through the narrow gap between the door and jamb. It was rude to enter a house uninvited. He waited for several seconds, but no one answered. He turned sidewise and slipped through the broken door into the front room.

Inside, the smell of smoke still hung in the air. The floorboards were largely intact except for the ones near the burnt openings in the walls. He kept wide of the blackened boards, taking four tentative steps inside, half expecting to fall through. The cracked window glass rattled, and the boards creaked as he inched his way from the vestibule into a dining room. Several broken chairs lay strewn across the floor. Sunlight filtered in through the tarry grime, casting a brownish glow over everything. The shadow of a table big enough to seat sixteen men still lingered on the damaged rug. He could almost hear the workmen laughing and the clink of silverware on plates as he walked past a chair. The bird had returned to its nest in the porch rafters and chirped at Jasper through the hazy window.

On the other side of a narrow corridor, he found a kitchen twice as large as the one where Aunt Velma did her baking. A huge cookstove with six burners stood in the corner. Its kindling bucket was still full. In the opposite corner, an old icebox stood open and empty. Everything else was gone. All the dishes and the pots and pans had been taken from the hanging racks and shelves. The washtub was gone. The plaster walls were blackened with smoke, but none had been eaten away by flames. Jasper looked back at the cookstove. It didn't seem to have been touched by the fire. He ran a hand over the dirty glass in the back door and looked out to see flowering weeds growing through the slats in the porch.

At the opposite corner of the kitchen, a set of steep stairs led up to the attic. They were covered in fallen leaves and debris from the trees outside. A ray of sunlight came pouring down the steps through a hole in the roof above. Jasper stared up at a piece of sky that had no business being inside the house.

It wasn't a good idea. The floor at the bottom of the stairway was littered with animal droppings and mud. Warning bells rang between his ears as he mounted the first step. The handrail held steady when he tested it. He gripped it hard and took another step. He shifted his weight slowly from foot to foot as he went, listening for a fatal crack, waiting for a step to give way. None did, and step by creaking step he made it to the top.

The roof rafters were black where they hadn't fallen away. Some hung in broken splinters or were cracked at their middles, and others had collapsed completely onto what remained of the attic floor.

Through the ripped-open roof, Jasper could see out over the fields that stretched from the west side of the house for over a mile until they reached the sky.

He watched his feet as he stepped away from the stairwell, testing the floorboards one at a time. On the opposite side of the attic, away from the missing rafters, he found what was left of two beds tucked under the eaves of the house. The blackened mattress covers bled white feathers onto the ground. He took a few tentative steps toward them and could see that some small creature had piled the stuffing into a makeshift nest in the far corner. It might be a raccoon, he realized, stopping in his tracks. *Raccoons are mean little critters,* that's what his uncle had said. One of them had killed his last hunting dog. It had rolled under the old boy and ripped his guts to shreds.

Jasper gave the nest a wide berth as he made his way across the floor to a small chest of drawers on the opposite wall. A wood dollhouse sat on top of the bureau. Between the warped and water-stained boards sat six tiny rooms. All the paint on the little blocks of wood that had served as furniture had worn away. Two blocks shaped like beds sat on the second floor of the dollhouse. Jasper picked one up and looked back at the torn-up beds behind him. The "Jack and the Beanstalk" feeling came back, and he imagined a giant hand reaching in through the hole in the roof and lifting him from the house. He quickly put the little block bed back down into its place.

He tried to open the drawers of the bureau, but the wood was too swollen with rainwater. The bottom drawer was the only one to give an inch, and he wrestled with it until it finally popped open with a puff of damp, moldy air. Jasper sneezed twice, then held his nose so he could inspect what lay inside.

A pile of dresses or nightgowns—it was hard to tell which, but whatever they were, they belonged to a girl because they had bows and flowers. He pulled one out and held it up to his chest. He laid it gently on the ground and tried to imagine the girl who had worn it. She would be taller than him. He pictured her long black hair set in braids. For a fleeting moment, he could see her standing in a doorway. Her dark eyes staring into his, pleading with him as though he had something to tell her. Jasper frowned and wadded up the dress.

In the bottom of the drawer lay a small book and a rag doll.

He picked up the doll and quickly set it back down. It was sticky and smelled like it had been buried in the dirt. The brown leather binding of the book had grown stiff and brittle. The edges of the pages were wavy and damp, but when he opened to the middle, they weren't stuck together.

Jasper couldn't read the scrawling writing, but he could tell flipping through that the letters were drawn by hand. Someone had filled page after page with swirly words set in narrow, straight lines. He squinted, not able to decipher any of them. The book was only half full. He flipped to the front, and his heart contracted.

Someone had written *Althea* in the middle of the first page.

Jasper looked up to the dollhouse then down to the dresses on the floor. It was her bedroom, he realized, glancing at the two beds behind him. It must be. Back when she was just a girl.

He tried to picture her again, sitting right where he sat, playing with her dollhouse. But he couldn't. The girl with the braids and dark eyes he'd imagined watching over his shoulder wasn't her at all. There were no pictures of his mother as a girl back home, and Jasper realized right then that he'd never seen one.

"Where did you go, Mom?" he whispered.

The doll in the drawer just stared up at him with dead button eyes.

He read the name *Althea* again, then hugged the book to his chest and cried.

CHAPTER 5

Let's start with something simpler then.
Any brothers or sisters?

"Jasper?" a voice called from outside the burnt house. It was Wayne. "Jas? You in there?"

It took a few seconds to find his voice. "Yep. I'll be right out," he called back, wiping his tears. The book was still in his hands. He had to hide it. If Wayne saw it, he might take it away or give it to Uncle Leo. Something told Jasper that his uncle wouldn't approve of him taking it or snooping inside the burnt-out house in the first place. It felt wrong and not just because the floors were crumbling.

Footsteps creaked below him. He slipped the book into the back of his pants under his pajama shirt before heading down the stairs.

Wayne was in the kitchen, waiting. "Whatcha doin' in here?"

"I don't know. Just curious, I guess."

"Don't ever let Pop see you in here, alright? He'll skin ya for sure." Wayne grabbed him by the arm and led him through the house and back onto the front porch.

"What is this place?"

"Used to be Grandma's house before she died. Pop grew up inside, you know."

"Did—did my mom grow up here too?" Jasper already knew the answer but wanted to hear it from Wayne.

"Sure enough. Pop, Aunt Althea, Uncle Alfred, and Aunt Pearl."

"What happened?" Jasper asked, pointing to the hole in the roof.

"There was a fire, dummy!" Wayne tousled his little cousin's hair.

Jasper squirmed away. "I'm not a dummy. I can see that. But I mean, why? How did it catch fire?"

"No one knows for sure. I heard it was wild Injuns!"

"Really?" Jasper's eyes grew wide. The closest he'd ever come to a real-life Indian was listening to the *Lone Ranger* show on the radio.

"Yep. See, the old Fox and Sauk tribes used to live around these parts back when it was nothin' but a forest. They used to fight the Iroquois nation in these great battles with bows and arrows and knives made from bone." Wayne fired an imaginary arrow at Jasper. "They buried their dead braves right where we're standin'."

Jasper looked down at his feet.

"They didn't like white folks like us buildin' a farm here, so one night they crept up on the house." Wayne lowered himself into a crouch and crept low through weeds toward the house. He reached behind his back for his imaginary bow and quiver. "They let loose flaming arrows right through the windows and sent the whole place up. Whoosh!"

Wayne leapt up making fire flames with his hands. "Poor old Granny! She didn't have time to get out. *Aaaahhh!*" he screamed and fell to the ground as if dead.

"She burned up in there?" Jasper whispered, staring slack jawed at the fallen roof. It wasn't funny. He'd never met his grandmother. She'd died long before he was born. Wayne seemed awfully lighthearted about the whole thing. Like it was just a story he'd heard on the radio.

"Yep. Pop came a-runnin'. He jumped on old Ginger and galloped after those Indians. Chased 'em clear to the next county." Wayne made a gun with his hand and galloped across the overgrown yard.

"Did he kill any of 'em?"

"Might've. Can't be too sure how many. See, that's why nobody comes out here no more. Those Injuns might come back for their revenge. Got it?"

Jasper nodded even though most of the story didn't make sense. If the Indians wanted revenge, they could just go to Uncle Leo's cabin down the road and burn that house down too. But there was no doubt that something terrible had happened there. He stared up at the broken window looking out from the attic over the fields and tried to picture her face behind the tarry glass. All he could muster was a shadow.

"We gotta get out of here before Pop sees us. He'd tan our hides for sure." Wayne led Jasper away from the house and back through the cornfield.

"Isn't he gonna skin me anyway?" Jasper asked. The corn leaves slapped at his cheeks, reminding him of the whupping that was waiting for him back at the cabin.

"Probably not too bad. He knows it's been tough on you." Wayne stopped and turned to Jasper. "You just got to start acting grateful's all. Pop thinks he's done saved you from a slow death in that city."

"A slow death?" Jasper immediately thought of his mother.

"'Can't no one breathe right there,'" Wayne imitated his father's gruff voice. "'If you ain't livin' off the land, you ain't livin' at all.' And that sort of thing."

Jasper nodded. The smoke of the mills and car factories did get thicker than fog in downtown Detroit. Then there were the streets he wasn't supposed to go near after sundown. *Does my mother think I'd die a slow death there?* he wondered. *Is she trying to save me?*

He dismissed the idea. All his life, she'd hated spending time at Uncle Leo's. After a few hours, she'd bellow from the front seat of the car that it was time to go, and Jasper would have to climb down from the hayloft in the barn or wherever he'd been playing. He usually threw some sort of fit about it, and she'd end up dragging him screaming through the dirt back to the car.

You get any dirtier, I'm gonna leave you here for Leo to plow under, she'd growl. *The only thing anyone gets in this godforsaken place is stink.*

But she'd left him there anyway. Jasper glanced back at the burnt house. The book in the small of his back pressed uncomfortably against his spine. Her eyes were red with dried tears the morning she left him. She looked scared.

Promise me you'll keep him safe.

The image of Wayne's wild Injuns crept through his thoughts, but he shooed them away. He doubted his mother had ever met an Indian in her whole life, but she was scared of something.

Wayne was too busy talking about other things to notice the frown on Jasper's face. "School's startin' in a couple weeks. Pop says you'll be walkin' with me this year. I think you'll like Miss Babcock. She's not as strict as some of them teachers I've heard about. You like school?"

I'm not going back home for school?

"I said, do you like school?" the older boy repeated like his cousin was thick.

"It's okay," he mumbled. Jasper had just finished third grade back in Detroit. His teacher mostly ignored him. He'd learned not to ask too many questions in class since all they seemed to do was irritate her. The older boys called him shrimp and stole his milk money every Friday. He wasn't going to see them in the fall. He might not see them ever again.

"What's your favorite subject?"

"I don't know." Jasper found them all fairly boring. He planned to say nothing more about it until another thought occurred to him. "I really want to learn to read better. Especially that curly writing people do."

"Cursive? Well, I can help you with that, kid. I'm the best." Wayne threw his arm around his cousin's shoulders.

Jasper shook it off, worried that his cousin might discover the book stuffed in his pants. "Isn't Uncle Leo going to be mad at me?"

"Nah. Just apologize . . . and offer to clean the chicken coop as penance. That should make Pop feel better."

The two boys had reached the road and headed back toward Uncle Leo's small house. It was so much smaller than the one that had burned down, and Jasper wondered for a moment why that might be. Up ahead, he could see the large man standing at the end of his two-track drive. He was holding a pitchfork in his hand, a pitchfork that might be meant for one ungrateful nephew. Jasper swallowed hard.

"Where'd ya find him?" Uncle Leo asked Wayne as they walked up.

"Down in the hay field. Think he must've got lost."

Jasper nodded pathetically, not looking his uncle in the eye. Leo put a palm on his shoulder. It felt like a boulder. The man's hands were strong enough to snap a nine-year-old's spine in two.

"This the last time you're planning on running away?" Uncle Leo squeezed Jasper's shoulder hard enough to bring tears.

"Yes, sir. I—I won't do it again. I'm sorry. Can't I do something to help out, like . . . clean the chicken coop?"

Uncle Leo let go and folded his enormous arms. He turned his iron stare to his own son. "What an interesting suggestion."

"I was gonna help him, Pop. I know it's my chore to do. He just felt so bad worrying y'all like that, he wanted to help. Right, Jas?"

Jasper nodded.

"C'mon. Let's get started so we don't miss breakfast." Wayne grabbed the younger boy by the arm and dragged him away before Uncle Leo could lay down a more severe punishment for them both.

CHAPTER 6

We'll get to the murder allegations, but first we need
to get to know each other. Understand?

Later that afternoon, Jasper crept back into the house while Wayne headed to the pump. The chicken coop had left them both covered in black straw and stray feathers. Jasper was sticky with sweat and the stink of twenty hens, but he had to do something before washing up.

The book was stuck to his skin. Once behind the bedroom curtain, he pulled it out of the back of his pants. Flipping it open, he quickly checked to see if the writing had been ruined. The pages were slightly damp but still legible. He prayed it wouldn't make all of his clean clothes stink like chicken shit as he shoved it under his long underwear and folded socks.

Shoving all the clothes he had over his buried treasure, something odd emerged from the bottom of the suitcase. A children's Bible. Jasper picked up the bulky tome and frowned at the pastel face of Baby Jesus, wondering why in the world his mother had packed it for him. They didn't go to church. They'd never even cracked the book open. It had just sat up on his bookshelf for years as her little private joke. *Everybody's a sinner, Jasper,* she'd say. *But as long as you have a Bible in the house, nobody seems to mind.*

And now the joke was his.

"Jasper! What are you doing in here? You're filthy!" It was Aunt Velma's voice just inches over his shoulder. "You know you are going to ruin that lovely Bible."

"Um . . ." Jasper spun to block her view. "I was just . . ."

"Didn't your mother pack you any handkerchiefs?" She pointed to his running nose, then pulled one from the pocket of her apron. "Here."

"Oh. Thanks." He took the cloth from her hand and wiped his face, grateful for an excuse. "I was lookin' for one."

Aunt Velma looked old and rough compared to his mother. She had mostly gray hair and deep lines in her face. "I need to have a word with you, Jasper." The lines grew deeper like they were mad. "I'm very disappointed in you."

"I'm sorry." Jasper dropped his eyes to the ground. "I didn't mean to run off like that. I was just . . ."

"Change is never easy, we all understand that, but if you're gonna live here and we're gonna be a family, we got to trust each other, don't you agree?" Her voice was soft, but that just made the anger behind it even more scary.

Jasper nodded, afraid to look at her.

"I won't tolerate secrets."

He nodded again. His heart began to pound, thinking about the book he'd taken from the burnt house. He didn't want to show it to her. It had been his mother's, and it was the only thing of hers he had left besides that stupid baby Bible. Aunt Velma couldn't possibly know about the diary already. *Could she?*

"Is there something you want to tell me?" she demanded.

The room closed in around him as her icy blue eyes bored through him. He shook his head, knowing it wouldn't do any good. She obviously knew something. His back was up against the bureau.

"You sure about that?" she insisted again.

His eyes circled the room. *What could she possibly know about the book?* His mouth opened to speak, but no words came out. Aunt Velma tapped her foot as he squirmed.

She sighed and pulled a wad of damp pajamas out from under his bed. "How 'bout now? You got somethin' you want to tell me now?"

His breath caught in his throat. He'd forgotten all about his accident and hiding his pajamas. Tears of relief mixed with utter humiliation stung his eyes. "I—I'm sorry."

"Dirty laundry ain't nothin' to be ashamed of, but I won't suffer liars. Understand?"

He nodded.

She crouched down in front of him with a gentler voice. "Don't nobody have to know about the laundry but me, okay? I won't tell, but if you leave it balled up like that, it's bound to stink and won't come clean."

The tenderness in her voice made him feel unbearably small. Part of him wanted to throw his arms around her neck and weep. The other part of him wanted to hit her. He just stood there and did nothing.

"If it happens again, you wait till after breakfast when everybody's gone and you tell me. Got it?"

He nodded glumly.

"Now go and get wa—"

Wayne burst through the front door. "Come quick! Sally's fallen into the well."

"What?" Aunt Velma tore back the bedroom curtain.

"Who's Sally?" asked Jasper, forgetting all about his humiliation.

"Pop's best milker. Come on! We gotta get the tractor." Wayne turned and ran back out the door.

Jasper dashed after him past Aunt Velma pulling the shotgun out from behind the door.

When Jasper caught up, Wayne mounted his pop's great green tractor. It was a twenty-five horsepower John Deere Model B. Its back wheels were taller than him. "Grab that rope!" he ordered Jasper, pointing to a coil hanging from a peg on the wall.

Jasper had to jump to reach it but managed to get the heavy coil over his shoulder. He ran to the rear of the tractor and hopped up onto the hitch. "What's a milker?"

"It's a cow, dummy. Hang on!" shouted Wayne over the roar of the engine. The tractor lurched forward and tore down the two-track drive that led past the house and the chicken coop to the well in the back.

Uncle Leo was standing next to their neighbor Paul Sheldon, staring into a hole in the ground in deep discussion. Wayne rolled the tractor up next to them and cut the engine. Both boys hopped down to join the two men. An earsplitting wail boiled up out of the ground, making Jasper jump half out of his skin. The bleating call came again and was followed by a mad snorting. It was worse than the sound of Roy losing his nuts. Sally was being skinned alive by the devil himself.

Mr. Sheldon shined a lantern down into the well, and they all strained to see. There were two hooves and a tail and a long streak of blood.

"How you reckon we do this?" Mr. Sheldon asked Uncle Leo.

Leo lay down on his belly and reached into the well all the way to his shoulder. "Can't quite reach her."

He stood up again and studied the well. It was about three feet in diameter and lined with fieldstones. The large flagstone cover sat next to the hole. Someone had left the cover off the well, Jasper realized. *It wasn't me,* he wanted to shout.

"If you hop down there, you're liable to push her farther," Mr. Sheldon said, then looked at the two boys. "We'll have to lower in one of them."

Uncle Leo nodded and turned to Jasper. "You're the lightest. You remember how to tie that slipknot I taught you the other day?"

"I—I think so." He gulped.

"Show me." Uncle Leo held out his arm and handed Jasper a length of rope. The cow let out another death wail from down in the well.

With trembling hands, Jasper looped the rope around his uncle's forearm and chased it around and pulled it through until a semblance of a slipknot formed.

"Not bad." His uncle nodded and grabbed Jasper's leg above the knee. "You're gonna have to set it over the tarsal joint, or we'll just pull the bones apart."

"I'm going to have to disagree with you on that point, Leo," Mr. Sheldon piped in. "The boy might get kicked in the head."

Jasper's mouth fell open, but nothing came out.

Leo paused, then nodded. "Okay, above each hoof then. Two ropes, and the knot's gonna have to be tight, got it?"

Jasper could barely nod. They were going to lower him into the dark well to get kicked in the head by a mad cow. It bleated again like a dying steamboat. A line was being tied around Jasper's feet, and before he could protest, the two men were lowering him headfirst into the darkness with a rope in each hand.

"Easy now," Uncle Leo grunted from above. "Wayne, give him some light."

A weak yellow beam followed Jasper down into the darkness. Blood glistened as the glow bounced from stone to stone down to the massive ass of the trapped cow. The smell of cow shit greeted him as Jasper got closer to Sally's hooves. Blood rushed to his head, making everything pulse red. All he could hear was the insane hiss of Sally's breathing. A sharp hoof swung toward him, missing his arm by inches.

"Ho!" a voice called from above, and Jasper stopped moving. He hung there mere inches from the cow's tail. It was swooshing frantically, throwing terrifying shadows. Jasper tied the first piece of rope around his waist for safekeeping, then, with trembling hands, looped the second rope around Sally's right hoof.

She kicked wildly, slipping the loop. He tried again without success. His eyes stung with sweat and methane gas, making the hoof harder and harder to see.

"Come on, boy!" his uncle called from above. "We haven't got all day. Grab 'er!"

"Maybe I should try," Wayne asked in a low voice, probably thinking Jasper couldn't hear him.

That did it. "Damn it, Sally!" Jasper growled, trapping her hoof with a loop of rope and pulling it tight. "Hold still!"

Two more loops and the hoof was knotted. He pulled the other rope free from his waist and made quick work of the other foot. He tugged them both as tight as he could manage while the hooves kicked wildly at his head. "Okay!" he shouted.

Two seconds later, Jasper was up and out of the well, blinking the big purple spots from his eyes.

"Lay down till your blood comes back around," Uncle Leo ordered him and patted him on the head in approval. He'd done it. All by himself, he'd done something right.

By the time Jasper's blood had equalized again, the two men had constructed a crude structure over the well. A large log lay across the hole and was tied back to two large trees to keep it from rolling off the hay bales they'd stacked on either side. Jasper's ropes were threaded up out of the well, over the log, and back to the tractor hitch.

"Okay, Wayne. Let's see how we did." Uncle Leo winked at Jasper, then gave the signal.

The tractor jumped to life. The ropes Jasper had tied to old Sally creaked as they rolled over the log, but they held. Tree bark cracked and crumbled as the two ropes slid forward inch by agonizing inch. The tractor roared louder than Jasper had ever heard it as the machine fought its way forward, but it couldn't drown out the sounds of the cow as it screamed.

Jasper stood shaking like a leaf as two bleeding hooves and a tail emerged from the ground. A gentle arm fell on his shoulder. It was Aunt Velma. He buried his face in her waist as the cow's bloody flank scraped free. She held him firmly to her side.

The tractor engine cut off. Voices shouted all around. "Clear! Back! Get back!"

Pounding hooves shook the ground. Jasper was jerked up off his feet. His chest crushed into Aunt Velma's ribs as she ran with him, her legs thumping against his. He lifted his head from her shoulder to see a blood-covered cow charging his uncle. Leo jumped out of the way just in time. The two men scrambled to the tractor. Jasper squeezed his eyes shut.

Then there was a gunshot. Then another.

Aunt Velma stopped running and set Jasper down. He didn't want to look but found he couldn't help himself. Sally had landed on her side in a pool of blood, her flank heaving up and down. The men climbed down from their embattlements and approached her slowly. Uncle Leo raised his shotgun as he circled around her.

"Back," he ordered the others. Then, without a prayer or apology, he shot her in the head.

CHAPTER 7

So what did your father do for a living?

Jasper's father finally came to see him the next day. The first thing Jasper said was, "Uncle Leo shot a cow." Then he crumpled into tears.

"Whoa. Take it easy there, slugger." His father grabbed his chin and gave it a little shake. "These things happen on a farm. You know that."

Jasper wiped the snot from his nose with the back of his hand. "Can we go home?"

"And miss all the fun?" His father gave him a weak smile. "Tell me more about this cow. What happened?"

Jasper filled his father in on his role in rescuing poor Sally, but he didn't tell him what happened next. Uncle Leo, Wayne, and Mr. Sheldon had spent hours cutting her up into meat. It still made him sick. Jasper had been told to fetch knives and hacksaws and had to stand there, watching a nightmare play out in the hot sun.

Wipe that green look off your face. Where do you think steak comes from, boy? Uncle Leo had chuckled as he sawed through her chest.

Come on, Jas! If you get on this side, you can see her guts come out. Cow's got four stomachs, you know. Wayne had waved him over to look, but Jasper just shook his head. It was different than looking at rat guts. Maybe it was because he'd tried to save old Sally. Maybe it was because of what Uncle Leo had said about his mother. Either way, Jasper worried he'd never stop hearing the sound of Sally screaming.

His father's voice broke in. "Well ain't that somethin'! Now let me take a look at ya. Did she try and kick ya?" Wendell spun him around, scanning him from head to toe like a doctor.

Jasper nodded. "But I still got the rope around her hoof. Are you proud of me, Dad?"

His father's eyes twinkled a bit as he chucked the boy's chin. "I sure am, but don't go and get yourself a big head about it. Everybody's gotta pitch in on the farm. You were just doin' your part. So, you been good? Doin' what your uncle asks?"

Jasper nodded again. "I cleaned the barn stalls, the chicken coop. Wayne even taught me how to hook up the milkers."

"That's my boy." His father straightened back up. "Where's your uncle?"

"I think he's out in the shed, working on the tractor."

"You go find your cousin for a bit. We'll play some catch before supper."

Playing catch was Jasper's father's answer to any problem that didn't have an answer. If one of his parents stormed out after a fight, the next day his dad would be oiling up his glove. Jasper frowned as his dad hobbled toward the shed. "But, Dad?"

"Yes, Son?"

The words *I want to go home, I want my mom* caught in his throat. They were the words of a baby.

Wendell nodded as if he'd heard each one. "We all do what we can, Son. You're lucky to have so many good people lookin' after you. Do your best to be grateful. Now go find Wayne."

He wasn't going to take him home.

Wendell Leary walked slightly bent at the waist, limping a little on his left side all the way to the shed. He'd been wounded in the First World War. He'd lied about his age and enlisted when he was only sixteen. Jasper only knew about it because he'd found a picture of his father in a military uniform tucked in an old book called *The Sun Also Rises*. The blurry young man in the photo didn't quite look like his father, but the words written on the back read, "Wendell I. Leary, 1917."

You don't want to hear about all that, his father had said. But Jasper had protested that he really did. *Don't go pokin' through other people's closets, Son. Them skeletons can be real mean.* And that was all he'd say.

His father's advice hadn't stopped him from snooping through drawers and bookshelves, looking for war souvenirs.

Instead of going to find Wayne, Jasper sneaked around to the back side of the tractor shed. Wayne liked to smoke cigarettes back there. He'd even let Jasper try one after Sally was shot, thinking it might calm his nerves. All it did was make him sicker than he already felt. But he had noticed that there was a good view into the shed through the siding boards back there. Mr. Sheldon and Uncle Leo had been inside sipping corn liquor after their hard-earned steak supper. That was how Jasper had learned that it was Uncle Leo who had forgotten to put the lid back on the well. That mistake would likely cost him over five hundred dollars in milk. He would only get fifty dollars for Sally's meat over in Burtchville.

Through a knothole in the shed siding, Jasper watched Uncle Leo climb out from under the tractor, covered in grease. He walked over and shook Wendell's hand. His uncle was taller than his father and had fewer gray hairs. "Nice to see you, Wendell. Feelin' any better?"

"Fair to middling. How's it been?"

"Can't complain." Leo shrugged.

"I heard you had some trouble with a cow?"

"My poor ol' Sally took a fall. It's a damn shame too. Her meat's tougher than an old shoe." He chuckled.

His father laughed back, while Jasper scowled at the both of them from behind the shed. He didn't really think it was all that funny. The ground where Sally had been butchered was still red with blood. He could still smell it on his hands from holding the knives.

"I hear the boy was some help to ya?"

"Yep. He ain't a bad boy. Not real used to this sort of life, though, is he?"

"I'm afraid he'll have to manage for a while . . . if that's alright. A boy his age needs a mother around, and I've been workin' all these extra shifts. I can't ask the landlady to do more than she already has. I can't in good conscience just leave him alone . . ."

"Still no word from Althea?" Leo went to the tool rack to grab a larger wrench, then climbed back under the tractor.

"Nope . . . She was by the bank the other day, I do know that. She withdrew every last cent we had. Must be one hell of a vacation she's takin'." He forced a laugh.

Uncle Leo's wrench stopped cranking. "What are you gonna do?"

"What's there to do? Half that money was hers, right? I just can't wait to hear her excuse . . ." His father shook his head and sat down on the rear axle next to where Leo was working. "What's the trouble? Drivetrain?"

"Oh, the old jalopy's got a bad gasket here somewhere. She's been droppin' oil like grease through a goose."

"John Deere's been known to have a bad crankshaft seal. Didya look there?"

The two men talked tractors and engines for the next ten minutes while Jasper sat there aghast. His mother had taken a bunch of money from the bank, and his father had no idea where she'd gone. And there he was talking about gaskets like it was nothing.

Jasper slumped down against the side of the shed with his head to his knees. He had to find her. He frowned and tried to think. She didn't have friends, none that he'd met anyway. All she did was work, and when she came home, she hated to sit still. She'd sit for just a few minutes before she'd leap up and start moving again. Once she painted the kitchen bright yellow in a single afternoon. Once she'd dragged him over the bridge to Canada just to buy a soda. Jasper could picture her standing at the kitchen sink with that look in her eye like she had to go. *But where?*

His father and Uncle Leo kept talking. "You see that new Model R they put out? Forty-three horsepower engine. You believe that?"

Jasper was only half listening. *Why did she always want to leave?* he wondered. *Did she hate being with me?* The little leather book filled with her writing was his only clue. He had to find a way to read it. He'd tried for thirty minutes that morning but couldn't make sense of her tightly curled penmanship.

"Pretty soon those machines will be puttin' us all out of business." Uncle Leo threw the wrench down with a clank. "Price of wheat keeps droppin'. Damn government won't let anybody plant more than fifteen acres of the stuff now as it is. Had some company man out poking his big snout around my field just last year. Made me cut out three acres."

Jasper sighed to himself. The conversation was going nowhere. He waited five more minutes and gave up. As he was standing to leave, he heard his father say a name he'd never heard before.

"You talk to Sheriff Bradley lately?"

"Nope. No need really."

"He still hangin' around the Tally Ho?"

"Beats me. I haven't been down to the tavern in months. It's the busy season, you know."

"What do you say we head on over after dinner tonight. I'll buy you a beer. Lord knows I owe it."

"I don't think he's seen her, Wen."

Jasper pressed his eye to the knothole at the word *her*.

"It won't hurt to ask. Besides"—his father hoisted himself off the axle of the big green tractor—"we could both use a drink."

42

"What are you gonna tell him?"

"Bradley? Not much . . ." He rubbed his face. "If he ain't seen her, that'll be it. Nothin' else to say."

"No. I mean, what are you gonna tell the boy?"

"Oh, he'll be fine. Althea's gonna turn up with her tail between her legs. She always does. Just can't say when."

Uncle Leo pulled himself out from under the tractor and asked the question that had been plaguing Jasper for five days. "What if she doesn't?"

CHAPTER 8

Did he drink much?

Ever lose his temper?

It was past ten o'clock when Wayne and Jasper slipped out of the bedroom window, landing on the grass with two soft thumps.

"Why are we doin' this again?" Wayne hissed after they'd scuttled away from the house.

"This Sheriff Bradley guy might know where my mom went."

"He isn't gonna talk to you. He's liable to just whip us both, or arrest us. The Tally Ho ain't a place for kids."

They scrambled up the two-track drive and out onto the side of the road. The half-moon shone high overhead, lighting their way down Harris Road all the way to Route 25. Uncle Leo and Jasper's dad had left about an hour before them.

"You know where it is though, right?"

"Yeah, it's just up and around the corner." Wayne stopped to light a cigarette with a wood match. "I still say this is nuts."

He handed it to Jasper. After the last experience, Jasper knew better than to inhale the smoke. Instead, he just sucked it into his mouth and blew the cloud out again. "I don't want to go inside. I just want to see if we can hear anything."

"Alright, but like I told you, anybody sees us, it's every man for himself. I'm gonna skin out, and I ain't waiting for you. Got it?"

Jasper nodded.

They walked in silence for several minutes until Wayne finally asked, "Where do you think she went?"

"I don't know . . . somewhere, I guess." He didn't want to say his greatest fear aloud—*she must be dead then.* He also didn't want to admit she'd disappeared before. She'd leave in the middle of the night, or sometimes she wouldn't come home from work at all. But she'd always come back the next day. Her eyes would be red, her hair would be a mess, and she wouldn't say a word about it. She'd just go to her room and fall asleep. His father would tell Mrs. Carbo that Jasper's mother was sick or had to work late and ask her to watch him.

Mrs. Carbo. He hadn't thought much about the big round woman since he'd come to the farm, but he missed her. Her hands were tough and thick from kneading bread all day, and she smelled like stale cookies. She always had a smile for Jasper, but her eyes went sad whenever she looked at him too long. It made him worry there was something wrong with him. He would go quiet and avoid looking back at her. If he did, she might hug him in her big, suffocating arms until he wriggled free. Mrs. Carbo was probably wondering where he'd gone.

Hundreds of stars gleamed overhead. It felt as though they were watching the two boys as they made their way toward the main road. If Jasper had been in a better mood, he would have stopped and stared back in wonder at them all. He'd never seen more than three stars at a time through the smog of the city. Even the moon looked brighter, a searchlight hanging over the dirt road.

Wayne finished his cigarette and ground it under his boot. "You think she'll come back?"

"I don't know." Jasper shook his head. It had been only five days since he'd seen her, but it felt like years. "She's never been gone this long."

In the past, after his mother would reappear, he would try to pretend like nothing had happened. Once she was done sleeping, she would be sad.

Jasper, honey. Come here. She'd grab his two small hands and squeeze them. *Let me look at you. You alright?*

He would nod. He had to be careful not to cry. If he cried, there was no telling what she'd do. Sometimes she'd cry too. Sometimes she'd get furious and begin screaming at him. One time, she left again. So he would nod and not cry.

Let's go get some ice cream. That was usually her answer for it. One time she took him to buy a new baseball glove. That was after she was gone for two days. If she were to come back now, Jasper had no idea what she'd give him. *Maybe a new bike,* he thought bitterly.

"She really as crazy as Pop says?"

"What do you mean? What'd he say?"

"Uh, you know. Stuff," Wayne mumbled as if he'd changed his mind about discussing it.

"Like what stuff?"

"I don't know. He's always goin' on about what a wild one she was growin' up. Always gettin' in trouble. I think she might've been the one that burned down the old house."

Jasper stopped walking. "I thought you said it was wild Injuns!"

"Shh!" Wayne stopped dead in his tracks and grabbed Jasper by the arm.

"What?"

Wayne pointed up ahead. A large furry creature crossed the road a hundred feet ahead of them. It was long, bushy, and low to the ground. They stood frozen until it had disappeared into the cornfield on the other side.

"What the heck was that?" Jasper whispered.

"Looked like a fox. Good thing the chickens are fenced in."

"A fox? They ever . . . attack people?"

"Only shrimpy nine-year-old boys." Wayne chuckled and socked him in the arm.

"Real funny." Jasper punched him back as hard as he could. He hadn't liked what Wayne had said about his mom. He wanted to ask why he thought she'd burned down the house, but a pair of headlights passed along in front of them about a quarter mile up ahead. They were close to Route 25.

"That's the Tally Ho." Wayne pointed across the dark wheat field on their right to what looked like a large house with all the windows blazing. "If we want to get there unseen, we're gonna have to cross the field."

Jasper nodded, trying not to think about the fox they'd just seen coming from that direction. Wayne climbed down five steep feet into the ditch that ran along the right side of the road.

"Come on. We gotta cross here."

The moonlight didn't reach the bottom of the ditch. Jasper had to find his way blindly down the edge. Muddy water seeped into Jasper's boot as it sank down into the muck. He tried to step out of it and pulled his foot right out of his shoe.

"Shit!" he hissed.

"What?"

"Lost my shoe."

"Well, find it, dummy!" Wayne was already at the other side.

Jasper felt around in the mud until he felt the stiff leather cuff. He yanked it out of the muck only to land his socked foot right back in again.

"Will you stop monkeying around down there," Wayne whispered.

Jasper scrambled up the other side of the ditch, holding his shoe. By now his sock, his pant leg, and the shoe were completely caked with mud. *Damn it.* There was no hiding dirty laundry from his aunt. "How am I going to explain this to your mom?"

"You'll think of somethin'. Come on, Agent J. Do you want to complete this spy mission or what?"

Jasper blinked the tears back and limped after Wayne through the wheat field in one shoe, stopping every now and then to rub his filthy boot on the long stalks. "They must hate me," he muttered.

"Who?"

"Your mom and dad. They didn't want to have to take care of me. They must really hate that I'm here all the time now."

"Don't be dopey. You're family, Jas . . . like a little brother. You know, I had a little brother once."

"You did?"

"Yep. I was a little younger than you. Ma's belly got all fat. They didn't say nothin' to me about it, but I could tell. It was just like when old Sally had her first calf. There was something in there besides food, you know. Then Ma got real sick one night. They sent me away to Mr. Sheldon's for a few days. When I came back, the belly was smaller. Then it just went away. They never told me what happened, but I knew."

"What happened?" Jasper had stopped walking.

"It died. Somethin' was wrong with it and it died. I saw it happen once with pigs. Ten pigs came out all wriggly and pink, and the last one came out gray and still. Pop buried that one in the orchard . . . Ma never said a word about the baby, but she was sad for a real long time."

Jasper put his head down and kept walking. Suddenly his muddy sock wasn't such a big deal.

"So you see, I think they're happy to have you come stay for a while." Wayne threw an arm around his shoulder, and this time Jasper let him.

The Tally Ho was just a big house with a hand-painted sign hanging above the door. It faced Route 25, with a large gravel parking lot off to one side. There were three pickup trucks and a tractor sitting on the lot. Yellow lights and chattering voices spilled out of the open windows into the warm night outside. There was a pair of windows on the other side of the house away from the parking lot. Wayne and Jasper crept up and sat under them.

"Clint! Tell Ronnie here how you picked the name Tally Ho!" a voice called from a table not far from the window where they hid.

"You don't know that joke?" a deeper voice asked. "You see, one day a rich Yankee sailed all the way to merry ol' England to go fox hunting with the gentry. So he mounted up his horse, and they had one hell of a hunt. Got three foxes, and our dear Yankee shot two of 'em. So imagine his surprise when during the feast after, no one would talk to him. He'd go into a room, and they'd all leave. No one would sit at a table with him. Finally, he'd had enough and asked, 'Why are you gentlemen being so rude? Didn't we have good hunt?'"

"I love this part. What'd they say?" the first voice asked with a slight slur. The entire tavern had gone quiet in anticipation.

The barkeep put on a thick British accent. "Dear, sir. When we spot a fox, we say, 'Tally ho!' We do *not* yell, 'There goes the son of a bitch! Let's git 'im!'"

The entire bar erupted in laughter. Even Wayne and Jasper snickered out under the window. A few voices shouted "Tally Ho!" and glasses clinked together. In the uproar, Jasper decided to risk a peek inside. It was a large, smoky room with eight wood tables scattered about and a bar with five stools in the corner. His father and Uncle Leo sat on two of the stools next to a bigger man Jasper didn't recognize. A fat, balding man with a thick mustache was stacking up glasses behind the bar. Half of the tables were empty, including the one pressed against the window. Jasper moved out of the square of light on the grass and watched from the shadow.

His father drained a beer stein and raised a finger to order another. Uncle Leo's glass was still mostly full. They were clear across the room, with their backs turned. There was no way to hear what they were saying.

Jasper crouched back down and whispered, "I can't hear. I'm going to the other window."

"What are you crazy? All the cars! Someone might see you."

"I'll only be a minute."

Wayne shook his head but said, "I'll stay here and keep a watch."

Jasper nodded in agreement and crept around back to the window closest to the bar. There were no bushes to hide in from the parking lot, so he did his best to stay in the shadows. As he approached the window, he heard his mother's name.

"Althea? Nope, I ain't seen her in . . . jeez, must be at least a year. She's still a wild one, huh?" It was a voice Jasper didn't recognize.

"Nah. Just goin' through a rough patch." It was his father talking now. "Had a little trouble at work, I guess. She hasn't been there in a week. Never did trust that boss of hers. Wouldn't put it past him to try somethin'."

"He wouldn't be the first." The voice laughed.

Uncle Leo and his father didn't say anything, and the laugh fell flat. Jasper risked a peek inside the window. The man talking was wearing a tan shirt and a badge. He had a full mug of beer in his hand.

"Althea never did seem to take to workin' much. You remember, Clint, back when she was waitressing over at Steamboat's? What was it, thirty-one or thirty-two? That night she blew up the still? I thought he'd shoot her for sure. Place about burned to the ground."

"The still?" his father asked.

"Oh, back then everybody was making up their own mash. Prohibition and all. Course I wasn't the law back then." The man chuckled and drained half his glass. "Turned out she was better at drinkin' it than makin' it. Wasn't she, Leo? I don't know how she got herself out of that one. Didn't hurt she was such a looker, though."

Uncle Leo slapped his mug on the bar. "That's my sister you're talkin' about, Cal."

"Hey. Take it easy, Leonard. You know I don't mean nothin' by it." The sheriff held up his hands. "Besides, she's a married woman now. You could go over and talk to Big Bill yourself, but I'm sure he ain't seen her in years. Last I heard he's runnin' a roller rink down in Burtchville."

"I thought he ran the creamery." Uncle Leo did not seem amused.

"He pawned that off to his son. Or a cousin maybe. I can't remember. That family of his is into everything."

A hand grabbed Jasper by the shirt. It was Wayne. He yanked him behind the building just as the door slammed open and two men walked out.

"Hey! Who's there?" a voice shouted after them. "Didya see that? Looked like kids."

"So what?" a second voice slurred. "C'mon, Ronnie. Let's get up to Black River while we're still young."

Jasper and Wayne took off running through the field of wheat into the dark.

CHAPTER 9

What about your mother?

Was she a drinker?

Three nights later, something Wayne had said out on the road came back to Jasper uninvited. His eyes flew open in the dark. "Hey, Wayne?" he whispered.

"Hmm?" His cousin was half asleep.

"What did you mean the other night? When you said my mom might've burned down the old house?"

The shadow of Wayne sat up in the bed. "What?"

"Outside on the road. You said she might've burned down that old house," he repeated in his quietest voice, not wanting to wake his aunt and uncle.

"All I know is that Pop said Aunt Althea ran off after it happened."

"She ran off?"

"Disappeared."

"Disappeared? For how long?"

"He didn't really say."

"How long ago was that?"

"Knock off all the chatter!" a voice boomed from the other room like a strap to the back. "Get to sleep, boys."

Both boys flopped back down. Wayne's feet were at Jasper's head, and his were at the older boy's belly. After several minutes of silence passed, Wayne answered in a barely audible voice, "All I know is she didn't come back again until you were born."

Then there was nothing but the sound of Wayne breathing and the chirp of crickets outside the open window.

Jasper's father came back the next weekend to play catch. Jasper could tell from the sag of his shoulders and the tired look in his eyes that he hadn't found her. Jasper overheard him explain to Uncle Leo that he'd taken on more shifts at the plant before handing over an envelope. His uncle tried to hand it back, but his father wouldn't take it.

Wendell didn't say nearly as much to Jasper. He just asked, "You behavin' yourself? Stayin' out of trouble?"

Jasper nodded.

"School starts in a week. You do what Wayne says there, understand? I don't want to hear a bad report."

"Yes, sir." Jasper threw him the ball and studied the knots in his baseball glove. It was the same glove his mother had bought him the year before when she'd left the house in the middle of the night. *Don't you worry, Jasper. I'll always come back for you. I'm not goin' anywhere. Okay. I promise.* She'd wiped a tear and said it again. *I'm not goin' anywhere.*

There were so many questions he wanted to ask his father, but all of them would mean admitting that he'd been eavesdropping. Most would prove he and Wayne had sneaked out that night and listened under the windows of the Tally Ho, so he said nothing.

His father didn't stay over that night, and there were no visits back to the tavern. He'd already left to go back to Detroit when the right question finally popped into Jasper's head. "Can we go roller-skating?"

There weren't many chances to ask that question in the days that came next. Uncle Leo and Wayne spent twelve hours a day working the fields, harvesting hay. Even Aunt Velma came out of the house and pitched in.

Jasper mostly rode the rear bumper of the tractor while Wayne drove the giant green machine up and down the fields, pulling the mower and then the rake. Uncle Leo followed behind it, raking loose cuttings into windrows and sneezing.

"Is Uncle Leo sick?" Jasper asked Wayne after he'd cut the engine at the end of a row.

"Nah. Just allergic."

"To what?"

"Hay . . . Kinda funny, right?"

Uncle Leo walked up, wiping his face with a wet handkerchief. His eyes and nose were running and beet red. "That's enough for one day. Wayne, take the tractor back to the shed. Jasper, go water the cows before supper. I'm gonna finish up here."

"Yes, sir," both boys said in unison.

Jasper raced across the cut hay field toward the barn. He filled each giant water dish so quickly he splashed half the bucket on himself, but he hardly noticed. He threw the pail back onto its nail and dashed back to the far corner. He glanced over his shoulder before pulling his mother's diary out from its hiding place between the siding plank and the girt.

His eyes traced her name several times before attempting once again to read the first entry.

August 1, 1928
I'm going to die here . . .

Jasper stared at the word *die*, not sure if he was reading it right. "Die?" he whispered. He looked at the date again as he always did. His mother had been fourteen.

"Whatcha doin' in here?" a voice called from the barn door. It was Wayne.

Jasper spun around, hiding the book behind his back. "Uh. Nothin'."

"Oh, yeah?" Wayne smirked and walked over to him. "What's that you're hiding?"

"None of your b—"

Wayne whacked Jasper's arm before he could finish. The diary went flying, landing just outside the pigpen. Poor Roy snorted at it and walked to the other end of the pen like nothing had happened.

"Hey!"

"Hey, yourself." Wayne picked up the book and turned it over. "What is this?"

"None of your business!" Jasper yelled and swiped at the diary in his cousin's hand.

"Where'd you find it?" Wayne asked, holding the book high over Jasper's head and thumbing through the pages.

"It's mine, dammit! Give it back!"

"It's your mom's," Wayne stated the obvious and then finally looked down at his cousin flailing his hands. "Can you read it?"

Jasper's arms went limp. "No."

"Do you want to? I can help."

Jasper frowned, thinking about it. "I don't think she'd like that very much."

"So? She's not here. C'mon. I'll show you." Wayne sat down with his back to the side of the barn and ran his finger under each word.

August 1, 1928
I'm going to die here on this farm.

Jasper reluctantly squatted down beside him and followed his cousin's dirty fingernail as it navigated the page.

It's already happening. I can feel it in my bones. Every day is the same awful routine. Milk the cows, wash the dishes, clean the laundry, haul the water, feed the pigs, weed the garden. There's no end in sight! I'm supposed to keep slaving away day after day until what, I ask you? Until I get married to a sweaty, sunburnt, dirt-poor farmer of my very own? I'm amazed my mother hasn't dropped dead a hundred times already.

If I stay here, my fate is sealed. Mama doesn't even want to send me off to high school. She says there's really no point in it anyway. What good would it have done her? She says once Pearl is married off, she'll hardly be able to manage even with my help. Then she gives me that disappointed look of hers, and I know what she's thinking.

My mother never really wanted me. I was the last one born, and I can see it in her eyes whenever I don't dry a dish the right way or miss a weed in the vegetable garden. She figures she should have stuck with three. I figure she should've run screaming from the start.

But instead, I get to be the unlucky, unwanted, unnecessary number four. It's like I'm that ugly weed I didn't pull today, that prickly flower that hurts your hands when you yank it from the dirt. I'm not a hearty potato like Alfred. I'm not a hayseed like Leonard. I'm not a lovely, little daisy like my older sister, Pearl. I'm a weed.

It's only a matter of time before they find some excuse to pull me up and throw me away. That would suit me just fine. I'm so tired of being rooted here in the dirt. I'd stow away on the creamery cart to Burtchville just to escape the ever-loving smell of manure. No matter how many times you wash, you can never seem to lose the stink of it on your hands and clothes. It just gets under your skin. Papa might call it the "smell of money," but to me, it's all just shit.

Wayne let out a low whistle. "You better not let Pop find this."

Jasper agreed. His mother's bad language would earn them both a whipping just for reading it out loud, but it was still his best hope of finding her. "Will you keep it a secret for me?"

"No problem, kid." Wayne tousled his hair. "C'mon, we'd better get cleaned up for supper."

CHAPTER 10

They ever have any run-ins with the law?

The next morning, Jasper woke to the sound of tires rolling down the gravel driveway. They stopped, and an engine cut off. He sat up in bed with a start. Squinting out the window, he saw a black sedan was parked in front of the barn.

Mom?

It was a stupid thought, he realized. He'd never seen the car before. A hard knock on the door shook the house. His aunt answered it.

"Can I help you?" she asked.

"Are you Mrs. Leonard Williams?" a gruff voice asked.

"Yes."

"I need to speak with your husband."

"Of course . . . Come in, Officer. Can I get you a cup of coffee?"

"No, thank you." Hard footsteps slapped the floorboards, and a chair was pulled out from the table with a stuttering scrape. "Is your husband here?"

"Yes, out in the barn. Make yourself at home. I'll go get him."

The door opened and closed. The kitchen chair creaked as a large weight sank onto it. Jasper peeked out from behind the curtain at the back of the police officer's head. He was wearing a light-blue shirt and a wide-brimmed hat, but it wasn't a policeman's uniform. A gun hung from a shiny leather holster at his side. Jasper glanced over at Wayne peeking through the other side of the curtain from his pillow. They exchanged bewildered looks.

The police officer let out a low whistle as he surveyed the room. Both boys ducked behind the curtain.

The front door opened again, and two sets of feet came into the house. The chair sputtered as the officer stood back up.

"Morning, Officer," Uncle Leo said.

"Good morning. I'm Detective John Russo. Are you Leonard Williams?"

"I am. What can I do for you, Detective?"

"I'm investigating the disappearance of a woman—a Mrs. Wendell Leary. I understand you know her?"

"I do. Which police department did ya say you're with?"

There was a pause as the detective flashed his badge. "Detroit PD. Perhaps we should talk outside."

Through the curtain seam, Jasper could see the detective motion to the alcove where he and Wayne were listening.

Uncle Leo nodded. "Why don't we step out to the barn. You caught me right at feedin' time."

The two men left the house, and it was all Jasper could do not to run right after them. Wayne grabbed him by the shoulder and motioned to the window. Catching his meaning, Jasper threw on his pants and shoes and went to open the sash.

His aunt's voice stopped him cold. "Good morning, you two," she sang, pulling the curtain wide open.

Jasper spun around. Precious seconds ticked by. "Morning, Aunt Velma."

"Hey, Ma, who was that man?" Wayne asked.

"A police officer from Detroit."

"No foolin'? What'd he want?"

"That's really none of your business, young man. I need the two of you to collect extra eggs this morning in case our guest wants to stay for breakfast." She handed a basket to Wayne.

"I'll—I'll get started." Jasper snatched the basket from his cousin and was out the door before his aunt could object.

He ran a wide loop past the chicken coop and straight to the back side of the barn, where he'd be hidden from the house. It took several moments, darting from slat to slat, to locate the voices of the men inside. Uncle Leo was slopping the pigs.

"I don't know what you're talkin' about," Leo was saying.

"They didn't have any problems?"

"It's not really any of my business if they did."

"What sort of man is Wendell Leary in your opinion?"

"Old Wen's a nice enough guy. We were all happy when he came along."

"Is he prone to violence? He ever smack her around?"

Uncle Leo slammed the slop bucket on the ground. "I don't know where you were raised, Detective, but where I come from, you don't insult a man with those sort of questions. Wendell is good, God-fearin' folk, and if you're implying otherwise, we're gonna have words."

"Fair enough. We have to ask these things, sir. Nine times out ten, in these sorts of cases, the husband is to blame."

Jasper gaped at the detective through the wood planks. His dad had never laid a hand on his mother as far as he knew. Once she'd even screamed in his face for him to hit her. He never did. He'd just picked up Jasper and taken him to play catch.

"Are you suggesting that there's been a crime?" his uncle asked.

"We haven't ruled it out. According to her employer, a Perry Galatas, she's been missing work for quite some time."

"People up and quit jobs all the time." The sound of another bucket of slop hitting the trough drowned out the detective's response.

When the noise let up, he was saying, ". . . don't often leave their car in the woods and disappear, do they?"

Uncle Leo stood rooted to the spot for a beat. "Where'd you find it?"

"A farmer a few miles up the road went looking for his dog in the woods. He stumbled on a forty-seven Chevy buried under a pile of branches. Looked like someone had gone to some trouble to hide it. There was no sign of Mrs. Leary. No hospital has any record of her. County sheriff didn't know a thing about it. The car's been down at the impound lot in Port Huron for almost a week. No one's come to claim it."

"Why didn't they contact Wendell?"

"They did. He was hoping she'd come back for it, at least that's what he says. He finally filed a missing person report. They're processing the car as evidence today."

"Evidence of what, exactly?"

"Well, for starters, I understand she's wanted by the sheriff for questioning . . . Abandoning a car on county land isn't a serious offense, but it does raise some questions. And then, of course, there's the possibility that someone else was involved."

There was a long silence.

"I'd hoped we might find her here. Hiding out. Pulling a Houdini like that makes a husband pretty angry. You sure she wouldn't come back here?"

"I am. She was never afraid of Wen. Besides, she never really took to farming life."

"Yes, I hear around Burtchville she was a colorful sort. I understand she has a son?"

Uncle Leo didn't answer right away. "Yep. He's been stayin' here with us for a while."

"Since when?"

"About two weeks. Althea brought him up here, said there was some things she had to do."

"Was this unexpected?"

"A bit."

"She ever leave him here before?"

"Sure. We're family, ain't we? Nothin' strange about a nephew coming to visit for a few days here and there."

"She ever leave him this long?"

"Oh, I don't know. Back when he was about a year old, he came and stayed here for a spell."

Jasper's mouth fell open. He had no memory of being left the first time.

"How long?"

"A few weeks. Frankly, I encouraged it. City's no place to raise a boy. Besides, the wife really enjoyed having another little one around for a bit."

"Did Althea tell you what she was doing or where she was going this time?"

"Not really. Just said there was something she had to do. I've learned not to ask too much."

"Why's that?"

"Because Althea's a private person." His uncle sighed. "There's nothin' wrong with that. Last I checked, it ain't a crime. I'm pretty private too, and I can't say I'm liking all these questions. What's it to you way down there in Detroit anyway? Isn't this a bit outside your jurisdiction?"

"Althea's a Detroit resident. The county sheriff here called it in to see if we had an open case."

"Do you?"

"Not yet. Let's just say we have our interests, but nothing for you to worry about. We're the good guys in this. Did she ever mention any enemies to you? Anyone she felt threatened by?"

"You don't really think somethin' like that's goin' on, do you?"

Something like what? Jasper wanted to scream.

"We're not ruling it out. Will you answer the question?"

"No. She never talked about anyone, but she never talked much to begin with. Christ, Althea . . ."

"She seem nervous last time you saw her? Jumpy?"

Jasper remembered her hands gripping the steering wheel, trembling when she screwed open the flask.

"A bit."

"Take my card. If you hear from your sister or think of anything at all . . ."

A hand slapped over Jasper's mouth.

"We gotta move," a voice hissed in his ear. It was Wayne. Jasper had no idea how long he'd been there listening too. He dragged him away from the barn by his arm and over to the chicken coop. "Sorry, kid, but he was done with the pigs. He always comes out to the pump after."

In the distance, Jasper could see his uncle rounding the side of the barn to the well pump. He was carrying two buckets. Wayne grabbed the basket from Jasper's hands. He'd forgotten he was holding it.

"I don't think Detective Russo will be stayin' for breakfast," Wayne said and swung open the wire door to the chicken coop. A flock of feathers flew up at them as the hens scattered about. Wayne flopped open the wood ramp to the outdoor run, and most of them scrambled away. Jasper just stood there in a stupor while Wayne did the rounds, collecting eggs from the old apple crates.

A loud squawk snapped Jasper back to his senses. The family rooster pecked at his legs and then tried to eat one of his shoelaces. Jasper kicked him off. Wayne finished collecting and pushed him back out the door.

"Wayne?"

"Yeah?"

"Did I come stay with you when I was a baby? For like two weeks?"

"I remember somethin' sort of like that. I was a lot younger than you are now." He held the door to the coop open for Jasper, then latched it shut. "I remember being all excited about being a big brother. I kinda hoped you'd stay."

Jasper stared at the ground and said nothing.

CHAPTER 11

Did you ever feel like they were hiding something?

Later that afternoon, Jasper dragged Wayne back into the barn.

"I don't understand what you think this has to do with anything," his cousin protested.

Jasper didn't respond. The smooth prints of hard-soled shoes scarred the ground where the detective had stood and accused his father of terrible things. He tried to imagine his mother burying their family car under branches deep in the woods. It didn't make sense.

Did she ever mention any enemies to you? Anyone she felt threatened by?

"She wrote that stuff years ago, you know," Wayne continued, but he let himself be pulled along by the younger boy anyway. Probably because he felt bad for him. Jasper didn't care why. The dried leather binding felt stiff in his hands as he pulled it from the gap between the siding slats and the girt. The yellowed paper still smelled of smoke and crackled as he ran his fingers over her name.

"You have to show me how to read this." Jasper sat down in the dirt with the book in his lap.

"Why?"

"Because I need to know what it says," Jasper pleaded, grabbing his cousin's arm and pulling him down to the ground. He shoved the book into his cousin's hands.

"All this thing says is your mom was a big blabbermouth as a kid."

"Shut up!" Jasper was on the verge of tears. "It's all I have, and if you don't help me . . . I'll . . . I'll . . ."

"Oh, for Pete's sake." Wayne smacked the top of Jasper's head. "Don't give yourself a hernia. If I do this for you, whatcha gonna do for me?"

"I'll do all your chores for a week."

"Hmm. Two weeks and we have a deal."

"Fine." Jasper sighed.

"Alright. Then school's in session. If you want to read this stuff, all you have to do is recognize the letters. It's the same alphabet as before. You can read, right?"

Jasper nodded. He'd been reading since he was four. *Don't go thinking you're something special just because some things come easy, baby,* his mother had warned when he started showing off. *Knowing how to read don't make you smarter than anybody else, and thinking you are is the surest way to ruin your life.*

"Good. Then you can read this stuff once you get used to it. A few letters look a bit strange, that's all. There's *L*. There's an *S*. The ever-important *I*. Doubt you'll even see a *Q* in this—them's pretty rare. Now see if you can follow along with me." Wayne cleared his throat and put on his best girlie voice.

> *August 5, 1928*
> *Mama called me a liar again today. She says there's nothing worse in this world than a dishonest woman. I'd like to argue that point, but what's the use? Of course I know I shouldn't lie, but I'm telling you it's really not fair. You*

lie about one silly little thing like saying your prayers at bedtime or washing the dishes and you're branded for life: Liar. And a young woman to boot. I guess I'm doomed.

Papa says I don't have the sense of a headless chicken. Isn't that a gruesome thought? Me just running around the yard with my head cut off, possessed with a twitching ghost? If anybody bothered to ask me, I'd say the fact he doesn't understand me doesn't make me stupid. It's more of a commentary on his intelligence than mine, don't you think?

Perfect Pearl is hardly a sister at all the way she's constantly telling Mama all my secrets. She's probably reading this right now, and if she is, she'd better understand that if she keeps reading, I'll tell Mama all about her kissing Davey Harding behind the schoolhouse. I'm not kidding, Pearl. I've booby-trapped this book, and I'll know if you've gone snooping.

My brothers are hardly any better. All Leonard cares about are tractors, and my oldest brother, Alfred, hardly knows my name. He spends all his time over at the high school in Port Huron. It's like I don't exist at all.

Wouldn't that be nice? To not exist? To just up and vanish in the night? To fly away? My next life I want to be a bird. That's assuming you get more than one, of course. Dear God, I sure hope I do.

Wayne stopped to take a breath. "See what I mean? Just a bunch of girlie whatnot. You sure you want to read this mess?"

Jasper just kept staring at the twisted-together words. His mother wanted to fly away. Maybe she'd finally gotten her wish.

"Fine. It's your funeral. See if you can do it. Try that one again."

Jasper spent the next hour reading and rereading the first two entries until he had a grasp on her penmanship.

"Not bad, kid. Maybe you don't have rocks for brains after all. You read the next one."

In a slow, faltering voice, Jasper sounded out the words.

August 12, 1928
Today was a terrible day. Papa was right. I'm worse than
a headless chicken. Mr. Hoyt caught me in his barn.
Mother's always telling me not to go snooping where I'm
not wanted, but I just had to see that new . . .

"Colt," Wayne interjected.

. . . colt. Papa was talking all about it just the other
day. Mr. Hoyt's been trying to get the . . .

"Neighbors."

. . . neighbors to invest in his new plan to breed
racehorses. He says a single horse can fetch over $1,000.
What a . . .

"Schemer!"

That's what Papa called him, anyway. Of course, he
decided it sounded too good to be true. I don't think Papa
believes in anything that doesn't involve sweating yourself
to death out in the sun, least of all horse racing. But
imagine that! A $1,000 horse living just over the creek. I
had to see it. It might've had golden hooves.
Turns out he was just a normal sort of baby horse,
all . . .

"Wobbly."

> *. . . wobbly and skinny. I sat down next to him and stared him right in his big black eyes, looking for some sort of sign that he was something special. A $1,000 horse should look like something, but I didn't see nothing but the reflection of my own dopey face, the poor thing. I couldn't help but pet him. He was just a baby after all. What was Mr. Hoyt going to do when he found out this prize pony was nothing but a plain . . .*

"Quarter horse. Look at that—there's a Q."

> *. . . quarter horse? All I could think running my hand down his flank was that he would never be worth more than the plow he'd pull. It made me want to love him. He was so smooth and soft, but under the skin something wild trembled. Maybe he had some racing in him. Or maybe he was just cold being all alone without his mama. I put my arms around him and tried to make him warm and still. It wasn't his fault he was stuck in that barn. I felt so bad for him, I began dreaming up ways to help him escape.*
>
> *Right about then, Mr. Hoyt kicked in the barn door yelling, "Who's in there, God . . .*

"Damn it!" Wayne raised his eyebrows and grinned, daring Jasper to cuss out loud.

> *. . . damn it!"*
> *I must've lost my voice, because I just stood there dumb. He came stomping through, checking stalls until*

he found me with my arms wrapped around his new horse and pointed a double-barrel shotgun right at my head!

"Wow!" Wayne piped in. "She's lucky he didn't shoot her. You don't go messin' around Old Hoyt's place. He's liable to kill you! Pop said he was robbed once, and that sort of thing leaves a mark."

Jasper thought about this for a minute before continuing.

He looked so surprised to see me, you'd have thought I'd sprouted horns. "Don't shoot! It's just me, Mr. Hoyt. Althea." I gave him a real stupid smile. Papa always said it was important to be a good neighbor. Doesn't that include horses? I think so too, but Mr. Hoyt didn't seem to agree. He just kept on staring at me down the barrel of his gun.

"Who said you could be in here? What're you doin'? Get away from him! When I tell your father about this, you're gonna wish you'd had more sense! It ain't right sneaking around someone else's place like this."

I must've looked like I'd seen the devil himself, because out of nowhere he just starts laughing one of those laughs without any sound . . .

"Boys? You out there?" Aunt Velma called from the driveway. "Time for dinner!"

"Be right there, Ma!" Wayne hollered back, then hissed, "Hurry up before she comes in here."

Jasper dropped his voice to a whisper.

. . . laughs without any sound, just a lot of hot air blowing out.

*Then he lowered his gun and smiled at me. It didn't
look like a real nice smile, though. His lips were smiling,
but his eyes were doing something different. I didn't like
it. "Say, maybe we could keep this between us, Althea.
We're friends, right?"*

Jasper stopped, not sure he'd read the last line right.

Wayne jumped in, whispering the words twice as fast as Jasper
could manage to get to the end.

*I'm not sure if I said anything back. He didn't look
like my friend, but Papa would tan my hide if Mr. Hoyt
asked him too. They're the ones who was friends.*

*"Maybe you could do me a favor instead?" His
strange smile got bigger. Doing a favor would be better
than getting a whupping, right? "You come back here
tomorrow, and we'll figure something out."*

*So I backed my way out of the barn and ran home.
Now we have some sort of deal, I guess. But I really don't
want to go back there.*

Wayne snapped the book shut and tucked it back into its hiding
place. "We should get back to the house."

Jasper reluctantly followed him out of the barn. Halfway to the
cabin, he stopped and stole a glance out over the back fields to the
split-rail fence that separated his uncle's farm from Old Hoyt's place.

I don't want to go back there.

CHAPTER 12

Children hear things. Sometimes they see things
they're not supposed to. Did you?

Labor Day came without so much as a break in the work or a chance to go back to the barn and read. Jasper couldn't help but think of the kids back in Detroit as he helped his cousin and uncle rake the endless windrows before the hay baler rolled over them. They'd be playing in the park or begging the shop owners to open up a fire hydrant. Mrs. Carbo would've made her red, white, and blue frosted cookies down in the bakery, and the whole apartment would've smelled like burnt sugar.

"Hey! Quit daydreaming over there!" Wayne barked over the grumbling baler. "You're gonna get run over!"

Jasper jumped out of the way and picked up his rake.

The sense of adventure had left the farm weeks ago. He missed his home. He missed running water and flushing toilets and the playground and his old bed. He missed the way his father would read him parts of the Sunday paper over toast.

Most of all he missed her.

The next morning, Jasper woke with a start. He'd dreamed he was falling again, only this time it was down a dark well. The echo of Sally screaming hung in his ears long after he jerked himself awake. He sucked in a breath and blinked the sleep from his eyes. The first tinge of dawn was still tucked behind the fields.

His pajamas were wet again. He climbed off the mattress, careful not to jostle Wayne, and assessed the damage. The extra towels Aunt Velma had put under his sheet were damp, but the bed beneath was dry. Jasper hung his head. Wayne hadn't said anything about the towels, but he must've noticed. Jasper tore off his wet pajamas, letting his angry fingernails rake his skin raw.

Damn it!

He threw the wet pajamas and towels into the laundry basket Aunt Velma had hidden under the bed.

Cursing made him think of his mother. He slumped onto the side of the bed and pictured her in their kitchen, standing over the shards of some broken plate. *Damn it!* she'd yell. Then she'd remember Jasper was right there. *Sorry, hon . . . Hear no evil. Right, baby?*

Huh? Jasper would pretend to be deaf.

This almost always made her smile. Jasper squeezed his eyes shut before the tears could come. Her smile was the sun after a long cold rain.

"You nervous?"

Jasper jumped up at the sound of his cousin's voice. "Huh? No . . . Well, sorta. Did I wake you?" He quickly pulled on his pants, mortified that Wayne might've been watching him the whole time.

"Miss Babcock is real nice. Don't worry." Wayne slid off the mattress. "Let's get the chores done so we can get there early."

The two boys fed the pigs and milked the cows before breakfast, with Wayne chatting the whole while. "The school's called St. Clair Primary. It's over on Jeddo Road about a mile from here. It'll take us about fifteen minutes walkin'."

"How many kids go there?"

"About fifty or so. They all come from the farms around here. School only goes up to eighth grade. I'll have to go down to Port Huron in two years for high school," Wayne explained, carrying two full buckets back up to the house.

"Fifty kids and just one teacher?" Jasper trailed after him with a basket of eggs plucked from the henhouse. He wasn't really listening. All he could think about was her. It had been three weeks.

A half hour later, Wayne and Jasper were heading down the two-track drive out into the fields. The sun was warm, and the air smelled of fermenting apples and cut hay. The day would have been perfect if he wasn't heading off to some strange school. Back in Detroit, the bus to Southpointe Elementary would be pulling away from his block right about then. He never really liked going to that school, but the fact that he wasn't on the bus told him he might never go back.

In the distance, the stand of trees hid the crumbling house where his mother had grown up. His feet itched to go back there.

Wayne kept talking. "We could've gone down Harris, up St. Clair, and over to Jeddo, but this is the fastest way to go on foot." He led Jasper through the field. They crossed over a small creek on a makeshift footbridge and hopped a low fence. "We're on Mr. Hoyt's land now. He don't mind us cuttin' through, but you don't hop the fence unless you know Nicodemus is in the barn, understand?"

"Nicodemus?"

"Old Hoyt's bull. He's real mean. That son of a bitch almost gored me last year. He's got horns like two daggers, and that bastard's fast. If I didn't know better, I'd say he's out to kill me."

Jasper's eyes widened at the description of the bull and his cousin's foul language. He scanned the field. There was a blood-red barn three hundred yards from the creek. The door was closed. "How'd you know he's in the barn?"

"You see 'im?"

Jasper shook his head. "But how do you know when he'll be out?"

"I don't." Wayne grinned. "Race ya!"

With that, the twelve-year-old took off running for the far fence. Jasper's short legs were no match for his cousin's long ones, but he was faster than he looked and took off after Wayne. As he sprinted the four hundred yards, he imagined the demon Nicodemus right on his tail. He could feel its hot breath on his neck. He glanced back and there was nothing there, but the more he thought about it, the faster his legs went, until he couldn't think at all.

The two boys slammed into the fence at nearly the same time. "Shoot, Jasper! I didn't know you could run like that."

Jasper tried to smile, but the unbridled terror was still coursing through his veins. An image of his mother ran through his mind. Something was chasing her. He shook it off and pulled himself over the fence and headed down to Jeddo Road with his cousin grinning after him.

Halfway down the road, Jasper glanced back over his shoulder at the clapboard house where Old Hoyt still lived. The white paint was peeling and one of the green shutters hung loose from a nail.

A curtain moved aside in Hoyt's window. A pale face peered out from behind the glass. Jasper squinted at the hanging jowls, sagging eyes, and a frown of mouth.

"Hey there, Mr. Hoyt!" Wayne called out and waved.

The curtain fell closed again without a response. Jasper whipped his head back around and kept walking, but he could feel a pair of eyes following him the whole way to the schoolhouse. Wayne didn't seem to notice.

The teacher greeted the two boys at the door. "Good morning, Wayne!"

"Morning, Miss Babcock. This is my cousin Jasper Leary."

"Hello, Jasper!" She knelt down to size him up. "Welcome to St. Clair Primary. How old are you?"

"Nine," Jasper replied, keeping his eyes on the ground.

"Well then. You'll be sitting in the third row." She stood to hold the door open, and the boys stepped into a large room. There was a slate blackboard at the front of the room and five rows of wood desks lined up like church pews. A black woodstove sat unlit in a corner. There was a hand-painted sign next to it that read "Wandering Hands Get Burned."

Jasper found a seat in the third row, and Wayne picked a spot in the back. They were the first kids in the room, and Miss Babcock followed Jasper to his seat.

"Did you finish third grade, Jasper?" she asked, standing in front of his desk.

He nodded his head, keeping his eyes on the hem of her long skirt.

"Did you like it?"

He kept his eyes down and nodded again. He hated his old school, but at that moment he missed it so bad it hurt.

"Well, you'll find school here to be a little different. You don't have to stick to only fourth grade lessons. You can do fifth or sixth grade lessons if you like. You can do third grade things too. There's only one rule in this school."

He waited for her to continue, but she didn't. Finally, he had no choice but to look up at her face. Her eyes were kind but not smiling anymore.

"You must be your best self while you're here. I will not tolerate lying, cheating, stealing, interruptions, or laziness."

He glanced up at the wooden paddle hanging above her desk then back down at the wood-plank floor.

"Can you be your best self, Jasper?" She crouched down in front of him and lifted his chin until they were eye to eye. For a split second, he was terrified she was looking right into his soul and could see all the ugly things inside it. All the things that had made his mother leave him.

He shut his eyes and nodded.

CHAPTER 13

Tell me about your neighbors.

Were you particularly close to any of them?

August 13, 1928
I hoped he'd forget. But I've never been lucky. I was born under a bad moon, that's what Mama told me that time when I accidentally broke her favorite vase. Seemed like an awfully mean thing to say over a really ugly piece of pottery she'd gotten across the river, but maybe she was right. Maybe I was born bad.

Mr. Hoyt came by today to talk to Papa about something boring, but then he motioned me over and patted his knee for me. I'm fourteen years old and far too big to sit on a lap, but I did it anyway.

"Althea here's growin' up to be a fine young lady, John. Don't you think?" he said, smiling that strange smile of his.

"She sure is, Art. Sometimes I think she's gettin' a bit too big for her britches." Papa laughed. He didn't seem bothered at all that Mr. Hoyt had his hand on my shoulder.

"Could you spare her a couple afternoons a week? My Alice is having a harder time keepin' up with the housework since Maureen up and got married. We'd pay. How does a nickel an hour sound?"

I wanted to jump off Hoyt's leg and scream, but Papa just seemed pleased as punch. "Well, sure."

"But, Papa!" I practically yelled. "I—I have so many chores here. And in a few weeks there'll be schoolwork."

"Althea, hush. A little hard work never did anybody any harm. You're always asking for new dresses and the like. Now you can earn the money for 'em. I dare say Mr. Hoyt here's being all too generous."

And just like that I was sold into slavery by my own father!

"Wonderful. Why don't you send her over tomorrow after lunch then." Mr. Hoyt patted my back, then put his hands on my waist and lifted me off his knee.

The minute he left, I begged Papa to undo the deal, but he wouldn't have it. He said we've been hurtin' for money for too long and it was high time I was put to good use. I screamed at the top of my lungs that I did all my chores every day and I worked hard in school and how could he single me out and not Perfect Pearl or Leo.

Turns out, I got my whupping anyway.

Jasper read the entry again nice and slow just to be sure. Wayne wasn't there to help him this time and complain about all the girlie whatnot, but he'd done his job. Jasper could see the words coming out of the mess of swirled ink. The same thing had happened when he was four. One day he picked up his favorite book about the little blue engine, and he didn't just see the letters his mother had taught him. He could see all the words he knew by heart jumping off the page.

Pride over his achievement was short-lived as he read the words again and thought of his mother sitting on Old Mr. Hoyt's lap with his pale face and sagging frown.

August 14, 1928

Well, that was unexpected. I showed up at Mr. Hoyt's farm today just as planned to go and help his wife, Alice. I expected to do dishes, wash clothes, and other horrible hand-cracking things. Instead, Mr. Hoyt met me at the front door and led me straight away into the barn.

"You seem like a real bright girl, Althea," he said as he closed the door.

"I do? I was just thinking the opposite," I said. Mrs. Hoyt was nowhere to be seen and Mr. Hoyt had on that strange smile again.

"How'd you like to make some real money?" he asked and put an arm around my shoulder. "Pretty girl like you can go far."

"What do you mean?" Being a girl has never been anything but a burden to me on the farm, and something told me that wasn't about to change.

"You ever tried giggle water?" he asked. He went over to a corner of his barn and pulled out a big brown jug. He bit the cork out and waved it under my nose. Whatever was inside burned my nostrils.

"No, sir." I took a big step back and eyed the door. Whatever he was suggesting was sounding pretty bad to me.

"Good. I don't want you sampling the wares." He rammed the cork back into the neck of the jug. *"I need you to make deliveries."*

"Deliveries?" I felt the squirrels in my stomach quiet down. I could make deliveries.

"Can you drive a horse cart?"

"Of course. Papa's been having me drive since I was six."

"Excellent. I'll load up a cart, and you'll drive it to the places I say. Understand?"

"Is that all?" No washing, no chopping wood. Just driving. It was too good to be true. I would just have to ignore what Papa says about those types of things. Papa and I don't agree on much anyhow.

"Yep. Got my first delivery tomorrow. Can you be here at three?" he asked.

I agreed and followed him out of the barn past that pathetic little horse of his. I paused to look at the colt. I don't know why I asked, "What's his racing name going to be?"

Mr. Hoyt started laughing that hot-air laugh again and said, "You wanna name it?"

I shook my head and told him I didn't. I've always been bad luck.

"Hey, kid. Get your nose out of that book before someone sees you." Wayne smacked it out of Jasper's hand and handed him a shovel. "We have to clean out the stalls today. You know, I really don't think you should be reading that."

"I thought you said it didn't matter since she's not here." Jasper scowled at his cousin and snatched the book off the dirt.

"Well, maybe I was wrong. Maybe this stuff isn't for a little kid to read. Ever think of that?" Wayne grabbed the diary and shoved it back between the siding boards. "Just don't let Pop find you reading it."

Jasper's eyes widened at how easily his cousin had crept up on him. He made a mental note to be more careful. It also occurred to him that Wayne with the disapproving look in his eye might just take the book away himself. He'd have to find a new hiding spot.

The two boys spent that Saturday morning shoveling manure out of the barn and laying down fresh straw. Every time a car rolled down Harris Road, Jasper would stop in his tracks and wait for that rusted pickup to appear. It never did.

After lunch came and went, Jasper realized his dad probably wasn't coming.

Around three o'clock that afternoon, Wayne came and found him sitting under a tree by Sally's well. The stone cap was back in its place, and the ground no longer stank of bile and blood. The tree where he sat still had scars from where the tieback ropes had broken the bark.

"Hey. You alright?" Wayne kicked his boot.

Jasper shrugged. His first week of school had been relatively uneventful. He'd learned the names of everyone in all the grades but hadn't made any real friends yet, except Miss Babcock. But she didn't really count.

"Say, I know what'll cheer you up. I think I just convinced the old man to take us into Burtchville after supper. Want to go try roller-skating?"

"Do you really think your pop will let me go?" Jasper leapt to his feet with only one thing on his mind. According to that sheriff at the Tally Ho, Big Bill knew his mother.

"Sure. Go get changed."

The roller rink was called Mr. G's Skating Club. Uncle Leo dropped the two boys off with fifty cents each. "Be back in a couple hours. You two better stay out of trouble. Understood?"

Both boys nodded as they scrambled out of the truck. Wayne went racing to the door, but Jasper stopped and turned to his uncle. "Thank you, sir. I'm . . ." He couldn't find the words for what he wanted to say. It was somewhere between a sorry and a thank-you. He was still a guest in his uncle's house and didn't know when either of his parents might come back for him.

Uncle Leo waved a hand at him. "Try to have some fun. Go on and git."

Jasper nodded and ran after Wayne.

The roller rink looked like a big blue barn from the outside, but inside it was like nothing Jasper had ever seen. Big flashing lights of every color lit up the walls and the polished wood floor. Music blared over the loudspeaker, and what seemed like hundreds of kids were racing by in a squealing blur. There were food stands lining the edges of the rink, selling hot dogs, soda pop, and penny candy. The smell of fresh popcorn hung in a buttery fog over everything.

Wayne was over at the main counter getting a pair of roller skates. Each pair cost fifty cents to rent for two hours. Jasper had never skated before in his life and watched with fascination as his cousin traded his filthy work boots for a pair of green-and-red shoes with shiny black wheels on the bottom.

"Ain't nothin' to it!" Wayne said, lacing up the skates. He stood up and spun around Jasper in a tight circle. "Go get yourself a pair. I'll be out there."

With that, Wayne flew off to the rink to join the other boys and girls circling the floor. A clinking piano rang out over the PA. A brassy woman's voice belted out a song about candy.

A grizzled giant stood behind the counter, oiling up skates. He had gray stubble all over his fat cheeks and a half-chewed cigar hanging from his mouth. He tested the roll of a skate with a hand that looked tough enough to crush stone. His name tag read "Bill." From his enormous belly, Jasper could only assume this was the Big Bill that might know where his mother had gone.

"Ex—excuse me?" Jasper stepped up to the counter.

"Can I help you?" the man barked.

"Um . . . I—I don't know."

"You're gonna have to speak up, kid." Bill pointed to his ear.

"Are you . . . are you Big Bill? From Steamboat's?" Jasper shouted as loud as he dared.

The man dropped the rag in his hand and let the skate roll down the counter. "What the hell you know about Steamboat's?"

"Not . . . nothin' really. I heard my dad talkin' about it."

"Who?" The man seemed angry. He snatched the skate and stuffed it back in a cubby below the counter.

Jasper's feet wanted to run, but he forced them to stay put. This might be his only chance. "I think . . . I think you knew my mom?"

"Did I?" Bill lowered his elbows to the counter and glowered over the edge at Jasper, who was feeling shorter by the second.

"Her name is Althea. Althea . . . Williams." Jasper guessed Bill wouldn't know her married name.

The man's hard face softened into a grin. He straightened up and laughed. "Althea Williams. Well, I'll be a son of a bitch. You're Althea's boy? Let me look at ya." Bill grabbed him by the chin and studied his face. "Yep. You sure are, aren't ya?"

He stubbed out his cigar and lumbered out from behind the rental desk. Clapping Jasper hard on the shoulder, he led him to a bench and sat him down.

"What's your name, boy?"

"Jasper. Jasper Leary."

"What's your pop's name?"

All the questions were making him nervous, but he answered, "Wendell Leary."

"Don't know him. Hmm. Your mom was really somethin', kid. Used to turn heads and then some. What's she up to now?" Big Bill craned his neck and scanned the walls, looking for her.

"I—I don't know." He didn't want to say any more, he realized. He'd probably already said too much. Jasper's heart tightened thinking about her car hidden away in the woods. *What if she was hiding too?*

The consternation must have been written all over his face, because Bill nodded ever so slightly. "You don't know."

Jasper didn't say a word.

"Huh. Wish I could say that surprises me. Althea had a way of finding trouble. Or letting trouble find her."

Jasper couldn't help but ask more. "I heard that once she sorta . . . blew up something and that you . . . you might've shot her?"

Bill raised his eyebrows but looked a little less amused. "Sounds like someone's been listening to other people's stories."

Jasper shrugged and studied his feet. The man wasn't wrong. "Did she work for you?"

"She worked over at the old diner for a while. Back when she was just a messed-up kid. Like I said, trouble seemed to find Althea wherever she went, but I'd have never shot her. Besides, I don't think that fire was all her fault. She'd gone and got herself mixed up with them wild folks over at the res. Motega came in and started raising hell. I warned her to stay away from him."

"Motega?"

"Hey, little snooper. Don't get any ideas about pokin' around over there. Black River ain't no place for a kid. People get killed messin' around up there. Heard a bunch of 'em just got run up for murder. That poor girl . . ."

"What girl?"

Big Bill shot him a warning look. "You better just start mindin' your own business."

Wayne sailed by on skates and gave him a scowl. Jasper hardly noticed. *What girl?*

The giant man next to him nodded like he could hear the wheels turning in Jasper's head. "Shoot. You're just like her, ain't ya?"

Jasper straightened his back. "No. I'm not."

"Ain't nothin' to be ashamed of. Not really. I always did have a soft spot for Althea. She was such a beauty. Too bad she couldn't help stickin' her nose where it didn't belong. You can see where that got her." The man patted him on the back.

The unwanted gesture made weeks of anger boil up in Jasper's blood. He stood up and shouted, "Have you seen her or not?"

Big Bill chuckled and stood up from the bench. He made Jasper follow him all the way back to the counter before he answered, "Nope. Not in a while. But you tell her to come see me when you find her. She and I should talk."

"What do you mean?"

The man didn't answer. He just studied the boy's face like he was looking for something that was missing. Two men walked up to the counter, and Big Bill turned his attention to them. "Perry! Taki! How you boys doin' tonight?"

"Just fine, William. Looks like business is booming." The older man grinned. He had silver hair and thick black eyebrows. He set a briefcase down on the counter. "Who knew this roller-skating was such a gold mine?"

"It's these kids. What can I say? Seven days a week, they love it. The money practically prints itself." Bill rolled a pair of skates over to Jasper. "That'll be fifty cents, kid."

Jasper knew it was his cue to leave, but he couldn't give up that easily. "What did you want to tell her?"

The two men turned and raised their bushy eyebrows at him. The second, younger man looked like he'd been in a fight. His face was a map of cuts and bruises.

Big Bill just laughed. "Sorry, kid. I haven't seen your little friend. Now, go have fun."

CHAPTER 14

Don't you want to identify all potential suspects?
Then answer the question.

Jasper woke up early the next morning to the dull thump of Aunt Velma throwing fresh logs in the woodstove on the other side of the curtain. Wayne was still snoring at the other end of the bed. Jasper waited until the front door opened and shut again and the cabin went quiet before sitting up.

Utter relief washed over him when he felt the dry mattress. He climbed out of bed in silence and pulled on his clothes in the pink morning light filtering in from the window. Wayne rolled over but kept on snoring. Jasper carried his shoes to the door, not putting them on until he was out on the porch.

Twenty feet behind the cabin, he caught sight of his aunt disappearing into the outhouse. With the coast clear, he scuttled across the driveway and into the barn. The cows stirred in their pens as he slipped by them to the far corner under the feed bins where his mother's book was waiting.

August 15, 1928
It was just as easy as he said it would be. I showed up at
Mr. Hoyt's barn at three o'clock, and he had a cart loaded
with ten brown jugs like the one he'd had me smell.

"Now, just take this up to Burtchville to a little café
called Steamboat's. It's on Lake Road. When you get there,
ask for Big Bill. Can you do that?" he asked.

I told him I could.

"If anybody stops you to ask, I want you to tell 'em
you're haulin' buttermilk. Alright? And if anybody wants
to check, let him sniff the last jug on the right."

He pointed to a jug that looked like all the others.
I must've looked worried, because then he said, "Don't
worry. No one's going to stop and bother a sweet young
thing like you. Just look like your papa will whup you if
you're late, and they'll let you go."

"Steamboat's. Big Bill. No problem," I said and took
off with Hoyt's rickety old mare, Josie. The cart creaked
and squeaked the whole way, and the jugs clanked and
rattled as I tried to forget what Mr. Hoyt had called me.
He'd called me a "thing." I passed four carts on the road,
but no one even looked at me sideways.

Steamboat's was a small six-table restaurant just like
the others that lined Lake Road. You could only pick
it out by the tiny handwritten sign hanging from two
hooks over the door, but I found it. When I walked in,
there was nobody there but an old lady behind the lunch
counter. I begged her pardon and asked, "Is there a Big
Bill here?"

"You got a delivery? He's in the back." Her voice
sounded like a rusty nail, and I wondered if she knew

*what I was delivering. Mr. Hoyt called it "giggle water,"
but the lady looked like she hadn't laughed in years.*

*I pulled the cart around to the back of the restaurant
and found an enormous man with black hair sitting on
a stool by the grease trap. It smelled worse than any gut
wagon I'd ever whiffed, and I almost lost my lunch on
his splattered apron.*

"Are you Big Bill?" I asked.

*He just looked up at me with his fat, stubbled face
and didn't say a word.*

"I've got a delivery from um . . . Mr. Hoyt."

*Big Bill smiled with these big yellow teeth biting a
cigar and asked, "You got a name, cupcake?"*

*Cupcake. How do you like that? I didn't know if I
should tell him my name. I would have given him a fake
one if I could've thought that fast. "Althea," I said, dumb
girl that I am.*

*"Nice to meet you, Althea." Then he shook my hand
like I was an actual grown-up and not a cupcake at all.
"Let's see what you got."*

*After he unloaded the jugs and placed them in the
back room of the restaurant, he did something absolutely
shocking. He gave me ten one-dollar bills like it was
nothing. "You tell Hoyt I said hello."*

*"Yes, sir!" And then I just hightailed it out of there
before Big Bill could change his mind. I had half a mind
to just drive right on past Hoyt's farm and head to the next
town with the cash. I played the fantasy out in my head
the whole ride home. I'd get a room in a boardinghouse.
I'd say I was fifteen and looking for work. Maybe I'd get a
job with a seamstress or at a diner. If anyone asked about
my family, I'd say I was an orphan.*

It was a good plan, but I couldn't seem to keep the horse on the road to Croswell. Instead, Old Josie found her way back to Hoyt's barn, and I gave him his ten dollars. I nearly fell out of my shoes when he handed one of the dollars to me. It was the first whole dollar of my very own.

"See, now that wasn't so bad, was it?"

I just stared at that green paper.

"I'm sure you understand that I'd like to keep this little transaction between us. Don't you, Althea? Can we make this our little secret?"

I didn't say nothing. I was too busy calculating. The dollar in my hand was enough to buy a new dress.

"You keep that dollar for yourself. You earned it. Now here's a dime for the housework you did for Alice. Go and give that to your daddy, alright?"

And that's just what I did.

"Jasper? Is that you down there?" It was his aunt standing at the entrance to the barn.

"Uh. Yeah." Jasper turned toward her, stuffing the book down into the hay behind him.

"What are you doing back there?" She walked over to him with an empty milk bucket in each hand.

"Oh . . . I . . . uh," Jasper scrambled for an answer. "I thought I heard a rat rustlin' around. I really wanted to catch one."

"Good God. Why?"

"I thought . . . it'd make a fun pet?" He didn't mean to make it a question. It just came out that way.

"Nuh-uh. Not in my house."

"Yes, ma'am."

"Well, since you're out here, might as well make yourself useful. Here." She handed him a bucket and pointed him to a stool near one of the cows' gigantic pink udders. He settled down next to the animal and began pulling milk until his aunt went back to the house.

The minute her white apron turned the corner, he rushed back to the book. He read the entry again, letting his eyes linger on the words *Big Bill* for a moment before tucking it back in its hiding place.

CHAPTER 15

Did you do well in school?

"Hey! What's your story, shrimp?" A huge sixth grader named Cecil Harding shoved Jasper in the shoulder that day at school. They were outside in the yard for recess.

Jasper didn't answer. He scanned the school yard, hoping someone would intervene. Miss Babcock was still inside grading papers. The door to the school was open, but her head was down. All seven of the girls had gathered at the fence to admire Lucille's new dress. The boys were scattered about playing games. Wayne was at the far corner with his buddy Mel, practicing walking on his hands.

Cecil pushed him again. "You deaf, boy?"

Jasper shook his head.

"Why don't you talk? You stupid or somethin'?"

"No," Jasper said softly. In fact, he was quickly learning he wasn't stupid at all. Miss Babcock had already bumped him up to sixth grade math, and he could read some of the seventh grade books.

Cecil, on the other hand, was sort of stupid. He was supposed to be in sixth grade but had to do some of his math on the chalkboard with the third and fourth graders. He shoved Jasper again. "Why don't you talk, huh? Is it true what they're sayin'?"

"I don't know," Jasper mumbled. "What are they saying?"

"That you're staying with Wayne Williams's family instead of yours. That right?"

Jasper didn't want to answer but finally shook his head. "Wayne's my cousin."

"Is it true your mama just up and left you there?"

Jasper studied his shoes and didn't say a word. A couple of the other younger boys had wandered over to listen.

"My ma says she wouldn't be surprised if she did."

Jasper looked up at this revelation.

"She says Althea Williams was the most notorious hussy in all of Burtchville. A real hell-raiser. Ma says I ought to be nice to you 'cause you had the misfortune of bein' the hussy's son. So, what do you think?" He grinned. "Should I be nice to you?"

One of the older boys snickered at this, and Jasper could already see the song, *Your mama's a hussy! Your mama's a hussy,* dancing in their eyes. He didn't know what the heck a *hussy* was, but he could tell from the smug smile on Cecil's face it wasn't good.

Jasper balled his small hands into fists. If getting beat up at school in Detroit had taught him anything, it taught him that you had to nip this sort of thing in the bud or it would haunt you all year. He was too angry to care that the boy was bigger. In fact, if he wanted to make an impression, he suspected the bigger the better. Besides, he'd been dying to hit something ever since Big Bill had left him with nothing. No answers. No hope of finding her. Just more goddamned questions.

You tell her to come see me when you find her.

Without a word, Jasper punched the boy hard in the stomach. The blow caught him by such surprise that Cecil doubled over to where Jasper could reach his big, stupid head. With a low growl, he slammed his fist into the giant boy's nose.

Blood instantly came pouring out of it.

One of the girls at the fence screamed. The boys that had gathered took a step back. Jasper braced himself for Cecil's retaliation, but the boy just stood there, eyes bulging, holding his bleeding nose.

"Jasper Leary!" Miss Babcock shrieked from the doorway.

He dropped his fists.

She stormed over to him and grabbed him by the ear. "What in God's name do you think you're doing?"

Jasper knew better than to answer. He looked out in the yard for Wayne. His cousin was staring at him slack jawed and holding up his hands as if to ask, *Jasper, are you crazy?*

As she dragged him back to the schoolhouse, he realized with a sinking heart that he must have been crazy indeed.

The other kids poured into the room after Miss Babcock and her hostage, taking their seats for the show. She pulled him over to her desk, grabbed the paddle off the wall, and slapped it down on her desk. "I do *not* tolerate fighting in this school."

She left Jasper gaping at the paddle and walked around to her seat to pull a first aid kit from a drawer. "Cecil? Come here."

The older boy obeyed. Blood was still running from his nose. He shot Jasper a knowing glance and took a wad of gauze from the teacher. She inspected his face and asked him a few questions. *How many fingers am I holding up,* that sort of thing. Jasper stood frozen at the front of the room, trying not to look out at the beady eyes of his classmates staring up at him and the paddle.

When Miss Babcock had finished with Cecil and sent him back to his seat, she turned her attention to Jasper. A breath caught in his throat. He knew better than to try to explain why he'd hit the older boy, and she didn't ask.

"Cecil, how many lashes would be fair?"

Jasper's jaw dropped. He couldn't help but look at Cecil, sure he'd see a wicked grin spread across his stupid face. But Cecil didn't smile at all. The boy didn't seem to want any part of it. In the back, Wayne was shaking his head.

"Cecil?" she prompted again.

"Five." The word was barely audible.

"Jasper, grab the chair."

With shaking hands, he grabbed the wood. No one made a sound as the paddle whistled through the air and landed with a deafening *thwack!* It took all of Jasper's strength to not cry out. *Thwack! Thwack! Thwack! Thwack!*

By the last crack of the paddle, Jasper's legs were rubber and silent tears were streaming down his face. The tears were just as much from the humiliation as the pain. He'd been spanked plenty of times before but never in front of a whole school.

"Back to your seat," Miss Babcock commanded. Jasper hobbled back to his chair with his head down, trying like hell not to snivel.

"Cecil?"

"Yes, ma'am."

"Are you satisfied?"

"Yes, ma'am."

"Do you feel any need to fight this boy?"

"No, ma'am."

"Good. If I hear of any of you attacking this boy or fighting in any way here at school or on the way to or from, there will be ten lashes for each of you. Understood?"

"Yes, Miss Babcock," the class said in unison.

"And Jasper?"

It took Jasper a moment to find his voice. He wiped his face with his sleeve. "Yes, ma'am."

"If I ever hear of you starting fights at this school again, you will *not* be welcome back. Am I making myself clear?"

"Yes, ma'am."

"I will be sending a note home to your family about this."

A murmur swept through the classroom. A voice in the back muttered, "You're dead meat." It might have been Wayne.

"Enough!" Miss Babcock barked. "Now. I want you all to write a hundred-word essay explaining why fist fighting cannot be permitted in a civilized society. Little ones, you may draw a picture showing better ways to handle problems that don't involve fighting."

Jasper suffered through the rest of the school day with his eyes locked on his desk. As the pain in his rump faded, the feeling of dread grew in the pit of his stomach. Miss Babcock was sending a note home to his aunt and uncle.

What will they do to me?

The knowledge that he'd made the worst mistake of his life swelled inside him until he was certain he was going to throw up.

When the teacher dismissed the class at the end of the school day, the kids poured out in twos and threes, none of them looking at Jasper. He didn't move.

"Jasper?"

Jasper looked up from his desk and realized he was the only pupil left in the room.

"Take this note home to your aunt and uncle." Miss Babcock held up a crisp piece of paper that surely spelled his doom. "I don't know what sort of school you came from, but we do things differently here. I trust you won't make this mistake again."

There was almost a hint of sympathy in her eyes as he stood up and took the paper from her hand. *Almost.*

Jasper shuffled out of the building to find a pack of boys waiting for him at the edge of the school yard. Cecil was among them. He had the beginnings of a black eye, and his nose was swollen. Jasper looked over his shoulder, not knowing if his teacher's warning would hold outside the schoolhouse. Miss Babcock had her head down in a book. Wayne was nowhere in sight.

The five boys were all bigger than Jasper. Three were sitting up on the split-rail fence. A huge boy named Bobby was standing next to Cecil. Jasper remembered something Wayne had said about them being cousins. He debated running the other way but figured there was no point. He was fast but not fast enough. Besides, his uncle was going to murder him when he got home anyway.

Jasper took a breath and walked straight up to Cecil. "What do you want?"

"Hey, kid. I just wanted to say sorry. I shouldn't have said that stuff about your mom."

Jasper couldn't have been more surprised if balloons and fairy dust had shot out the boy's ass. "What?"

"I didn't know you'd be so bothered by it. It was pretty stupid." The other boys sort of nodded. They were all at least two years older than Jasper, but they were looking at him with something akin to respect.

"Sorry about your nose," Jasper said and realized he actually was sorry.

"Nah. I've had worse." Cecil socked him in the arm hard enough to let Jasper know he could've whupped him something fierce. "You got a decent swing."

Jasper shook the sting out of his arm and managed a smile.

"You gonna git killed at home?" Bobby asked as though he knew the answer. All the boys nodded.

"I'm not sure. Probably. Never seen Uncle Leo get really mad before."

Cecil patted Jasper hard on the back. "Just grab the chair and hold on."

CHAPTER 16

How did your parents punish you
when you broke the rules?

Jasper took the long way home. He didn't want to risk running into Hoyt's bull, Nicodemus, but mostly he was terrified of what would happen when he arrived back at his uncle's cabin. The dirt roads were deserted as he walked the two miles back to the tiny shack where his mother had left him without any explanation a month earlier. He tried not to think of their '47 Chevy driving away.

The wind whipped up a chill in the air. Summer was over.

A huge oak tree towered over the far end of Harris Road. Squirrels chattered at each other, and acorns rained down, pelting the ground like hail with each gust of wind. Jasper stood under the great tree and gazed up at the leaves that would soon be dying. A few low, thick branches reached out over the road. Jasper considered climbing onto one and hiding there until the whole world forgot him. A broken tree swing hung from a frayed rope looped over one of the far branches. The other rope had snapped years ago. Jasper walked over to it and lifted the splintered board that had once been the seat. It might've been his mother's swing back when she was small like him.

He dropped the board and wondered what she would do with him if she were the one to get the note in his hand. She'd spanked him before but never the way Miss Babcock had done. His mother always lost heart after two or three whacks. She'd end up looking like she'd been the one getting hit and didn't seem to notice if he was crying or even breathing. It would take hours of him acting happy before she'd crack a smile again. Once she smiled, everything would be all right.

Acting happy wouldn't cut it with Uncle Leo and Aunt Velma. Jasper could still see his uncle pointing a shotgun at his favorite cow's head. The man hadn't even flinched when he pulled the trigger. He'd loved that cow, probably more than he loved his good-for-nothing nephew.

Jasper trudged along the last bit of Harris Road and turned down the two-track drive to his doom. Wayne stopped him before he'd reached the door.

"Pop's out in the shed," he said. "You need to go talk to him. Ma already knows."

"You told her?"

"Yeah. She usually knows how to break bad news, and I didn't want you to go in cold. Pop can sometimes . . . well, he can get real mad if you don't talk to him right."

"What do I say?"

"Ma says he's already in a mood because the damned tractor's still leakin'. So what you gotta do is go in like a man. No snivelin', no excuses. Just tell 'im what you done and don't leave nothin' out. If he reads somethin' in that note you didn't say yourself, he'll whup you double hard."

Jasper nodded, then dropped his eyes. "I didn't read the note."

"Give it here." Wayne grabbed the note and read aloud:

Dear Leonard and Velma Williams,
I regret to inform you that your nephew caused a disruption
in school today. Please discuss this issue with Jasper so that he
may continue his education here.
  Sincerely,
  Miss Ellen Babcock

"So what do I say?" Jasper asked. Miss Babcock left out some major details.

"Tell 'im everything. You leave somethin' out, I guarantee he'll find out about it, and there'll be hell to pay. Farmers talk, and I wouldn't put it past 'im to go up to the school himself."

Jasper nodded again and turned his feet toward the barn. For some horrible reason, he thought of Sally the cow and the sound of her screams. The spit dried up in his mouth.

"Don't chicken out now." Wayne nudged him. "Worst whupping I ever got, I lived through it just fine. Couldn't sit for a week, but I lived. Didn't even leave a scar."

This didn't make Jasper feel any better. By some inner machinery beyond his control, his feet started moving toward the shed.

The unforgiving smell of motor oil, metal, and sweat greeted him at the door.

"Uncle Leo?" he whispered to the pair of boots sticking out from under the tractor.

The boots didn't respond.

"Ex—excuse me? Uncle Leo?" he said a little louder, crouching onto his haunches so he could see the rest of his uncle. The kerosene lamp lit up the undercarriage of the tractor. It was an upside-down metal labyrinth of a world.

"Hmm?" Uncle Leo dropped a hunk of metal with a clank. "Hand me that socket wrench."

Jasper searched the toolbox on the ground. *Socket wrench.* He picked up something that might've been a socket wrench and set it in his uncle's huge, greasy hand.

"Dammit, boy! This here's a pipe wrench," the man barked, sliding out from under the tractor. His face was spotted with oil, and his eyes were filled with disappointment. He flipped through the different metal things in his toolbox, tossing the unwanted ones down with a crash. Jasper felt each one drop. His uncle finally found the one he'd been looking for and pointed it at him. "This. This is a socket wrench. Got it?"

Jasper nodded, too terrified to speak.

The top half of his uncle slid back under the tractor with the wrench. He had to tell him, he realized. He couldn't just sit there all day, stalling. Each second that ticked by was one more lick he'd have to take.

"Uncle Leo? Sir?"

"What is it, Jasper?" Uncle Leo started cranking on something. The whole tractor rocked back and forth.

Jasper swallowed hard. "I have . . . a letter here from my teacher."

"Oh, yeah?" The tractor stopped shaking. "What's it say?"

"It says I caused . . . a disruption in school today."

There was a long silence. His uncle still had the wrench in his hand, but he was staying under the tractor for the time being.

"I—I punched somebody." Jasper's voice had shrunk to a whisper.

"Speak up, boy!" his uncle growled.

Wayne had said to be a man. Jasper straightened his back and said loud and clear, "I punched somebody. On the playground."

Uncle Leo said nothing.

After a few agonizing seconds, Jasper decided to keep talking. "It was a bad thing to do. I realize that now, sir."

Still nothing.

Jasper couldn't help it. The tears just came. "I'm awful sorry about it. I won't do it again. I promise."

After a full minute of listening to Jasper sniffling, Uncle Leo started working the wrench again. The tractor seemed to lurch even more than before.

Jasper was at a loss. He just sat there and tried to pull himself together, jumping every time his uncle shifted his feet, waiting for the man to come barreling out from under the tractor and take off his belt. But he just kept on working.

After what might've been an hour, Uncle Leo finally pulled himself out from under the tractor. He seemed surprised to see Jasper cowering there at his feet. "You still here?"

Jasper was too petrified to move.

His uncle stood up and brushed himself off. He put his tools away, all the while ignoring his nephew, still sitting there like a cornered mouse. After everything had been cleaned up, his uncle turned off his lamp and left the shed.

Jasper sat there in the dark for several minutes, debating what to do. The note was still hanging from his hand. He realized his fingers were stiff from holding it. *Am I supposed to stay here?* he wondered. *Am I still welcome in the house?*

Eventually, he stood up and felt his way out of the dark shed. The sun was setting over the fields, and the lights burned in the cabin windows. The smell of the pork roast Aunt Velma was cooking for supper wafted across the yard.

He crept up onto the porch and peered in through a window at the kitchen table. There were four chairs set around the worn wood tabletop. Ears of corn, bread, beans, and mashed potatoes spilled over plates. He could smell it all through the window, and his stomach tightened when he saw only three places had been set.

Uncle Leo was cleaning the motor oil off his hands at the kitchen washtub. Aunt Velma pulled a bubbling brown chunk of meat out of the woodstove. They were talking to each other too quietly for Jasper to hear. His uncle shook his head.

They were going to make him leave. He was sure of it. Jasper backed away from the window, stumbling off the edge of the porch. They never wanted him there in the first place, and now he'd embarrassed them and brought shame on their family. He really was rotten inside. No one wanted him anymore—not his dad, not his mother, no one.

The golden sky reeled overhead as he staggered away from the cabin, sobbing harder than he could ever remember crying. There was nowhere else to go. The grass seemed to fall away from his feet as he stumbled past the barn. He didn't want to look where he was going. He didn't care if he crashed into the corncrib. He didn't care if he fell in the well. In fact, he'd rather he did.

"Jasper?" It was Wayne calling his name somewhere behind him.

He didn't want to see Wayne. His eyes stayed shut as he plowed away from the voice. He couldn't stop the stream of tears and snot and spit running down his face. He couldn't keep from wailing. His feet stumbled over a tree root, and he crumpled down into a ball. *No one.*

"Hey." Wayne shook his shoulder. "Hey, kid. It's alright. Shake it off. You'll live."

Wayne's warm hand made everything worse. He jerked away from it.

"Jeez. He didn't use the crop, did he?" Wayne pulled his hand away. "He only used that on me once, but that was for giving Millie too much horse tranquilizer. It about killed her."

Jasper shook his head and sobbed. "Go away."

"I'm supposed to come get you for dinner."

This made Jasper go quiet. He wiped his face with his shirt. "What?"

"Ain't you hungry?"

"But there's no place for me. They don't want me."

"Don't be stupid. Ma wasn't sure you was coming. Pop said you might just spend the night in the tractor shed."

The tears wouldn't stop. "That's where he wants me then."

"No, he don't. It'd be better if you cleaned yourself up and act like you took it well. That's what I do. I pretend like it's all okay with me, and pretty soon it is. You know?" Wayne tousled his hair. "You can't let a little whupping break your back."

"But he didn't whup me," Jasper sniffed. "He didn't even say anything."

"You told him?"

"Yeah. I told him everything, and he didn't do anything. He didn't even . . ."—Jasper had to fight back a sob—". . . look at me."

"Shit." Wayne sat back in the grass next to him and nodded. "No wonder . . . Maybe they just want to let your own dad handle it. Maybe Pop feels out of place doin' it himself."

"He hates me."

"He don't hate you, dummy. He's the one that told me to go check on you."

"Really?" Jasper wiped a long string of snot onto his arm.

"Yeah. Now let's get you cleaned up. C'mon."

Jasper sat silently all through dinner, waiting for his aunt or uncle to say something about a punishment. He had handed the note to Aunt Velma when he'd come in the door. She'd taken one look at his swollen face and put the note in a drawer. Jasper couldn't tell if she was angry or not. He just kept his head down while his aunt and uncle talked about the weather and the coming harvest over the food.

After dinner, they all listened to the radio. In between the *Lone Ranger* and *The Adventures of Ozzie and Harriet*, the governor came on the air to announce stiffer punishments for illicit drug use and trafficking under something called the Boggs Act, but all Jasper could hear was the thundering silence of his uncle.

At bedtime, Aunt Velma poked her head behind the curtain to say good night to Wayne. Jasper's heart leapt when she also said good night to him. He had to steel himself from whimpering, *Do you still like me at all? Do you wish I was gone?*

As she was closing the curtain, he managed to say, "I'm sorry, Aunt Velma."

She stopped and looked at him with watery blue eyes. "I know."

When the lights were off and the house was silent except for the crackle of the fire in the woodstove, Wayne sat up and whispered, "Hey, Jas?"

"What?"

"What did Cecil say that made you so mad?"

Jasper didn't know how to answer. He still didn't know what *hussy* meant, but he knew he'd be betraying his mother if he said it again.

After a long silence, he whispered, "Nothing."

CHAPTER 17

Did they ever hit you?

Jasper's father didn't come back that Saturday morning.

After lunch, Jasper stole away into the barn to read more from his mother's book under the guise of feeding the goats. Just as he pulled the diary from its new hiding spot, his uncle's voice came booming from the doorway.

"Hey, Jasper?"

"Uh. Yes, sir?" Jasper nearly dropped the book. He half turned, hiding it against his oversized pant leg.

"Whatdya say you come with me and Wayne down to the creamery? Might be an ice cream in it for you." From the doorway, his uncle didn't seem to notice the thin volume pressed to his flank.

"Sure! Okay." Jasper forced a bright smile. In truth, he was thrilled his uncle was still speaking to him.

"Well, what are you waiting for? Let's go." His uncle waved him over.

There was no chance to tuck the book back where it belonged. His uncle watched Jasper drag his feet to the door as the boy's mind searched for a place to stash it. Uncle Leo finally turned to grab one of the full milk canisters next to the door, and Jasper stuffed the book into the pocket of Wayne's hand-me-down overalls, praying the legs were wide enough on his small frame to hide it.

"Get the lead out, boy!" Uncle Leo barked over his shoulder. "I need you to lower the hitch for me."

"Yes, sir!" Jasper scurried past him with the book swinging from his hip. His uncle didn't seem to notice.

After loading twelve milk canisters into the back of his uncle's truck, the three of them piled in and headed the four miles down Route 25 to the Burtchville creamery. Jasper and Wayne rode in the open bed the whole way. The wind whipped past them at fifty miles an hour, and every bump in the road was a carnival ride as they both fought to hold on. By the time they arrived in Burtchville, Jasper was laughing.

The creamery was just a giant warehouse with a bunch of refrigerated holding tanks and a few storage sheds in the back. Uncle Leo pulled his truck up to the receiving dock, and Wayne and Jasper hopped out.

"Don't wander too far, you two. Meet me back here in twenty minutes." His uncle walked over to the booth and talked to a short, hairy man about his delivery.

"C'mon! Let's go see what new baseball cards they got over at Calbry's." Wayne grabbed him by the arm and dragged him out of the warehouse and down the street.

The sidewalks were crowded with farmers and their families out collecting the weekly supplies. Just outside the doors to Calbry's General Store, two women with long black hair and tan skin were sitting behind a card table covered in beaded necklaces. A hand-painted sign that read "50 Cents" hung from the edge of the table next to another sign that read "Will Work for Food."

Jasper stopped on the sidewalk to read the signs. The older woman smiled at him and beckoned him toward the necklaces on the table. Next to the jewelry lay a small photograph of a teenage girl with long black hair. A small hand-painted sign below it read: "Do You Know Who Killed Me?"

Jasper read the words again and studied the girl's face. The feeling that he'd seen her before crept into his head. Her eyes. They'd been sad. She'd been standing in the doorway.

"You know her."

"Huh?" Jasper blinked up into the weathered face of the older woman. Her lips were set in a frown.

"You knew Ayasha."

Jasper took a step back, shaking his head.

"No necklaces today, thanks!" Wayne told her with a broad smile and pushed his cousin through the door.

"Wait. Who are they?" Jasper asked.

"Ladies from the Indian reservation. Don't mind them. They just want your money. They're always sellin' stuff."

"But it said a girl was killed."

"I don't know anything about it. Do you? C'mon. Pop will be cashin' out any minute."

Jasper let his cousin drag him by the arm into the store but looked back over his shoulder at the two women.

Do you know who killed me?

The rest of the afternoon was spent collecting bars of soap, thread, needles, and a new gasket for the tractor from the various shops in town. That and the biggest ice cream cones Jasper had ever laid eyes on. He was still licking the chocolate from his lips when they pulled back down Harris Road around dusk.

A familiar truck was parked at the end of the drive as Uncle Leo's headlights drew nearer. The shadow of a man was hunched over the steering wheel. It was his father.

Uncle Leo cut the engine and climbed out behind Wendell's truck. Wayne cranked open the passenger door and glanced back at Jasper still glued to his seat next to the gearshift. "Don't worry so much, kid. It'll be fine."

Outside, Uncle Leo was talking at the driver's side window to his father. Jasper's guts knotted up. He didn't want to get out of the car. It wasn't just the whupping he was about to receive; it was the fact that his father hadn't come to see him the week before. It was some of the things the detective had asked his uncle. It was the idea that his mother had hidden the car deep in the woods where she'd hoped no one would find it.

"Come on, Buck Rogers." Wayne pulled him down out of the truck. "Time to go to the moon."

Jasper's feet hit the ground like they were made of lead. His father was still sitting behind the wheel of his borrowed truck. The barn loomed darkly in the other direction, and Jasper considered making a run for it. Wayne tugged on his arm, but his feet wouldn't move.

Uncle Leo came around the hood. "Wayne?"

"Yeah, Pop?"

"Time to head inside, Son." Uncle Leo's eyes fell on his nephew for a few moments before he turned to the house.

Wayne patted Jasper on the shoulder and then followed his dad into the cabin.

Jasper's legs were rubber as they made their way around the bumper. Wendell's head was resting on the steering wheel as he approached the driver's side door. It was like looking at a total stranger. His father's gray hair was worn thin at the top, and he looked smaller than Jasper remembered.

He heard himself say, "Hi, Dad."

His father lifted his head from the steering wheel and looked at him with pale eyes. They were heavy and tinged red. "How've you been, Jasper?"

"Okay." He studied his feet, swallowing all his questions about his mother. *Children should be seen and not heard.*

"Your uncle tells me you've had a little trouble at school. Is that right?"

Jasper kept his eyes on his shoes. "Yes, sir. I was fighting in the school yard."

"How big was the boy?"

"Huh?" Jasper looked up with a scowl.

"Was he smaller than you?"

"No, sir. He was bigger. Cecil's in sixth grade."

"Why'd you hit 'im?"

"He said some things." Jasper debated confessing the horrible things Cecil had said. *Your mama's a hussy.* He couldn't say it. "He just wouldn't leave me alone."

His father nodded. "Can't blame you too much then, but you did break the rules. Didn't you?"

Jasper forced a nod.

"If I don't whup ya, your uncle's gonna feel like he has to do it. He's already doin' too much." His father sighed and hauled himself out of the truck.

"But . . ."

"No buts, boy. Come on. Let's just get it over with." His father grabbed his arm and pulled him toward the barn. "I don't like this any more than you do, but it'll be worse if Leo does it."

The tremor in his father's hand vibrated up Jasper's arm. The old man's foot hit uneven ground, and he staggered a bit off balance. *He's drunk,* Jasper realized. It took his father a solid minute to get the kerosene lamp lit in the barn. By the time the light went on, Jasper was furious and convinced he could take the wobbly old man in a fight.

"This isn't fair! That boy was picking on me. You always told me you got to stand up to bullies." That was true. When the bigger boys had stolen his milk money, his dad had acted like it was Jasper's fault. He'd even showed him how to make a fist.

"Bein' a man ain't easy, Jasper." His father was struggling with shaking fingers to take off his belt. "Even when you do the right thing, sometimes you gotta pay."

"But it's not fair!" None of it was.

"Who told you life was going to be fair? Huh?" his father growled. "What do you know about fair? You got a roof over your head and food on your plate and people lookin' after you. You think everybody's got that? *You think I had that?* You don't know how good you got it! You think you're the only one's ever lost somethin'?"

Jasper felt himself shrinking. "No."

"Now you broke the rules. Ain't nothin' I can do about that. The law's the law."

"The law?" Jasper thought of the detective and felt his anger return. "You know what the law said last week? Huh? A police officer came here Monday. He said they'd found her car buried in the woods. He said Mom's missing! They think there might've been a crime! He said it might be *your* fault!"

"What?" Wendell lowered the belt and grabbed Jasper's arm in his fist. "Who said that? *Who?*"

There was a fiery red alarm flashing in his father's eyes, but Jasper could hardly see it through the tears streaming down his face. The man hadn't come to see him in two weeks. "A detective from Detroit. He wanted to know if you ever smacked her around."

"If I ever *what?*" his father roared.

"Smacked her around!" Jasper shouted back. Suddenly, the detective's accusations didn't seem so outrageous. All their screaming fights. Her teary eyes the morning she'd left Jasper alone on the farm.

He wrenched his arm free and gave his father a running shove. "Did you? Did you hit her? Why didn't you tell me about the car, huh?"

The old man sputtered, "Why you little—"

Jasper shoved his staggering father again and screamed, *"Where is she, goddammit? What did you do with her?"*

Wendell grabbed him by the shoulders and slammed him to the ground. The man's hand crashed into Jasper's face with a blinding white pop.

CHAPTER 18

Did they ever leave bruises or marks?

Pain pounded his temples with each beat of his heart. A steady vibration hummed all around him. Jasper blinked his eyes open and saw nothing but black. The smells of cigarette smoke and gasoline worked their way into the back of his mouth. A beam of yellow light passed overhead, and he felt his body lurch forward as the rumbling beneath him slowed. He must've dozed off.

Jasper tried to sit up, but the pain in his head kept him on his back. The brakes squeaked as the vehicle pulled to a full stop. He was curled up on the bench of the truck. Down on the floorboards, his father's worn boot let off the brake and stepped on the gas.

The truck picked up speed again, and another streetlight blew by. The shadow of his suitcase sat on the floor beneath him.

"Just sit and wait here," his father had told him after dragging him to the truck. They were the first words either of them had spoken since it happened. Jasper had sat in the front seat too dazed to even cry until Wendell came back with the bag. He set it down at the boy's feet without a word.

The suitcase lurched forward as his father's boot laid on the gas.

Jasper was leaving the farm. He'd been praying for it for weeks, but now it wasn't clear where they were going. His father still wasn't talking. He might not ever talk to him again.

Tears welled up as the horrible scene replayed in his head over and over again. The words he'd screamed. His father's furious eyes. His father's hard smack, rattling his teeth. He didn't have to reach up a hand to feel the swelling around his left eye. His father had hit him. He'd screamed in his father's face, and the man had hit him hard.

His father had never hit him before.

Afterward, his father had just stood there gaping at him. That look. That deflated, disappointed, utterly devastated look brought tears to Jasper's eyes as he lay there next to the man.

A chill clung to his inner thigh. Shame washed over him when he realized his pant leg was wet. He wanted to die.

The truck lurched to another stop. His father cut the engine. Wherever they were going, they'd arrived. Jasper feigned sleep as his father opened the driver's side door. Wherever it was, he didn't want to go.

A panicked thought ran through his head. *Orphanage.*

For a few blessed moments, Jasper was alone in the truck, hoping against hope that his father would change his mind. He'd said terrible things. He'd accused the man of hitting his mother and doing God knows what else. He'd gotten him so angry his father had revealed a side of himself Jasper hardly knew was there. *You think you're the only one's ever lost somethin'?*

Wendell Leary was an orphan. Jasper's mother told him that once after one of their fights. His father had lost *both* his parents when he was just a boy. She'd been drinking and muttering that they were meant to be together because of their broken hearts, but Jasper didn't understand what that meant. His father had never spoken of it before.

No doubt his father hated him now. He would be happy to be rid of him. Jasper rolled onto his side and buried his face in his hands. His left eye felt like a ripe plum about to burst. It was the eye of a monster.

Jasper fought back a sob and prayed that his father would forgive him. The passenger side door wrenched open.

"Time to get out, Jasper." His father's voice was hoarse.

Jasper shook his head, still hiding his face in his hands.

"Stop foolin' around, Son. Let's go."

His father pulled him by the elbows until he was sitting up in the seat. A wave of nausea came and went at the sudden movement. Jasper tried to blink his eyes straight. His left eye didn't match his right. Everything pulsed with red.

Out the window, he saw a familiar sign. "Carbo's Bakery." He blinked twice, but it was still there. They were home.

Home.

Jasper leapt out of the truck. "Are we—?"

"Easy, kiddo." His dad reached out a hand to steady him.

"Are we going home? Is Mom . . . is she here?"

The pained look in his father's eyes was his answer. "Come on. Let's get you cleaned up."

His dad led him up the stairs and down the narrow hallway to their three-room apartment. The door to 2B swung open, and it was all Jasper could do not to run through the dark living room straight to his bedroom and his pillow and his books and his few treasured toys. Wendell set the suitcase down by the front door and flipped on the lights.

"Jesus, Mary, and Joseph," his father whispered.

The apartment was in shambles. Piles of clothes and books and dishes were scattered across the floor. The cushions of the couch were torn open, and white and yellow stuffing was scattered across the rug. Jasper sucked in a breath and checked the number on the door again.

Wendell pushed past Jasper and waded into the mess. The kitchen cabinets and drawers all stood open. All the books on the shelves had been thrown on the floor.

"What happened?" Jasper gaped at it all from the doorway.

His father didn't answer him. "Althea?" he called out, crashing through the living room. He ran down the short hall to their bedroom, calling again, "Althea?"

"Is she here?" Jasper whispered and took a timid step into the room.

"Goddammit!" his father bellowed from the bedroom. "I'm gone one day. One goddamned day, Althea. What the hell have you done now?"

He stormed back to Jasper in a fury. For a terrifying second, Jasper thought he might hit him again. He staggered back, falling over a broken lamp with a crash.

"Christ, Jasper!" his father barked, but then he saw the look on his son's face. He held up his hands. "Hey, Son. Relax. I'm not gonna . . . Oh. Jesus."

Wendell crumpled onto a chair and put his head in his hands.

Jasper stayed where he'd landed, afraid to move. Afraid to breathe.

All the color had drained from his father's face. After an agonizing minute, the man cleared his throat loudly and straightened himself. "You alright, Son?"

Jasper forced a nod and whispered, "Is she here?"

"Nope. Looks like a pair of burglars just paid us a visit . . . Why don't you . . . uh . . ." Wendell shook himself as if to wake up. "Why don't you get yourself cleaned up and head down to Mrs. Carbo's. I have to do some things here. Understand?"

"Yes, sir. I just have to get . . . something." Jasper pulled himself up off the ground where he'd fallen and staggered into the mess that had been their home. Broken dishes covered the linoleum floor in the kitchen. His mother's favorite flower vase had been shattered.

Passing the bathroom, he could see the contents of the medicine cabinet had been dumped onto the floor. At the end of the hall, the door to his room stood open. Clenching his fists, he forced himself through it and saw that everything he owned had been thrown from its shelf. His bed had been stripped bare.

Who would do this? Jasper wanted to scream. His eyes darted from the open closet to the corners as if the perpetrator might still be there, lying in wait. His father was right. He had to get out of there.

Jasper snatched a clean pair of pants off the floor. As he ripped the wet ones off, he remembered the book he'd stuffed into the pocket. He pulled it out and tossed the wet overalls into the garbage can in the corner. By some miracle the diary was dry. He hugged it to his chest and scanned the wreckage again. His father had shouted, *Althea!* But there was no possible way she would've destroyed his room. She got angry if he left a sock on the floor.

"Jasper! It's time to go," his father's hoarse voice commanded.

"Yes, sir." Jasper shoved the book into the waist of his clean pants and hurried down the hallway. As he passed by his parents' bedroom door, he glimpsed the mess inside. His mother would have died at the sight of it.

His father sat slumped near the doorway.

"Tell Mrs. Carbo we had a break-in. It just ain't safe here tonight. Okay?" Wendell's pale face contorted into what was supposed to be a reassuring smile. He patted Jasper on the head. "It's going to be okay, Son."

"Yes, sir." Jasper knew better than to question it, even though his father didn't look okay at all. He picked up his suitcase and headed down the corridor to 2A.

Mrs. Carbo threw the door open on the second knock. "Jasper!" She pulled him into her apartment. Her housecoat smelled like oatmeal cookies as she wrapped her arms around him. "Where have you been, my little lamb? I've been so worried!"

His spine went limp as she held him, and he had to fight not to cry. He hadn't realized how much he'd missed her.

"Let me take a look at you." She held him out and studied the bruise on his face. "Sweet Jesus, Jasper! What has happened to you?"

"No—nothing," he stammered, avoiding her eyes. He knew he'd have to do better than that, but he couldn't admit what he'd done to his father. "I, uh, fell roller-skating."

"Roller-skating?" Her lips pressed together as though she wanted to share his pain. "You should be more careful."

"Yes, ma'am."

"Oh, you silly boy." She kissed him five times on the cheeks. "Come inside. Let's get you some milk and cookies."

If she noticed his suitcase, she didn't mention it. He set it down by the door and followed her into the kitchen. She didn't ask him any more questions until he'd had three oatmeal raisin cookies and a tall glass of warm milk. He ate them slowly, knowing the questions were coming.

"Where have you been staying, love?" she finally asked in a gentle voice. "I've been looking for you these past few weeks. I even knocked on your door."

"My uncle's farm," he answered with a mouth full of cookie. He quickly swallowed and could see by the worried look on her face that he needed to tell her more. "It's really neat. I have a cousin there, and there's cows and chickens . . ."

"Wow. That sounds exciting." She handed him a napkin.

Jasper took it obediently and nodded. The clock on the stove read 11:05 p.m. "Um, Mrs. Carbo? Do you mind if I sleep here tonight? I'm really tired and . . ." He let his voice trail off. He didn't want to have to explain about the apartment. Or his mother. *My father will fix it,* he told himself. *In the morning everything will be fine.*

"Of course, love." She patted his hand. Her eyes were sad as she smiled. It wasn't just sadness. It was worse.

CHAPTER 19

How did you get those scars?

Yellow sunshine streamed in through the window sheers. It took several blinks for Jasper's aching head to focus in the light. He was lying on the blue couch in Mrs. Carbo's living room. He rolled onto his side but recoiled as his face hit the pillow. The bruising around his eye had become an alien thing stuck to the side of his face. His fingers traced the edges of the swelling, half expecting to feel it move.

Jasper could still see the look in his father's eyes right before the blow landed. It wasn't just an angry look. It was more like something had snapped loose. The eyes didn't even look like they belonged to his father at all. They belonged to some other man.

The fight replayed again in his head.

He sat up. He had to go find him and say he was sorry. His father would never hurt his mother. The sun hung high in the sky out the window. The morning was half gone. A panic swept through him that it was too late. He jumped up from the couch only to find his pajama pants were wet. There was a small circular stain on the couch cushion.

He punched himself hard in the leg and looked down the hallway leading to Mrs. Carbo's bedroom door.

The door was shut.

He stripped off his damp pajamas and tried his best to soak up the stain with them. Mrs. Carbo would be furious, but he couldn't face her. He tiptoed to his suitcase at the front door. He threw on clean clothes and clicked his bag shut as quietly as he could.

Jasper was carrying his balled-up pajamas to the kitchen trash can when he heard a muffled voice behind him. It was Mrs. Carbo. He turned toward her closed bedroom door at the other end of the hall.

". . . yes, Officer. You told me to call if I heard anything new . . . Right. Well, he came home last night . . . Mmm-hmm. He'd been gone for weeks. Then there was this knock on my door around eleven o'clock. He looked terrible . . . Yes, it's worse than I feared."

Jasper stopped breathing.

"Oh, goodness! Gunshots? . . . No, I didn't hear a thing. I was down in the bakery all day yesterday, and you know how loud the delivery trucks can be . . . Yes. Sergeant Kilburn stopped in for his usual coffee around nine a.m. . . . I thought he just went back to his stakeout or whatever it is you fellas are doin' outside here . . . He didn't say anything about a break-in . . . Maybe he just left early. You don't think . . . No. Wendell couldn't possibly have . . . But what will happen to Jasper? I'd hate to see that boy in an orphanage. You hear such terrible things . . ."

The word *orphanage* sent Jasper running to the apartment door. He stuffed his feet into his boots.

Mrs. Carbo's voice murmured from down the hall. "Yes, of course. Thank you, Detective. Okay. I'll see you then."

The faint click of a phone handset made him freeze. She'd probably scream if she saw him standing there, about to sneak away. He heard a dresser drawer open and close behind the bedroom door. He couldn't risk another second. Jasper silently pushed the security chain out of its slot and pulled the door open. It creaked, stopping his heart for a beat as he waited for Mrs. Carbo to burst out of her room. Nothing happened. He picked up his suitcase and eased the door shut.

The lights in the hall glowed burnt yellow. Jasper slipped under them and around the corner to his own apartment door. The brass number still read "2B" but there was a piece of paper nailed right under. It read "Crime Scene—Do Not Enter" in big black letters followed by a bunch of smaller ones he didn't bother to read. It was like he was standing outside someone else's door. *Do not enter,* he read again, but Mrs. Carbo would be leaving her room any second. She would soon see he wasn't lying there on the couch. He looked down at his empty right hand and realized she'd find the wet pajamas on the floor of her hallway. Cheeks burning, he tried the handle and was relieved when the door swung right open.

"Dad?" he called out softly, closing the door behind him.

There was no answer.

Jasper set his suitcase down and threw the dead bolt. His mother had always told him to keep the door locked when he was home alone. *Don't open it for nobody. Not even the president of the United States,* she'd say.

Jasper turned and faced the room. It still looked like a storm had torn through it. He swallowed hard. "Dad?" he tried a little louder this time. He didn't leave the safety of the doorway for a full minute as he listened for an answer.

A delivery truck lumbered down the street outside. The apartment felt deserted. *Crime scene.* The familiar smells of brewed coffee and his father's cigars had been overpowered by the putrid aroma of dirty dishes and trash. It didn't even smell like home anymore.

He took a few cautious steps away from the door. "Hello?"

No one answered.

Growing braver, he picked his way down the dark hallway past the bathroom to his parents' room. Their bedroom door was shut. He reached out for the handle but couldn't help but remember the time he'd opened it and caught his mother changing her clothes. She'd snatched her robe from behind the door but not before he had glimpsed a long, angry scar running down her stomach. It matched several others on her arms. She grabbed his chin too hard. *Closed doors should stay closed!* she'd shouted and slammed it in his face. A few minutes later, she'd emerged to find him balled up in the corner of his bedroom. *Sweet, sweet, Jasper. No. No. No. Don't cry. Mommy loves you. Some things are just private, baby. Some things you should never see . . .*

He'd looked at his parents' door with suspicion ever since, but he'd never tried to open it again. Until now.

Jasper pressed his ear to the door and listened for the familiar sound of his father's snores. He couldn't hear a thing. He raised his fist to the wood and took a long pause before rapping it lightly with his knuckles. Nothing. He knocked harder. Still nothing.

"Dad?" Jasper called out again, then turned the handle and peered inside.

CHAPTER 20

It says here you ran away from home at a young age.
What set you off?

At first, the room looked no better or worse than the others in the apartment. Clothes were scattered across the ground. All the drawers had been pulled from the bureaus and tossed in heaps onto his mother's favorite rug, its violet and pink flowers crushed by the broken wood. A shattered lamp lay in the corner.

Jasper took a cautious step into the room. His mother's jewelry box had been dumped onto the floor next to the open closet. Under the pile of rhinestones and plastic pearls, his mother's favorite necklace lay facedown on the rug. He snatched it up off the floor. Its beaded pendant was heavy in his palm. Two of the tiny shells were cracked. The rest wove together into tight concentric circles, forming a mosaic of colorful flowers in a field of white. When he was younger, it had been the exact size of his palm. Curled up on his mother's lap, he would trace the swirling colors and the symbol in the very center that looked like an *S* laid on its side.

What does it mean? he'd ask, running his finger over the odd emblem.

It's just pretty. That's all. Not everything has to mean something, she'd say.

It *was* pretty. The shiny beads spun on their threads as he rubbed them between his fingers. He scanned the floor again and saw the rest of his mother's favorite things. Her blue dress. The fluttery blouse with the ruffled collar. Her red shoes. He frowned as he cataloged each of them. Everything she loved was still there, trampled on the ground.

He squeezed the necklace, then slipped the beaded loop over his head. The pendant looked silly on him, hanging down to his belly button, but she wouldn't want it left on the floor. She'd be furious if she could see her room. The bed had been stripped of its sheets and blankets, leaving the mattress naked and skewed on the frame. Dark yellow and brown stains dotted the fabric. It was like glimpsing under his mother's skirt by accident. He shouldn't be in there.

He spun back to the open doorway and startled at what he saw.

Odd colors were sprayed across the wallpaper in a large plume the size of a beach ball. It looked like an exploded firecracker. It wasn't quite red, but it wasn't quite brown. Several large drips ran down from the center toward the floor.

A streak of rusty red ran in a crooked smear down the wallpaper next to the door. Squinting at it, Jasper reached out and touched a frozen drip with his fingertip. It crackled to pieces. He studied the dried flecks of color on his skin. It looked just like the crust that had come off Wayne's hands after he'd helped butcher Sally. It was blood.

Jasper's heart thudded in his ears. He could see it everywhere now. Brown spots on the mattress. A spray of black across his mother's carpet and on the wood floor at his feet. Dark droplets on the floorboards passed under his boots and trailed out the door.

He followed the scattered stains out into the hall. He tried to tell himself the dark spots could be mud as he traced them past the kitchen, through the living room, and to the front door. There was a red smear below the doorknob.

Two fingerprints were pressed in red. He reached out to touch one of them but stopped himself.

Burglars. His father had said it was burglars. Jasper scanned the room behind him, searching for anything missing in the wreckage. They didn't have much. His father was a line worker at the auto plant, and his mother worked at the dairy. She hated it but said she had no choice. They needed the money, that's what she said.

Althea! Jasper could still hear his father calling out to her as he'd plowed through the mess the night before. He turned back to the blood on the door. His mother's hands were large for a woman. She kept her nails short so she could work the register and adding machines. Jasper reached up to touch one of the fingerprints.

A hard pound on the door knocked him back on his heels. The doorknob rattled.

"Jasper? Jasper, are you in there?" a deep voice demanded. "This is Detective Russo."

Another hard knock. Jasper clamped his mouth shut. The detective was there to take him away to God knows where. He'd take him away from his father, he realized, feeling the bruise around his eye. He'd wanted to know if his father had slapped his mother around. His black eye would be proof his father was the villain. There was blood all over the apartment. Jasper knew in his heart his father hadn't hurt her, but no one would believe a kid. He held his breath, hoping the man would go away.

The door pushed against the dead bolt.

Jasper staggered back. His suitcase was sitting right next to the entry. The diary inside it was still his best hope of ever finding her. He snatched the bag off the ground and flew down the hallway to the first open door. It was the bathroom. He slipped inside and locked the knob.

The front door slammed open. "Jasper? You shouldn't be in here, kid. This is a crime scene . . . Mrs. Carbo is very worried about you . . . I need you to cooperate with me. We'll keep you safe."

Jasper backed up into the bathtub and slid the shower curtain closed. The good little boy he'd been raised to be knew he should obey the man, but his guts told him not to.

He stared through the blue flowered curtain, realizing what a lousy hiding place he was in. Any second the policeman would find him and snatch him away forever.

If any strangers come to the door, you hide, baby. You hide and stay hidden, his mother had said to him the last time she'd left him home alone so she could go to work.

What if I can't? he'd asked, panicked at the thought of having to hide. She'd always told him not to worry when she'd leave, but that time it was different. He could tell by her voice. *What if they find me?*

You gotta outsmart 'em, she'd said. *You know this place better than any stranger, right? What do we do when there's a fire? Remember?*

Jasper shook his head.

Sure you do. What are those ladders for outside the windows? What are they called? Think, baby.

Fire escapes?

That's right. You can climb out any window on the east side, and there's a ladder. Strangers don't know about them. Understand?

Jasper had nodded even though he was fairly certain she'd gone crazy. The fire escapes were old and rusted, and he was scared of heights. And he'd been confused. She'd always told him to go find Mrs. Carbo if he needed help, and no one ever came to their door.

Except once, he realized. He'd been much younger. There had been a soft knock, and he had whispered through the closed door, *Who is it?*

The detective's heavy steps rumbled past the bathroom door to the bedrooms. "Jasper? I can't help you unless you answer me, boy." His voice sounded angry.

Jasper spun around to the window in the bathtub wall and pulled back the yellowed linen. Outside the glass, the black iron railing of the fire escape hung in midair. Staring through the metal grate, he could see the sidewalk twelve feet down. Jasper swallowed hard and unlocked the window.

Down the hall, the door to his bedroom slammed open, and he could hear the detective sifting through the debris and moving furniture aside in the room next door. He lifted the window sash as quietly as he could. Its counterweights clanked inside the wall. Cool morning air hissed into his face, billowing the shower curtain behind him. He slid his suitcase onto the fire escape and climbed out onto the metal landing on his hands and knees.

Fear sent jolts of electricity through his limbs as he pulled himself up onto the rickety platform. Behind him, narrow stairs led up to the third floor and then onto the roof. In front of him, an iron ladder reached up into the sky, leading nowhere. It took several moments for Jasper to figure out it had been lifted up off of the ground. Its rails were attached to wheels. He grabbed a rung and gave it a gentle tug. It didn't budge. *This is a huge mistake,* he thought, looking back through the open bathroom window. He was disobeying a grown-up. He was running away from a policeman. But it was worse than that. There was blood everywhere. *Maybe they'll think it's my fault. Maybe someone died. Maybe it was her.* His knees buckled under him.

There was a pounding on the bathroom door. An angry voice bellowed, "Jasper?"

No. It'll be okay. Jasper forced himself back up. *The detective will know what to do. I'm just a kid.* As he slid the window shut behind him, he heard the locked doorknob on the opposite side of the bathroom rattle violently.

"Son of a bitch!" the detective muttered.

Bam!

It sounded like a kick to the door. There wasn't any time.

Jasper threw his suitcase from the second-floor landing down into the alley below. It popped open on impact. He nearly lost his nerve.

Bam!

Jasper jumped onto the raised ladder as hard as he could. The lowering mechanism slowly screeched to life as the rusted wheels began to turn. Jasper grabbed the side rails and slammed his feet down on the rung over and over, dropping the stubborn ladder farther and farther until it screamed to a halt two feet above the sidewalk.

As he leapt to the ground, a window over his head slammed open.

"Jasper!" the detective shouted from the bathtub. "Where the hell do you think you're going, boy?"

Jasper kept his bruised face turned to the pavement and didn't answer. He gathered up his mother's diary and the rest of his things into his suitcase and took off running down the alley. As he rounded the corner onto South Main, he glanced back at the window. The detective was gone.

Jasper could hardly feel his legs as they carried him to the next block. *This is crazy.* He was going to get caught. His father would never forgive him. There was no place to hide. A police siren would scream up behind him any minute. He was a criminal. They would probably throw him in jail. They might even give him the electric chair.

He sprinted past Mickey's Convenience, the dry cleaner's, and Sampson's Auto Repair. All the shops had "Closed" signs hanging in the windows. It was a Sunday. He wanted to scream for help, but the street was empty. He turned the corner and bolted down the next street and then the next.

The signs and awnings became a blur of colors as the wind fell out of him. He couldn't run anymore. The suitcase hung limply from his hand as he staggered down the sidewalk. He had no idea which street he was on.

A block ahead, a door stood open. Jasper gathered another deep breath and barreled toward it. He didn't stop to read the sign. Inside was a small shop with pictures of ladies on one side and a tall wood counter on the other. There was nowhere to hide. The women plastered across the wall leered at him with dark eyes. Many were bending over and some were lifting their skirts. He stepped back aghast and bumped into the counter. The bell on top jingled softly.

A snort came from the behind the counter.

A bleary-eyed old man stood up from his chair. A cigarette dangled from his lip with a long column of ash hanging from its end. "Can I help you?"

"Uh, yes. Excuse me, sir. Do you have a bathroom?" Jasper panted.

"Does this look like the public restroom, boy? This place ain't for kids. Beat it." The long ash fell onto the countertop. He didn't seem to notice; he just waved Jasper to the door and plopped back down again.

Jasper nodded, glancing back at the ladies on the wall. The man was obviously right, but there was nowhere else to go. Somewhere out there, Detective Russo was waiting for him, and he was furious. He would take him to jail or an orphanage or wherever really bad boys go. He'd never find his mother or his father now.

The ladies on the wall glowered at him as he sank against the counter and put his head in his hands.

A noise came from behind the counter. There was some mumbling and then another snort. It took a second for Jasper to register the sound. The clerk had fallen back to sleep.

Jasper peeked over the top. The man's head had lolled back against the wall with the cigarette still stuck in his mouth. Looking frantically around the shop, he caught sight of a narrow doorway in the far corner. It might lead to the restrooms or to some place he could hide. The clerk would think he'd left.

Biting his lip, Jasper picked up his bag and took a tentative step toward the doorway. The snoring just got louder. Inch by inch, he made his way past the counter and slipped into a dark corridor.

Once he was out of sight, he breathed a little easier. It took a few seconds for his eyes to adjust. The dimly lit hallway was lined with doors. There were ten of them. Jasper crept past several, debating which one to open. Out in the shop, he heard the ring of a bell.

"Anybody home?" a deep voice asked. It was the detective.

There was a loud snuff and snort before the clerk finally answered. "Yeah. Can I help you?"

Jasper scrambled to the end of the corridor, searching for an exit. All the doors were shut.

"I'm looking for my son," the detective's voice echoed down from the lobby.

Son? Jasper stopped.

"No sons here. This ain't a kid-friendly shop, if you know what I mean."

"He's lost. I saw the open door, and I thought he might have wandered in. Do you mind if I look around?"

"Yeah, I mind. This ain't lost and found," the clerk barked. "You wanna come in, you gotta pay just like everybody else."

"Perhaps I'm not making myself clear." A loud thump reverberated down the hall.

Jasper scrambled to the nearest doorknob. Locked.

"Whoa. Hey, buddy. Take it easy. Take it easy . . ."

A door opened next to him, and a woman's heavily made-up face poked out of a pool of light. She locked eyes with Jasper for a beat and opened her mouth to yell. Her gaze darted from his bag to his black eye. Her face softened, and she motioned him toward her.

"There's nobody back there, man. But go ahead. Help yourself." The clerk's voice sounded like someone had squeezed the air out of it.

The woman whisked him inside.

CHAPTER 21

Where did you go?

"Whatcha doin' here, honey?" the woman whispered. She was wearing nothing but her underwear and a pair of black stockings full of little holes.

"I don't . . . I'm sorry, ma'am. I just . . . ," Jasper stammered. The detective would be there any second. He could hear doors being opened down the hall. He peered up at her painted face and begged, "I need help."

"He do that to you?" she frowned and ran a finger next to his black eye.

It was too difficult to explain, so he just nodded.

"My pops used to do stuff like that too. Come here." She grabbed him by the hand and led him through a dark room into another one filled with mirrors and glittery costumes. "Climb in. Quick." She motioned him into a large locker. A red purse was hanging from a hook, and black rain boots sat at the bottom.

He hesitated before standing his suitcase up on its side and climbing in next to it.

"Don't worry, honey. No one's gonna look in here." With that, she closed the door.

Inside the locker, there was just enough room for Jasper to sit down on the edge of his suitcase. The steel box was pitch-black except for three narrow slats of light streaming in through the vent at the top. Her high heels clicked away from his hiding place. A moment later, the light went out.

All Jasper could hear was his own shaky breath hissing in the dark. Fatigue set in as the adrenaline pumping through his veins ran out. For the moment, he was safe. He leaned his aching head against the wall of the locker and shut his eyes. The dried blood on the wall of his mother's room flashed in his mind. His lids snapped back open. *It's not hers,* he told himself over and over. But his father had called out her name the minute he saw the wreckage of their home. *Althea!*

His breath became a deafening rasp, rushing in and out of his lungs as he tried not to picture the red handprint by the door. *Take it easy, Jas,* he imagined Wayne's voice talking. *Keep your skirt on. Everything will be alright.*

His father would be knocking on Mrs. Carbo's door any minute, he told himself. There'd be hell to pay for running off, but it would all work out. It had to. The look on his father's face the night before told a different story. Jasper shuddered. *He's gonna kill me.*

Muffled voices grew louder through the walls. It sounded like fighting. Jasper strained to hear but couldn't quite make out what they were saying. A door slammed open nearby, and the three stripes of light over his head flicked back on. Jasper sucked in a breath. *One, two, three . . .*

"You can't come back here." It was the half-naked lady talking. A set of high heels clacked toward the locker.

"The hell I can't," the detective barked.

"I'm tellin' ya, John. I ain't seen him."

"Then you won't mind me looking around. Will you?" The shadow of the detective passed by the locker vents.

"Fine. Help yourself." She sighed and lowered her voice to a purr. "But come on now, Johnny. Is that really why you wanted to bring me back here?"

The detective's feet stopped moving.

"Bet your wife don't do it as good as I can. Five dollars and you can find out."

"That's a lovely offer, but I'm working. Open the lockers."

"Fine, but I can't open 'em all. Some belong to the other girls."

Metal doors crashing open shook the box where Jasper hid. He nearly yelped as the one next to him slammed.

"You the only one here?"

"Yeah. Sundays are slow."

The handle to Jasper's locker rattled. He covered his mouth to keep from whimpering out loud.

"Whose is this one?"

"That one belongs to Dixie. She ain't here."

A flashlight clicked on and poured into the locker. Jasper crouched down as the beam of light danced over his head.

"Come on, baby. You sure you couldn't go for a little somethin'? I'll treat you real nice." The lady's voice got husky again on the other side of the thin sheet metal, and the flashlight stopped moving. The sound of a zipper opening was followed by kissing sounds. "It's fixin' to be a real slow day."

Something heavy crashed against the locker next door followed by a slap. "I told you. I'm working. I could haul your ass in for solicitation, but I won't. If you see a little boy roaming around, you better call this number or I'm comin' back, and you're not going to like it. Now show me the rest of the booths."

Even, hard-soled shoes strode past the box where Jasper hid, followed by stumbling, clicking ones. The lights went out again. Jasper stared into the dark with his mouth hanging open. He was repulsed by what he'd heard the strange woman say but felt incredibly grateful all the same. She'd saved him. She'd even been willing to kiss the horrible detective to help him.

But the woman didn't come back.

The room stayed dark and silent. After the first handful of minutes, Jasper began to panic. *What if she forgot about me? What if the detective arrested her and took her away?* He was still too scared to make a sound, so he sat there as the seconds ticked by one by one.

After what felt like an hour, Jasper stood up and stretched his cramped legs. The locker was big enough to lift his arms up but not big enough to turn around, not with the boots and his suitcase on the floor. As he stretched, his arm bumped into the lady's purse. He felt the lumpy leather in the dark and could hear something metallic jingle. *Keys,* he thought with rising hope. *Surely she wouldn't leave without her keys or her purse.* He sat back down and waited.

The blood in the apartment splattered across the walls in his mind again. He put his head in his hands and whispered, "It's not hers. It's not hers." But he didn't believe it.

Who else's could it be? he asked himself in Wayne's voice. *Come on, Jas. You're pretty smart. Whose could it be?*

Jasper sat back down on his bag and stared into the dark, imagining a masked villain in black storming through the apartment, breaking everything in his path. Maybe it was his blood. Jasper shook his head. If the blood belonged to the villain, that could only mean that someone had tried to stop him. *But who?*

It wasn't his father. He was pretty sure of that, given the shock on the man's face at the sight of the mess. *Was it Detective Russo?* Police are supposed to be the ones that foil the crime, but Jasper didn't think so. Detective Russo didn't seem like a hero at all. *Son of a bitch!* he'd hissed through the bathroom door. That wasn't the way a hero talked.

Jasper strained to remember what Mrs. Carbo had said on the telephone behind her bedroom door. She'd seemed really upset about something. *Oh, goodness! Gunshots?* . . .

Was that what she said? She'd also mentioned some sergeant. Didn't she?

Her words muddled together in his head until the only one he was sure about was *orphanage.*

The half-naked lady still didn't come. The longer he sat there, the louder the terrible thoughts whispered in his head. He pictured the masked villain dragging his mother into her bedroom by her hair and throwing her against the wall. He could hear her screaming.

No!

Jasper stood up and clawed at the sides of the metal box. He couldn't breathe. Each breath hissed out louder than the last as his throat tightened. It reminded him of Sally stuck in the well, only now it was him. He was Sally. He had to get out of there. He felt blindly along the seams of the door. A bulky mechanism stuck out along the right jamb. He fumbled with it, tried to push and turn it. Nothing happened. He pushed against the door with all his might. It didn't budge.

"Hello?" he croaked into the dark room. *The detective must be gone by now.* He risked saying it again, louder. "Hello?"

Still nothing.

"Hello? Anybody?" he hollered and pounded the door with his fist. "Let me out!"

He pounded and kicked, growing more and more hysterical, braying and bleating. "Let me out! Let me out! *Help!*"

The lights clicked on. Jasper froze in terror. *What if it wasn't her?*

A second later, the door flung open.

"Jesus, baby! You want Moe to find you? Quiet down." It was the painted lady again. Her thick makeup was smudged with sweat, but it was her.

Jasper fell out of the locker, sobbing.

"Shh!" she hissed, scooping him off of the floor. "Hush up."

He sniffed and snuffed until he managed to speak. "I thought . . . I thought you'd gone."

"Don't be silly. My shift don't end till five." She set him down on one of the stools and took the one next to it. She grabbed a tissue and dabbed her sweaty face. "What's your name, sugar?"

"Jasper," he said and grabbed a tissue for himself. The mirror cased in lights gave him a shock. His face was a distorted patchwork of red blotches and snot, and his right eye was a pulsing mess of purple and blue.

"How old are you, Jasper?"

"Nine."

She whistled low and slow, then gave him a hard look in the mirror. "Where you plannin' to go?"

He bit his lip and looked down at his hands. He had no idea where his father had gone, but he couldn't risk going back to the apartment. He couldn't go to one of his old classmates' houses looking like he did. They'd call the cops. Mrs. Carbo was his only grown-up friend, and she'd called Detective Russo. There was only one place else he could think to go. "My uncle's farm."

"Where's that?"

"Off Old 25, north of Port Huron."

"That's pretty far off. How you gonna get there?"

Jasper just shook his head.

She turned and cocked a half grin. He could tell by her appraising look she wasn't in the charity business. "You got anything to sell?"

Jasper frowned and tried to think. The only things in his suitcase were his clothes and his mother's diary. The clothes couldn't be worth much, but the bag was encased in leather. "My suitcase?"

She didn't even look at it. Instead, she reached out and lifted the necklace from his chest. "This here's real nice. It might fetch you bus fare."

"No!" His eyes widened in horror. "No, I can't. It—it's my mother's. She's been gone."

"Well, if she's gone, she can't miss it, right?"

"But she might come back," he pleaded, trying to keep his chin from quivering. "She will. I know she will. She has to."

"Okay. Okay, baby. Maybe there's somethin' else we can work out." She dropped the necklace. "You know how to mop?"

He nodded.

"Well, moppin's the worst part of the job around here. I'll give you a dollar if you do it. Deal?" She held out her hand.

He nodded, and they shook on it.

"One more thing," she said, still holding his hand. She leaned in close, and Jasper could see the dark circles below her eyes under her makeup. "You got to leave tonight. I don't know what you done, honey, but you have no idea who you're dealin' with."

CHAPTER 22

What did you do for money? For food?

Jasper spent the next several hours in the dressing room while the half-naked lady finished her shift. *I don't even know her name,* he thought as he sat there, hidden under the makeup counter. He tried to sleep, resting his head against the wall. His legs went numb from sitting on the hard floor. His stomach rumbled in protest at missing lunch.

His father would be out looking for him by now, he figured. He wouldn't just leave and not come back. Jasper fidgeted in the dark, thinking about his dad rushing through the mess to the bedroom. *Althea!*

"No," Jasper whispered. The villain hadn't found his mother. *Maybe there were two burglars and they got into a fight with each other.* Jasper climbed out from under the counter and stood up, shifting his weight from foot to foot as the blood returned to his legs in splintery needles. That made more sense, he decided. They were probably furious that they had gone to all that trouble and didn't find anything worth much money.

The muted sound of music came throbbing through the wall behind the lockers with a slow, pounding drumbeat. Jasper slumped back down to the floor. Something was seriously wrong with the lady who was keeping him hidden in her dressing room. She wore too much makeup and too few clothes. She didn't look anything like the other ladies he knew. Mrs. Carbo and Aunt Velma wouldn't be caught dead running around in black lacy drawers like that. They never wore all that black gunk around their eyes or so much red and pink on their cheeks and lips. It was like she was dressed up as some sort of clown. Only she wasn't funny. She was something else. Remembering the sound of a zipper outside the locker made him frown. *What had she tried to get the detective to do exactly? Pee?*

He knew the thought was stupid, but he felt even more stupid that he didn't know the answer.

Jasper surveyed the row of high heels lined up along the far wall. There was a red pair that wasn't that different from the ones his mother owned. He stared at them. His parents had once gotten into a hellacious fight about red shoes. His mother wanted to wear them someplace, and his father had thrown an absolute fit about it. Jasper couldn't remember all the words that were shouted, his head was buried under his pillow at the time, but he'd gotten the impression that the red shoes might just turn her into something. Something bad. Like they had evil powers. Jasper remembered wanting to sneak out of his room and steal the shoes. Maybe he'd try them on and they could make him fly or read minds. But he knew those thoughts were dumb. He already had a pair of red rain boots, and they didn't do anything special to him. *Red shoes must only work on girls,* he'd thought.

Jasper walked over to the high heels and picked one up. *Aunt Velma would never wear these.* Just like she'd never be caught dead walking around in lacy underpants. He began to wonder why his mother would have the same shoes as the painted lady in the next room. She never walked around in her underpants. She never wore all that gunk on her face.

Holding the shoe, he could hear Cecil saying, *Althea Leary was the most notorious hussy in all of Burtchville.* The word *hussy* sounded damning, like *liar* or *thief.* But worse.

Jasper put the shoe back and dragged his suitcase out from the painted lady's locker. The music was still thudding somewhere behind the wall. He pulled his mother's diary out of his bag.

He started at the beginning and reread all of the entries up to the one where his mother met Big Bill. *Giggle water.* He strained to remember the conversation he and Wayne had overheard at the Tally Ho. Sheriff Bradley had said something about a *still* and everyone making their own *mash* back when he wasn't the law.

That Mr. Hoyt had been up to something. Something bad. *Can we make this our little secret?* Jasper wanted to answer for his mother. *No, Mr. Hoyt. We can't.* But she had. She had taken the dollar from him in the end. Jasper looked over at the red shoes sitting along the far wall then back down to the book.

August 25, 1928

Mr. Hoyt keeps having me do more things I know aren't right, but I can't seem to find a way to stop. I've been snooping around his stinking barn for days trying to figure out where all those jugs come from, thinking maybe there's something I could accidentally break and put an end to all this. The dollars aren't worth it. I'd rather be scrubbing Mrs. Hoyt's rotten pots. But I hadn't found a thing until today.

Old Hoyt just told me flat out that all the giggle water is made up at the Indian reservation still. He says it's heaps cheaper than the stuff running over the border. He's sending me up the road to get more tomorrow. He's sending me right up to the wild men!

"You can't make me go there!" I shrieked. "I'm liable to get scalped or worse by those heathens. My Lord! What would my father say?"

Hoyt just laughed. "What, you think I'm gonna tell him? Hell no! And you ain't gonna tell him neither."

"The hell I'm not!" I yelled back, hoping someone might hear. "This ain't right. This ain't Christian! You're sending me to the slaughter. I won't do it!"

Then he slapped me dead across the face. "You go. I dare you. You go and tell your daddy that you've been cartin' moonshine all over town for me and Big Bill. You go and tell him that I've been paying you dollar bills to break temperance and that I'm a no-good bootlegger. You really think he's going to believe that? We've been goin' to the same church for years. I'm a goddamned deacon!"

I just stood there stunned for a minute. He had it all figured out. But I couldn't give up that easy. "I have the dollars to prove it!" I shouted.

"There's lots a ways for poor girls like you to get dollars. Pretty little girls without morals. You catch my meaning?"

I sure didn't.

He walked over and grabbed my backside with his big, hard hand to help me figure it out. "Your daddy would sooner think you've been lifting up these skirts and giving those town boys with money a nice taste. I'm a respected man in this community. You're just a little liar, a hustler, and everyone knows it."

He laughed his hot-air laugh right in my face. I squirmed myself away from him as quick as I could, but he was right. Papa never trusted me, not one day of my whole miserable life. I've lied enough times about stupid things, but it's more than that. He and Mama decided a long time ago that I was just born rotten somehow. He never looks at Perfect Pearl the way he looks at me, like he's horribly disappointed. He thinks I'm a no-good schemer. Just like Old Hoyt.

Jasper read and reread the entry, trying to make sense of it, certain he must have deciphered the words wrong. He finally slammed the book shut, not wanting to read any more, and curled into a ball with the words *hustler, hussy,* and *taste* turning over and over in his mind. *My mother isn't any of those things,* he argued. She sang in the shower with a voice that would make him stop and listen. She made pancakes shaped like Mickey Mouse just for him. But then sometimes she would leave him alone in the dark apartment when she thought he was sleeping. *She didn't mean to,* he told himself. *Maybe she didn't have a choice.* But the other side of his mind didn't believe that.

Jasper hugged his head with his arms to shut up his brain. He didn't want to think bad things about her anymore. He didn't want to think anything. *Sleep,* he thought, *just let me sleep.* He shut his eyes and laid there until he got his wish.

Through the fog of a fitful dream, he heard a knock at the door.

He sat up and found himself in his own bed back home.

The knock came again.

Jasper got out of bed and crept through the empty apartment to the door. He knew he was dreaming when he saw his mother's favorite vase back on its shelf where it belonged. Still he kept walking. *Who's there?* he whispered.

There was no answer.

His mother always told him to never answer the door, but she wasn't there. He was too short to look through the peephole, so he dragged a chair from the kitchen and climbed up onto the seat to peer out into the hallway through the tiny glass eye.

The face of a girl peered up at him. A pretty girl with dark, pleading eyes.

Do you know who killed me? she asked.

The door to the dressing room slapped opened.

Jasper sat up with a start and cracked his head on the underside of the counter. A pair of shiny black high heels clicked over to him, stopping inches from his nose.

"I'm glad you got a nice nap there, kid." The lady poked at him with her pointy shoe. "Rest time's over. A deal's a deal."

Jasper rubbed the top of his head and tried to get his cramped limbs to move again. Everything hurt. He quickly checked his pants and was relieved to find them dry. An itchy feather boa was stuck to his cheek. The lady stood in her lacy underpants next to a yellow mop bucket. It was an odd enough sight to make him crack a small smile. No one mops in their underwear.

"Here." She rolled the bucket toward him. "Moe's gone home for the day. Front door's locked. You need to go into the booths and mop up the walls and floors. We only used five today. They're the ones along the left-hand side."

Jasper nodded and pulled himself to his numb feet.

"You know which one's the left?" she asked, holding up her left hand.

"Yep."

"Well, if you're not sure, just follow the smell. I gotta get changed." With that, she ushered him and the bucket out into the dark hallway and closed the door.

Two rows of closed doors lined the hall, barely lit by the flickering bulb at the far end. Jasper stood for a moment, listening to the silence before pushing the mop bucket to the first door on the left.

He wasn't sure what to expect when he stepped inside. The first thing he saw was a big room with a velvet couch lit up with pink spotlights. The purple walls matched the couch, and a white fur rug covered half the floor. He blinked for a moment and realized he wasn't actually in the room with the couch. A pane of glass separated the tiny booth where he stood from the stage. The booth itself was just barely big enough for a grown man to turn around. There was a black leather rail about chest high to Jasper and a brass foot rail running along the bottom. Between the two rails was a black leather wall panel. It was spotted with spilled milk.

Jasper frowned. All people did in there was stand and look at the purple room with its purple couch. *Why?* It all looked pretty boring to him. He lifted the mop from the bucket and scrubbed the milk from the wall. The mop water reeked of ammonia, but that was fine with him. He hated the smell of sour milk, especially after being around cows for weeks. He rinsed the mop and scrubbed some more. It took five minutes to clean the wall and floor of the booth.

He opened the next door and found the exact same thing. Each booth looked at the same purple couch. He was deep in thought about it when a spot in the purple wall behind the couch suddenly opened like a door. He dropped his mop into the bucket and stared as the painted lady walked into the room and over to the sofa. She was wearing normal clothes, and the thick makeup was washed from her face. She bent to grab a water glass from the end table next to the sofa, then stopped and squinted at Jasper in the booth. She waved at him and gave him a wink. He waved back and stared after her as she left the room with her drink in her hand.

Ten minutes later, she met Jasper in the hall as he was closing the door to the last booth. "All done?" she asked.

Jasper nodded and wheeled the bucket toward her.

"The janitor closet's that way," she pointed and helped him walk the bucket to the far end of the hall. "So whatdya think of your first day in the business, kid?"

Jasper shrugged weakly. He didn't know what to say, especially since he'd figured out that people paid money just to look at her on the couch in her underpants. Or maybe to watch her take off her underpants. He couldn't even think it without blushing.

"I felt that way too, honey." She chuckled. "But you do whatcha gotta do, right? Here's that buck I promised ya."

She handed him a dollar after he'd dumped the bucket and hung up the mop.

"Thanks," he said, afraid to look at her. Something was really wrong with her. Or with him.

She crouched down to face him and grabbed him by the chin, forcing his eyes up to hers. This time, he didn't see a painted face. She just looked like an ordinary woman. Her blue eyes didn't look that different from his mother's. They were hard at the edges but soft in the middle. She gave him a small smile and said, "Don't mention it. You hungry?"

He nodded voraciously.

"Let's grab a sandwich on the way to the bus station." She stood up and offered him her hand.

After a moment's hesitation, he took it. "Okay."

The two of them walked past the closed booth doors to the back of the shop and grabbed their bags. She led him out into the alley and snapped off the lights.

As the door swung closed, Jasper turned and asked her, "What's your name?"

"It doesn't matter, Jasper. That's one thing you oughta learn quick."

"What?"

"Never tell strangers your name."

CHAPTER 23

Do you expect us to believe you relied
on the kindness of strangers?

The lady led Jasper down the alley and around the corner to Woodward Avenue. The fresh air outside felt like a much-needed bath. He stole glances up and down the sidewalks as they went, but the detective was nowhere in sight.

They passed three blocks before turning into a small diner with a hand-painted sign that read "Stella's." A short, fat woman with gray hair and thick glasses was standing behind a register near the door.

"Lucy! How are you?" She had a thick accent and a warm smile.

"I'm fine, Mrs. Valassis. How are you?"

Mrs. Valassis didn't answer, she just looked at Jasper and raised two bushy gray eyebrows. "Two tonight?"

The lady holding his hand nodded, and their hostess grabbed two plastic-covered menus. She led the odd couple to one of the six booths lining the left side of the narrow restaurant. There were four square tables pushed against the opposite wall with mismatched chairs. Jasper and Lucy were the only ones in the restaurant except for two old ladies in the last booth.

"Tonight's special is the moussaka," Mrs. Valassis announced proudly.

"We'll just have two hamburgers and two Cokes. Thanks."

The old woman seemed put out. "Moussaka is very tasty. It was my yaya's recipe."

"Next time."

The old woman scuttled away with the menus and came back an instant later with two amber glasses filled with water, slapped them on the table, then disappeared again. Jasper grabbed the cup and drank the whole thing in one go.

"Is your name really Lucy?" he asked when he came up for air.

"No, but you can call me that if you want." She gazed out the greasy window. Her eyes had gone dark, like someone had closed the curtains.

Jasper tried to ignore the hundred embarrassing questions he wanted to ask about the purple couch and looked around the tiny restaurant instead. The old ladies two tables behind them were hunched over their dinners. Mrs. Valassis was slouched behind the register, writing something in a book. A set of shelves on the wall next to the door held odd-looking pastries and breads Jasper had never seen before. A wave of hunger made him close his eyes.

He left them closed for a few minutes. He'd never been so tired in his life. His night on the couch at Mrs. Carbo's had been full of fits and starts and blood splattered on the walls in his dreams.

Do you know who killed me?

Jasper's eyes snapped back open.

A shuffle of feet approached the table. Mrs. Valassis was back, clutching a blue ledger to her huge bosom. "Lucy, you want your usual numbers?" the woman asked under her breath.

Not Lucy nodded and slipped a dollar across the table. Mrs. Valassis made a quick note in her book before taking the money and waddling back to the register. Jasper wanted to ask what the dollar was for but didn't. Not Lucy went back to staring out the window.

The walls of the restaurant were covered in a yellowish-white wallpaper with brown and gold pictures. There were ladies in flowing robes and men with long beards. They all had leafy crowns on their heads. The dresses were falling off the women. Jasper found himself staring and stood up. "I'm going to the men's room."

Not Lucy didn't even blink.

Jasper tried not to ogle the multi-breasted wallpaper as he found his way to the back of the restaurant and down a narrow hallway to the bathroom. He took his time, hoping to burn up the minutes before the food would arrive. His hunger bordered on madness now, and he could feel the need to whine about it creeping in. He didn't want to do it in front of his new friend, but he might not be able to help it. He washed his hands slowly and carefully, thinking about the dirty mop bucket he'd touched and the men staring at the purple couch. The walls of the men's room were scarred with written notes and numbers. Jasper tried to decipher them as he pulled the hand towel loop down and down until a clean spot emerged.

The walls of the long wood-paneled hallway back toward the dining area were covered in photographs. Jasper paused and studied the pictures. Men with slick, combed hair and ladies with perfect curls all smiling out at him like they wanted to tell him a secret. Jasper frowned back. Some of the photos had swirly black ink scrawled across the corners. One of the men looked vaguely like someone he'd seen somewhere, but he couldn't place it. *A movie?* He cataloged each face as he approached the dining room, until one of the pictures stopped him cold.

It was his mother.

He blinked his eyes and checked again. There she was with her dazzling smile, pinned hair, and the faint mole on her left cheek. The name *Thea* was scrawled under her chin. It was her, but it wasn't. She was much younger, and her dress was cut low and tight across her chest. It reminded him of Not Lucy in her underwear. His father would have a fit.

He reached up his hand to lift the picture from the wall. It wouldn't budge. He grabbed it with two hands and pulled with all his might. *She shouldn't be here with all these strangers dressed like that.* The frame had been nailed down. He fell back against the opposite wall and stared up at her face. He hadn't seen it in so long he couldn't help but feel tears.

A light hand brushed his shoulder. "Thought you might've fallen in. You okay?"

Jasper nodded his head, but he wasn't.

"Food's here. C'mon, let's eat." She pulled him away from the photograph and back to the table.

The heavenly taste of burger and onions was almost enough to take his mind off her picture. *She shouldn't be here* was all he could think every time he looked up at the hallway leading to the toilets. *Why is she here?*

"Lucy! How nice it is to see you!" The voice of a strange man startled Jasper out of his thoughts. He strode over to their booth.

Not Lucy dropped her sandwich. "Perry! What are you doing here?"

"I own this place. Why should I not come and visit my customers?" He was a rotund older man with bushy eyebrows, just like the old lady behind the register. Jasper had seen him somewhere before but couldn't remember where. "Who is this young friend of yours?"

Jasper kept his head down.

"Oh, him?" Not Lucy waved her hand at Jasper like he was a stray dog. "I'm watching my neighbor's kid for the afternoon. Earning a little spare change. You know how it is."

He chuckled. "I certainly do. I'm hoping to see some of this spare change myself."

"I know I'm behind, Perry. Just give me another week, and I'll have the whole thing for you."

Perry patted her shoulder. "I'm sure you will, Lucy. One way or another . . . You know, you could always come do some work for me. I got a lot of boys up north that would love to meet you."

"Thanks, Perry, but I've got a job." She smiled sweetly up at him, and for a split second, she looked more like a little girl than a woman. "I'll get it to you. I promise."

Perry tapped Jasper's shoulder. "Make her take you to the playground. Make her earn that money your mama's paying, alright?"

Jasper kept his head down and nodded. He didn't want the man to notice him or the fact that they'd seen each other somewhere before. The way he made Not Lucy stiffen in her seat and smile told him he was not to be trusted.

The man put his hand on the back of Not Lucy's neck and gave her a loud kiss on the cheek. "You have until Thursday."

With that, he left. When the door had swung shut, she grabbed her napkin and wiped the kiss from the side of her face.

A half an hour later, Jasper and Not Lucy were sitting in the bus station. Outside the sun was setting over Grand River. The ugly gray haze that hung over the skyline every day lit up in majestic shades of scarlet and orange, and the black soot running down the faces of the buildings faded away. For the briefest moment, the city was beautiful. Not Lucy seemed to notice it too, and neither of them talked for several minutes.

Finally, she asked, "Why's John Russo lookin' for you, honey?"

Jasper thought about it before answering. "I think he wants to take me away."

"Why?"

"I'm not sure." The mess in the apartment, the blood on the wall, his mother's picture, Mr. Hoyt, Big Bill, it was all a blur. A tear ran down his cheek. "I think something really bad happened to her."

"To who?"

Jasper wiped away his tear and looked up at the strange woman whose name wasn't Lucy, not sure how much he should trust her. She herself had told him not to talk to strangers. His mother had once told him the same thing. But Not Lucy wasn't exactly a stranger anymore. She'd bought him dinner. She'd hidden him in her locker. She'd helped him figure out which bus went past Port Huron to Burtchville.

"My mom. She's missing."

"Well, she must be into something pretty big and bad if John's lookin' for her." Not Lucy studied him with those hard but soft eyes. "He isn't a regular cop."

Jasper frowned at this.

"Who was she, honey?"

Jasper thought of the picture hanging in Stella's diner on a wall full of strangers. "I'm not sure anymore."

Not Lucy nodded and lit a cigarette.

"Who was that man? Back at the diner?"

"Him?" She blew out a cloud of smoke. "He thinks he's some kind of gangster. He's really just a two-bit hustler."

"What's a hustler?"

She cracked a half smile. "Someone who makes money the wrong way."

"There's a wrong way?"

She laughed. "There is if you ask the police. Know what I mean?"

Jasper really didn't. He thought of the blood in his apartment and the burglars. Maybe the man with the bushy eyebrows was one of them. "What's his name?"

"You don't want to know him or his family, hon." She shook her head and gazed out at the tall buildings. "Trust me."

"But I feel like I've seen him somewhere before. Who is he?"

"Perry Galatas."

CHAPTER 24

Did anyone take advantage of you?

The bus was mostly empty on a Sunday night. Jasper sat in the back row with his suitcase balanced on his knees as the blue bus rumbled out of the station. Out his window he could see Not Lucy making her way up Woodward Avenue with her head down. She didn't look back or wave; she just headed down the street to wherever it was she was going. Home maybe. Jasper pressed his forehead to the cool glass. *Home.*

The streetlights faded as the bus lumbered up the Dixie Highway and out of the city. The sky was going dark, with only a clouded moon hanging low in the sky. Up north in his uncle's small cabin, Aunt Velma and Wayne would be cleaning up dishes from dinner. Ozzie and Harriet would be on the radio while they worked. Pretty soon, they'd shut the lights and go to sleep. Nobody stayed up late on the farm. The work started too early, and his uncle was always complaining about how keeping the lights on wasted electricity.

Clumps of tightly packed houses rushed by his window. Lamps were still lit in some of the windows, but many had gone dark. It would take over an hour to get to Burtchville. It would be too late to knock on

Uncle Leo's door. *What am I gonna tell him?* he wondered and leaned his head on the back of the seat in front of his. The bus ticket had cost him seventy-five cents. He had a quarter in his pocket, but it wouldn't be enough to get anywhere else for the night. He had no choice.

The bus plunged farther into the dark, leaving the dimly lit suburbs behind. His father would be furious he'd left the city. Of course, he'd be furious he'd run away from a policeman and talked to a half-naked woman too. His father would eventually come looking for him at the farm, and he'd have to tell him something. He'd have to tell his uncle something as well. No matter how he sliced it, he was going to have to lie to somebody.

Jasper chewed his fingernails down to the quick, wondering what to say. *Kidnapped.* He could say he'd been kidnapped and thrown in the back of a car, and when the villains weren't looking, he'd made a daring escape. He'd hidden in an alley until a bus came along, and he'd flagged it down. Or he'd hidden in a ditch until sunrise and found his way back home to the farm on foot. Jasper stared out into the dark fields rushing past his window. It was the best story he could think up. He could even say something about the mess and the blood in the apartment he found right before the kidnappers pounced. It was always good to mix some truth into a lie to make it more believable.

The bus turned onto Gratiot Avenue in Port Huron. The street lamps of the town center flooded into the bus, lighting up the hats of the three men slouched in the seats in front. A hairy arm reached up and pulled the bell, and the bus's brakes let out an earsplitting squeal as they rolled to a stop at the town square. All three of the other passengers stood and stretched, then lumbered out. A farmer in his straw hat, a businessman in his fedora, and a younger man in his flat cap all climbed down the steps, one by one.

The bus driver stood up and lit a cigarette. "Anybody left back there?" he barked.

Jasper raised his hand. "I'm here."

"Oh. Right," he mumbled. "Where ya headed?"

"Burtchville, sir!"

"Never heard of it. Where the hell's that?"

"Um . . . it's not far. Ever hear of the Tally Ho tavern?" Jasper peeked his head out into the aisle. He couldn't see if the name of the tavern registered on the man's face, but he seemed like the sort that would drink.

"Nope."

"Just head north a few more miles. I think you'll find it."

"Mmm-hmm," the driver grumbled with the cigarette hanging from his mouth and slid his big belly back behind the steering wheel.

The bus started moving again. The station clerk had told him the 91 bus was going to Croswell and would pass right through Burtchville, but it took a moment for him to find the tiny village on the map. The lights of Port Huron were disappearing behind the bus as it rumbled up the road. Jasper watched them out the back window. A red exit sign hung over the glass.

The highway was perfectly dark on all sides except for the yellow headlights at the front of the bus. The moon drifted under another cloud out the back window as Jasper debated whether he would wake up his uncle or sleep in the barn that night. The barn sounded more appealing.

The squeal of the brakes interrupted his thoughts. The driver cut the headlights and shut down the engine. Outside, there wasn't anything but dark fields.

Jasper stuck his head out into the aisle. "Excuse me, sir? This isn't Burtchville."

"Need to take a pit stop," the driver said with a low chuckle and stood up from his seat. But instead of opening the front door to take a leak, he started heading down the aisle toward Jasper. "Been wonderin' why the hell I'm goin' all these extra miles for some kid."

He said it like he was telling a private joke to someone else on the bus, but there was no one there. Jasper wanted to shrink back into his seat, but his gut told him to stand up. "I—I thought this bus went all the way to Croswell."

"Nobody goes to that shit-hole town. Not on my Sunday route." The man was getting closer. He unhooked one strap of his overalls. "Haven't been there in months and can't say a single soul complained."

Jasper backed away from him until the emergency exit handle was pressed into his back. He glanced out the side window again. He was miles from anywhere. "I can pay extra," he blurted, reaching into his pocket. "Here, I've got another quarter. Take it. I just want to get home, mister."

Jasper held out his hand to show the man the shiny coin. The driver grabbed him by the wrist with big, meaty fingers. "Nah. I've got somethin' better in mind, boy."

The quarter bounced to the floor.

Jasper's mouth fell open as he tried to pull himself free, but the man's hand was a vise.

"Let me go!" he shrieked.

"Don't make it harder on yourself, kid. Just relax." The man grabbed Jasper's other hand and forced it into his drooping overalls.

Jasper's eyes bulged from his head. He couldn't even put thoughts to the shock and horror. The man was clearly insane, and inside his pants was nothing short of a monster. Hard, hot skin and hair assaulted Jasper's palm as the man moved his hand up and down, forcing him to pet some hideous creature. The man was breathing hard and nodding his approval. Jasper wrenched his arms with all his strength to absolutely no effect. The man just shoved his hand down farther, and Jasper could feel more hair and something soft dangling between his fat thighs.

A word finally came to Jasper's stunned-dumb mind. *Balls.* That one word snapped Jasper out of his stupor. The man was rubbing his hand on his balls.

In a fury, his hand grabbed the nuts just like he'd seen his uncle do right before he castrated poor Roy. The driver loosened his hold on the boy in surprise.

You gotta grab and cut quick, or the boar will eat you alive, Uncle Leo had told him.

There was no knife, so Jasper squeezed and twisted the man's testicles as hard as he could, hoping to tear them off instead. The man let out a deafening scream and released his grip on Jasper's wrists for a precious second.

He ripped his arms free and gave the bus driver a sound kick in the crotch. The fat man toppled back on his ass, doubled over, and bleated just like Uncle Leo's pig.

Once you're done, you better clear out of there, 'cause he'll be madder than a nest of hornets.

Jasper spun and cranked the emergency door handle with all his might. The latch came undone with a loud clank, but the door didn't budge. "C'mon! Come on, you son of a bitch!" he screamed and kicked the door open.

Behind him, he could hear the driver groaning and trying to pull himself up, but he didn't look back. Jasper hit the road at a blind run and tumbled down into the side ditch with a small splash. Not daring to stop, he scrambled along the bottom of the trench, staying hidden in its shadow.

"Get back here, you filthy little fucker!" the man shouted from the bus's back exit. "When I find you, I'm gonna tear you in two! Ya hear me? I'll make you wish you was never born!"

Heavy boots thundered down the road. Jasper kept crawling as fast as his hands and knees could carry him along the floor of the muddy ditch. The moon had gone behind a cloud, and the only lights were the stars. Up ahead, Jasper could just barely make out the shadow of dirt piled into the ditch for a field access path and a big cement pipe going through it. He squeezed himself inside the culvert and out of sight.

The bus driver's footsteps grew quieter as he headed the other way, bellowing more threats of what he planned to do to him. Jasper balled up inside the concrete pipe. Muddy water crept up his back. He'd never been more confused and terrified in his life. All he knew was that he wanted to chop off his hand. He scraped the palm of it against the concrete wall.

The driver was losing patience out on the road and tried a different tack. "You're going to die out here, ya know. There's nobody around for miles. Coyotes gonna catch ya and eat ya for supper. You come with me, I'll make sure you get home safe and sound . . ."

Jasper would rather be eaten by coyotes. He stayed silent in his hiding place under the access track until the bus driver finally gave up. "Fine! Burn in hell, you little shit!"

The loud, wet thump of something being thrown into a ditch was followed by the slam of a door. A moment later, the engine of the bus cranked up and rumbled away. It was only when the sound had faded completely that Jasper's tensed muscles began to tremble. He turned to the side and threw up his dinner.

CHAPTER 25

We're not here to pass judgment.
We're here for the truth.

Jasper stayed balled up in the drainpipe all night. It was out of the wind, but more importantly, he was too terrified to move. He eventually fell into a fitful sleep, a sort of waking nightmare filled with hairy bus drivers and the sound of poor Roy squealing.

He woke with a start. The muted-gray beginnings of dawn lit the sky above the ditch. It would be another hour until sunrise, but he was already running out of time. He pulled his stiff arms and legs out of the culvert and forced himself to stand up. The first frost of autumn hadn't come yet, but the promise of it blew in the air. He shivered in his damp clothes and marched his aching body along the bottom of the trench. The suitcase had landed in the mud next to where the bus driver had pulled over.

A tightness in his throat warned him he'd gotten too cold lying there in the dark puddle. He could hear his uncle's voice in the back of his ears. *The surest way to freeze to death when you're out huntin' is to let yourself get wet.*

Heeding this warning, Jasper hurried to his suitcase and pulled it out of the muck. By the thinnest slice of luck, it hadn't popped open. Clutching it in his freezing hand, he scrambled up the far side of the ditch away from the road. A grove of trees loomed a hundred yards ahead. Behind it sat the shadow of a farmhouse. He'd have to be quick. The farmer would be up any minute to tend to the livestock.

He darted into the cover of the trees and stripped off his wet, muddy clothes. Even his underpants and socks were damp. Naked and shivering, he relieved his bladder against one of the thick oaks, then opened his bag. Two sets of clothes. That's all he had, but they were dry. He pulled on his shirt and pants and instantly felt warmer but not quite warm enough. He considered his other set of clothes in the suitcase and the pile of muddy garments on the ground. The wet clothes would ruin the rest along with his mother's diary. He grabbed the book up from the bottom of the bag and checked to see that the pages were all still there.

One of the farmhouse windows lit up through the dark trees.

Jasper pulled the second pair of clothes on top of the first and threw his filthy, wet rags into the suitcase. The door to the farmhouse fifty yards away swung open with a loud creak as he stuffed his mother's book into the waist of his pants. Jasper ducked behind a tree.

A woman walked out onto the front porch with a pail. She stood and stretched for a moment, staring out into the grove. Jasper held his breath, certain she'd seen him and would scream bloody murder. She didn't. She just picked up her pail and headed toward the barn behind the house.

Jasper snatched up his suitcase and darted from tree to tree, making his way toward the field of corn flanking the road. A dog barked somewhere out behind the farmhouse. *Shit.*

Jasper took off running for the furrows between the cornstalks. The thick leaves flapped against his shoulders as he ran, not stopping until five hundred yards separated him from the house. He slowed to catch his breath and listened. He couldn't hear the dog or anything else following him. Above his head the sky was growing lighter, not yet pink with sun but light enough to see.

He reached up and grabbed a ripe ear of corn from the stalk next to him. Starving, he hardly managed to strip off the leaves and silk before taking a bite. He'd devoured the first ear of corn and had started on another before he took off walking again. Several feet to his right, he heard a car pass by on the road. He had to get going.

He had no idea how many miles lay between him and his uncle's farm. *Five? Ten? Less than ten,* he decided. His father'd once told him that Burtchville was ten miles from Port Huron, and the bus had gone at least five before pulling to its terrible stop.

Jasper shuddered and tried to shake off the memory of the driver. Maybe his uncle had been right to castrate poor Roy. *Maybe nuts do make you crazy.* His hand reached down involuntarily and probed his own anatomy. It bore no resemblance to what he had been forced to pet. None whatsoever, but he jerked his hand away all the same. He felt sick.

Jasper dragged his bad hand down the row of corn, hoping the scrape of the leaves and slap of the stalks would undo what had been done.

By the time the corn turned to wheat, he'd gone at least three miles, crossed two creeks, and climbed one fence. Behind the tufts of grain, the golds and reds of the rising sun bled out into the sky. Every half mile or so, he poked his head out of the field to check the road. Lake Huron peeked out from behind the shoreline buildings here and there. Just when his hopes were climbing, he ran out of wheat field.

A wire fence blocked him from the large road crossing ahead. Beyond it lay Burtchville with its little shops and houses. It was both a comforting and worrying sight. He couldn't wander through town with a muddy suitcase. He would run into grown-ups who knew his uncle. They'd want to know what he was doing and why he had a suitcase with him. Jasper hunkered down in the wheat to rest his tired legs and think.

He could ditch his suitcase and tell anyone who asked that he was running to the store for his uncle. That wasn't so unusual. Kids got sent to town by themselves all the time. Wayne was always running raw milk to the creamery. He stood up and squinted at the buildings across the road. He could swear that the gray one three blocks over was the creamery. He plopped back down, wishing he'd paid closer attention to the roads when they'd gone for ice cream. The only other option was to try to go around and avoid town altogether. St. Clair Road flanked the west side of Burtchville and led north. It crossed Harris Road west of his uncle's farm. He walked that way home from Miss Babcock's schoolhouse.

Mind made up, Jasper got to his feet and turned back into the tall wheat. He followed the edge of the cross street west in search of St. Clair Road. It would be better not to have to talk to other grown-ups. He didn't know how many lies he could keep straight in his head.

"Oh, what a tangled web we weave, when first we practice to deceive," he whispered to himself. It was one of his father's favorite quotes. It was kind of how he felt, like a sneaky spider hiding in the grass.

"Hey! Who's out there?" a voice came booming across the field.

Jasper dropped to the dirt at the sound.

Rustling footsteps were making their way toward him. He debated whether he should run to the street or deeper into the field. He was fast at a sprint, but he was tired and dragging a suitcase full of wet clothes. *The road,* he decided. He sprang up to make a dash for it and ran straight into the chest of a large boy.

"I got him, Pa!" the boy shouted.

When Jasper's dazed eyes came into focus, he saw it was his classmate Cecil Harding, the sixth grader who'd called his mother a hussy.

A large straw hat appeared attached to an enormous man with a full beard. He had a rifle in his hand, and it was pointed at Jasper. He lowered the gun and looked down at the boy with a mix of irritation and bewilderment.

Cecil clapped Jasper on the back and laughed. "We thought you was a fox. Mean little sucker's been gettin' into the henhouse lately."

"Oh. Uh—I'm sorry" was all Jasper could think to say.

"What on God's green earth are you doin' in my field?" the man demanded. "Don't you know you could've been shot?"

Jasper just blinked at him, at a loss for something to say.

"Where's your parents?" Mr. Harding stood the gun up next to him and studied Jasper's face.

"He don't have parents," Cecil answered for him, then added, "I mean, he's stayin' with his aunt and uncle."

Jasper nodded, hoping that might be the end of it.

Cecil's dad looked down at his muddy suitcase and back to his face. "Where are you going, son?"

"Back home to my uncle's farm," Jasper said, studying his feet. It was true. He didn't want to be a sneaky spider weaving webs, but the truth just seemed to exasperate the man.

"Why are you by yourself? Walking through my fields?"

"I was on a bus and . . . ," Jasper started. He couldn't tell the man what had happened, especially not in front of Cecil. He'd rather die. "And it broke down. I was so close to home, I thought I could walk the rest."

The man nodded with his mouth in a hard line, waiting for more. Finally, he said, "You still haven't answered my questions."

"Oh. Sorry . . ." Jasper frowned. He'd have to be a spider. "My dad had to work today, so he sent me on the bus. When it broke down, I was worried I'd be late for school, so I . . . tried to take a shortcut. I guess I got a bit lost. I'm sorry, sir."

The man stared hard into Jasper's face. It was only then that he remembered about the black eye. Jasper grimaced and lowered his head.

After a long silence, the man asked, "You had breakfast?"

"Sir?" Jasper looked up.

"Have you had breakfast?"

Jasper shook his head.

"Well, come on then. You can eat with Cecil. He's headin' to school soon too." With that, the man picked up Jasper's suitcase and headed back into the wheat field.

CHAPTER 26

Did you ever tell anyone what happened?

Jasper followed behind Cecil's dad across ten acres of wheat to a small white house with green shutters. He tried to stay silent along the way.

"You really take a bus by yourself?" Cecil asked under his breath so his father wouldn't hear.

Jasper nodded.

"Wow," Cecil said, obviously impressed. "How'd ya get the shiner?"

Jasper didn't answer. He just kept walking, trying to figure out what on earth he was going to say to Miss Babcock. He hadn't thought about school until Cecil's dad had cornered him. It was a Monday. He'd been to school that past Friday. Miss Babcock wouldn't know anything about his trip back to Detroit. She would think it was just another day.

A low whistle blew next to him, and he looked over at Cecil. "Man, I knew you'd get a whuppin' at home, but I never seen a kid catch a black eye."

Jasper caught his meaning. Everyone at school knew he was facing punishment for fighting at school, he realized. Everyone would figure his uncle had given him the black eye. From the look on Cecil's face, he saw that this was a bad thing. It was the same look Mrs. Carbo had given him. Like something was wrong with him.

"No," he blurted out. "I just got hit . . . We was runnin' around in the hayloft. You know? Ran smack into the crossbeam."

Sneaky spider. His uncle had warned him time and time again not to go running through the loft. It was dark and hot up there, and the framing timbers were covered over with hay.

"Ouch!" Cecil nodded and grinned. "I guess that'll teach ya."

"Yep."

They finally reached the house, and Cecil led him around back to the well pump to wash up. The house was twice as big as Uncle Leo's two-room cabin. It reminded Jasper of the half-burnt house out in his uncle's back fields, or the way it must've been before the fire. There was an upstairs and everything.

Cecil, his little sister, and his parents all had chairs at the big round table. Cecil grabbed a small stool from the kitchen for Jasper, who squeezed in between the large boy and his father.

"Come, Lord Jesus, be our guest, and let this food be blessed. Amen," Mrs. Harding said softly with her head bowed.

Jasper bowed his head and repeated, "Amen," with the rest of the Harding family.

Forks and knives clinked and clanked, but Jasper kept his head down, wishing he could disappear. He didn't want anyone to notice him there or to ask any more questions. His breakfast of stolen corn was better than nothing, but the smells of ham and bacon were almost too much to bear. His eyes flitted to the edge of Cecil's plate now piled high with flapjacks.

"Jasper," Mrs. Harding said in a scolding voice. "Aren't you hungry, dear?"

"I'm okay." He didn't dare look her in the eye.

"Cecil, help your friend here to some food," Mr. Harding commanded.

Cecil promptly scooped eggs and bacon and flapjacks onto Jasper's plate. He seemed slightly annoyed Jasper hadn't done this for himself.

"Thanks," Jasper whispered and dutifully picked up his fork.

"So, Jasper," Mr. Harding began, "I understand you gave my son a bit of a whuppin' the other day."

Jasper stopped chewing and forced his eyes up to the man at the head of the table. He didn't know what to say. He glanced back at Cecil, who still had the shadow of a bruise under his left eye. "I . . ."

"Oh, I don't doubt he deserved it." The man cast a glance at his son. "What prompted a little guy like you to take on this big galoot?"

"I—I don't know . . . it was just a misunderstanding." The last thing Jasper wanted was to get Cecil in trouble, especially since they'd sort of made friends after the incident. Jasper prayed he could leave it at that. An uncomfortable silence fell over the table, and he knew he'd have to say more. "I thought he called me stupid. But he didn't."

"Hmm," the man grunted. He was about to say something else, but he was interrupted by Cecil's mother.

"So, Jasper, Cecil tells me you're staying with your aunt and uncle. Is that right?"

"Yes, ma'am." Jasper stiffened. It was Cecil's mother who had declared his mother something despicable.

"Leonard and Velma are such good neighbors. We haven't seen them at the Rotary Club in ages. You will tell your aunt that I said hello, won't you?"

"Yes, ma'am." He gave her a wide grin. It was the first time he'd dared look at her.

"Good gracious, Jasper." She set down her fork. "How did you get that black eye?"

"He was running in the hayloft," Cecil answered with a mouth full of food. "Smacked right into a beam."

"She wasn't asking you, Son," Cecil's father snapped.

"Honey, don't talk with your mouth full," his mother added.

Jasper turned back to his food and stayed quiet, but he could feel the woman's eyes on him for the rest of the meal.

After they were done eating, Jasper helped clear the table and offered to clean the dishes.

"We're gonna be late," Cecil warned his helpful little friend.

"Yes, you should get going," Mrs. Harding agreed. She brandished a wet washrag and wiped her son's face, giving him a full inspection before releasing him out the door.

Jasper turned to follow him but was caught by the wrist. He jerked his hand away on instinct before realizing it was Cecil's mom.

She took an offended step backward and lowered her washrag.

"Oh. Sorry, ma'am. I didn't mean to . . ."

Mrs. Harding gave him a long, cool appraisal like a cat might study a mouse. She offered him the rag and said, "You have a bit of syrup, dear, right there on your cheek."

"Uh, thanks." He took the rag and wiped his cheek.

"What do you have there?" she asked, raising an eyebrow. She touched the string of white shells hanging from his neck and disappearing under his shirt. It was his mother's necklace.

"No—nothing," he stammered.

"It doesn't look like nothing." She pulled the string of shells out of his shirt until the hand-beaded medallion emerged with its beautiful flowers and secret symbol. Her eyes narrowed. "Where did you get this?"

"It's my mother's," he said, taking a step backward. It seemed like she was accusing him of something.

"She gave it to you?" The word *thief* was written all over her face.

"Yes, ma'am," he said slowly. "She told me to keep it safe and to always think of her. Before she left."

"Before she left?" Her eyebrows raised. There was a smug smile in her eyes, and Cecil's words that day on the playground came back to him. This woman did not like his mother. "And where did she go exactly, dear?"

Jasper could tell by the hidden smirk on the woman's face that she knew he had no idea where his mother had gone. She knew Althea Williams was a bad woman, a hussy. He felt the overwhelming urge to punch her in the nose just like he'd punched her son. Instead, he lied, "She had to work longer hours at the dairy in Detroit. She's being promoted . . . to a manager. She might even be president of the dairy someday."

"Hmm," she sniffed. "I guess that's a good reason to leave your son." The way she said it told him she thought the opposite was true.

He frowned and turned to leave. *What does this dumb lady know about anything?* But it felt like she'd put a stain on him he'd never wash away. There was something wrong with him just like there was something wrong with his mother.

"Did she tell you what it means?" Mrs. Harding forced him to turn back.

"Huh?"

"It's Indian, you know."

"Indian?" He looked down at the necklace despite himself.

"It came from the Black River Reservation. Our church group had a mission there back when I was a girl." She lifted the pendant in her hand. "It's a wedding necklace."

"A wedding necklace?" he repeated.

"In a way. It wasn't good Christian marriage out there. Our minister tried to consecrate the ones he could for the good of the children. We even gave them rings to use, but they preferred these." She dropped the necklace. "I don't seem to remember Althea helping with the mission. Shoot, I hardly remember seeing her in church. Ever ask her how she got it?"

He just shook his head.

She flashed a self-satisfied smile. "You better git. You're going to be late for school."

CHAPTER 27

Were there any adults you trusted?

Jasper stuffed the necklace back under his shirt and hurried across the yard after Cecil, with his suitcase thumping behind him. Glancing back, he could see Cecil's mom standing at the doorstep, watching after them. The smug, knowing look on her face haunted Jasper the entire two-and-a-half-mile hike to school.

He'd been right in that the paved street he had planned to follow did indeed meet up with St. Clair Road. The pavement turned to dirt as it headed north past Burtchville. When they crossed Harris Road, it occurred to him that Wayne might be heading right for them. Jasper stopped and squinted toward his uncle's farm. It had turned into a warm autumn day, and he was sweating under his two layers of clothes.

"You see 'im?" Cecil asked from over his shoulder.

"Nope. He must've took the shortcut through the field. Give me a sec." Jasper walked over to the huge tree and laid his suitcase down in the tall grass. He didn't want to have to explain it to the whole school.

"Good idea," Cecil said as Jasper came back to the road. "Walking around with that looks sorta funny."

Jasper nodded, and the two boys headed up St. Clair to Jeddo Road.

"That bus really break down like you said?" Cecil asked.

"Yep," Jasper answered without missing a beat. "Blew a gasket. Driver said it'd have to be towed."

"Can you tow a bus?" Cecil seemed skeptical.

"I didn't stick around to see." Jasper tried to hide his consternation. He had no idea if buses could be towed and decided to eliminate that part from his story.

As they turned down Jeddo Road, Jasper could make out a tiny figure out in front of the schoolhouse that was probably Miss Babcock sweeping the front porch. A few kids had gathered in the yard. It hit him as they approached that he'd been assigned homework over the weekend, homework that he hadn't been able to complete. Miss Babcock would be furious.

"Jasper!" a voice called from the yard as they drew near. Wayne came running up and clapped his cousin on the back. "Hey, kid! I didn't expect to see you here today."

Jasper smiled weakly. Before he could open his mouth, Cecil was blabbering the whole story. "His bus broke down this morning. Me and Pa almost shot him walkin' through the fields. Thought he was a fox."

"A fox?" Wayne repeated with raised eyebrows, then studied Jasper's face. "He sure is, ain't he? Nice shiner!"

Before Cecil could blab Jasper's lie about the hayloft, Miss Babcock rang the big bronze bell hanging over the door. All the kids poured into the schoolhouse and sat by age in the rows of desks.

"Pass your assignments to the aisle," Miss Babcock instructed.

Jasper kept his head down, avoiding her attention until he felt a light tap on his head.

"Don't you have anything to turn in, Mr. Leary?"

He shook his head.

Miss Babcock lifted his chin up to her impatient eyes. They softened a bit at the sight of his bruised face, but she didn't let on. "See me at recess," she commanded, and then raised her voice to the room, "Class, please remember rule number one. If you want to learn, you have to work. Knowledge does not come free. Now, if you would all get out your composition books . . ."

Two hours later, Miss Babcock snapped her book closed. "Twenty-minute recess. Everyone out!"

All the kids stood at once and clomped outside in a rumble of chairs and feet. Everyone but Jasper. Once the others had left the room, Miss Babcock shut the door.

"Do you want to tell me about it?" She pointed to her eye, and he realized she was talking about the purple bruise around his.

Jasper shook his head. He didn't want to lie to her if he could help it.

She walked over to him and brushed the hair from his forehead to take a better look. "Everything alright?"

"Yeah. I just fell roller-skating."

"Is that why you didn't finish your assignment? You were roller-skating?" she asked, a little spark of irritation flared in her eyes.

Jasper couldn't bear the idea of her being mad at him too. "No. I had to go with my dad back home to Detroit and . . . ," his voice trailed off. Now he'd really stepped in it. He couldn't possibly tell her everything that had happened. An image of Not Lucy in her lacy underpants danced in his head. And then there was the bus ride.

Miss Babcock nodded expectantly, waiting for more.

"And I'm sorry. We forgot it."

Expectation deflated to disappointment as she studied him. "Well then. I'm going to need you to write the words 'I will not forget my homework' one hundred times."

"Yes, ma'am."

She handed him a stack of papers. He began writing, and Miss Babcock opened the door to watch the children running around the school yard for a moment. She sighed under her breath and walked back to her desk. Perched on the edge of her chair, she began to shuffle through the pages of returned homework, making a few marks here and there.

Jasper was on his sixty-fifth line when he stopped to stretch his cramped hand. He glanced around the room at the letters and numbers Miss Babcock had hung over the blackboard and the shelf of books on the far wall. He was squinting, trying to read the titles when her voice startled him.

"You like books, Jasper?" she asked.

He nodded and turned his head back down to his sheet of paper. His sore hand began again. *I will not forget* . . .

"Were you looking for anything in particular?" Miss Babcock pressed him.

"No, ma'am," he said, keeping his head down.

"It's all right, Jasper. Books are the most precious things we have in this world. Anything you might want to know, you can find in a book. What do you want to know?"

He scowled up at her. It was crazy talk. He needed to know so many things, and there was no way any of them were in one of those books.

"You don't believe me." She smirked. "Give it a try."

"Um . . ." He thought for a moment. "I want to know what a still is."

She dropped her pen. "A what?"

Jasper instantly regretted asking. "N—nothing."

"It is not nothing. Where did you hear that word, Jasper?"

Now he'd done it. He couldn't have her sending another note home to Uncle Leo. It would be the death of him. "I . . . um . . . overheard it. Some grown-ups were talking about a place in town a long time ago called Steamboat's."

Miss Babcock studied him carefully, and for a second, Jasper was certain she'd send a note home anyway.

"I'm sorry. I shouldn't have asked."

"No, it's fine. There are no bad questions, Jasper." She gave him a slow smile. "Still is a slang term for distillery. Do you know what a distillery is?"

"No, ma'am."

"A distillery makes liquor. Making liquor used to be against the law, and in my opinion, it should have stayed that way."

Jasper bit his lip.

She took it as confusion. "You'll learn more when you study Prohibition in high school. Unfortunately, this part of American history is not in our curriculum, and I only have a small collection of books here in the classroom. You can find many volumes on the subject at the public library in Port Huron. I suggest searching the card catalog for the key words *Prohibition, rum-running,* and *organized crime.*"

"Organized crime?"

"Who do you think ran the stills when making liquor was against the law?" She leaned across her desk, pleased she'd piqued his interest, and whispered, "Gangsters, killers, and thieves."

Jasper just gaped at her.

"It's good to study your history, Jasper. If you don't understand the mistakes of the past, you're bound to repeat them. Remember that."

Miss Babcock went back to grading the homework assignments. Jasper's hand continued writing his assignment over and over as his mind repeated the words.

Gangsters, killers, and thieves.

Several hours later, school was dismissed. His classmates gathered their assignments and books and poured out the door. Jasper didn't move.

"Are you alright, Jasper?" Miss Babcock raised her eyebrows at him, surprised to see him still sitting there.

"I had another question."

Her eyes lit up. "Shoot."

"Do you have any books about the Black River Reservation?"

She blinked at him for a moment. "What would you like to know about it?"

Jasper unconsciously pressed his mother's necklace against his belly. "I don't know. I want to know about the people who live there, I guess."

"We do have a few books about the Indians. Let me see." She got to her feet and crouched down in front of the bookcase, thumbing through the volumes until she came up with one. "Here."

She set a children's book titled *The First Book of Indians* onto his desk. His eyes widened as he looked at the fierce hunters on the cover chasing down a buffalo. He flipped the book open, almost forgetting she was there. Arrows and tomahawks were flung across page after page. The red-skinned warriors looked mad with rage, and Jasper swallowed hard. *Killers.*

"You be careful, Jasper."

"Ma'am?"

"Books are like people. Sometimes they lie."

CHAPTER 28

We understand you tried to reconcile with

your family. Is that right?

Jasper left the schoolhouse that afternoon with the book in his hand. Wayne met him in the yard.

"Takin' the shortcut today? I think Nicodemus is back in the barn."

"No. I'll take the long way." At the moment, Old Hoyt's bull was the least of Jasper's worries. He wasn't eager to explain where he'd been to his aunt and uncle.

"Whatcha got there?" Wayne asked, pointing at the book pressed to his chest.

"Nothin'. Just a book Miss Babcock lent me."

"Can I see?"

Jasper handed it to Wayne, and they tromped down Jeddo Road, kicking up a trail of dust behind them. Wayne whistled at the cover of *The First Book of Indians*. "Since when are you interested in Injuns?"

"I don't know. I always liked Tonto on the *Lone Ranger*."

"Yeah, but he's not like a real Indian, you know. He just talks funny. 'Me no like where train go.' They don't talk like that."

Jasper stopped walking. "How do you know? You ever met a real Indian?"

"Sure. The reservation's not far. Sometimes Pop needs an extra hand in the fields. Indians work for real cheap. Nobody likes to hire 'em."

"Why not?"

"You know, people think they're wild and crazy and call 'em savages. Pop says the only thing savage about 'em's the way they've been treated. Says it ain't Christian, but people do it 'cause they can get away with it."

"Is that why you said they set Grandma's house on fire?" Jasper studied the book again. A screaming brave was throwing a spear across the cover.

Wayne shrugged. "I just wanted to give you a little scare. Besides, Pop always says Indian justice ain't like regular justice."

"What do you mean?"

"They can't put you in jail if you break a deal, but they might make you disappear. So don't cross 'em."

"Disappear?" Jasper couldn't help but think of his mother.

"You hear talk. One rumor went around a few years back that a farmer named Patchett over in Croswell was desperate to get his beans out the ground, but his sons were all grown and left. He was broke too. So he tricked a couple of braves from the reservation to do the work and didn't pay up, not even when the money came in. Then one day, poof! He was gone. Never heard from again."

Jasper had stopped walking. All he could think of was the blood on the bedroom wall. *Had his mother crossed them? Big Bill had said she'd gone and got herself mixed up with them wild folks over at the res.* His cousin grabbed him by the arm and pulled him down the road. Jasper managed to find his feet again, but he couldn't feel them.

"I guess that's why folk around here don't trust 'em. Pop says it's just because they're different, but I can tell they worry him a bit too."

"How can you tell?"

"Oh, I don't know. He tells me not to talk to 'em too much. He never invites 'em to supper in the house. Has 'em eat out in the barn. Stuff like that." Wayne cracked open the book and looked at the drawings of Indians hurling arrows. He flipped a few pages and snapped it shut. "They don't really look like that either. Least not the ones I seen."

Jasper took the book back. "Do you think . . . I could meet one of 'em?"

"Sure. Next time they come round. Maybe they'll come help with the harvest this year. Pop was just sayin' he wasn't sure how he was gonna get the wheat and the corn picked before the rains come. You think you'll stay that long?"

Jasper didn't answer. The two boys turned back down St. Clair Road in silence. His uncle's farm was less than a mile away, and he still didn't know what he'd tell him.

"So, why'd you come back so soon?" Wayne asked, kicking a rock down the dirt road.

"My dad had to go back to work." Jasper decided he'd better stick with the same lie he'd told Cecil and the Hardings. *Farmers talked.* God only knows what Mrs. Harding might say. The thought made his stomach go cold.

"Thought he said he was taking you on a camping trip up north. He told Pop he needed to spend some time with you to straighten you out."

Jasper's heart sank. He loved camping with his dad more than anything, but the man hadn't said a word about any of that to him. *And why would he after what I did?* Tears stung the corners of his eyes. "I guess the trip got canceled."

"He really put you on a bus all by yourself?" Wayne gave Jasper a sideways glance. "Why didn't he just give you a ride?"

That was a good question, and Jasper didn't have a good answer. He just shrugged and ran up ahead to the oak tree on the corner. His suitcase was still sitting in the long grass right where he'd left it. He wished he'd been able to walk home alone as he picked it up. He didn't want to answer any more of Wayne's questions. He didn't want to go back. Uncle Leo would know he was lying. But he couldn't tell the truth. The tangled web was tightening around his neck. Jasper sank to his knees.

"Hey. You okay?" Wayne pushed his way through the grass and knelt down by the boy's side.

Jasper just shook his head and hid his face so Wayne couldn't see his tears. He needed to tell someone what had happened—the apartment, the blood, the detective, the bus driver—but he didn't want anyone to know about any of it. He couldn't tell Wayne. Jasper pressed his hand into his black eye until the pain was all he could feel.

"I'm fine." Jasper lurched up and grabbed his bag.

"Hey, don't forget this!" Wayne came trotting up beside him, holding the book.

"Right. Thanks."

"So why you so interested in the Indians?" Wayne asked again.

Jasper forced his feet to keep moving. They didn't even feel like his own. "I think my mother knew them."

"Who told you that?"

Jasper didn't want to say anything about his conversation with Cecil's mother and her horrible smile, but someone else had mentioned Indians. "Big Bill over at the roller rink."

The beaded necklace was bouncing lightly against Jasper's chest. He'd have to hide it, he realized. Aunt Velma might find it and start asking questions. He could just tell her that his mother had given it to him, but she wouldn't believe him. She'd think he'd stolen it, and he sort of had.

"What'd he tell you?" Wayne asked.

"That someone named Motega might know her." Jasper stopped walking. Big Bill had told him a lot of things. *People get killed messin' around up there. Heard a bunch of 'em just got run up for murder. That poor girl . . .*

The photograph of the girl outside Calbry's flashed behind his eyes. *Do you know who killed me?*

CHAPTER 29

What happened when you went home?

His uncle's cabin loomed at the end of the two-track drive. Its whitewashed siding piled together in the middle of a giant field of tall grass flanked by autumn-red trees. Looking down at it from where Jasper stood, the house was as small as his thumb. Its stone chimney was smoking. Aunt Velma would be cooking something for supper.

Wayne strolled down the gravel drive, leaving Jasper standing there alone at the edge of Harris Road. Aunt Velma greeted Wayne at the front door, then stepped out onto the crooked front porch with her hand shielding her eyes from the afternoon sun. She waved toward Jasper. He just stood there, rooted to the spot.

"You gonna stand here all day?" a voice asked from behind him. It was his uncle Leo. He had his shotgun slung over his shoulder, and a dead goose hung from his hand.

Jasper's mouth fell open, but nothing came out.

"Help me with this thing." His uncle handed the webbed feet of the goose to Jasper. Blood dripped from two small holes down its neck and onto the ground. Jasper set Miss Babcock's book on his suitcase and grabbed the feet as he was told. The twenty pounds of goose that hung from them sent him staggering off balance. Its black leathery skin stretched tight over hollow bones still felt warm, like it might still be a little bit alive. Uncle Leo picked up the boy's book and suitcase and headed down the driveway without another word.

Jasper followed him, struggling to hold the goose high enough to keep its head from dragging on the ground. It was nearly as tall as he was. Its huge wings flapped half open, catching the air and making its body swing. The way the bird hung taut and springy in his hands, Jasper wouldn't have been shocked at all if the head swung up and bit him. It left a trail of blood along the driveway. The stained hallway of the apartment back in Detroit flashed in his mind, stopping his feet. Red drops fell onto his shoe.

"Velma." His uncle waved to the front porch. "You got that water ready?"

She nodded and ducked back inside, returning two seconds later with a giant pot hanging from the handle in her oven mitt. She set the steaming cauldron on the porch.

"Take this, will you, dear?" His uncle handed her Jasper's suitcase.

Aunt Velma's eyes flitted from the hard leather bag stained with mud down to Jasper frozen in the driveway. Then she took the things inside without a word.

"Stick her in there, boy," his uncle instructed, pointing to the pot.

Jasper swallowed hard, then stepped onto the porch. The poor goose's head thunked against the wood step, splattering it in blood.

"Go on. She's not gettin' any deader."

Hoisting it up with his rubbery arms, Jasper managed to clear the rim of the pot and lowered the bird's head with its glassy, dead eyes into the steaming water. Its long neck and half its body followed. The water level rose up until hot liquid poured over the edges, washing the red stains from the porch. The bird hit the bottom, but its tail and feet still stuck up out of the water as though it were diving for fish.

"We're going to need a bigger pot." His aunt chuckled from the doorway, sounding pleased at the size of it.

Aunt Velma bent down with a giant iron spoon until she was face to face with Jasper. He was certain the spoon was meant for him. Instead, she dipped it into the steaming water, now pink with blood, and shifted the bird around until its feet and tail were submerged and its drowned head hung over the side, staring up at him.

Uncle Leo put a hand on his shoulder.

Jasper jumped.

"Take this inside before it gets hurt." His uncle was holding Miss Babcock's book.

"Yes, sir." Jasper grabbed the book and hurried away from the blood on the porch. *Crime scene—do not enter.*

"You look like you seen a ghost," Wayne chirped with a mouth full of food. He was sitting at the kitchen table eating a sandwich. There was a second one set on a plate in front of Jasper's usual seat.

The floor seemed to roll under his feet. *It was her blood on the wall, her hand on the door.* "What if she's dead?" Jasper whispered.

"Who's dead?" Wayne dropped his sandwich.

Jasper grabbed the edge of the table to steady himself. "Uh, nobody. Your dad shot a goose."

"Great! I love goose. Hate pluckin' 'em, though. Lucky for me."

"Lucky?"

"Yeah. Pluckin's a job for the youngest. Have fun!" With that, Wayne stuffed the rest of the sandwich in his mouth and headed out the front door again. Jasper could hear him through the door say, "Nice one, Pop!" before whistling away.

Jasper's stomach turned when he looked at the sandwich on his plate. He ran to the tiny alcove where he shared a bed with Wayne and threw his book on the mattress. His muddy suitcase was back in its perch on top of the bureau next to the bed frame. It was open and empty. That meant his aunt had found his muddy clothes inside, still wet from sleeping in the culvert the night before. Jasper bit his lip and considered crawling out the window and running into the fields. Instead, he pulled his mother's necklace out from his shirt and held it in his hand. *Where are you, Mom?*

The front door opened. "Jasper? I could use some help, dear." It was his aunt calling him from the front porch.

"Coming," Jasper called back. He stuffed his mother's necklace and her diary under the thick feather mattress and wiped his eyes.

When he stepped back out onto the porch, his uncle was gone and the goose was hanging from one of the rafters. The black webbing of both feet had been pierced by a sharp hook. Aunt Velma pulled a knife from her apron and swiftly cut the bird's neck from its plump chest. Jasper sucked in a breath as the blood poured from the stump into a fresh pan.

Noticing the look of horror on his face, Aunt Velma chuckled. "Where do you think gravy comes from? These necks really add some flavor too if you can get the feathers off." She snapped off the head and tossed it into a slop can, then made short work of it, running the dull edge of her knife over the long neck in brisk strokes. Strips of damp black fluff fell into the large bucket at her feet. Soon something resembling a red sausage emerged. She dipped it into the hot pink water of the soaking pot before tossing it into the pan full of blood.

The stump of the bird had stopped leaking by then. Aunt Velma stood and handed the bucket with the black fluff to Jasper. "Catch the feathers, dear," she said and began yanking out the long feathers from its wings. The bird jerked and twitched as she methodically robbed it of everything that made it a bird. When the large feathers were picked clean, she handed him a wicker basket. "This is for the down. We can get a few dimes in Burtchville for goose down, but I'm fixin' to make a new pillow."

He stood holding the basket over his head as fine feathers rained down in clumps. He caught them the best he could as the bird transformed into meat before his eyes. He had always loved his aunt's roast goose. It used to be his favorite holiday meal. The holes widened in its black feet as the corpse swung violently from the hook.

"You alright, Jasper?" She didn't look at him, but he could tell from her tone she wasn't talking about the goose.

"Yes, ma'am."

"Wayne tells me you took the bus back from Detroit all by yourself this morning. Is that right?"

"Yes, ma'am."

"Did your father put you on that bus?"

Jasper fell silent. He didn't want to lie to Velma.

"You're droppin' feathers, hon."

Jasper raised up the basket. "Oh. Sorry."

"I'm going to send Leo over to the Tally Ho tonight to use their phone. We need to let your father know you made it back here alright. Is there anything you want to tell me before we do that?"

The bird had stopped twitching. Jasper looked up at her and could tell from the way she was studying his face that she was talking about his black eye. The bucket of feathers he was holding drooped a bit. The tenderness in the set of her brow made him nervous she might try to hug him.

He dropped his eyes to her hands, sticky with blood and covered in feathers, and shook his head.

The knife she was holding went back to scraping the feathers from the meat. "Alright then," she said and without warning ripped the bird down from the hook, tearing the rusty metal right through its feet.

Jasper nearly toppled the basket of feathers as he lurched back. She didn't seem to notice. In three quick movements she snapped off one foot, then the other, and handed them both to Jasper. "Put these in with the neck," she said.

They were cold and clammy and no longer felt like feet at all. He dropped them as quickly as he could into the pan with the blood and the angry red sausage. Aunt Velma set the rest of the carcass into the pink water and picked the cauldron up by the handle. She stopped in the doorway and smiled at him. "It's nice to have you back."

CHAPTER 30

Didn't they suspect something

was wrong with you?

Jasper struggled to eat his supper that night. The oily smells of goose and gravy that he used to welcome with such relish made his stomach turn. He kept his eyes on his plate and forced himself to eat bite after bite. There was no greater insult on a farm than uneaten food.

Never leave food on your plate, Jasper. You gotta respect what the world's gone through to put it there, his father had said once when their family had come up for a Sunday dinner. His mother hadn't said anything. She'd just put her fork down and stared out the window. Jasper tried to remember her face at that moment, but all he could see was her thick black hair. It always smelled like flowers after getting set in curls at the hairdresser's. After a long day at the creamery, it smelled like sour milk.

His aunt and uncle were busy talking about something other than him, which was a relief.

"Been thinkin' about heading over to Black River tomorrow," his uncle said.

"Do you really think we have the money?" Velma asked.

Uncle Leo cleared his throat and dropped his fork and knife onto his plate in a metallic reply.

"I'm sorry, but hired hands cost," Velma said, mostly to herself, then got up to clear the dishes. Jasper didn't protest when she took his half-eaten meat. She shot him a glance of disapproval before scraping the bits of goose back into the pot.

His uncle sighed. "Wheat and corn stuck in the field costs more, now, doesn't it?"

"You're right." His aunt held up a hand in surrender. She came back to the table with an apple pie and fresh cream.

"You wanna come?" Uncle Leo asked. It took a minute of awkward silence for Jasper to realize his uncle was talking to him.

He looked up. "Me, sir?"

"Well, you seem to be mighty interested in Indians."

"I do?" Jasper squeaked, picturing the necklace hiding under his mattress.

"Kids don't usually borrow books about things they're not interested in, do they?"

"I guess not." He forced a smile.

"It's settled then. We'll head over to Black River when you get back from school tomorrow."

"Can I come too?" Wayne piped in. "I found some more arrowheads in the back field."

"I can't see the harm in that. Can you, Mother?"

"No. Just be sure to get your chores done in the morning," she said, giving each boy a double helping of pie.

"The Manitonaaha will sometimes trade you for arrowheads," Wayne said to Jasper. "Last time I got a nickel each."

Jasper stuffed his mouth with pie so he wouldn't be tempted to ask too many questions. Like whether Indians really did kill people.

A minute later, Uncle Leo stood up from the table. "I'm headin' out. You boys better hay those cows before bed. Understand?"

"Yes, sir," both boys answered.

"Invite Wendell for supper Sunday, will you, dear?" Aunt Velma asked.

Uncle Leo looked long and hard at Jasper and his black eye. He finally said, "Will do."

Even in the chill of the fall evening, the hayloft was sweltering hot from the day's sun. Square bales were stacked to the rafters, leaving only a narrow path from the ladder to the open chute in the center.

"We'll need three bales," Wayne decided. The older boy grabbed a giant hook hanging from a crossbeam and handed a second one to Jasper. They each plunged a hook into either side of a fifty-pound bale, and together they dragged it over to the chute. They unhooked and shoved it the last foot through the hole. It fell fifteen feet to the barn floor. *Whump.*

"So, what'd they say?" Wayne asked as he hooked into a second bale.

"About what?" Jasper decided to play dumb. He seated his hook and helped his cousin drag another square bundle of hay to the opening. *Whump.*

"About you taking the bus home?"

"Nothing." Jasper walked to another bale.

"No. Not that one. Pop wants us to mix in the timothy grass till we run out." Wayne motioned to a different stack on the other side of the chute.

Jasper picked his way carefully in the light of the kerosene lantern past the large hole in the hayloft floor. *Lots of people been known to get hurt in haylofts, Jasper,* his mother had warned him the last time she'd caught him horsing around up there. She'd squeezed his arm hard and said it again, *Lots of people.*

"They really didn't ask?" Wayne pressed him as they dragged the third bale.

"Your mom asked about it a little, but she didn't say much."

Whump.

"Must be nice," Wayne said, hanging the giant hooks back where they belonged.

"What's nice?" Jasper picked up the lantern.

"Give me that," his cousin ordered and took the light. "One spark and this whole place will go up like a firecracker."

Jasper followed Wayne back down the ladder. "What's nice?"

"Must be kinda nice not havin' to answer to a mom and dad." Wayne hung the lantern from a hook and pulled a pocketknife out of his jeans. He'd cut the twine from two bales before he noticed the sour look on Jasper's face. "Shoot. I didn't mean nothin' by that."

Jasper shrugged, trying to show his cousin that his stupid words didn't bother him. *It was sort of nice,* he told himself. He'd be like Tarzan in the jungle or Peter Pan from the storybooks. He wouldn't have to worry about getting in trouble anymore if he were a Lost Boy.

But he wasn't lost. He'd been left on purpose.

Wayne cut open the last bale and handed Jasper a pitchfork. "Each cow gets two good loads, but you have to break 'em up like this." He stabbed the hay bale, breaking it apart. "Give each lift a good shake too. The side rake sometimes picks up nails and scrap. Vet pulled a fistful of metal outta one of Pop's best cows last year. You know, after they put her down."

Jasper speared a good forkful and shook it hard. All the hay scattered to the ground.

Wayne laughed. "Okay, maybe not that big of a shake."

Three more tries and Jasper finally got the hang of it. It still took the better part of an hour to get all ten cows fed and watered. When Wayne finally hung up the pitchforks, they each had a fine layer of itchy hay dust clinging to their clothes.

"I'm gonna go wash up. You comin'?" Wayne asked.

"In a minute." Jasper didn't want to go back. His uncle would have talked to his father by now. Both men would be looking for blood.

"Alright. Bring the lantern with you. And watch out for Lucifer. He's on a mean tear lately." With that, Wayne left him alone with the sounds of cows chewing hay.

Jasper picked up the lantern and rushed past the swishing tails in the stalls to the far corner. The rafters creaked as a brisk wind whistled through the open slats in the siding. He glanced over his shoulder. The sounds of mice skittered across the wood planks overhead. Somewhere up there the black cat was stalking after them, but otherwise the barn was empty.

He sat down with the light and pulled his mother's diary from the waist of his pants.

> *August 26, 1928*
> *I went up the hill today with nothing but Hoyt's empty cart and a sick feeling under my skin. Mr. Hoyt thinks he owns me now. He squeezed my backside again as I climbed up onto the driver's seat.*
>
> *I have no idea what that grinning bastard meant by giving rich boys a taste, but I know it wasn't good. It was dirty. And I can tell by the way he looks at me now that he thinks I'm dirty too.*

Jasper grimaced at the word *dirty*. That's exactly how he'd felt when that bus driver had made him touch the beast inside his pants. He'd never be able to wash the dirty off. He rubbed his palm against his overalls until it hurt, but he could still feel it.

> *It took all I had not to kick him in the teeth! My fanny felt strange where his hand had been the whole day. Like it wasn't even mine anymore.*

The entire five-mile ride I plotted ways to get right again with the world. I'd burn down Hoyt's barn. I'd drive the cart straight to the sheriff's office on Lake Road and tell him everything. I'd take the ten dollars I'd earned for doing Hoyt's dirty work and leave town for good. I'd do something, but I couldn't seem to figure what.

In the end, I just did what I was told. Hoyt was going to tell Papa I'm worse than everybody thought. He'd tell him I'm lifting up my skirts and doing dirty things with boys. God knows what else he'd tell him. I almost ran the cart off the road I was crying so hard.

I nearly drove past the entrance to the Indian reservation. The narrow drive up into the woods was only marked by a dead tree and a tiny splintered signpost that read "Door of Faith Road." I had to read the sign twice. "Door of Faith." What does that even mean? It didn't seem like something a heathen Injun would write. For a second there, it made me feel a little braver. Like God might be watching me at that very moment, but dear Lord, what would God say? Here I was, the worst sinner under the sun, hoping for his protection. I had to practically beat poor Josie to get her up the hill.

I'd never met an Indian before. I'd seen two of them once in town, walking on the sidewalk. No one lets Indians into their shops or cafés, so it was a real novelty to see them there in Burtchville. I pointed at one with long black hair and asked my mother who it was. "Don't point, Althea." That's all she said.

I found out who they were, with their strange clothes and shoes, at school. Delilah Cummings knew them from her family's church group. "They're Manitonaaha Indians," she said in that bossy voice of hers. "Didn't you know there are actually many different kinds? They're more like animals than like us, but they do have some strange language that they sort of talk. I once saw one that could even speak English, although not too good. My mother says it's important to teach them about Jesus, but I personally don't really see the point."

Between you and me, I don't see the point either. I hate sitting in church hearing about all that hellfire waiting for us sinners. Unless Jesus forgives us, of course, and we get to go to heaven. That's what I'm supposed to hope for, but when I pray to him, it feels like I'm writing letters to Santa Claus. But I sure was praying my heart out as I led my cart up that hill.

This is what I was doing when a very tall brown-skinned boy with long black hair stopped my cart in the road. He wasn't wearing a shirt, but he had on pants just like Papa wears. He just stood there staring at me like I was some sad creature that had lost its way.

"Hello?" I said real slow and then muttered a bunch of nonsense like, "Do you speak English . . . um . . . no of course you don't. I don't—I shouldn't have . . . I'm sorry. I should probably leave." I started to turn the cart around, certain that the boy would pull out a tomahawk any second and try to cut off my head.

"What are you doing here?" he asked in perfectly fine English. I was so surprised I nearly ran old Josie into a tree! He talked to me like he knew me. He was actually sort of smiling.

I didn't know what to say. I just sat there with my mouth hanging open like a gaping fish.

"You okay?" He seemed really amused that I was so stupid. That made me mad.

I straightened myself up and said, "I'm here to pick up a delivery for Mr. Hoyt."

"You want firewater," he said and frowned at me like I was crazy. "Why'd he send you? You're just a girl."

I didn't have a good answer until I realized he might send me back empty-handed. Part of me wanted him to, but then I'd have to deal with Mr. Hoyt. I could barely stand him when he was pleased with me. The few times I'd made him angry, he'd smacked me dead in the face.

"I can drive a cart just fine, thank you," I said in the haughty voice Papa hates.

"Do you know what firewater will do to you?" He was not amused. "You know what the sheriff can do to you if he catches you? Go home, little girl."

"The sheriff won't bother me." Now I was getting rather annoyed. "I'm just a little girl. Don't you see?"

He nodded with his head, but his eyes did not seem to agree. I'd never seen eyes like that—so black, like the eyes of a crow—and when they looked at me it was like they could see every bad idea I'd ever had. I guess he gave up on changing my mind, because he said, "Follow me."

So I did. I followed behind him in my cart as he led me past tents and scrap-yard huts and a clutch of small cabins. I kept my head down the whole way, but I could feel a hundred eyes on me, I swear.

He had me pull the cart up just outside the door to a large barn. Inside were three large copper tanks and hundreds of jars and jugs like the ones Mr. Hoyt had in his barn. The tall boy talked to an older man with a long gray braid running down his back in a language I didn't understand. The man looked up at me and laughed the way Hoyt likes to laugh at me. Like I'm some dirty joke.

Two younger men were sitting on the ground, passing a hand-painted jar between them. They started laughing too.

I started to get down to give those hyenas a piece of my mind, and the boy held up his hand. "It would be better if you sat."

The two younger men began loading the jugs. Each had a long knife hanging from their belts and a dark look in their eyes. I sat back down and stayed there until the cart was full. The old man said something softly to the boy in the strange language before he led me back down the road. When we reached the sign at the bottom of the hill that read "Door of Faith," the boy turned to me. "Tell Hoyt he must pay it back before the next full moon."

I agreed.

He looked at me a long time with those black eyes before he asked, "What is your name?"

At first I didn't want to tell him. I was there on criminal business after all, and he was a Godless Indian. But he didn't seem so Godless. Besides, even if he went to the sheriff himself, no one would believe him. No one trusted Indians. So I told him.

"Be careful, Althea," he said and then headed back up the hill.

"Wait!" I called after him. "What's your name?" I don't know why I wanted to know. It was something about the way he'd looked at me. No one had ever looked at me that carefully before. I felt like it was the first time anyone had ever really seen me at all. Until that moment, I didn't really exist.

"*Does it matter?*" *he asked. It was a fair question, considering we would probably never see each other again. But he was the first Indian I'd ever met.*

"*It matters to me,*" *I said.*

He raised his eyebrows like he was surprised. Maybe I was the first white girl he'd ever met. "*Motega. My name is Motega.*"

"*Thank you for your help, Motega. It was nice to meet you.*" *I gave him my most winning smile.*

Motega didn't smile back.

CHAPTER 31

Tell me about the night of the fire.
How did it happen?

It was getting late. Uncle Leo would be back soon. He would have found out that Jasper had run away from Detroit and gotten on a bus without his father's permission. There would be hell to pay.

Jasper tried to close the book but couldn't bring himself to do it. It was clear that Motega was one of the organized criminals Miss Babcock had warned him about. But so was Big Bill and Mr. Hoyt and God only knew who else. And there was no denying it now. His mother was a criminal too.

Jasper turned the page.

August 31, 1928
I can't stop thinking about that boy Motega. He was so
nice to me. It's been so long since anyone was nice to me.
I asked Hoyt if I had to go back to the reservation for him
anytime soon. I even tried to make it sound like I really
didn't want to go, so he might send me. He says he won't

have another large pickup for at least a month.

In the meantime, I'm still going to his barn three afternoons a week for small deliveries. It's shocking to know how many neighbors keep moonshine hidden near their houses. Check the haylofts if you're ever wondering. Half the Christians in the county are hiding Indian hooch, and no one else knows it but me and Mr. Hoyt.

It was funny at first, knowing everyone's big secret. But secrets have a price. Every time I show up with those jugs from Mr. Hoyt's barn, I can see the look in their eyes. They don't trust me. They think I'm up to some no-good even worse than the no-good they're all up to. They think there's something wrong with me. They whisper about me as I leave. I can see the whispers in their eyes. They don't like me.

The only person that seems to like me is Mr. Hoyt. Him and his greedy smile hover all around me, but if I drop a jug or forget a message from one of the customers, he slaps me hard enough to bring tears. He tells me I'm his favorite girl one day and then the next threatens to march me right over to my father's house and announce to the whole family what a filthy girl I am.

He's making me dirty. I can feel it every time he looks at me. He keeps inviting me up into the loft and trying to get me to drink from a jug with him. He watches me load up the cart. He stares at me so hard it's like he's grabbing me with his eyes. His eyes seem to whisper things about me too.

The memory of the bus driver crept up behind him as he flipped to the next page and then the next. His mother's words bled together on the page until he couldn't read any more.

Jasper slammed the book shut and threw it clear to the far wall. Tears burned his hay-dusted eyes. *What did that son of a bitch do?* He didn't want to know. He really didn't. He couldn't take it. Wayne was right. He shouldn't be reading any of it. His eyes followed the arc where he'd thrown the book despite himself.

He jumped to his feet to go after it and knocked one right into the lantern.

The glass broke with a crash, and kerosene splattered across the ground. The loose straw scattered about lit instantly. The flames spread faster than Jasper could follow until a fire taller than he was blazed all around him. He couldn't even think to scream. It wasn't until his pant leg started smoking that he managed to move. Jasper leapt from the flames and fell to the ground. He slammed his leg against the dirt until the embers went out. The straw fire had shrunk in height but was still burning. He searched his panicked head for a way to put it out. If he burned down the barn, his uncle would kill him.

Water.

Jasper scrambled to the nearest stall. Inside it the old cow was chewing away, oblivious to the danger raging behind her. "Move!" Jasper yelled in her ear and squeezed past her giant body to the full water trough on the ground. He could barely move it. Grunting, he dragged it inch by inch past the cow's udder, splashing water on his arms with each tug. He finally managed to get the enormous tray past the gate.

The fire had gone from a solid mass to several hot spots scattered around the broken lantern. It was running out of straw but had begun to lick the wood framing of a stall. Jasper dragged the water dish the last few feet and tried to hoist it up to empty it out. But he couldn't lift it. He pulled with all his might, but it wouldn't budge. Desperate, he began bailing it out with his hands, splashing water as far as he could reach. The flames attacking the stall hissed with smoke, but others popped and scattered with each splash. *Shit.* He jumped up and stomped on the blazes with his boots, kicking up dirt and mud until they each went out one by one. Jasper coughed as he breathed their smoke in.

Before long, all he could see were a few glowing embers. He stamped the tiny red lights until they all had gone out. It was only when it was perfectly dark that he realized he was screaming. His throat burned with smoke. Dizziness took hold, and he sank down to the wet, charred ground. His pants and boots smoldered beneath him, and he stripped them off, tossing them all in the trough.

The cows were still chewing, not bothered by the fact they'd all almost died. Water seeped into Jasper's underpants. He ran a hand down his legs and found what felt like a sunburn on his left shin and ankle. His other leg was sticky and wet. The shard nicked his finger when he ran his hand up his shin. A piece of broken glass had lodged in his right knee. It didn't even hurt as he picked it out. That scared him.

A voice out on the driveway brought Jasper back to his senses. It was his uncle. "Christ Almighty! What the hell's goin' on in there?"

He was going to kill him. Jasper was certain of this. He'd broken a lamp and nearly burned down the barn. He pulled himself to his feet and headed deeper into the dark.

"Wayne? That you in there?" Uncle Leo roared from the doorway. "Answer me, boy!"

Jasper felt his way back to the hayloft ladder and silently began to climb.

Footsteps scraped across the dirt floor, and then the sound of metal tools clanked against the far wall. A second later, the rip of a match flooded the lower barn with light as Uncle Leo lit another lantern.

"Son of a bitch," he muttered. The sound of broken glass clinked across the barn floor.

Up in the loft, Jasper crept away from the ladder to the stacks of hay and wedged himself behind a large pile.

"Whoa! What happened, Pop?" Wayne asked from the doorway.

"You tell me, boy." There was murder in his uncle's voice.

"I—I didn't. I swear. Jasper was the last one in here. He must've h—"

Thwack! Wayne grunted.

"Who told you it was alright to leave a nine-year-old nitwit in the barn with a lit lantern? Huh?"

Thwack! Thwack! Thwack! Jasper flinched with each lick. *It. Wasn't. Wayne's. Fault.* He wanted to leap down from the loft and take his punishment. But his body wouldn't move. Hot tears just spilled down his face.

Thwack!

"Ah!" Wayne cried out over and over until the beating was done.

Uncle Leo didn't say another word. All Jasper heard was the sound of something big being pulled from the wall with a metallic scrape. *Oh God. He's going to kill him.* Jasper lurched to his feet ready to scream.

"I—I'm sorry, Pop," Wayne managed in a strong voice. *He's not allowed to cry.*

"Here," his father growled. "Clear the straw and dump some dirt on that. Them embers can start back up unless they've been properly smothered. Clean up that glass too."

"Yes, sir." The sound of a shovel scraping the ground immediately went to work. Jasper sank back down behind his hay bale and cried his eyes out for Wayne in silence since his cousin wasn't allowed to cry for himself. *It's all my fault. I'm no good. It's all my fault.*

"Where is he?" Uncle Leo demanded.

"I ain't seen him since we finished haying the cows."

"Jasper!" Uncle Leo's voice boomed loud enough to make a cow join in.

Jasper didn't move.

"You in here, boy? You can't hide from this. You can't hide from me. You hear me?" The sound of heavy footsteps mixed with the scrape of Wayne's shovel as his uncle searched the barn. Cow stalls opened one by one.

"This good, Pop?" Wayne asked.

"That'll do. Go get your mother and then get your ass to bed."

"Yes, sir." The sound of a shovel being hung up was followed by silence. Jasper barely breathed. Something small rustled in the hay not far from where he crouched. *A rat,* he thought. *A rat just like me.*

"Jasper?" Uncle Leo's voice boomed from the hayloft ladder. He was not ten feet from Jasper's hiding place.

Something landed on the hay bale above him with a thump. He nearly yelped out loud. A bright light shined toward the noise. "Jasper? Is that you?"

Footsteps vibrated the wood boards beneath him. The light grew brighter as his uncle approached. He was going to be caught. Jasper squeezed his eyes shut as if it might make him disappear. Then he heard a yowl.

"Dammit, Lucifer!" His uncle sighed. "Go catch a rat."

The thump bounced down to the ground then padded off into the hayloft.

"Leo?" his aunt's voice called from the barn door.

"I'm coming," he called back. The light quickly faded back down the ladder. Jasper released the breath he'd been holding.

"My goodness! What happened?"

"Looks like Jasper knocked over a lantern."

"Is he alright?"

"Can't seem to find him. He ran off again."

"Oh, dear . . . He's hurt. Look at these." She must have been looking at his pants. The blood on his leg was drying. The sunburn on his left shin was starting to smart a bit.

"Stupid is what he is."

"Oh, Leo. Don't be unkind. The poor thing must be scared to death."

"He should be."

"Go easy on him, dear. He did manage to put out the fire, didn't he? That couldn't have been easy."

"He had no business bein' alone in here in the first place. Shouldn't be here at all. Jesus, I don't know what the hell she was thinkin'."

"Well, he can't help that . . . This could've been so much worse."

He told himself it was true. *It could've been worse.* The whole barn could have gone up in flames just as easily. It didn't make him feel any better.

Uncle Leo just grunted.

"What'd his father say?"

"Not a damn thing. I couldn't reach him. The home line's gone dead. I left a message for him with Mick at the plant."

"Still no word from Althea?"

"Nope. Nobody's heard a thing. Who the hell goes and leaves her kid? Huh? I ask you," he growled. "Damn woman's been nothin' but trouble since the day she was born. Always stirring things up with her craziness. Burnin' down the damn house, then running away . . . The old man couldn't live with the torment. Jesus, she cost us *everything*! I swear if I ever see her again, I'll wring her neck."

"You don't mean that."

Uncle Leo didn't answer.

Jasper squeezed his eyes shut and pressed his hands to his ears. *It wasn't her fault,* he wanted to scream out in her defense. Something terrible had happened to her. Mr. Hoyt had done something terrible. Jasper's eyes flew open. *The diary.* He'd thrown the diary to the far wall near the feed barrels. It was trapped somewhere down there, alone.

"There has to be a good reason for it."

"Right. You go on ahead and get to bed. I'm gonna sleep a fire watch out here."

"What do you want to do about Jasper?"

"He'll either turn up or he won't."

"He's wandering around in the freezing cold in nothin' but his Skivvies. Aren't you worried about him?" Aunt Velma obviously was worried. That just made Jasper feel worse.

"Even a stray dog's got the sense to get out of the rain. He'll find his way back. Shoot. He managed to find his way back sixty miles. He'll be back."

"He's just a little boy."

His uncle sighed. "Don't coddle him, Velma. The sooner that boy grows up, the better."

CHAPTER 32

Were you injured?

Coiled up in the dark between the bales of hay, Jasper thought of his grandmother's house crumbling in the back field. His mother was to blame. *Maybe she'd knocked over a lantern too.* Even if it had been an accident, it was clear her brother Leo would never forgive her. He'd never forgive his no-good nephew either.

Down below the hayloft, his uncle set about making his bed. He could hear the cot for the county fair being pulled off the wall. Then the barn door swung shut. More footsteps scuffed across the ground.

"Someone steal your water, Myrtle?" his uncle asked. The sound of a water dish clunked to the ground and was followed by splashing as it was refilled. "You're lucky you gave it up. Thanks for not kickin' him, ol' girl. But you got my permission to bite him next time you see 'im."

There was a light patting sound and the creak of a stall door. "Stupid son of a bitch is gonna freeze out there, runnin' around with no britches on," his uncle muttered to himself. "Ain't got the sense of a shithouse rat."

Jasper frowned in the dim light that seeped up through the floorboards. Uncle Leo was right. He was stupid. He couldn't hide in the hayloft forever. If he escaped to Detroit, his father would just send him back to the farm. *A boy his age needs a mother around . . .* But it wasn't just that. He suspected if his father didn't hate him already, he sure did now. He might just drag Jasper to some orphanage himself. The swelling around his eye had gone down, but it still felt funny when he blinked.

The sooner that boy grows up, the better.

A whisper came from below. "I'm trying, Mother. I'm trying real hard to take care of her like you asked, but she sure ain't makin' it easy, now is she? How you found the strength to still care after . . ." There was a long pause as Uncle Leo cleared his throat. "You always said it wasn't her fault. I want to believe that, I do. Not for her, but for you. I pray for you . . . and Dad . . . may you both rest in peace tonight. Dear Lord, I pray for the strength to forgive the past. I pray for the wisdom to guide us through this storm. Amen."

The light went out in the barn below.

Up in the loft, the darkness was so complete Jasper could no longer see his own hands in front of his face. His heart beat out the seconds as the minutes passed one by one.

I pray for my uncle's forgiveness. I pray my father still loves me. I pray that my mother is safe out there somewhere. I pray that she comes back home.

An eternity went by before the sound of his uncle's snores rumbled beneath him.

He'd never heard the man so angry before. He'd never heard Uncle Leo speak about his grandparents either. They'd both died long before Jasper was born, and his mother never said one word about them. He'd never even seen a picture. He puzzled over each of his uncle's words. *The old man couldn't live with the torment.*

Tiny feet skittered across the floorboards not three feet away from where Jasper hid. A brisk thump fell next to them. Then a hiss. The screeching, thrashing sounds of hell followed as Lucifer battled with the rat. Within ten seconds, the racket of the fight died off into the wet, slimy sounds of teeth feasting. Jasper curled tighter into his ball with his hands over his ears, trying not to picture the rat's guts splayed out in a ring.

I pray I don't get eaten.

A few moments later, something soft and furry brushed against his leg. Jasper stopped breathing, certain that Lucifer had come to dine on him next. The cat brushed against him, nuzzling his head against the boy's bare legs until he settled on a spot and curled up next to him. Too terrified to move, Jasper just lay there frozen while the beast beside him purred, occasionally licking its lips. The cat was falling asleep, he realized to his horror. Lucifer's half-inch claws had left scars up and down Wayne's arm. Jasper worked up the courage to gently nudge the animal with his knee. The old tomcat didn't move.

His uncle snored and the cows chewed their cud while Jasper lay pinned by a cat, struggling to find a way out of his predicament. He had to talk to his uncle. There was no way around it. He would have to stop hiding. *It's time to grow up.* He knew it was true but was too terrified to move. Every few minutes, Lucifer would twitch his tail.

As the hours passed with Jasper staring into the dark, he found the warmth of the cat against his bare legs more and more comforting. The burning in his left shin and the growing ache in his cut knee made it harder and harder to think of anything but the pain. Lucifer stretched out against him, and the brush of soft fur provided moments of relief. He didn't want to risk petting the tomcat, uncertain now if he was more afraid of getting scratched or of it running away. At that moment, the ferocious animal was his only friend in the world.

There would be school tomorrow. *Will I even go?* he wondered, wishing more than ever that he hadn't been such a coward.

I pray for the strength to face my punishment.

In the darkness, his worst fears came calling one by one. Blood spurted from his mother's black curls onto the apartment wall. The girl with dark eyes banged on his door crying, *Do you know who killed me?* Detective Russo came crawling through the hay to drag him off to an orphanage where his family would never find him. The surly bus driver crept up behind him with Uncle Leo's castration knife and a dirty gleam in his eye. Mr. Hoyt hovered over his mother, making her scream and scream and scream . . .

Stop.

And then the terrors would start again.

Sometime before dawn, he heard the crow of the rooster down in the yard. He sat up with a start, sending Lucifer scampering away to a far corner. The hayloft was still pitch-black, but his uncle would be up soon. He had to make it right, one way or another, because he couldn't take another minute alone with his nightmares.

Jasper pulled himself to his feet and nearly fell when he tried to put weight on his cut leg. It was hot and swollen like it had been pumped full of poison. He forced himself to walk on it, wincing with the pain. He deserved it. He deserved whatever he got. He inched his way around the hay bale toward the ladder, straining to see through the dark. *Don't fall through the chute. Please don't let me fall through the chute.*

He slid his feet slowly along the boards, feeling for the edge of the hole in the floor where the ladder ended. His mother's voice haunted each step. *You be good for Uncle Leo. Make Mommy proud.* His uncle's snores were growing louder and less even. The hay beneath his feet brushed against the wood, telling him where he was. The pain in his cut leg took his breath away with each step. Finally, his toe found the ladder.

He almost cried out in agony as he crouched to find the first rung, but he didn't stop. The cool air of the barn below struck his bare haunches as he made his way down the ladder one rung at a time. Pale light leaked through the wood siding. The cows were waking. He could hear their restless hooves moving in their stalls. Their udders had grown heavy and painful overnight. Jasper vowed he would do all the milking that day and all the rest of the days it took to make it up to his uncle.

"I see you made it back."

Jasper's heart contracted. He turned to face the shadow of his uncle sitting up on the cot. He opened his mouth to say how sorry he was and how he'd never do anything bad ever again but thought better of it. The man wouldn't believe him. He was no good, just like his mother. Instead, Jasper limped over to the far wall and pulled the riding crop from its hook. He limped back and handed it to his uncle. It didn't matter if he beat him, not even if he beat him to death. He probably deserved to die, if that's what it took to beat the bad out of him.

Uncle Leo took the crop and set it down next to him. "Get me a match, boy."

"Yes, sir." Jasper nodded and limped over to the side of the barn door where the wood matches were kept. His knee was on fire now. Each step made his eyes lose focus, but he kept walking and handed his uncle the match.

Uncle Leo struck it against the side of the lantern and the barn filled with light. "Let me take a look at ya."

He leaned down and examined the boy's legs. Jasper startled as he looked at them himself for the first time. His right leg was caked brown with dried blood. His left shin was blistered purple where the fire had got him. Both legs were covered in dirt and flecks of hay. His shirt was charred black at the edges, so were his hands.

His uncle let out a low whistle. "You really did it to yourself but good, didn't ya?" His voice was hard, but as he glared at him, Jasper could see a twinge of sympathy in his eyes.

"Yes, sir." He felt a tear fall down his cheek and brushed it away. He wouldn't cry. No matter what happened, he wouldn't cry. He looked down at the crop and then back to his uncle expectantly. He deserved everything Wayne got and then some.

His uncle followed his gaze. "Don't you mind that. That there's to make a lesson stick. Nothin' more. Looks like you took care of that one yourself. Come 'ere. We got to get you cleaned up." His uncle stood and scooped the boy up into his arms. The gesture filled Jasper with such a tidal wave of relief and humiliation he nearly started bawling. *I won't cry.*

"I—I can walk," Jasper whimpered and struggled to get down.

"Like hell." His uncle pushed the barn door open with his shoulder. "Save your strength, boy. I promise you, when we're done saltin' those wounds, you're gonna wish I'd whupped you instead."

CHAPTER 33

Were you hospitalized?

Uncle Leo made good on his promise. He carried Jasper up to the cabin and set him on the kitchen table. Aunt Velma was at the stove.

"Oh, Mary Mother of God!" she gasped when she saw him come in. "Jasper! What were you thinkin'?"

Jasper didn't answer. He just watched her put a large pot of water on the woodstove and stoke the fire. She grabbed the can of salt from the shelf and dumped half its contents in the water.

"What's goin' on?" Wayne asked from his bed.

"Jasper's back, honey. You never mind that. Get up quick and go tend to the cows," Velma said as she ripped a large cloth into rags and dumped them into the pot on the stove.

"Yes'm." Jasper could hear Wayne thump out of bed and pull open drawers. A second later, he was at the boy's side, staring at his legs. "Dang. You really did it, huh?"

Jasper couldn't look him in the eye. "I'm—I'm so sorry, Wayne."

"Hey." Wayne socked him in the arm. The dull pain was a brief distraction from the horrible burning in his legs. "Don't worry about it."

"Wayne! Git!" Aunt Velma swatted at her son.

Wayne squeezed Jasper's arm before leaving. "It's gonna be alright, kid," he said, as though he didn't really believe it, and then pushed through the door.

"Leo, I'm gonna need you to wash up." Velma was scrubbing her own hands in the washbasin with lye soap. Then she pulled one of the rags from the pot. "We're gonna start easy, baby," she cooed.

She began wiping the dirt and dried blood from his legs. The water felt warm and soothing at first. Jasper stared at the ceiling. He tried to count the nail heads in the boards to keep from squirming. Trickles of salt water seeped over his skin to the edges of his wounds, sending sparks of pain up his spine. He flinched despite his best efforts. *I won't cry.*

After two rags were filled up with blood and hay, Uncle Leo's face floated over him in front of the ceiling. "You're gonna need to bite on this now, son."

The word *son* distracted Jasper to the point where he barely noticed his uncle putting a leather belt between his teeth. It tasted like shoe polish. Jasper wanted to spit it out, but the look on his uncle's face told him he better not.

"We're gonna do this as quick as we can," Leo said to Jasper. He then pinned the boy to the table with the trunk of his body.

Jasper thrashed in protest but couldn't move under his uncle's weight. His knee exploded in pain as Aunt Velma set about attacking the wound. In that terrible moment, Jasper lost all sense of himself and became something else. Something wild and inhuman, screaming and thrashing against the weight of his uncle. White lights flashed as he pounded his head back against the table. His teeth bit down on the belt hard enough to crack them all.

"Easy. Easy now," his uncle said from a million miles away. "We gotta clean it out."

"Bits of glass are lodged in there," Velma said over the gagged screams. "I'm gonna need to get the brush."

The pain eased up just enough for Jasper to stop thrashing. His uncle let him up and pressed a bottle of brown liquid to his lips. "Drink some of this, boy. It'll help the pain."

Jasper opened his clenched eyes, and the entire room pulsed. The liquid burned his mouth, and it was as though he'd forgotten how to swallow. His uncle thumped him on the back, and the hot stuff poured down his throat. It hit his stomach like a fireball and headed back up again. His uncle slapped a hand over his mouth, forcing him to swallow it again. His head began to spin.

"What'd you give him?" a muddled voice asked.

"Corn mash. Just a little."

"Good Lord, Leo. That'll make him sick."

"You got a better idea?" Jasper could barely understand them. Their voices warped and wobbled.

It wasn't quite clear what happened next.

Over an hour later, Jasper woke up, cold and trembling. A lump throbbed on the back of his head, and his right leg felt like it had been half eaten by a monster—a monster with steel nails for teeth. When his eyes managed to focus, he could see a bloody rag tied to his right knee. His left shin was slathered in some thick white paste. They weren't legs anymore, they were meat. The whole room was stuck at a funny angle, like a giant had picked up the house and set it back down crooked. It took him several minutes to see he was lying in bed. He tried to sit up and groaned.

"You comin' back to us?" Aunt Velma asked from the curtain that separated Wayne's bed from the kitchen.

Jasper tried to say *yes*, but nothing but a garbled moan came out.

She came to his bedside and put a hand on his forehead. "You got a fever, baby. Cuts like that go septic real fast in a barn. You should've come to me right away."

"I'm so sorry," he tried to say but couldn't be sure what words got out. The warmth of a gentle hand on his skin made it impossible to hold back the pain, and soon the room was shaking with his sobs. He wanted his mother.

Aunt Velma scooped him into her arms and held him as he cried. He bawled like a baby and didn't even care. He wept until her shirt was drenched and he could almost breathe again. She didn't let go even when he'd calmed down a bit. Her rocking back and forth was comforting and nauseating at the same time. He didn't want her to stop but was certain he was going to throw up all the same. He groaned and lurched until she eased him back down to the pillow and placed a cool compress on his head.

After she left the room, Jasper fell in and out of nightmares as he lay there slowly going crazy. Blood dripped down the walls. The monster in the bus driver's pants. Lucifer eating a rat. Mr. Hoyt laughing. The bed shifted like a feeble raft as the room tossed and turned. The blanket smothered his screaming skin. His entire body was a knee, a throbbing, pus-filled knee.

Eventually, a face resurfaced at the bedside. It was Uncle Leo. "We're gonna get you dressed and head over to Dr. Whitebird. I got business out there anyway. Can you stand?"

Jasper tried to nod.

His uncle pulled him up until he was sitting on the edge of the bed. Jasper struggled not to vomit from the dizziness. Leo pulled a clean shirt over his head and looked the other way so Jasper could use the chamber pot. Getting pants on over his injured legs proved much harder, and they eventually settled on Wayne's old summer short pants.

The cool air outside the cabin hit Jasper's overheated skin hard enough to focus his eyes for a moment. His uncle helped him limp over to the truck, hobbling on his burnt leg, until Leo just gave up and carried him. Jasper didn't have the strength to be embarrassed anymore.

Uncle Leo cranked the engine, and the boy leaned his throbbing head against the cold metal of the car door. He shut his eyes and didn't open them again until the car had stopped moving.

"We're here," his uncle announced. "Black River Reservation."

Jasper forced his head up so he could look out the windows. He expected to see tepees or wigwams like he'd seen in his book, but there was nothing but rows and rows of small cabins and a few scattered trailers. "What are those?"

"Forget what you've heard, boy. These are regular folks, just like us."

Jasper nodded.

"Be polite to Dr. Whitebird, and whatever you do, don't ask if he's a real doctor. He gets real offended by that." Uncle Leo opened his door. "He got his MD from Wayne State, and he's the best damned doctor this side of Port Huron. Understand?"

His uncle got out of the car before Jasper could answer. The passenger door cranked open, and his uncle scooped him up and set him down a few strides later on a folding metal chair inside a small cinder block building. Then he rang the silver bell set on the card table opposite the entrance.

A minute later, a brown-skinned woman appeared through a blank door behind the table. She didn't have a feather in her hair. Her long black braids were the only thing that looked Indian about her. She wore a simple dress almost identical to the one Aunt Velma had been wearing that morning.

"Can I help you?" she asked.

"Tell Dr. Whitebird Leonard Williams is here to see him. My nephew's in need of some help."

"Just a moment."

Uncle Leo took the seat next to Jasper and put a hand as rough as sandpaper on the boy's smoldering brow. He dropped it and shook his head. "You ever get the chance again to pick between a whuppin' and some real-life punishment, what are you gonna pick?"

"A whuppin', sir," Jasper whispered. The room was starting to tilt under his chair. He shut his eyes and pressed the lump on the back of his head to the wall.

"Damn right."

A door clicked open. "The doctor will see you now."

"Come on." Uncle Leo hauled Jasper off the chair and helped him through the door and down a narrow hallway to another room. Inside sat a hunting cot and a locked cabinet. His uncle laid Jasper out on the cot and leaned against the wall next to him.

A few minutes later, an older man appeared in the doorway. He was wearing a button-down shirt, a white coat, and a tie. A stethoscope hung around his neck. Jasper blinked at him with his fevered eyes. It took several minutes for him to confirm that Dr. Whitebird was actually an Indian. His long gray hair was tied back, and he had a tattoo of a bird on the back of the hand he extended to his uncle.

"It's been a long time, Leo," the doctor said as they shook hands. "How's the family?"

"Been doin' real well, thanks."

"And who is this?" Dr. Whitebird asked, crouching down to look at Jasper.

"My nephew Jasper. He decided it'd be a good idea to knock over a lamp in the barn last night."

"I see," the doctor said, studying Jasper's face. His deep brown eyes were kind, but they stared at him longer than anyone had ever bothered to look at him before. For an instant, Jasper panicked that they could see all his thoughts—even the bad ones he was afraid to think out loud. The doctor touched Jasper's cheek, then peeked under his bandages. After this brief examination, he stood up. "Where are his parents?"

"Away," Uncle Leo said in a tone that made clear he wouldn't be answering more questions on the topic. "I'm his guardian at the moment."

"Hmm," the doctor grunted and contemplated this for a moment. "This boy needs a penicillin IV and a tetanus shot. How do you plan to pay?"

"I'm lookin' to trade if I can."

The doctor chuckled. "Now I know why you come here first. What do you have for trade? Corn? Wheat?"

"His mother gave him this before she left."

Jasper sucked in a cry as his uncle pulled his mother's necklace out of his jacket. The men pretended not to notice.

"I'm sure she'd do anything she could to help him now," Uncle Leo added, handing the beaded pendant over to the man.

Dr. Whitebird took the necklace and studied it, turning it over and over in his hand. Finally, he said, "The boy must stay here for two nights at least. There is too much danger now for him to leave. If the infection spreads to the blood, he will be in the hands of the Great Spirit."

"I understand," Uncle Leo agreed and then looked down at Jasper, who was gaping up at him in tears. He grabbed his nephew by the chin and looked him hard in the eye. "He's a strong boy, Doc. He's gonna be fine. Aren't you, son?"

Jasper clamped his trembling lips together and nodded.

CHAPTER 34

Do you believe it was your fault?

Uncle Leo held Jasper still so the doctor could put a needle in his arm. And then another. The pinpricks felt like nothing compared to the madness in his legs. Dr. Whitebird hung a glass jar of medicine over his head, connected to the spike in his arm. The nurse got Jasper a straw pillow and put a colorful blanket over him.

"Don't mess with that line, boy," his uncle warned him.

"Yes, sir," Jasper whispered, trying not to look at the bloody bandage that held in the needle.

"We'll come check on you tomorrow." Then Uncle Leo left him alone in the room.

A few minutes later, the nurse came back. It was the same woman from the front desk. "Drink this," she said, lifting his head up with one hand and holding a warm mug to his lips. "It will cool the fever. You should try to sleep. Sleep will help the medicine."

It was a bitter tea, but Jasper did what he was told. The warm liquid hit his queasy stomach and immediately calmed it downs then spread to his arms and legs, quieting the chills in his bones. It was such a relief he couldn't form the words to thank her. Jasper was out before she left the room.

Hours later, the sound of footsteps pulled his eyelids open. He squinted in the darkness of the room, unsure what had woken him. He didn't know where he was. There was no window or clock. The tug of the line in his arm reminded him he was lying on a cot at the Black River Reservation. The pain in his knee was still there but had been muted. Maybe it was getting better. It might even be normal again someday. He lowered his head back to the pillow and let his eyes close.

"Jasper," a voice whispered next to him.

He sat up with a jolt.

"Relax, honey. Lay down." The voice was startlingly familiar.

He strained to see in the dark. "Mom? Mom, is that you?"

A warm hand reached out and cupped his cheek. "Shh! Lay down, sweetie. You're hurt."

He slowly lowered his head back to the pillow. Her hand moved from his cheek to his forehead.

"Your fever's coming down. That's real good. You're gonna be fine." Her voice trembled with tears. "You're gonna be just fine."

It hurt to hear her crying. It hurt to hear her voice. He started crying too. "Where did you go? Why? Why did you leave me?"

"Shh, baby . . . I'm so sorry. I had to leave. I had to . . . but you shouldn't worry about that now. You need to get better."

"But—the apartment. I thought someone might've . . ." He felt himself growing more and more hysterical. *Her car. Detective Russo. The blood on the wall. The diary.* He fought to lift his fevered head back up. "What'd he do to you?"

Her gentle hands pushed him back to the bed. "Don't worry, baby. Just get better, okay?" Her voice drifted up and away from the cot.

Jasper struggled to sit up again but didn't have the strength. It was as if her hands were still on his shoulders. They still felt warm. "Wait," he called after her weakly. "Don't go."

"I love you, honey. No matter what happens. I'll always love you." Her voice was fading.

She was gone.

"Come back!" His wails turned to screams. "Don't go! *Come back!*"

"Jasper?" A pair of hands shook his shoulders. "Jasper."

Jasper opened his eyes. The room was filled with blinding light, and Dr. Whitebird was staring down into his face. Jasper's clothes and the blankets were drenched.

"Your fever broke," the doctor said. "This is a good sign."

Jasper blinked, trying to adjust to the jarring reality happening all around him. The doctor changed the medicine jar over his head. The nurse came in a minute later and changed his bandages. The shock of the air on his open wounds woke him so completely it left no doubt. It had all been a dream.

On reflex, a hand shot down to the leg of his pants. It was dry. He set his head back down on his pillow and bit back tears, not knowing if he was more miserable she hadn't really come to see him or that he had woken up at all. The nurse finished re-dressing his wounds and left.

"They are looking better," Dr. Whitebird said from behind Jasper's head. He pulled up a stool and gazed into the boy's eyes with that probing stare. "The body is healing, but I see the spirit is still sick."

Jasper looked away to hide his face.

"Bad dreams?"

He didn't answer.

"Hmm," the doctor grunted. "Sleep tea can loosen bad spirits. It is important to let them go."

Jasper shook his head at the wall. His mother was not a bad spirit. He didn't want to let her go. He needed to go back to sleep and find her.

"You cannot walk in dreams, little Ogichidaa." The man patted him on the shoulder.

Jasper turned and scowled at the leathery face of the doctor. "What did you call me?"

"Ogichidaa means warrior."

Jasper frowned. He wasn't a warrior. He was a coward—a crybaby coward that ruined his leg so bad it'd cost him the only thing that mattered anymore. He hadn't said he was sorry, he realized. He hadn't told his mother he was sorry he'd lost her necklace. He flexed his legs against the bandages until the pain blocked out his guilt.

"Your uncle, he said you knocked over a lantern, yes?"

Jasper didn't answer.

"Did you run?"

"No, I . . . ," his voice trailed off for a moment. "I ran away after."

The doctor looked down at the bandages on his legs and nodded. He reached into his white coat and pulled out the necklace Uncle Leo had given him. "This is very special to you."

Jasper bit his lips and nodded.

The doctor smiled and placed the necklace back into Jasper's hand. His mouth fell open. "But the medicine? We can't pay . . ."

The doctor patted his hand. "When you grow up, young Ogichidaa, you will come back and pay."

"When I grow up?" Jasper clutched the necklace to his chest.

"When you are old enough to have a fair trade, you will come back. Taking something that does not come to you freely is baataamo—a curse. Remember that."

"How do you know I'll come back?"

The doctor chuckled and held up his hands. "I don't."

"I will. I promise. I will come back."

"Good. Promise to live and grow up. That is payment enough for now." The doctor patted his head and stood to leave.

Jasper opened his hand and looked down at the beaded pendant with its strange symbol. "Doctor?"

"Eya?"

"What does this mean?" he asked pointing to the symbol in the middle.

"It is an old symbol," he answered. "Nimaamaa. It carries with it a mother's love."

Jasper ran his finger over it. He could still feel her lips on his forehead.

"A wise man once said, 'Every child has many mothers, and every mother has many children.' Do you understand this?"

Jasper shook his head. He only had one mother, and she was gone.

"The mother that births us, gives us life. For some nimaamaayag, that is all they can give. Even that is a blessing. Do not forget."

"But," Jasper protested and then couldn't find any words to say except, "someone told me it was a wedding necklace."

The doctor raised his eyebrows. "Manitonaaha weddings are not about jewelry. Farmers know very little of our ways. Most call me a witch doctor." He wiggled his fingers at Jasper with a broad smile, then headed to the door.

Jasper stared after him and asked in a tiny voice, "Did you . . . know her?"

The doctor turned back to the small boy on the cot. "Your mother?"

He nodded with pleading eyes, not wanting the doctor to leave.

Dr. Whitebird looked pained for several seconds before he finally answered. "Eya, I knew her."

"But how . . ."

"No more questions now, Ogichidaa. Save your strength." With that, he was gone.

CHAPTER 35

What happened after the fire? Where did you go?

After the doctor left, the nurse brought Jasper a plate of venison and mashed corn. The meat tasted strong and bloody, but he devoured it anyway. He couldn't remember the last time he'd eaten. After he'd cleaned his plate, she brought him another cup of the tea. He drank it fast and flopped down on his pillow, hoping to see his mother again. The nurse gave him an odd little grin and flipped off the lights.

Jasper lay in the dark, holding his mother's necklace. He would tell her how Dr. Whitebird had given it back and the vow he had made. He had vowed to grow up. He had vowed to come back and pay his debt. She'd be proud of him, he decided. He ran his finger across the hundreds of tiny beads. *Nimaamaa.*

As Jasper drifted away, he swore he could feel the summer sun warming his face. A light breeze blew through his hair. He was back at his grandmother's house, only it wasn't buried in the tall grasses of Uncle Leo's back field. It was surrounded by flowers and cut grass. The air was thick with the smell of freshly stacked hay. A woman stood on the porch. She was beating a rug with a broom. He didn't recognize her but knew it must be his grandmother. He stared at her as she worked in her long cornflower dress with her dark hair pinned up like his mother would sometimes do. She was beautiful. Her head tilted up to where he was standing, but she looked right through him as though he weren't there, then disappeared back into the house.

"Come back," he whispered and struggled to follow her inside. His feet were rooted to the ground as though he were just another maple tree protecting the house from the wind.

It was a cheerful-looking house, he decided. White with green shutters and a wood shingle roof. The second-story window stood open, catching the summer breeze. Something behind the glass moved. It was his mother's room. He called her name, but nothing came out. The only sound for miles was the steady hum of the locusts in the trees. Silently cursing, he watched the window, desperate for another glimpse of her.

The sky grew dark and dotted with stars. The windows of the house glowed yellow. Then he heard shouting. Then the crash of a dish hitting the ground. The faintest smell of smoke began to waft into his nose. It could have been a distant cigar, but then it grew stronger. *The house.* Wisps of smoke came billowing from his mother's window. The light inside it began to flicker.

"No!" he screamed, but his voice was silent. He yelled again, but nothing came out. He fought to free his feet, but they stayed planted in the ground. Plumes of smoke were wafting from the ridge of the house now, but no one came out. His mother's yellow sedan was parked in the driveway in a spot that had been empty moments before. The door to the car stood open.

From deep in the house, he heard a scream.

Jasper bolted up from the cot. The line in his arm yanked hard as he struggled to the door. He was screaming.

The light flipped on, and a woman he didn't recognize ran to him and forced him back to the bed. "Easy. Easy, little one," she said firmly. "You were dreaming."

"The house. It was burning. She couldn't get out," he wailed, flailing his arms.

"You are not going to save her today," the lady said, grabbing his wrist. "Now hold still."

Jasper shook his head, trying to shake loose the image of the beautiful house on fire. The woman held his arm steady as she pulled off the bandage where the needle had nearly ripped out of his arm.

It was the sight of his own blood that finally calmed him down.

"You are not ready for the hook to come out, little fish. It is not time to swim away." She worked quickly, reinserting the needle and securing it with fresh tape. Jasper felt a pinch but held still for her. She had dark skin and long hair like Dr. Whitebird.

"I—I'm sorry," he whimpered.

She gazed down at him with smiling eyes. "We sometimes see bad things when we are close to the spirit world, but you are getting better now. The dreams will get better too."

Jasper lay back down, wanting to go back to sleep and save her.

"You have a visitor."

His eyes snapped open. "I do?"

She nodded and went out the door. His heart leapt at the thought of who it might be, but he did his best to quiet it. His uncle said he'd be back tomorrow. He had no idea how long he'd been on the cot, but it was probably tomorrow. Maybe Wayne had come with Uncle Leo. He glanced down at the beads he was still gripping in his hand. Uncle Leo would be furious he'd taken them back.

Just as the door opened, he buried the necklace under the blanket.

"Jasper?" a shaky voice asked.

His father emerged from behind the door and hobbled toward the bed. He was leaning on a cane. The mild tremor he'd carried home from his time in the war had multiplied. The man lowered himself with some difficulty onto the stool next to the bed.

"Let me get a look at ya," Wendell said, giving the yellow-and-red-stained bandages on Jasper's legs only a glance. Instead, he leaned forward and examined his son's face. Jasper wondered self-consciously if the bruise around his eye had faded away. The tortured look on his father's face told him it hadn't.

"I'm okay," Jasper whispered.

His father nodded and lowered his face to a shaking hand. "I thought . . . I thought I'd lost you," he choked and then cleared his throat with a wet cough. It took a full minute before he could look Jasper in the face again. "How'd you manage to get here, Son? I looked for you everywhere. Everywhere. When Mrs. Carbo said you'd gone . . ."

"I'm so sorry." Jasper couldn't look at him. "I was afraid. That detective came for me, and I didn't—"

"Shh . . . shh." His father patted his head. "You get all worked up, they won't let me stay. You know, you're damned lucky you're in the hospital, or I might've beat you something fierce—scaring me half to death like that."

Jasper shrank against the far wall.

"No. I'm sorry. I never should've . . ." He opened his hand as a peace offering and fell silent for another minute. He managed a weak smile and reached over and took Jasper's hand. "The important thing is you're here. Thank the Lord, you're here. I'm the luckiest bastard on earth. They treatin' you alright?"

"Yes, sir."

"Your uncle says you really did it to yourself good. How's the leg?"

"Okay, I guess. The doctor says I can go home tomorrow."

"That's real good. Sounds like you gave the devil the slip on that one. Lucky for me, you got nine lives, Son. I just don't know what I'd do if . . ."

Jasper swallowed hard. "Dad, what happened back at home? The blood . . ."

Wendell held up a hand to silence him. "You shouldn't be worrying about that now. Probably just burglars havin' themselves a scuffle. The police took half the night going over it with their cameras and collecting their evidence, then dragged me down to the station for hours . . . to fill out their damn papers."

"Was it . . . Mom?"

"Don't be ridiculous." Wendell clenched his trembling hands together and gave Jasper a weak smile that had the opposite of the intended effect. "She's fine. She's just fine. She's gonna turn up. She always does."

"But the detective said they found her car . . ."

His father's eyes hardened. "Now, look it. Every police officer in Detroit's out lookin' for her. We just have to let them do their jobs, alright? She wouldn't want us losin' our heads, would she?"

Jasper went quiet again and nodded as though he agreed with him, but he knew his father would never tell him the truth. Not if the truth was bad. Not if the blood was hers. He was just a kid, and his father would try to protect him.

"Here. Your uncle thought you might like this." Wendell handed Jasper *The First Book of Indians*. "You know, to pass the time."

"Thanks." Jasper set the book in his lap, keeping his eyes on the screaming faces on the cover.

Wendell reached out and took Jasper's hands in his. There were red welts on both his wrists like matching bracelets under his shirtsleeves. "You like staying with Leo and Velma?"

Jasper knew it really wasn't up to him, but he thought about it to humor the old man. Uncle Leo was tough but fair. He even seemed to forgive him for knocking over the lantern. Then he thought of Velma rocking him in her arms. *Every child has many mothers, and every mother has many children.* "Yeah. I like it there okay, I guess."

"Good." His father gave his hands a squeeze and let go. "As long as you don't try to burn the barn down again, I think they'd be happy to have you back. But don't you worry. I'm not going anywhere. I'll come visit every weekend. You're the best thing I've got goin'. Don't ever forget that."

Jasper forced a smile, but there were still so many questions he needed to ask. "Dad?"

"Yes, Son?"

"What about that detective?"

His father looked him hard in the eye before answering, "What about him?"

"Mrs. Carbo said he might take me to an orphanage."

His father leaned forward and squeezed his shoulders. "Over my dead body. Nobody's takin' you anywhere. Understand? Nobody. I won't let 'em."

He pulled the boy into his arms and held him tight. It was a bit of a shock. Jasper could count on one hand the number of times his father had really hugged him. It just wasn't what people did. He would have been overwhelmed by it if it weren't for the unsteady tremor in his father's arms . . . and the feeling that the man was hiding something.

CHAPTER 36

Is that when you started drinking?

Jasper lay in the bed with his mother's necklace in his hand and tried to remember every true thing he could about her. She drank her coffee black. *Sugar just covers up the real taste of things, Jasper,* she'd say from her morning perch next to the kitchen sink. She always drank two bitter cups before leaving for work. The acrid residue of the coffee would cling to his cheek as she kissed him good-bye.

He reached up and touched his face, then squeezed his eyes shut to plug the tears.

She loved to dance. She'd once taught him the fox-trot in their tiny living room. *Left, together, up . . . Right, together, back. That's good, Jasper. Go easy. Don't push a woman around the floor. Just move like you know what you're doing, and she'll follow. That's the key to it all, baby . . .*

Jasper must have drifted back asleep. The next thing he knew, he heard angry voices coming from the hallway outside his room. Something thumped hard against a wall.

"Don't you use that voodoo witchcraft on me!" a man howled. "It ain't Christian. It ain't!"

"Sir, you have a laceration. It requires stitches," the voice of Dr. Whitebird calmly responded.

"It's just a cut, you crazy red bastard! I need a doctor." The drunken slur of his voice made Jasper cringe in the dark.

"I *am* a doctor, and you will bleed out if you don't keep that elevated. You need compression."

The crash of a metal tray hit the ground just outside Jasper's room.

"What made me bleed out was that rigged poker room you Injuns got!" His voice fell to a mumble Jasper had to strain to hear. "That and that little hussy that drank up all my money . . . I swear to Christ, I been robbed!"

Something louder thumped against a wall.

"Get Motega," the doctor said to someone.

Jasper sat up at the name.

"I'm callin' Galatas. He promised me a nice little time up here with you heathens. Buy the little red girls some drinks, he said. Give 'em a little cash for their habits. They'll show you a real nice time, he said. Bullshit! What kind of brothel is this?"

"*This is not a brothel!*" Dr. Whitebird thundered.

"Like hell it ain't. I need a phone!" the drunk man yelled back. "Hey! Get your dirty hands off me! You can't touch me . . . *Police!*"

A deeper voice answered, "Your police will not come here. You better listen to the good doctor."

"Or what you gonna do? Go on the warpath?" The man laughed. "Gonna throw a spear at me?"

"No, but I will gladly watch you bleed to death." The deep voice seethed. "Black River is closed."

The drunk man let out a squeal. There was a loud thump, and then he went quiet.

"Thank you, Motega." The doctor sighed. "Help me get him onto the table."

"We should let him bleed out in a ditch."

"We are not murderers, Motega. You can find a ditch for him after the medicine."

"They are the murderers!" Motega roared. "How many must die? How many fields must burn? This drunk gookoosh will light more fires, and it might be *you* they take to jail for it."

"Killing this drunk won't bring her back, Motega. We fought and lost this war years ago . . . long before you were born. We must find peace with these people or the Great Wind will sweep us away. Take heart." The doctor chuckled. "Between the liquor and the loss of blood, he won't remember his name tomorrow."

"And if he does?"

There was no answer.

"He will have bandages to explain," Motega insisted. "He might file a report with the federal marshal. Then what? I have been to their prison. How many more must go?"

"Eya." The doctor grunted. "He will have nothing to report if he wakes up at the Tally Ho. I will call Clint Sharkey and make the arrangements."

"I still say we crash his car into a tree."

Jasper's mouth fell open as the voices faded down the hall.

Not a minute later, Jasper heard footsteps approach his door. He slammed his head back into the pillow and shut his eyes. He didn't dare move as the doctor, or whoever it was, peered in at him. Three seconds later, the door closed again.

As soon as it did, Jasper sat back up and gaped at the slivers of light leaking in from the hallway. He hadn't understood half of what had been said, but the words *They are the murderers!* still hung in the air like a storm cloud. *Killing this drunk won't bring her back.*

Her.

The only thing he knew for sure was that he'd heard the name Galatas before. Jasper lay back down and gazed up at the ceiling.

Smoke rose up from the horizon of Jasper's mind. A field had been burning the day she left him. *Just someone burning a fallow field,* she'd said as if it were nothing.

But it didn't seem like nothing anymore.

Dr. Whitebird came to check on Jasper the next morning.

"How are we feeling today, Ogichidaa?" he asked, placing a warm hand on the boy's head.

"Better." That was the least of his worries. "Who was that man? The one that was yelling earlier?"

"You have keen ears, little rabbit." The doctor flashed a small smile and then opened up his bandages. "I see the healing is well underway. This is good."

Jasper wouldn't let the doctor change the subject. "Who was he?"

"Just a lost man from the city. I must apologize for him. Some of my tribe like to drink whiskey with strangers and play games for money. Such things always lead to trouble. But it is hard for our young men to find good work."

"He was so . . . mean to you," Jasper said.

"I do not let the bad spirits of others come and bother me." He pointed a finger at Jasper as if this were a warning.

"What will happen to him?"

The doctor laughed. "He will wake up with a terrible headache tomorrow, but he will live."

"But . . ." Jasper didn't think it was funny. There had been talk of murder, burning fields, and prison. "Will you get in trouble?"

"All of our troubles come to us invited . . . with open hands." The doctor studied his palms for a moment, then clapped them together. The doctor closed the bandages and smiled at Jasper. "Don't worry, Ogichidaa. These are not your troubles . . . You are healing well. You can go home when this is done."

The doctor pointed to the half-full glass jar over his head. The liquid dripped steadily into the tube attached to his arm. Time was running out.

Jasper wanted to ask a million more questions, but the most burning ones wouldn't come out. *Did Motega kill my mother? Did he hide her car in the trees? What did you mean when you said, It won't bring her back?* He finally managed, "Who was that other man? Motega?"

"He is the son of Ogimaa. Ogimaa is the head of our tribal council."

"Did he and my mother have some sort of . . . fight?" Jasper whispered. "Someone told me she was in trouble with someone named Motega."

The doctor raised his eyebrows. "You do have long ears, little rabbit. Who told you this?"

"A man named Big Bill. He owns the roller rink in Burtchville."

"Ah." He nodded. "Be careful when you listen to others speak. Life is a story of many voices and the truth lies between them."

Jasper frowned at this. Dr. Whitebird liked to talk in riddles, and it was starting to get on his nerves. "Did Motega know my mother or not?"

The doctor studied Jasper's scowl a moment and answered, "Eya. But I know of no fight between them."

"Were they friends?"

"Eya."

The boy sat up. "Why was he put in jail then?"

Dr. Whitebird gave him a hard look. "Motega is a good man. The men that hold the keys to your jails do not see always good or bad. They see Manitonaaha, and that is crime enough."

Jasper realized he had offended the doctor, and his eyes fell in shame. "I just . . . I heard there was a murder."

"Have no fear, Ogichidaa. It was not your mother." Dr. Whitebird held up a hand to stop the questions. "I will speak no more of the dead."

"I—I'm sorry." Jasper knew he should stop but couldn't. "How did you know my mother?"

"It is not my place to speak for her."

"But someone has to speak for her! She's gone, and I don't know where she went." His eyes welled up. "She left me all alone. It's like she doesn't care about me at all!"

"No," Dr. Whitebird commanded. "Never doubt the love of your nimaamaa. If she has gone, it is only to protect you."

"How can she protect me if she's not here?" Jasper buried his face to hide his tears.

"Let me tell you a story." The doctor put a warm hand on his shoulder. "One day a Manitonaaha mother and child were walking in the woods, hunting for wild berries. Do you like berries?"

Jasper forced a nod but kept his face in his hands.

"They picked a big basket of berries and were headed back to the village. But the mother heard the growl of a wolf deep in the woods behind them." The doctor let out a low growl. "What should she do? She picked up her child and began to run, but they run too slow. She puts down the basket of berries and runs faster. But still she runs too slow. The wolf was getting closer." The doctor patted his knees making running sounds. "Its growls were getting louder." He let out a loud roar.

Jasper looked up at the sound.

"Do you know what she did?"

He shook his head.

"She put the child up in a tree. Without the child, she runs faster than before, and she leads the wolf away. Now, you must decide, young Ogichidaa. Does the mother still love him?"

Jasper thought about it for a minute, then nodded. "If she hadn't put him in a tree, they both would've been caught and eaten."

"Very good." The doctor smiled. "Now, your mother has left you with your uncle, yes?"

"Yes," he whispered.

"Does she still love you?"

"I—It's not the same!" Jasper protested, catching the doctor's meaning. "We aren't in the woods! There's no wolf chasing us!"

"Oh? How do you know? Wolves come with many faces. Some even live inside us." The doctor patted his own chest for emphasis. "You don't want to meet the wolf. Your mother doesn't want you to meet it either. You must have faith, Ogichidaa. You must believe she loves you."

Jasper thought of the detective chasing him from his apartment. It was sort of like running from a wolf, but he'd been alone without her. He closed his eyes and tried to remember the warmth of her lips on his forehead. "Did she . . . Did she come back here? Have you seen her?"

"I wish I could tell you that I have. But she is with you. Her love is with you here." The doctor patted Jasper's cheek and pressed the necklace into his palm. Then he stood and headed to the door.

"Wait." Jasper stopped him in the doorway. "You didn't finish your story. Did she ever come back?"

The doctor turned a puzzled face down to the boy on the cot.

"After the mother runs and leads the wolf away. Does she ever come back?"

The doctor pressed his lips into a thin line of regret. "No. The wolf passes under the tree where the child hides and goes back to his den, not hungry."

"But what about the child?" Jasper shouted in protest. "What happens to him?"

"He cries for his mother for three days and nights. Then her voice returns to him in the songs of the birds. She tells him there is nothing to fear. She tells him that she gave her life to save him, but she would always be near—in the birds, in the wind, in the sky. And do you know what he does?"

A tear slid down Jasper's cheek as he shook his head.

"He climbs down from the tree all by himself, Ogichidaa."

With that, the doctor left the room.

CHAPTER 37

Do you think you have an illness?

After the doctor left, Jasper sat up in the bed and wished he could rip the tube out of his arm. He didn't want to be stuck up in a tree. He wanted his mother.

She might not be far. Her car had been found only a few miles away. She could even be hiding somewhere at the reservation. The clear fluid in the jar over his head dripped one slow drop at a time. He laid his head back on the pillow and sighed.

There was nothing to do in the tiny room but sit and stew. Jasper snatched the book about Indians up off the floor and read it. Then he read it again. There was a lot of talk about the buffalo, tepees, and battles, but nothing about wolves.

Jasper pulled the necklace out from under the covers and studied it again. Dr. Whitebird knew her. Frowning, he looped the necklace over his head and tucked it under his shirt. He vowed to himself that he'd ask her about it when she came back. Even as he thought the words, they clouded with doubt.

The mother in the story never came back.

The door to his room finally opened, and the nurse came in with more food. "You are looking quite shiny today, little fish," she said and set the food on the cot. "You happy to be going home?"

"Yes, thank you," he said, eyeing the tray. More venison and corn. He glanced up at the glass bottle attached to his arm. It was still a quarter full.

"You are tired of being on a hook," she said, noticing his frown. "Don't worry. I think you are almost done. Eat your food, and I will come and take out the line."

He grinned at the news and immediately began devouring his plate. The nurse chuckled and left the room. Jasper ate every crumb, eager to be declared healthy again. Truthfully, he still felt quite tired, and the itch in his leg was like a hatch of fleas. It was going to take all his strength not to claw through his bandages, he could tell, but he didn't care. He wanted to escape the windowless room.

The nurse finally came back. The glass jar had a half inch of fluid left, but she made good on her promise and pulled the needle out of his arm. He went to stand up, and she gently eased him back down to the bed. "Not yet, little fish. Let me change these wrappings one more time."

She pulled off the bandages. Jasper half expected to see a nest of wriggling maggots chewing at his skin. The wounds were getting smaller, and the skin had tightened up at the edges. "They itch!"

"The itch is good. That means the wounds are healing." Her voice turned stern. "You are going to have to change these bandages twice a day for the next week. No running around or rolling in the mud until then, okay?"

"Okay."

"Your family isn't here just yet. You will have to wait."

"Do you mind if I walk around a bit outside?" he asked, trying not to sound too eager. "I miss the sun."

She stopped and thought about it for a minute. "I cannot let you go missing, little fish. You are a stranger here. You do not know our village."

Jasper's face fell as his one chance to go looking for her slipped away.

"Oh. Don't lose your shine. Wait here."

He debated whether he should just escape on his own.

The nurse returned before he'd made up his mind, and she was not alone. A brown-skinned boy not much taller than Jasper stood by her side. "This is my son, Pati. He can walk with you for a little while."

Pati studied Jasper like he was an interesting new bug.

"Hello." Jasper gave him a little wave.

The boy didn't wave back.

"Okay. You two go outside for a while." The nurse turned to her son and said several other things in a language Jasper didn't understand. The boy nodded and went over to Jasper and grabbed his hand.

Together, the two boys walked down the hallway to the sparsely furnished waiting room. Jasper could hardly remember being there, but it had only been two days. Pati led Jasper out the front door and into the blinding sun. It was late afternoon and unseasonably warm out. A stand of trees shielded the clinic from the narrow dirt road that led down the steep hill to Route 25. According to his mother's diary, it had once been marked the "Door of Faith," but he didn't see a sign anywhere.

The thought of the diary sent a jolt of regret through him. He'd thrown it across the barn in a rage. He could only hope it was still lying behind the feed bins, undiscovered.

As soon as they were out of the nurse's sight line, Pati dropped Jasper's hand. "So, where do you want to go?" He spoke with no accent at all.

"I'm not sure," Jasper said, not knowing how much he should tell the strange boy. "I'm sort of looking for someone."

"Here at Black River?" The boy cocked a grin, sizing Jasper up. "Indian or white?"

"Um . . . white."

"There is only one place the white people go here. I'll show you, but you can't tell my mother. Deal?"

"Deal." Jasper nodded and held out his hand to shake on it.

The boy just gave him an odd look and started walking down to the dirt road. Jasper dropped his hand and followed. Pati wore clothes very similar to the clothes on his own back. There were no moccasins or leather tassels, just boots and jeans. Pati did have long black hair tied back into a tail. Besides that, he could have been just another kid at school.

The two boys followed the dirt road farther up the hill and away from the clinic. They walked past a group of trailers where adults sat in clumps, enjoying the warm sun. A few campfires were lit, and the air smelled of burning leaves. One man was roasting a whole fish on a spit. He waved to Pati and said something Jasper didn't understand. Pati answered in the same language and motioned to Jasper. The man laughed and waved them on.

"What'd he say?" Jasper asked once the man was out of earshot.

"He wanted to know why you were here. I told him you were looking for your drunk father."

Jasper stopped walking at this comment.

"Don't worry. Most of the white men that come here get drunk. He will not remember you."

Jasper opened his mouth to respond, but Pati had turned his back and kept walking. Jasper followed him despite the insult. If he wanted any chance of finding his mother, he had no choice.

After Jasper walked over a mile on sore legs, a large barnlike building emerged from between the trees. Several pickup trucks were parked around it in the open spaces between the pines. "This is the game house," Pati said, motioning at the building. "White people come to play games they cannot play out there."

Jasper remembered what Dr. Whitebird had told him. "Games for money."

"Yes." Pati led Jasper through the stand of trees to the side of the building. "We are not allowed inside, but you can see through here." He pointed to an opening in the siding.

Jasper pressed his face to the boards and squinted to see. The room inside was dark and full of smoke. Low voices and clinking glasses mixed with scratchy music from a record player. Four men sat holding cards at a table right in front of him. There were stacks of blue and red chips beside them. At the next table, a woman stood handing out cards. Jasper's heart leapt when he saw her dark hair, but it only took another second to see she wasn't his mother.

Around the room there were several more tables half full with people. A man was sitting facedown at an empty table in the far corner. There were two other women walking around. One was handing out cigarettes. The other was handing out drinks. Neither of them was her. In the far corner, an old man sat at a full table with a young woman on his lap. He was whispering something in her ear. She laughed. The sagging, pale face of Arthur Hoyt was unmistakable as he grinned and nuzzled her neck. On reflex, Jasper shrank away from the wall.

Somewhere up in the hayloft, a door slammed. He couldn't make out what was up there through the dark, but he didn't smell any hay. Just smoke and sweat.

"Why uh . . . why do they come here to play games?" Jasper whispered, keeping his eyes on Hoyt and the girl. His aunt and uncle played cards with the neighbors from time to time. It didn't seem like such a big deal.

"It's against the white laws," Pati whispered back. "But police don't come here."

"Why not?"

A crash came from the far side of the room. It was a man throwing his glass to the floor. He stood up, shouting at another man holding the cards. Jasper recoiled. It was Big Bill.

"Goddamn it! You bluffed me! You dirty red son of a bitch! You bluffed *me!*" the enormous man bellowed and threw his cards into another man's face. "This whole place is rigged. You bastards are cheatin'. You've been talkin' in signals this whole time."

Jasper watched with growing alarm as two large Manitonaaha men grabbed Big Bill by either arm and pulled him toward the exit at the end of the barn. The door was just around the corner from where the two boys were crouched. Jasper stepped back, scanning the bushes for a place to hide.

"You know him," Pati said.

"He can't find me here," Jasper hissed.

Without a word, Pati grabbed Jasper by the collar and dragged him behind a high stack of firewood separating the dumpsters from the parking lot. On the other end of the building from where they hid, a door slammed open.

"You stupid Injuns. Don't you know who I am? Get your hands off me!"

A voice answered him in a low tone that Jasper couldn't quite make out.

"I don't give a goddamn about the house rules. That featherhead's a cheat! You better get me my money back and then some, or I'm gonna have the lot of you arrested! Gamblin', prostitution, you name it! Ol' Duncan will have a field day! He'll set fire to the lot of you."

The voices were getting louder. Jasper and Pati crouched behind the woodpile as they approached. On the other side of their hiding place, two trucks and a sedan were lined up. Jasper caught his breath when he realized that's where the men were headed.

"Save your fire. I will talk to Sakima," a familiar voice answered. Jasper squinted through the gaps in the pile at the backs of two heads.

"Fuck you, Motega," Big Bill slurred. He was drunk, but not too drunk to shove the taller man in the chest. "I want my money now."

"You will get your money," Motega said in a barely controlled voice. "If I disrupt the games, it will be chaos."

"Here's your chaos." Bill spit and pulled out a gun. "Now get me my money."

"If you cannot wait, you will have to shoot me." Motega smiled and stepped toward the drunk. "I am not afraid of death. Are you?"

Big Bill staggered back. "It'd better be here tomorrow, understand? All three hundred."

"Of course." Motega took another threatening step forward. Jasper could see his menacing profile. His stone jaw clamped in rage.

Bill thrust his gun in Motega's face again. "And I want to know where she went! We know she came back here."

Motega shoved him against his car. "I told you. She is not here. Tell Galatas to leave our people be."

"You're giving orders now?" Bill let out a drunken snort. He pushed Motega off his chest and pointed the gun at his head. "You can't touch me. I could shoot you right here, and no one would even blink an eye. You think Marshal Duncan would waste one sheet of paper on you? Now where is she?"

Motega swatted the pistol from Bill's hand as though it were a fly and grabbed him by the neck. "You cannot hide from what you've done. Justice will come for my people. One way or another."

Big Bill let out a strangled wheeze, and Motega released him. "You dumb son of a bitch," he coughed, stumbling. "No one's gonna listen to you. Shit, I'd be surprised if Duncan don't hang that last collar right around your neck. Poor girl, brutalized like that. It's a real shame the way you wild folks turn on each other."

Motega punched him dead in the face, sending Bill sprawling across the hood of his car. Jasper clamped a hand over his mouth.

Big Bill rolled back onto his feet and laughed. His big yellow teeth were red with blood. "Ya see how violent you people are? That right there's assault and battery. All I have to do is go to the marshal with this here bloody nose, and you're finished. You just made his job a whole lot easier."

Motega glowered down at him and said in a barely audible voice, "All sorts of people go missing out here in these woods. Remember that policeman from Detroit you boys brought a few days ago? The one with a bullet between his eyes . . . What makes you think they would ever find *you*, my friend?"

A bullet between his eyes. Blood splattered and dripped down the wall of the apartment in Jasper's mind. Mrs. Carbo had said something about a gunshot on the phone. And a sergeant.

Bill chortled and patted Motega on the shoulder. "I'm glad we understand each other. Listen, you're gonna help us find her or Marshal Duncan'll sweep in here with a paddy wagon and the dogs. Imagine when the good people of this state learn what you savages been up to out here. What will your children eat this winter? Huh?"

"I do not have children," Motega growled in his face, and for a moment it seemed as though he would tear out the man's throat with his teeth.

"Well, that's too bad . . . But think about all the other families." Big Bill staggered around to his car door and climbed inside. "You tell Althea to call me. You got two days . . . I'd hate for something to happen to *her* family."

He sped off before Motega could say another word. The large man watched him leave, then walked over to the side of the parking lot and picked up the gun.

CHAPTER 38

Did you ever do anything you regret?

The two boys waited until the sedan had squealed away and Motega had returned to the game house before climbing out from the woodpile. They walked back to Dr. Whitebird's clinic in awkward silence. Jasper could tell Pati felt just as unnerved about what they had seen as he did. A part of him wanted to apologize for dragging the boy out there and for every bad thing Big Bill had said, but he was too busy replaying the conversation over in his own head.

Galatas. Marshal Duncan. Poor girl. It all jumbled together, but one sentence repeated over and over in his head. *You tell Althea to call me.*

Finally, Pati spoke. "Did you find the one you were looking for?"

Jasper shook his head and glanced over at the boy next to him. His dark eyes were like Dr. Whitebird's. They seemed to know things. Jasper hoped they did. "Do you know that man? The white one talking to Motega?"

"He works for the head white man they call Galatas. It was Galatas that built the game house, and Galatas keeps the money. My mother says it has been nothing but a curse on our people." Pati spit on the ground for emphasis.

"But why do you let them come here? Doesn't the land belong to your tribe?"

"Nothing belongs to our people. Not anymore." Pati sighed at Jasper's ignorant frown. "Nimaamaa says they tricked us. The game house was supposed to bring our people money for supplies and food, but it was a lie. The white men come and take our money. They come to get drunk and do things much worse than gambling. She says they have brought a great shame upon us and poisoned our people. They are killers. Fucking bastards."

Jasper's eyes bulged at the curse and the shock of everything else he'd said. *Killers.* The picture of the girl, the girl with brown eyes. He could see her standing outside his door. His voice dropped to a whisper. "What happened to the poor girl he talked about?"

"Nimaamaa won't tell me." Pati kicked a rock down the dirt path. "I just know that during the last moon Ayasha came to the clinic very hurt, and then she died."

Jasper stopped walking. "Did they find out who hurt her?"

"Nimaamaa and Dr. Whitebird believe it was one of the white men who like to gamble and drink."

"Did the police find him?"

"What police?" Pati held his hands up to the sky in surrender. "Tribal police can't arrest the white men. They are not allowed. Your sheriff does not protect us. These men come and do what they want, and the police do not come. The only one that comes is the federal marshal. And when the marshal comes, it is only to take our fathers to your prisons."

Pati put his head down and kept walking. Jasper stared after him, unable to move.

"Are you coming?" the boy called over his shoulder.

The campfire where the man had sat roasting his fish was still burning, but the man and his fish were gone. Jasper forced his aching legs to keep moving, searching for something to say. He finally whispered, "I'm sorry."

"Why? You did not kill her."

Jasper walked in silence for a minute, then said, "There has to be something you can do."

"Ogimaa has tried. But the white men are dangerous. Galatas will burn our cornfields so we might starve. They burned one already. They say Black River owes money to Galatas for the buildings and the general store they built. If we do not pay the debt, they will take our medicine and all the food. They will arrest our fathers for the white men's crimes and drag them to jail. No one will believe us."

Jasper studied Pati with a raised eyebrow, not wanting to believe any of it. "Did your mom tell you that?"

Pati's black eyes flashed with anger. "You think I lie."

"No! I just don't . . . It's just that grown-ups don't tell kids that stuff."

"Nimaamaa tells me plenty. She tells me I must learn to be careful around the white men. I must learn to look after my sisters and friends. I must never drink the firewater or try their bad medicines. Careless boys go to jail. Careless girls get dragged away. White men do what they please."

Jasper stared at his feet, feeling like he was somehow to blame. All the farmers, even Uncle Leo, were suspicious of the Manitonaaha. "Motega said something about a policeman from Detroit. The one shot between the eyes. Do you know what he's talking about?"

"No one speaks of the dead, but new graves appear in these woods now and then. The white men bury their dead here when they don't want them found."

New graves. The two boys were almost back to the clinic. Jasper thought of his mother's car buried out in the woods. "Do you know the woman Bill was looking for?"

The boy stopped walking. "He was looking for your mother."

Jasper's mouth fell open, but Pati held up his hand to silence him. "We all know her here. Do not worry. We won't help him find her."

The Indian boy pulled open the door to the clinic. Jasper walked through it in a daze. Before he could think of anything else to say, Pati was gone.

"Did you have a nice walk?" The nurse's smile fell as she looked up from the desk. "Oh, goodness. Sit down, little fish. You look pale."

She rushed over to him and eased him onto a seat. Her warm hand felt his forehead, and her fingertips pulled his eyelids down so she could check the color.

"I—I'm fine," he stammered, finding his voice. "I guess I just got a little tired. I'll be okay."

"I will get you tea," she said after she was satisfied he wasn't going to keel over. She stood up from his side and swept through the doorway.

Jasper slumped back in the chair, not feeling any better. Bill's voice seethed in his ear. *You got two days.* The words stuck in his head as the nurse came back through the door with a steaming cup in her hand.

"Here. This will warm the blood." She knelt down next to him and tipped the cup to his lips.

"Thank you." He took the hot mug in his hands.

She placed a gentle hand on his cheek with a pained expression on her face, as though looking at him hurt her insides. Like something was wrong with him.

"I'm okay," he repeated, not liking the way her eyes held his.

She nodded and went back to her desk. "Your uncle will be here soon."

"Thanks." Jasper took another sip of tea and wondered what he should tell Uncle Leo. He didn't want to betray Pati by revealing their trip to the game house, but he felt like he should say something about what he'd heard. A policeman was dead. He gazed up at Pati's mother and thought of the girl who had died during the last moon. *Do you know who killed me?*

Before he'd decided what to tell his uncle, the door to the clinic swung open. Uncle Leo and Wayne both grinned when they saw Jasper in the corner sipping his tea.

"How are we feelin' today?" Uncle Leo beamed. "You still got both legs?"

Jasper forced a smile. "Yep!"

"They still work?" his uncle said, tapping him gently on his good knee.

"Yeah. I just got back from a walk."

"You don't know how lucky you are, kiddo!"

"Yeah," Wayne agreed. "Last year Jim Jenkins stepped on a rusty nail, and they had to cut off his whole foot!"

Jasper's smile dropped at this revelation, and he stared down at his bandages.

"Take it easy, Wayne." Uncle Leo shot his son a look. "Let's see what we have to do to get Jasper out of here."

His uncle went over to the nurse to discuss his discharge. She handed him a stack of bandages and started giving instructions on cleaning and caring for the wound for the next week. Wayne plopped himself down on the chair next to Jasper.

"What was it like staying at the res?" he whispered. "Didya see anything strange? Did they dance around a fire?"

"No," Jasper hissed, glancing up at the kind nurse. "They were really nice."

"Did they do any witch doctor stuff?" Wayne elbowed him in the ribs.

"No . . . Well. Sorta . . ." *The sleep tea.* It had brought his mother back for one fleeting, precious moment. But he hated to hear Dr. Whitebird being called a witch doctor.

Thankfully, it was time to leave. The nurse's voice stopped him in the doorway. "Wait. Don't forget these." She handed him Miss Babcock's book and a second one he almost didn't recognize.

"Oh, thanks." He shoved the embarrassing cover of *The First Book of Indians* under his arm and scowled at the second book she gave him. It was his children's Bible from back home, the one his mother had shoved into the bottom of his suitcase. *Everybody's a sinner, Jasper.*

"You take care, little fish."

His uncle placed a hand on his shoulder and steered him through the door. "They feed you okay in there?"

"Uh . . . Yes, sir." Jasper held up the Bible and asked, "Why did you . . . ?"

His words fell flat against his uncle's back as the man climbed into the truck.

"C'mon, Jas!" Wayne pulled him by the arm. Jasper let himself be dragged into the cab and just set the two books on his lap. Uncle Leo had probably brought it, thinking he needed all the prayers he could muster. He covered Baby Jesus's face with his hands and gazed out the window at the rows of beat-up trailers and tiny cabins as they pulled down the hill. *As long as you have a Bible in the house, nobody seems to mind.*

"Well, your aunt is fixin' a proper feast in honor of your return. Steaks and all!"

"Yeah?" Jasper tried to sound enthusiastic.

He memorized landmarks all five miles back to Harris Road.

It wasn't until they were pulling down the two-track drive to his uncle's cabin that Jasper noticed something bulging under the cover of one of the books. He waited until his cousin had climbed out of the truck before opening *The First Book of Indians* to see what had been left there. It was a black-and-white feather. An eagle feather, he decided after studying it for a few moments. He'd read in the book that eagle feathers were given to young warriors after their first battle. He frowned as he picked it up from the pages and turned it over in his hand.

Under the feather, some words were scrawled lightly in pencil: "Have faith, little warrior." Jasper read the words twice.

"You stayin' out here all night?" his uncle asked, holding the driver's side door open.

"Uh. No, sir." Jasper snapped the book shut and climbed out of the truck.

Jasper didn't say a word at dinner. His father had driven in from Detroit to join them in celebrating his recovery. Jasper sat next to him and managed to smile as Wendell slapped him on the back. He still hadn't told his father how he'd found his way back to the farm, about Not Lucy or the insane bus driver, and he was glad. It was as if it had happened in another lifetime. None of it seemed to matter now. Not with Big Bill's warning hanging over his head.

Two days.

"... what he lacks in good sense, he makes up for in luck. Don't he?"

"That and his father's good looks." His uncle and dad had a laugh over the steak. His father squeezed his shoulder, and Jasper tried not to wince. There were so many questions he needed to ask, but—

"I don't know what in the world is so funny. It's a miracle he survived at all," Aunt Velma protested halfheartedly. This only seemed to make the men laugh more.

She cleared the plates and served up chocolate cream pie for dessert. On any other occasion, Jasper would have asked for seconds, but he could hardly choke down a single bite. She might still be out there somewhere. *Hiding.* He thought about how terrified he'd felt crouching in the hayloft just three nights earlier. He dropped his fork.

"You feelin' alright, hon?" his aunt asked.

Everyone stopped eating and looked at him.

Jasper squirmed in his seat. "I'm just a little tired."

"Of course you are, dear. Get yourself to bed. I'll be there in a few minutes to change those bandages." Aunt Velma waved him from the table.

Jasper nodded. His legs were sore and itchy, and he couldn't bear to sit there for one more minute, pretending everything was fine. It wasn't fine. It would never be fine again. Some poor girl was murdered, and a policeman had been shot, and his mother was missing, and Big Bill was going to do something terrible if she didn't turn up. He shuffled away from the table and ducked behind the curtain into the tiny nook where he and Wayne slept. Even though he was technically in the same room as the rest of them, he breathed a little easier behind the linen divider. The table conversation quieted down and turned to discussions of the harvest.

Jasper removed the clothes he'd worn for the last two days, careful not to let the tiny beads of his mother's necklace rattle together. He pulled the heavy loop over his head and searched the room for a place he could hide it. His uncle had found it in the mattress. His aunt would go through his suitcase. Nowhere was safe. He slipped it back onto his neck and pulled his nightshirt over it. He'd have to find a proper hiding place tomorrow, he decided, but he liked having it with him, her beads next to his heart. *Nimaamaa.*

On the other side of the curtain, the grown-up voices were discussing how many days they'd have to borrow Old Hoyt's thresher. *That son of a bitch Hoyt.* His uncle still thought of him as a friend and neighbor while the old bastard sat drunk in the gaming house with some poor girl on his knee. It was enough to make Jasper want to scream.

His father offered to come help with the harvest that Saturday in between the clinks and scrapes of forks and knives.

"Thank you, Wen, but I'm afraid the rains are due early this year," Uncle Leo said. "I already talked to Motega. Four men from Black River are coming tomorrow. Velma, we'll need three days' board."

Jasper gaped at the curtain.

"I'm not sure I've got the stores for that," Velma said with a faint hint of irritation in her voice.

"We'll have to make do. I'll slaughter a pig in the mornin'." Aunt Velma must've made a face because he added, "It's a harvest, Mother. Not the end of the world."

"I sure wish I could take off work," Wendell muttered.

Uncle Leo cut him off. "Now, Wen, we'll take what help we can, but this ain't your farm. You handle your own business."

"This is too my business. As long as Jasper's here, it's my business. I'll be here Saturday at six a.m. You better leave some work for me." A fist hit the table, and the silverware jumped.

"You got it, old man."

Jasper lay in his bed, listening as the conversation wound down. A chair stuttered away from the table. A moment later, his father pulled back the curtain. His unsteady shadow loomed in the doorway, blocking the light from the kitchen. "You alright, Son?"

"I'm okay."

His father hobbled over to him and sat himself on the edge of the bed. "No more barnyard adventures for you. Agreed?"

"Yes, sir."

"Good." He patted Jasper's hand and got up to leave.

"Dad?"

"Yes, Son."

Jasper sat up, not sure what he wanted to ask first. "Where do you think Mom went?"

His father sat back down and let out a long breath. "I wish I knew, Son. I really do."

"I really . . . I miss her." Jasper's voice broke, and he hid his face.

"We all do, Son. We all do." His father squeezed his shoulder and went quiet for a moment. Then he let out one breath of a laugh. "Remember how she used to sing when she was cookin'? Like she thought no one could hear. Man, she had the voice of an angel. It's why we got married, you know. Did I ever tell you that story?"

Jasper looked up.

"She was singing at this club downtown. Sylvie's I think it was called. This beautiful girl gets up on stage. Thea. You should've seen her. It nearly broke my heart that voice of hers. I didn't care what anyone said. I just knew . . ." His father shook off the memory, then patted Jasper's knee. "We were married a week later. And then you came along. She made me the happiest man on earth. She really did . . ."

Jasper could see his mother's black-and-white face smiling from its frame down the dark hallway of the diner back in Detroit. He waited for more. It was the most the man had ever said about her, but it wasn't enough. He finally blurted, "I think someone is looking for her."

"Of course someone is. Lots of people are."

"No, I mean someone bad." Jasper wiped a stray tear and bit the inside of his cheek hard for courage. "Someone who might . . . hurt her."

His father didn't say anything for a moment. "What in the world gave you that idea?"

"I heard some things. Over at the reservation . . ." Jasper struggled for words that wouldn't get him or Pati in trouble and couldn't find them.

"What sort of things?" Jasper could feel his father's eyes boring through his head even though he couldn't see them in the dim light filtering through the curtain.

"Big Bill is looking for her . . . he said she's only got two days to call him before they do something terrible!"

Wendell just sat there. Jasper could tell by the hitch in his breathing that he was furious.

"It's Galatas, isn't it? This isn't just about her missing work, is it? Why is he looking for Mom?"

"Don't you worry about that, Son. Mommy's business isn't for you to worry about. You have *got* to stop listening to other people's conversations. Understand?"

His father squeezed his hand so hard Jasper worried it might break. He shrank against the pillow. "Yes, sir."

Wendell let go and rubbed his eyes for a minute, seeming lost in thought. "You get some sleep." With that, he got up and left the room.

On the other side of the curtain, he heard him say, "Leo, can we talk a minute?" Then the door to the cabin opened and shut.

Jasper sat up and held his breath, but all he could hear were the dishes clinking together in the washbasin. He pulled himself out of bed and pressed his ear to the cool window glass. The faint tones of men sounded in the distance, but he couldn't make out what they were saying. A moment later, an engine roared to life. The headlights of his father's truck lit up Jasper's face in the window and then pulled away.

An hour later, after Aunt Velma had changed his bandages and wished him good night, Wayne's shadow slipped into the room. Jasper pretended to be asleep as his cousin stripped down and threw on pajamas. He didn't want to talk about Indians or witch doctors.

Wayne crawled into bed and let out a low whistle. "You really done it this time."

Jasper sat up in bed. "What do you mean?"

"I heard 'em. After dinner, when Pop and Uncle Wen stepped outside, I headed out to the barn. If you know what I mean."

"What'd they say?" Jasper whispered, keeping his eye on the curtain. His aunt and uncle's bedroom door was only ten feet away. Their muffled voices were recapping the day.

"Your dad was hoppin' mad about somethin' you said. He wanted to know who had visited you at the clinic and if that Detroit detective had been back. He even asked about Big Bill from over at the roller rink."

Jasper stared out the window. "What'd your dad say?"

"He said your pop needed to calm down. I thought they were gonna have a scuffle right there."

Jasper felt a knot tying itself up in his stomach. "Did he say anything else?"

"Yeah." Wayne didn't seem to want to say anything more. An uneasy silence fell over the house. Uncle Leo and Aunt Velma had gone quiet. Out in the kitchen, a piece of burning wood cracked in the stove.

"Well, what was it?" Jasper nearly yelled.

"Hey!" Uncle Leo's voice boomed from the other side of the cabin. Both boys hit the deck. "Pipe down! Get some sleep, you two!"

"Yes, sir!" they both answered.

Jasper let a full minute pass before propping himself back up on his elbow. He nudged Wayne under the blanket and whispered, "What'd he say?"

Wayne sat up and cupped his hand over Jasper's ear. "He said that your mom is in some sort of trouble with gangsters."

"What?" Jasper gasped too loudly. Wayne swatted him on the head to shut him up.

"If anyone comes here lookin' for you, we're supposed to tell him you're not here."

"But . . . what am I supposed to do if they see me?"

"I dunno. Hide?"

CHAPTER 39

What was the worst thing you ever did?

Jasper spent half the night staring up at the dark ceiling of his uncle's cabin. *Hide.*

It's what his mother wanted. She'd left him on the farm so he could hide up in his tree. Somewhere out there, she was running from Big Bill and Galatas. *But why?*

Jasper pulled the beaded pendant out from inside his shirt and held it up in the moonlight.

Wayne began to snore in his low, steady saw. Across the cabin, he could hear the same noise coming from Uncle Leo's bedroom, only louder. Jasper rolled over, but his eyes wouldn't stay closed.

Her tearful voice from his dream haunted him. Her warm lips on his forehead. *No matter what happens. I'll always love you.* It sounded like a good-bye but for good.

Jasper sat up. *What if it wasn't a dream?* She might be sleeping in one of the trailers at Black River right now, not five miles away. He should have looked harder when he was there. It was all he could do not to get up and climb out the window to go find her. Five miles wasn't so far. He could walk it.

Out the bedroom window, a full moon hung overhead. A harvest moon. It would be enough light to walk by, he decided, but forced his head back down to his pillow. She would be furious with him if he went out in the night when he was supposed to be hiding. He stared up at the ceiling.

But in the story, the mother dies. He sat up again.

He grabbed the book about Indians from the bureau next to him and pulled out the feather. Its black and white stripes were a mournful blue and gray in the moonlight. He couldn't just let her die.

The strangled rage he'd heard in his father's voice reminded him again to stay in bed. He was just a boy. *My dad's the one that knows what to do,* he told himself. He tucked the feather back into the book. *Have faith.* He should have faith.

An hour later, he was still lying awake, listening to the logs dying in the woodstove. Men from Black River would be coming to the farm that morning. Motega was coming. Jasper might have a chance to talk to him. He remembered the way the huge Indian had growled at Big Bill before he'd knocked the gun out of his hand. *All sorts of people go missing out here in these woods.*

Jasper curled himself into a ball. Her car had been found buried in those woods. *The white men bury their dead here when they don't want them found.*

Dr. Whitebird must know where she was hiding, he decided. The kind doctor wouldn't let anything happen to her. Maybe he could get her a message. Jasper invented elaborate secret codes in his head, warning her about Big Bill, reassuring her he was okay, begging her to come get him, until he dropped off into a fitful dream.

Crawling along the forest floor, he picked his way silently over the damp fallen leaves. He was an Indian warrior stalking his prey. A set of tracks pressed into the mud before him, leading down a dark and winding path. They were the paw prints of a large dog. A wolf. He stopped. There were drops of blood on the leaves. Up ahead he heard a low growl. He rushed toward it. The drops of blood grew into puddles. His hands and knees splattered in red. Then he saw it. Gray fur standing up on end, crusted with blood, hovering over something soft and pink with the wet sounds of Lucifer chewing.

Jasper jerked himself awake. It took a full minute for him to stop seeing blood as his eyes adjusted to the moonlight streaming in through the window. Wayne snorted and rolled over. The house was cold and quiet. Outside, the sky was slate gray. The shadowy form of a woodchuck rustled in the grass across the field. A stiff autumn wind whistled softly through the gaps in the window, but Jasper could still hear the wolf in his head, tearing through the carcass at its feet. *Nimaamaa!*

He buried his face in his hands and shook with a silent sob. The cold beads of her necklace pressed against his stomach. He had to find her. There had to be a way. Something he'd missed in her diary, something he'd heard Pati say, there had to be something. He sat up.

Everyone would be up soon anyway. He would just say he'd decided to get an early jump on his chores. Mind made up, Jasper climbed out of bed and stripped off his pajamas, hardly caring that they were wet. He kept his eyes on Wayne as he pulled on his pants and shoes, but his cousin didn't move.

Jasper crept across the creaky floorboards through the kitchen to the front door. Even though he had a good excuse to be leaving, his heart still halted at every sound. He glanced back through the dark of the cabin to his uncle's closed door. He was still snoring. The cock would crow any minute, and he'd be caught. Jasper grabbed his jacket from the hook. The front door opened without a sound, and he slipped out before the hinges could think to squeak.

The brisk air snapped Jasper fully awake as he darted across the driveway to the barn. He made his way past the stink of ten dirty cow stalls to the back corner where his uncle stored the feed bins.

You rat bastard, Hoyt! he cursed as he rummaged through the feed, the buckets, the straw. *She was just a girl, and you made her do your dirty work. You sent her to the reservation.* Pati's words raged in his head. *Careless girls get dragged away. White men do what they please.*

Her diary was gone. He checked again and again, frantically throwing straw and dirt, but it wasn't there.

Jasper sank down onto the ground. A girl he'd seen before somewhere had been killed a month ago. A police officer had been shot between the eyes, and his mother could be next. If she was still alive at all. He didn't notice the tears running down his face as he scanned the floor one last time.

He lurched to his feet, ignoring the burn in his legs and the sag of his bandages. His aunt or uncle must've found it when he was at the clinic. *Did they even read it? Do they know?* His uncle probably took one look at her foul humor about growing up on the farm and tossed it into the woodstove. *No.*

Jasper took off running out of the barn and down the driveway to the back fields. There had to be more. More pieces of her somewhere in that house.

He should have told Wayne where he was going, he realized as he sped past the tractor shed and then the chicken coop. All the birds were nestled in their roosts as his feet kicked up the gravel outside. The unmistakable flap of a rooster's wings made him run faster.

The fields were still shrouded in the gray before dawn. Cold dew clung to the tufts of cut hay. Five strides into the field, his shoes and pant legs were drenched. His bandages were getting wet. Aunt Velma would skin him, but he didn't care.

He stopped at the tall stand of wheat in front of him and glanced over his shoulder before barreling in. The dark sky disappeared into the sweet-smelling boughs. He couldn't see a foot in front or behind him as he fought his way through. For a terrible minute, he panicked that he'd forgotten where he was going and gotten himself lost. Then he glimpsed the tip of a chimney among the branches of a distant stand of trees in between the stalks.

Jasper memorized his bearing and plunged deeper into the field. The ground was soft and unsteady as he followed the furrows toward the chimney. Somewhere behind him, the rooster began to crow. His aunt and uncle would be waking up now. He scrambled faster toward his grandmother's house.

The wheat finally gave way to overgrown grass, and what was left of his mother's childhood home emerged. The edges of the sky had turned a golden pink, but the house looked like night had never left. Black and gloomy, everything inside it was dead. Jasper felt his spirits go dark. He wouldn't find anything but a pile of old clothes and an abandoned dollhouse inside.

For no good reason at all, he surveyed the tall crops that surrounded the house on all sides, searching for a sign of her. There was no road to the house. No cars parked nearby. It was a deserted island. He would have to swim back through the wet fields alone. He gazed down at his mud-soaked legs, defeated. His aunt and uncle would be furious with him. Again.

There had to be something inside that would help him find her, he argued with himself. Jasper glanced back into the fields and listened. He didn't hear anyone calling his name. If he gave up, there would be nothing left to do but go home and wait. Determined not to just sit in his tree, he climbed the creaking steps up onto the porch and slipped through the front door.

Inside, the house was perfectly dark. The torn drapes and soot clouding the windows blocked the rising light. He picked his way through the living room, past the broken chairs, and into the shadow of the kitchen.

He bumped his arm into the corner of the cupboard. "Ouch!"

Squinting through the dark, he could just make out the outline of the back door in the pink glow filtering down the stairs. He felt his way to the doorknob and gave it a hard tug.

The room flooded with the pale morning light. It looked just like it had the first time he'd seen it. He scanned the cupboard and drawers for photographs or letters or any trace of her. There was nothing but broken dishes and animal droppings.

"Damn it," he hissed.

He turned to the stairwell that led up to the room where his mother had once lived. The piece of sky overhead lit his way through the broken roof as he climbed the creaking steps one by one.

A faint noise from above stopped him cold.

"Who's there?" a voice whispered.

CHAPTER 40

What happened?

"Jasper?"

The faraway voice was calling to him from a tiny opening high above. But he couldn't answer. He was trapped at the bottom of a well. There was water in his lungs.

"Jasper." A gentle hand shook his shoulder.

He could smell fire. The barn was burning down. He could hear screaming. The crack of a gun exploded in his head.

"No!" His eyes flew open. White light poured into his bruised skull. He squeezed them shut again and shook his head. *No.*

A warm palm fell over his eyes. "Easy, Ogichidaa. It is all right."

Jasper's eyelids fluttered against the shadow of the hand. "Dr. Whitebird?"

"Ah! You are alive." He could hear the smile in the doctor's voice. "This is good."

The large hand slowly lifted as Jasper's eyes adjusted to the room. He was back at the reservation clinic. He grunted as he tried to lift himself up onto his elbows. "Am I still here?"

The doctor lowered him back down to the pillow. "Easy. We are not there yet."

"Have I been here the whole time?" Jasper's words muddled together against his swollen lips. He lifted his arm to see the IV line. The needle was stuck in a different vein an inch away from a round bruise. His fingernails were blackened at the edges. There were cuts on his hands. Sandpaper burned in the back of his throat.

He closed his eyes, and he was standing in his grandmother's half-burnt kitchen again. He'd been looking for something. He'd heard a voice.

Jasper shot up, screaming, "Mom!"

The doctor forced him back down to the cot with firm hands. "Shh . . . You must rest, Ogichidaa."

Jasper flailed against the doctor. "No! I can't leave her."

"Your mother would want you to rest."

"But . . ." *Was it her?* He couldn't remember. Jasper turned his head into his pillow and sobbed.

The doctor pressed a warm compress to his head. "You have been through quite a lot. There is no shame in crying. Only tears can wash away blood."

Blood. Broken images assaulted the back of his eyes—blood splattered on the floorboards, yellow teeth grinning, giant hands gripping his wrists, hair catching fire, a gun crashing down. Jasper shook his head violently, his fingers clawing at his face.

"You are not ready to wake, Ogichidaa. It will be all right. No more dreams tonight."

Jasper felt a sharp pinch in his arm, and everything went black.

CHAPTER 41

It says here you tried to kill yourself.
Would you say that's true?

Jasper woke to voices. At first they were just muffled sounds in the distance, but they grew steadily louder until he realized the voices were in the room. They were talking about him.

"When can he come home, do you think?" It was his uncle speaking.

"We have to wait for his mind to settle. He's been in shock," Dr. Whitebird said. "He might come back to us tomorrow, but it could take longer. He will have to avoid any strenuous activity for at least two weeks to heal the concussion."

Jasper lay frozen, not wanting either man to know he was awake. It felt like there was a fifty-pound weight on his chest.

"What about his lungs, Doc?" a third voice asked. It was his father.

"The smoke inhalation wasn't severe. It shouldn't cause permanent damage."

"Maybe we should get him over to St. Catherine's in Port Huron. Damn the costs," his father pleaded. He sounded more worried than angry. In fact, he didn't sound angry at all.

"They will tell you no different, but there will be more questions. He needs his rest. The boy has been through quite an ordeal." It sounded like a warning.

The three men didn't speak for a few moments.

"Perhaps we should discuss this outside."

"Wen, he's right. Let's talk outside. Jasper needs his rest."

"I'll be the judge of what Jasper needs." There were tears in the old man's voice. "He's all I got left. I didn't even get a chance to talk . . ."

His father's voice faded down the hall, and the door to Jasper's room closed with a firm click. Jasper peeled open his eyes and turned his head toward the door. The sudden movement sent a blinding pain through his skull. Reaching up, he could feel a thick, damp bandage on his brow. Under it was an enormous lump.

The door to his room opened, and the doctor reappeared. "Ah. We are awake." He smiled at him. "How are we feeling?"

"My head hurts." Jasper's voice frayed to nothing but a whisper, like he'd been screaming at the top of his lungs. Maybe he had been.

"Yes. It should. Twelve stitches and a concussion. Do you know what a concussion is?" The doctor pulled the stool up to the side of the bed and placed a gentle hand next to the bandage.

Jasper shook his head, then winced.

"Your brain is bruised. You took a few good bumps to your skull."

Jasper frowned, trying to remember. All he could see were the stairs leading up to the attic. All he could hear was a whisper, *Who's there?* All he could smell and taste was smoke.

"Sometimes the brain forgets the things it does not want to remember. This can happen with a concussion. This is normal . . . sometimes this is best." He put the stethoscope into his ears and placed the cold disk on Jasper's chest. "Your lungs sound strong, Ogichidaa. This is good."

Jasper didn't speak until the doctor was finished checking him over. "Dr. Whitebird? What day is it?"

The man put his tools away and gave the boy his full attention. "Today is Sunday, September twenty-first."

Jasper's eyes flooded, and he turned to the wall. The two days were up.

"Take heart. The worst is over, Ogichidaa."

He could see Big Bill waving his gun at Motega. He could feel Bill's hands squeezing her neck as though it were his own. He'd failed her. He couldn't breathe. The hands were choking him. He gasped at the air like he was drowning.

"No, Jasper. You must breathe. Nice and slow." The doctor's voice sounded farther and farther away. "Nurse!"

Doors opened, and footsteps rushed back and forth while the world went out of focus.

Minutes or hours later, Jasper heard himself talking in choked whispers. It took him a moment to register what he was saying. "What happened? In the house? How did I get here?"

The doctor's voice answered, "There was a fire. You are safe now. This is all that matters."

A fire. Jasper could see it. His grandmother's house burning to the ground. The smell of smoke still clung to his skin. His breath could barely escape through the tightness in his throat.

"No one is angry with you, Ogichidaa," the doctor said. "You must rest your mind. You need your strength."

"Was it my fault? Did I start the fire?" Jasper could see an oil lamp shattering into—

The image went black like someone had cut it out of his head.

"If you did, I'm sure you did not mean to," the doctor tried to reassure him.

He searched his brain for the missing pictures. The swinging lantern. A pair of black boots. The floor. The rest were gone. "I can't remember."

"It is all right, Ogichidaa. Your brain will heal itself. Give it time."

"But what happened? He said he'd do something terrible if she didn't call. What if he did? What if he—" Jasper felt his face crumple and rolled onto his side. Hoyt. Big Bill. They blurred together.

"You must quiet your mind. There is nothing to fear." Dr. Whitebird patted his back. "Remember the story of the boy in the tree? Your Nimaamaa will never leave your side. Listen for her and you will see."

"What?" He wiped his eyes hard enough to hurt. "What does that even mean? I don't understand. She's not here. Is she?"

"When you are ready, you will understand, Ogichidaa. Now you must sleep." Dr. Whitebird left the room with his riddles.

Jasper fell back to his pillow. A voice had called to him from the attic, but the more he tried to hear it, the farther away it sounded. Until he couldn't be sure he'd heard it at all.

His hand instinctively reached for her necklace. It had been around his neck when he'd left his bedroom that morning to find clues. To find her. Groping fingers grew more frantic as they searched his neck and stomach and then the bed.

The necklace was gone.

CHAPTER 42

*Did you receive any treatment for acute stress
or depression after the incident?*

Several hours later, Jasper's door opened again, but he didn't bother to
look up.

"Hey, kid! You still alive?" It was Wayne. He was carrying a basket
filled with fried chicken from the smell of it.

Jasper couldn't bring himself to answer. He couldn't lift his head off
the pillow. It weighed eighty pounds.

Wayne pulled up the doctor's stool and set the basket on the cot.
It was warm. "Ma wanted me to bring you this. She figured you'd be
hungry."

Jasper nodded even though he couldn't feel his stomach. Everything
inside him had gone missing along with his memory of that night. All
he knew for certain was that something unspeakable had happened and
it was all his fault. Dr. Whitebird's reminder of the story about the boy
in the tree only worsened his fears. She wasn't coming back.

"Man. You sure are lucky. Pop says two more seconds and you
would have burned down with the house."

Jasper turned his head at this, which Wayne took as a sign to keep talking.

"You must've fell through the floor. Did you know that? You might've broke your back." Wayne paused to survey Jasper's various bandages, then grabbed a piece of chicken.

"I did?" Jasper croaked.

"Yeah. Pop says it's all his fault. That house has been just sitting there waiting for something terrible to happen. He called it a box of tinder. Said he should've torn it down years ago. He feels real bad about it."

"He isn't mad?"

"I wouldn't say he's mad. He's more worried . . . like maybe you wanted to burn the house down on purpose." Wayne gave him a wary glance. Like there might be something seriously wrong with him. "Did you?"

"No," Jasper whispered, but he wasn't sure of anything anymore. There *was* something wrong with him. Every time he closed his eyes, he saw terrible things. Things he couldn't even admit to himself.

"Phew! Glad to know you're not nuts, kid." Wayne gave him a halfhearted punch in the arm. "We're still gonna have to hide all the matches from you . . . So, what were you doin' out there anyway?"

Jasper frowned. His uncle thought he might've tried to kill himself. A gruff voice laughed knowingly in his ear. He jerked away from it, but nothing was there but the pillow.

"You okay?" Wayne looked at him sideways like he really was crazy.

Jasper tried to shrug.

"Can't say I blame you for bein' jumpy. Pop would've killed me right here in the clinic if I'd gone into that house."

Jasper agreed but said nothing.

"He's just relieved you're okay, I guess. Motega went and yanked you out himself. It was real lucky he was there early to pull the harvest."

In that moment, Jasper could see Motega's murderous eyes glaring down at him and feel his iron hands digging into his arms. He ran his fingers down his left shoulder and could feel the bruises.

The older boy kept talking. "He and his fellas are out in the fields now. They even cleared the wreckage of the house. Hauled it clean away. It's kinda weird havin' it gone. I always liked to think Grandma's ghost still lived inside it."

The gruff voice whispered in his ear, *Do you want to know how this place burned down, kid?*

Jasper wrenched himself away from it, slamming his bleeding bandage against the pillow until his brain flashed white. *Maybe I am crazy.*

"So . . . uh. Did they say when you can come home?" Wayne reached into the basket and pulled out another drumstick and tried to hand it to Jasper.

Jasper just shook his head.

The next day, the whole family came to escort Jasper back to the farm. He kept his mouth shut as Wendell settled the bill with the nurse. He glanced around the waiting room for any sign of her son, Pati, and was relieved he wasn't there. Pati would know he'd done something unforgivable. He'd see it.

Wayne helped him up into the back of his uncle's truck. "You okay, Jas?"

He nodded, afraid to speak. They all thought he was crazy and had burned down the house on purpose. No one said as much, but an awkward silence hung over the car all the way back to the cabin.

Once they arrived, Aunt Velma gently tucked him into bed like he was a porcelain doll and set about making dinner.

"Maybe I should stay here with him tonight." Wendell was pacing the kitchen floor on the other side of the curtain. "Mind if I bunk in the barn?"

"Not at all, Wen. You do what you gotta do," Uncle Leo said.

"I'm gonna run up to the Tally Ho and put in a call to work. Can I get you anything?"

"See if Clint will part with some of that scotch of his. I think we could all use some."

"Will do."

Jasper listened as his father left the house and fired up the engine of his truck outside, and then to the clinks and clanks of Aunt Velma cooking. Anything to keep the voices in his head quiet. He stared up at the ceiling, counting nail heads, afraid to sleep.

He wondered if Motega and his men were still out there somewhere. Part of him wanted to go find the man and ask what had happened, but the bigger part was too scared to find out. He didn't want to listen for his mother in the birds or wind or whatever gobbledygook Dr. Whitebird said. He wanted to believe she was still out there somewhere. The thought of approaching that house or whatever was left of it—

Jasper went back to counting nails.

The curtain opened, and Aunt Velma came in with a bowl of soup. "Jasper, honey, I need to sit you up." She set the bowl down on the dresser and gently coaxed another pillow under him. "You have to eat, sweetie. Dr. Whitebird said you need to if you're going to get better."

Jasper didn't want to get better, but Aunt Velma wouldn't have it. The weight of her jostled his aching head as she sat down on the bed and lifted a spoon to his cracked lips. He didn't budge.

She lowered the spoon. "We can do this the easy way or the hard way, Jasper."

He knew he was beaten. The warm soup slid past the burns in his throat down to his festering gut. The taste of the corn mash his uncle had forced him to swallow before his aunt had taken the brush to his leg came back up along with the smoke of the fire.

Five more agonizing spoonfuls later, the front door opened again. Aunt Velma abandoned her bowl for the moment to greet Jasper's father.

"Everything alright with work?" she asked on the other side of the curtain.

"Yep. Clint says hello and sent this along."

"Well, that was awful nice of him. Did you invite him to dinner, I hope?"

"I tried, but he's fixin' for a busy night there at the tavern. Bill Valassis over in Burtchville was just found dead."

Jasper stopped breathing at the name. *Big Bill.*

"Good Lord, what happened?" Aunt Velma's voice grew faint.

"Car accident. Real bad one, I guess. Did you know him?"

"Not well. Oh, his poor family. Did it just happen?"

"Early this morning. He ran his car straight into one of them fuel storage tanks. Must've been drunk as a dog."

"Wow! No foolin'?" Wayne piped in. A moment later, the curtain pulled back to their shared bedroom. "Hey, Jas? You hear that? Big Bill from Mr. G's just . . . oh, sorry."

The curtain pulled closed again. Behind it, Jasper kept his eyes shut, pretending to sleep, while the house burned over and over in his mind.

CHAPTER 43

Do you still think about killing yourself?

After the house had quieted down and Wayne had come to bed for the night, there was a hard knock at the door. Jasper gave up pretending to sleep and watched the shadow of his uncle pass by the thin curtain.

"Evenin', Officer. Can I help you?"

Jasper sat up.

"Good evening, Mr. Williams. I'm sorry to trouble you this late." It was the voice of Detective Russo.

Wayne's words of warning kicked over a nest of bees in his head. *If anyone comes here lookin' for you, we're supposed to tell him you're not here.*

Without making a sound, Jasper climbed out of bed and rolled onto the floor underneath the mattress. His bandaged head banged into the basket Aunt Velma had hidden there for his laundry, but he winced in silence. The bed frame squeaked as Wayne leaned over the edge to look at him down there, but he didn't breathe a word.

"I had some questions for your brother-in-law, Mr. Wendell Leary. Is that his truck outside?" the detective continued from the front door.

"I believe it is."

"You mind if I step inside?"

Jasper sipped shallow breaths and willed his heart to stop pounding like a drum, certain the detective could hear it.

"If you're lookin' for Wendell, he's out in the barn. What exactly is this all about, Officer?" Uncle Leo's voice faded as he stepped outside and shut the door behind him.

Wayne climbed off the bed and watched the two men out the window. He whispered to Jasper on the floor, "Whatdya think he wants?"

Jasper pressed his head to the floorboards and held his tongue, debating whether he had the strength to sneak out the window and find out. Debating whether he even wanted to know.

"Want me to go check it out?"

Before Jasper could answer, a loud crash rang out followed by shouting out in driveway. He scrambled out from under the bed to join his cousin at the window. His father was standing in the driveway in his thermals with a shovel in his hand.

"I don't give a goddamn about your so-called investigation," he yelled at the detective. "You boys haul me to jail, harass my family, and now you have the balls to say you need my help! You can go straight to hell!"

The detective backed up toward his unmarked car, with his left hand held out in front of him and his right hand on his gun. He said something neither boy could make out.

"She's gone, goddammit! And she's not coming back, you hear? File her under 'Dead,' you got me? She's *dead*. It's over. Now, if I ever see your face near me or my boy again, I swear to G——"

His father's voice cut off the minute he saw Jasper's stricken face in the window.

CHAPTER 44

Thank you for providing your history. Let's move on.
When did the alleged murder take place?

The snow came early that fall. A thick blanket covered the fields for miles in every direction in white silence. The animals stayed in their barn, feeding on the stores of hay and corn. No one spoke of Althea or the fire, burying the hurt as the snow buried the scarred ground. No word came from the world outside the frozen windows of the cabin, but every car that passed by on Harris Road was a reminder she was never coming back.

Every week, his father brought the chessboard to talk about strategy and logic and nothing else.

Every morning, Jasper helped Wayne empty udders and shovel snow. He trudged to and from school. He kept his head down and his mouth shut, knowing they all thought he was crazy. He kept his nightmares to himself, terrified they might be right, swallowing the screams when he'd jolt himself awake.

The cold months blurred together and eventually thawed to spring, but nothing changed.

Until June.

"Jasper?" Uncle Leo sneezed hard.

"Yes, sir?" Jasper stopped raking the hay. It had been nine months since he'd burned his grandmother's house to the ground, but he was still waiting for his punishment. Every time his uncle raised his voice, Jasper braced himself for a blow.

"You remember your lessons?" He waved at the tractor. Jasper had been practicing driving up and down the tracks to the fields for weeks.

Jasper froze for a minute, recounting each step he'd been taught, then nodded.

"I want you to give it a try. I could use Wayne's help down here. I want you to keep it in second gear and go real easy on the throttle. This ain't a race. Understand?"

Jasper nodded and stared blankly at the seat. He knew there was a time he would have killed to drive the tractor. He'd been absolutely green with envy that his older cousin got to sit at the wheel all the time.

"Ain't nothin' to it. Clutch. First. Gas. Wayne's been doin' it since he was younger than you."

Jasper just stood there.

"Wayne, why don't you help 'im start 'er up? Then hop on down here and give me a hand."

"C'mon, Jas! Don't tell me you're scared of a little ol' John Deere. She can't even go that fast."

Wayne started to make chicken sounds to shake the younger boy out of his stupor. Jasper forced a vengeful smile like a normal ten-year-old might give and hopped up onto the curved metal throne and took the wheel. He had to sit at the very lip of the seat molded to fit a giant man's backside to reach the pedals.

"That's right." Wayne nodded. "Push in the clutch. Slide 'er to first. Now give 'er some gas."

The great green beast roared to life. The two-stroke engine rumbled under Jasper's seat so loudly he was certain it would shake his teeth loose.

"Okay! Now giv—s—th—s!"

Jasper couldn't hear a thing over the twenty-five horses churning under his ass, but Wayne was making a turning motion with his hand. Jasper nodded and turned the wheel to reposition the tractor for another run down the field. He gave it some more gas, and the giant machine lurched forward, almost throwing him off the seat. His hand jumped off the throttle, and the tractor jerked to a stop hard enough to make Jasper hit his head on the steering wheel.

"Will you two stopping playin' around up there?" his uncle bellowed. "Radio's calling for rain. We got to get this field cut before supper."

"I don't know, Pop. Maybe I should do it," Wayne called back.

"No. Jasper here needs to learn somethin'," Uncle Leo insisted. His uncle was always trying to find ways to get Jasper engaged in something productive. His aunt and uncle gave him a pained look every time they caught him staring off into space or slumped against a tree. When they thought he couldn't hear, they'd discuss what should be done about him.

He had to make a bigger effort to laugh and pal around with Wayne. He hated making them worry. He always finished his chores and schoolwork on time, earning top marks in both, but it wasn't enough to ease their minds. Or his. It would never be enough.

Jasper threw the tractor into gear. The green beast lurched forward again, but this time he was ready for it and held tight to the wheel. The rig slowly swung around and inched its way forward, a bit unsteady but moving nonetheless.

"That's it," hollered Uncle Leo. "Now p—her up—econd!"

Jasper nodded and pushed in the giant clutch and slid the lever up a notch. The machine chugged slightly but then continued on a bit more quickly. Wayne slapped him on the shoulder and then hopped off the side. It was just him and the John Deere.

Driving straight was no problem. He just kept one hand on the throttle and one on the wheel. Everything was fine for three hundred yards, but he felt his arms tense as the end of the hay field drew nearer. He eased up on the gas and began to turn the wheel. The tractor ran off course a bit, so he turned the other way, but the corn tufts at the edge of the run were approaching fast. Using both hands, he cranked the wheel over. The tractor made a sharp turn. Too sharp. It began to roll up on one side.

A voice shouted from behind, but he couldn't make out the words as the tractor tipped. Sheldon's son had been killed the year before when his tractor rolled. *Never get caught under a tractor, boys.* His uncle's words had been beaten into his head. And now it was about to happen.

Jasper cut the throttle and climbed up the tipping deck to jump. For a split second he hesitated and willed the tractor to pull him under, but he could feel its momentum shift. Just as he lifted his feet, the giant machine slammed back down on the lifted wheels, launching all seventy pounds of him into the air.

The landing knocked the wind clear out of his lungs. Colors flashed. He could smell smoke. He closed his eyes and was back in the old farmhouse, lying on the floorboards, bleeding. He could hear the horrible grinding of metal on metal.

A pair of boots marched over to him lying there on the attic floor. A gun hung over his head. The point of a boot raised up to kick him. He braced for impact. Somewhere above him, he could hear screaming.

Then he heard laughter.

"That was quite a ride, huh?"

Jasper snapped his eyes open to see his uncle's boots. Leo reached down and pulled him off the ground. "You alright?"

"I—I think so," Jasper heard his disoriented voice answer after the air came back to his lungs. He regained his footing, moving each arm and leg cautiously. Nothing seemed broken. His back was sore where he'd landed, but that was about it. He blinked the fog from his eyes and focused on the rows of corn stretching out to the horizon.

"Man! I never seen anybody fly like that before! That was amazing!" Wayne came running up, beaming. "You're lucky we weren't pulling the baler!"

"Lucky, my foot. I'd never let a greenhorn driver pull that." Uncle Leo swatted his son's head. "Soft ground, light load, it's just how you learned, boy."

Wayne chucked Jasper in the arm. "I never got to fly like Superman, though."

Jasper tried to smile back.

"So now, Jasper." His uncle grabbed him firmly by the shoulder. "You ever gonna take a turn that fast again?"

"No, sir."

"That's what I thought." His uncle wiped his red nose with the handkerchief. "Now get back up there and drive. Don't forget to downshift at the turn. I want you taking those slow as molasses in January. Understand?"

Jasper nodded. He climbed back up into the driver's seat and surveyed the damage. The crushed sprouts of corn where he'd fallen left only the smallest scar in the endless field of green. Behind him he could hear his uncle and cousin laughing, replaying his amazing flight over and over. He put a smile on as he started the engine.

In his mind, a pair of black leather boots were still staring him right in the face.

CHAPTER 45

Can you describe the victim?

That evening, Jasper was playing in the barn with his baby goat, Timmy, when the storm rolled in. The low rumble of thunder sent the kid scrambling back to his nanny. By the time Jasper had the loose goats all penned back up, the wind was whistling in through the siding boards at a deafening pitch. The cows shifted their feet and bellowed restlessly. Jasper agreed with them. The air crackled with the feeling that something was about to happen.

He tried to ignore it and wandered back behind the feed bins the way he did every night. It was a penance now to look for his mother's diary. Once again, he retraced the path of its flight from where he'd thrown it. As he searched for the spot where it had landed, he mentally flogged himself for being so careless.

"You got 'em all secured?" Wayne shouted from the doorway so Jasper would hear him over the wind. "Pop says this one looks like a doozy."

His cousin trotted inside and double-checked the cow stalls. Jasper had learned in his months on the farm that milking cows produced the vast majority of the family's income. He came out from the feed bins and followed behind Wayne, checking water dishes and securing the milking hoses. When both boys were satisfied, they latched the barn door and trotted back to the cabin.

"All the stalls locked?" his uncle asked. He was standing on the porch, nailing boards over the windows.

"Yes, sir!" both boys answered.

"Then get your butts inside." Jasper could hear the anxiety in his uncle's voice. He didn't like thunderstorms. "That lightning is nothin' to mess with. It can demolish a solid barn in minutes, and don't you forget it."

Sheldon's barn next door had burned down thirty years earlier when it was struck by lightning. They all had lightning rods now, but Uncle Leo still brought it up during every major storm. It had nearly ruined that family.

Once they were in the safety of their room, Wayne whispered in Jasper's ear, "Did you know Sheldon's father hung himself the day they finished building the new barn?"

"He did?"

"No one knows why either."

Maybe he just couldn't bear having anything left to lose, Jasper thought to himself but said nothing.

Outside their bedroom window, the world had gone deathly quiet. Not even the birds were chirping. Jasper stared out and saw an unnatural green glow in the sky. A shelf of purple clouds hung out over the fields a half mile away.

"You ever see anything like that?" Jasper asked Wayne.

His cousin pulled off his shirt and gazed out the window. He'd grown into more of a man than a boy. His voice had dropped over the winter, and he towered over Jasper's shoulder. He let out a low whistle. "That's somethin'. This could be a real big one."

"What should we do?" Jasper thought of his baby goat hunkered down in the barn and felt a pang. A bolt of lightning struck a field a mile away. Not a second later, its thunder shook the cabin.

"There's nothing we can do besides watch." Wayne sounded more fascinated than scared. The green sky grew dark as night. Bolts of electricity jumped between the clouds. The wind picked up just as Uncle Leo finished boarding up their window. It grew steadily louder until it seemed to suck every inch of air out of the house. Not being able to see outside made it even more frightening every time the tiny cabin shuddered.

Jasper had never heard anything like it. The roaring wind was louder than ten freight trains. The window sashes began to quake. The stand of trees outside flapped like a million panicked birds.

A large hand grabbed Jasper by the shoulder and pulled him away from the rattling window. Uncle Leo shouted something that Jasper couldn't make out over the screaming wind. His uncle grabbed him and Wayne each by the arm and dragged them into the kitchen and forced them under the table. They huddled there together with Wayne's lanky frame draped over Jasper as the cabin lurched and trembled. Pots and pans fell from their hooks with a faint crash. The dishes tumbled from their shelves. Broken shards rained to the ground around them.

Jasper peeked out from under Wayne's arm and tried to find his aunt and uncle. All he could see was the front door. The wind had ripped it open. It banged violently against the porch wall. Outside, the rain blew past sideways. His uncle's truck had tipped over. Trees were being ripped up by the roots.

Another hard gust of wind slammed the door shut. The electric lights went out, and the house went dark. Jasper huddled under Wayne in the pitch-black as the wind tore open the world around them. He couldn't hear his own thoughts. A thunderclap ripped through the house, and the wind forced its way inside. The table above them flew away into the abyss. An instant later, Jasper was falling through the sky.

CHAPTER 46

How did she die?

Braying and bleating wails echoed all around him. Jasper rolled his head away from the noise, and his ear filled with muddy water. He was lying in a puddle. The sounds of dying animals flooded the spaces between the sheets of rain dropping all around him. *Am I dead?* he thought, unable to move. *Is this hell?* Another death wail rang out only a few yards from where he lay. In the distance, the wind rattled the trees. A giant crash shook the ground.

Feeling began to register in his extremities. His legs were tangled beneath him. His arm lay at an unnatural angle. It was as though his body had been ripped apart and put back together wrong. Somewhere in the distance, a woman was crying.

Mom?

He tried to look toward the noise, but all the lights had gone out. Invisible rain drenched his face. The soft sobbing continued, but he hardly believed it was there at all. His eyes might not even be open. *I'm dead.*

Somewhere in the distance, a voice called out. "Jas—per!"

His mind was playing tricks on him again. He didn't answer.

"Jas—per!" it called again.

He tried lifting his head. "Mom? Is that you?" he called, but the dry rasp of his voice was lost in the crack of a shotgun. Then another.

His mind broke open at the sound. He was outside his grandmother's house, lying prostrate on the grass. The fire roared hot wind. *Crack!* He could hear the floor collapse inside. *Crack!* Jasper could hear her crying. She was trapped.

"No!" Jasper flailed his arms and legs, trying to get up and run. A shock of pain in his shoulder made him scream.

"I found one!" a voice called out over the gunshots. The chorus of dying animals grew quieter with each blast.

A pair of hands lifted his head from the mud. From the rush of cold air down his back, he realized he was naked. Another gunshot rang out.

"Stop," Jasper whimpered. He realized he was crying. "Don't shoot her."

"Shh!" the voice murmured.

"Is he alright?" a deeper voice asked. Whoever it was sounded winded. A warm glow floated next to him, shining down at his face. Jasper recoiled from the light.

"I think so. Get me a blanket." It was a woman's voice talking.

A moment later, scratchy wet wool fell all around him. A yelp caught in his throat as strong hands lifted his shoulders off the ground. His arm dangled from his side in an unnatural way, and bolts of pain shot up his arm. He couldn't breathe.

"I'm going to need a board and a wrapping," the woman ordered.

Cold, wet mud seeped into his bare rump as she propped him up. As if she sensed his discomfort, she gently laid his head back down onto a pile of damp cloth. The voices of men shouted a few yards away.

"Grab the head!"

"Get her onto the side. We'll have to break her down here."

"I need a bigger knife."

The wind carried the pungent smell of fresh blood and entrails. He could taste it. Jasper heaved up the contents of his stomach into the puddle as muddled parts of a face appeared in his head. A hairy chin. Wet lips smiling a drunk, sweaty smile. Hot breath on his neck. A pair of hands gripped him. Struggling to escape, he sat pinned on a bouncing knee.

Jasper let out a strangled scream.

"It's okay. It's okay, baby. They're just butchering the cows. That's all. They're beyond our help now."

Jasper forced his eyes open to stop the terrible nightmare in his head. The blackness reeled overhead. Another gunshot fired in the distance. "Why?"

"It was the storm, hon, It picked us all up and threw us back down hard."

Jasper remembered falling from the sky. He seized as though he were plummeting again.

"Shh! Take it easy, baby. Can you feel your legs?" the woman cooed in her hoarse voice.

He turned toward her. In the yellow light of the lantern on the ground, he could only make out the side of her face. Her hair was short and unkempt. A thin scar ran down the length of her cheek. She reached down and patted his forehead gently. *Mom?* he thought again, but he knew it wasn't her.

"I got what you asked for." The man with the bright lantern trotted over with a wood board and an armful of long rags.

The woman had him set the supplies down, then swiftly slid the board under Jasper's back. Together, the two adults rolled him onto his side and began to tie his back and bad arm down to the board. They rolled him flat and straightened his legs out.

"Can you wiggle your toes?" she asked. Not waiting for his response, she ran a fingernail down the middle of each foot until they both twitched. "Good. You're gonna have to stay here a minute until the truck can get in."

The woman stood up to leave. He wanted to yell after her, *Don't go!* But by the time he'd mustered his voice, she'd gone.

In the distance, he heard other panicked calls out over the fields. "Cecil!"

"Mary? Where are you?"

"Eleanor? You out there?"

Tied firmly to his board, all Jasper could do was lie there. Trapped. Turning his head to the side, he saw the field nurse had left her lantern so the truck could find him. The putrid smell of bile and stomach acid spilled onto the ground as a cow was gutted nearby.

"Uncle Leo?" he called out in a weak voice. His lungs felt flooded, but he tried again. "Uncle Leo? Wayne? Are you there?"

Refusing to close his eyes for fear of what he might see, he craned his neck and tried to tell from the shadows of nearby trees and buildings where he was. His uncle's barn and cabin were nowhere in sight. Nothing in the landscape looked familiar. A large silo loomed off on the horizon. None of his uncle's neighbors had a silo.

"Where am I? Hello?" he called out. No one answered. Death was all around him. The air reeked of it. Fear began to squeeze his chest, making it harder and harder to breathe. *They're not dead,* he told himself. *They can't be dead.* He struggled against his bonds to sit up. The pain in his shoulder forced him back down. He couldn't move.

A man's voice breathed in his ear, *Stay down, boy. This isn't going to get any better for you.*

Somewhere far behind him another gunshot rang out.

"Stop it," he whispered, squeezing his eyes shut. The instant he did, he was back in his grandmother's house. The man was laughing.

"Leave me alone," he whimpered and opened his eyes at the black sky. "Make him leave me alone. I'll be good for Uncle Leo and Aunt Velma. I'll do good in school. I promise. I'll make you proud."

He realized he was talking to his mother. For the first time in months, he allowed himself to picture her. The backs of her fingers brushing his cheek. Her breath, warm with whiskey. The way her black hair fell across her forehead and curled around her ear. The beaded necklace hanging down from her long neck as she hovered over his pillow. Her smile . . .

"I'm so sorry, Mom," he wept. "I didn't know what to do. I'm sorry I did everything wrong. Please forgive me. Please." He shouted at the sky for all he was worth. "God, *I'm sorry!*"

The rain kept falling.

CHAPTER 47

Who discovered the body?

Jasper startled awake as two men he didn't recognize lifted him up into the back of a pickup. They laid him flat on his back next to a girl wrapped in a blanket. Her face was caked with dirt and dried blood, and her eyes were shut. He stared at her for several seconds, trying to see if she was breathing. "You okay?" he croaked.

She didn't answer.

The truck lurched forward through the mud. The driver moved slowly over the lumpy ground, and each bump sent fire up his arm. The girl didn't seem to notice. She had long dark hair, and for a dazed moment, Jasper wondered if she had brown eyes too. The black-and-white photograph on a folding table outside Calbry's floated behind his eyes. *Do you know who killed me?*

Jasper turned his head away from her and gazed up at the stars. All signs of the storm had cleared from the night sky. He searched for constellations to keep himself from hyperventilating.

After a quick examination, the nurse at the Burtchville clinic removed the board from Jasper's back. She determined that his shoulder was dislocated. What happened next happened too fast for anyone to argue. An orderly just held him down as still as she could.

The nurse barked, "One . . . two . . ."

Crunch.

Jasper screamed and thrashed against the poor woman.

"Shh! It's over, honey. It's over," she whispered. She held him until he'd quieted down. It was several more minutes before his shaking body could manage to sit up. The nurse wrapped his arm in a sling and told him he'd need to wear it for at least a week. Then she handed him a set of clothes.

"These were donated by the good folks of Burtchville," the nurse said in an apologetic voice as he unfolded a torn set of overalls. "I hope they fit well enough to get you home. Do you know where your folks are, hon?"

Jasper hesitated. From the look on the nurse's face, he could tell he was too young to be released on his own. She would make him stay and wait with nothing to do but think the worst. He had to go find them. He wouldn't let himself consider what would happen if he didn't. "Yeah. They're waiting outside."

Thankfully, things were too frantic at the clinic for her to question his lie. She held the door for him and wished him well.

The hallway was filled with battered people wrapped in bedsheets and blankets. Some were bleeding into red rags. Some were just staring. The sheriff was there in his uniform, talking with one of the survivors. Jasper caught a few words as he walked past with his head down, hoping not to be noticed.

". . . was the worst we've ever seen. State's calling it a category five. We'll be searching a thirty-mile radius for the next several days. You missin' anybody?"

The man nodded his head, but his eyes looked blank. His hand covered half his face. His shoulders were shaking. From the look of him, they were *all* missing.

Jasper scanned the waiting room for Aunt Velma, Uncle Leo, and Wayne. There was no sign of them. He checked again before pushing through the door.

Outside, the sun was rising. The sky glowed golden shades of orange and red as if nothing terrible had happened at all. Jasper found himself hating the sun as it peeked over the edge of the world. It would go on burning, no matter what happened to him or his family or the poor man in the clinic. It simply didn't care. By all rights, the damned thing should have fallen from the sky the day his mother disappeared.

Jasper sighted up and down Lakeshore Road. It was less than three miles up Route 25 to Harris Road. The blinding white pain in Jasper's shoulder had cooled to a dull ache. He could walk it, he decided. He didn't really have a choice.

Besides a few scattered tree branches, the shops and houses lining Lakeshore were untouched by the storm. Jasper wandered past them barefoot, wondering how a storm could tear apart his home and leave these unscathed. *Were these families more loving, more devout, more deserving?*

The sun rose higher in the sky, lighting the few scattered clouds in beautiful shades of silver and gold. If there was a God, he was toying with him, like Lucifer batting around an injured rat.

Jasper reached the top of the hill north of town, and the night's carnage splayed out before him. Uprooted trees and tattered lumber littered the ground where houses had once stood. Pieces of tractors and trucks lay scattered. The foot of a giant had stepped down and crushed everything beneath it.

"My God," Jasper breathed.

The wreckage grew more devastating as he approached his uncle's farm. The younger trees had been ripped from the ground. The older ones stood naked, stripped of their leaves and lighter branches. A signpost that read "Harris Road" was sticking out of the trunk of an enormous tree on the other side of Route 25. He walked over to it and saw the four-by-four post had been driven into the side of the giant maple as though it were a tenpenny nail. Jasper gaped at it, not believing that wind could do that to a tree.

Down Harris Road, he found a man dragging the trunk of a huge oak out of the road with his tractor. He stopped when he saw Jasper coming. "You alright, son?"

"Yes, sir." Jasper put his head down and tried to skirt around the man and his questions.

"I wouldn't head that way if I was you," the man warned. "There's not much left. Where's your family?"

I don't know, Jasper wanted to scream. "They're—um—down there already. I should go help." With that, he scuttled by the tractor and down the road before the man could stop him. A few seconds later, the motor started up again.

Huge tree branches lay strewn across the dirt roadbed like a child's Lincoln Logs. Jasper climbed over and under them as best he could with his bad arm, inching his way back toward the cabin. *They're fine,* he told himself. *Uncle Leo's probably mad I haven't shown up yet.*

He imagined his uncle chiding him. *Just decided to leave all the work for us, that it?*

As he approached Mr. Sheldon's farm, his imaginary conversation with Leo stopped short. Not a single building was left standing. A tractor stood half buried in the mud, its six-foot tires missing, its one-inch steel bolts sheared clean off. Mr. Sheldon and his wife were nowhere to be found.

Uncle Leo's farm was just three hundred more yards down the road.

Jasper raced past Sheldon's wreckage all the way to his uncle's two-track driveway, yelling, "Aunt Velma? Uncle Leo? Wayne? Are you there?"

They didn't answer. The stand of trees that shielded the house in winter had been stripped bare. The cabin was flattened. The roof was nowhere to be seen. The logs that made up the walls lay scattered. Jasper's feet slowed halfway down the drive. "Aunt Velma?"

By some miracle, most of the barn was still standing. Jasper trotted toward it. "Uncle Leo?"

The roof of the barn was half torn off, and the entire structure was listing to the east. As he approached it, he could hear a cow groan. Loose hay covered the ground. The hayloft at the top of the barn had exploded all around him. Jasper ran to the door and tried to pull it open, but it was so badly wracked, it wouldn't budge.

"Uncle Leo?" he shouted through the jammed doorway.

A cow answered. She sounded hurt.

"I'll get you out, girl!" he called back to her. Jasper ran around to the collapsed end of the barn. The end wall that had housed all his uncle's tools had been blown apart. None of the pitchforks or shovels had survived, and Jasper shuddered, thinking of them flying through the air like missiles, landing God knows where. The barn walls leaned over far enough to make him feel dizzy. One stiff wind and the whole place would collapse. Some of the cattle stalls had been sucked open while others were wedged shut. Over half the cows were still in their pens. Jasper didn't want to think about the rest of them.

His family was nowhere to be found.

The barn creaked as a breeze blew by. It was a warning. He had to get the livestock out of there. He ran to the far end where the goats were penned. Several planks of wood had fallen down into the stall. None of the goats could be seen.

"Timmy? Timmy, you in there?" Jasper shouted, lifting one of the boards with his good arm. He kicked it aside along with three more. Under them he found a huddled lump of gray and black hair. Lying on top, a goat's head was smashed with its eyes fixed open. It was Timmy's nanny. He grabbed her by the collar and pulled her off the top of the pile. The other nanny lay under her with her tongue hanging limp. Jasper collapsed to his knees. Timmy wasn't even six months old.

A muffled noise like a child crying made him lift his head. The dead goat was moving. Jasper stumbled back. Its fur was fluttering. Another high-pitched wail came from under it.

"Timmy?" he whispered, not daring to hope it was anything more than his imagination. The sound came again. He grabbed the other dead nag by the neck and lifted her up. Out from under the carcass, a baby goat came scrambling. Jasper pulled the kid loose and wrapped his free arm around his neck. "Timmy! Is that you?"

The baby goat staggered two uneven steps before lying back down. Jasper could see his back leg was broken. He wiped a tear and laughed, showing Timmy his sling. "Aren't we a pair, huh?" He hugged him again and helped him out of the barn.

It took the better part of an hour to get the rest of the animals out and into the yard. Jasper had to wrestle and kick at the wedged stall doors, but he managed to get them all open. He was drenched in sweat by the time he was finished.

The cows were grazing on the grass, stepping between the fallen branches as though it were the most natural thing in the world. Timmy was curled up under a tree that had been stripped of every last leaf. Jasper knelt down next to him and took a breath. In the branches overhead, a bird started singing. Jasper stared up at it for a moment in wonder, realizing he hadn't heard a single bird since the storm had blown in.

Her voice returns to him in the songs of the birds . . .

A cow bellowed across the yard. Udders were hanging like sandbags, and the old girls were starting to complain. He could hear his aunt warning him, *These cows need milking soon or they'll get mastitis.*

Jasper went back to the barn and gathered all the rope and buckets he could find, pushing Dr. Whitebird's riddles out of his head. The bird kept singing while he set up a stool and bucket and started in, roping each cow and milking it dry. After filling two storage containers, Jasper grabbed a spare water dish and filled it up with milk for Timmy.

The road stayed dead quiet the whole while. He gazed up the driveway every few minutes, hoping to see Aunt Velma or Uncle Leo trudging down all banged up. *Maybe they were all at some clinic somewhere getting broken bones set.* He tried not to think of the girl who had been lying so still next to him on the bed of the truck. He had no idea what had happened to her.

When the milking was done, Jasper stepped back into the empty barn to take stock. His uncle's toolbox had spilled out onto the ground. His father would say, *Good tools don't come cheap.* If the barn fell over, his uncle would have a hell of a time getting them out.

He plopped himself down and pulled the box back upright. The upper and center trays toppled out, sending screwdrivers and wrenches spilling to the ground in a metallic avalanche.

"Shit!" he hissed, knowing his uncle would be furious at the sound of his tools hitting the dirt. But it was for the best. He couldn't lift the full toolbox with only one arm anyway. He'd have to carry it out a few pieces at a time. He lifted the trays and tools one by one and carried them over to where Timmy was sleeping all alone under the tree.

Poor Timmy. He patted the kid on the head and told him, "It'll be alright. I'll take care of you. I'm not much of a nag, but—" He knew nothing he said would help.

Jasper gazed up the driveway again at the empty road, then headed back into the barn. As he went to close the lid of his uncle's giant steel toolbox, something at the bottom of it caught his eye. Under his uncle's pipe and tobacco was a small leather-bound book. Jasper reached down and picked it up, not quite believing it was really there. He opened the cover.

Inside, written in a girlish hand, was the name *Althea*.

CHAPTER 48

Why wasn't the murder reported?

Jasper sank down onto the floor of the creaking barn with her diary, not believing it had been right under his nose all those months. Her troubled life tumbled out all over again. Hating the farm, getting caught by Hoyt, running giggle water to Big Bill, driving an empty cart up Door of Faith Road. He hesitated to read the final entries for fear he might throw the book again and lose it for good.

He pressed the diary to his heart, steeling himself, then turned the page.

> *October 1, 1928*
> *There were no deliveries today. Hoyt had me watch his bull and his new heifer Clementine in the breeding pen instead. "You come and get me when he's finished with her," he said.*
>
> *I didn't know what he meant by finished. He had this sly smile on his face like he wanted me to ask, so I didn't.*

Clementine was such a pretty girl, just two years old and tawny brown. Hoyt's bull Pluto is a monster twice her size. I'd never seen what goes on in a breeding pen before, so part of me was curious. The wicked part of me, I guess. Papa always brings our heifers to Mr. Hoyt. After a few days, they come back, but they're not heifers anymore. A year later they're cows.

Mr. Hoyt had tethered sweet Clementine to one of the fence posts. She could take a few steps side to side, but she couldn't turn around. He let Pluto in the pen and then went up to the house, leaving me there to watch.

But I couldn't watch. Not after a minute. Not after I saw what was happening to poor Clementine. I crouched down into a ball, covering my eyes and ears, but I could still hear her crying. It sounded like he was killing her. I can't stop hearing it. My ears are ruined.

When it finally stopped, I just stayed there, crouched in my ball for Lord knows how long. Next thing I knew, Old Hoyt was tapping the top of my head. "I told you to come and get me." He chuckled. When I looked up at him, he seemed real pleased. He was happy I was crying.

Jasper quickly turned the page and scanned the next entry. It was frighteningly brief.

November 7, 1928
Papa's taking Blue Bell to Mr. Hoyt's bull tomorrow. I begged him not to do it. I cried. He called me a silly little girl. Heifers have to become cows or else they get eaten.

"It's better to be eaten," I shouted.

If I had the nerve, I'd kill her myself. My God I wish I did.

I gave her Hoyt's giggle water instead, and I told her not to cry. Only little girls cry and giggle, and we're not little girls anymore, Blue Bell. She didn't want to drink it. I'm so sorry, sweet girl. The burning water will make you feel nothing. Like you're not there at all. Like it's happening to somebody else.

Anybody but you.

The words wove together in loose and uneven ink as though the hand that had written them was half asleep. Or drunk. Jasper flipped to the next page and the next, but they were all empty. A sickness crept into his gut. He slammed the book closed and threw it back into the toolbox. He squeezed his eyes shut and was back in his nightmare, lying on the floor in his grandmother's old house. He could see his mother, pinned down to a filthy bed by a hulking man—

Jasper ground his fists into his eyes to pulverize the image, but he could still hear her crying. He could feel the sweaty breath of the bus driver on his neck. He jerked away from it and covered his ears.

That no-good, filthy, son of a bitch. What did he do, Mom? What did he do to you? Why d—

"Jas—per!"

It was a woman's voice. He stopped breathing and listened, convinced he'd imagined it. That damn bird was still chirping in the yard. A fly buzzed by his ear.

"Jasper?" the voice called again from the driveway. It was his aunt Velma.

"I'm here!" he whispered, then shook himself out of his stupor. He glanced at the diary in the bottom of the toolbox, then trotted out of the open end of the barn to the driveway, calling, "I'm here!"

"Oh, thank God in heaven! There you are!" Aunt Velma ran down the drive and swooped him up into her arms. Pain shot through his shoulder as she squeezed him, but he didn't care. "My sweet Jasper. Let me look at you." She set him back down and took stock of every bump and scrape and the sling wrapped around his arm.

"I'm okay." He tried to smile, but tears came up instead. "Really, I'm alright. Are you okay?"

"Oh, honey. I'm just fine now." Aunt Velma was dressed in a torn yellow dress he'd never seen before. There was a bloodstained bandage on her cheek, and the entire left side of her face was purple. The white of her left eye was red.

"Where are Uncle Leo and Wayne?"

"Out lookin' for you. They're a bit banged up . . . but that's all." She cupped his hands around his face. "The good Lord was watching over us."

Jasper gazed past her at Timmy lying alone under his tree but said nothing about his thoughts on *the good Lord*.

Uncle Leo and Wayne got back to the wreckage of the cabin less than an hour later. Their ill-fitting clothes were splattered in blood. His uncle grinned widely. "Hey, look who's decided to join us, Wayne!"

"Jas! You made it!" Wayne trotted up to him and tugged at his sling. "Some ride, huh? What'd ya do? Break it?"

"Dislocated. What, uh . . ." Jasper gaped at his cousin's crusted red hands. "What happened to you?"

"Oh, this ain't me. Me and Pop had to help a few folks break down cows. So where'd you land?"

"I—I'm not sure."

"I ended up on the other side of Jeddo Road. That twister threw me almost a mile. Ain't that somethin'?" Wayne was doing his best to brag about it, but tears had left tracks in the mud on his face.

Aunt Velma dug the washbasin out from under a pile of fallen timbers and filled it up at the hand pump. The two men stripped down and rinsed the blood off, while she busied herself taking stock of what was left of the kitchen. The woodstove had been thrown clear across the yard.

"Wayne, these flies are going to chew your ass to bits. Go see what you can find to wear." Uncle Leo picked a tattered curtain up off the ground and wrapped it around his waist. It was covered in pink flowers and would have been real funny if it hadn't been for the purple bruises running the length of his body.

Jasper followed his cousin as he picked through the remains of the cabin. The feather mattress the boys shared was nowhere to be seen. The bed frame itself was upended in the garden. The bureau full of their clothes was gone. Wayne found a tablecloth lying in the grass. The wind had ripped it to tatters, but he wrapped it around himself anyway and kept on digging through what was left. Jasper's ill-fitting overalls were suddenly a luxury. He made a motion to offer them to his cousin. Wayne waved him off. His entire back was scraped raw as if he'd been dragged down a gravel road.

"So, how's the arm?" he asked.

"It's alright." Jasper did his best to shrug even though he couldn't really move his shoulder.

Wayne's eyes lit with amusement at the gesture.

"How is it? Out there?" Jasper tried not to stare at the angry rash running down his cousin's spine.

"About like it is in here." Wayne surveyed the mess that was left.

"Stop gabbin', you two." Uncle Leo kicked his way through the rubble to where the boys were standing. "We have a mountain of work to do before nightfall. Jasper, I need you to go survey the yard for whatever you can find. Take the wagon and haul back anything that'll help us get through the night. Wayne, we need to go shore up that barn before it topples over. Jasper, you found my tools?"

"Yes, sir. Most of them, I think." Jasper tried to sound casual about rummaging through the bottom of his uncle's toolbox. His mother's diary was buried back under the old pipe tobacco where he'd found it. Her words were still scrawling through his brain.

Anyone but you.

Jasper turned toward the barn to hide his face.

"Good. When you're done searching, go help your aunt tend to the animals. We've been blessed, boys." His uncle wrapped an arm around each of them.

"Oh, I don't know." Wayne forced a chuckle. "Gettin' pulled out of the house, stripped naked, and thrown into the mud doesn't make me feel so special. How about you, Jas?"

"Hey." Uncle Leo smacked the back of his son's head. "Not many farms still have a barn standing or a pot to piss in. That chicken coop over there looks like nothin' happened at all, so you count your blessings, hear me?"

"Yes, sir," both boys answered.

Jasper did as he was told and walked a circuit around the rubble, dragging a rusted wagon behind him. Dish towels, bedsheets, spoons—items from the house were scattered across the yard like broken Easter eggs. He climbed trees and fought his way through pricker bushes, collecting one item after another and placing them as carefully as he could on the wagon.

When he lifted Aunt Velma's best soup pot up out of the mud, he found his old children's Bible stuck in the muck beneath it. The pitiful consolation prize his mother had left him in the bottom of his suitcase the day she vanished. His worried aunt had placed it up on a shelf to watch over him.

Blue-eyed Baby Jesus smiled up at him from the dirt like it was all a big joke. The tornado, the fire, Mr. Hoyt—all of it. *Everybody's a sinner, Jasper.*

He wanted to pick up smirking Jesus and throw him across the field.

Uncle Leo's words stopped him. *Count your blessings, boys.* He shouldn't be completely ungrateful. He still had family after all. And a pot to piss in.

His eyes found the place on the horizon where his grandmother's house had once stood. Jasper drew in a shaking breath and pulled the wagon onward, leaving Baby Jesus in the dirt.

CHAPTER 49

Murder is quite a serious charge.

Isn't there any other explanation?

The family spent the first night after the storm in the shored-up barn with the animals. They'd laid down what clean straw they could find for beds, and Wayne was stretched out a foot away from Jasper. He could tell from his cousin's breathing he was asleep. His uncle snored in the far stall next to Aunt Velma. They'd been up for over thirty-six hours, and the work of slaughtering animals and gathering their home into piles had rendered them all dead tired. All except for Jasper.

A warm wind whistled through the open end of the barn. His eyes darted between the crossing shadows of mismatched timbers Uncle Leo and Wayne had nailed up wherever they could reach. Scraps of sawn lumber braced the walls against the ground like broken crutches. The whole structure creaked and shuddered with each strong gust, making Jasper flinch. The dull ache in his shoulder was a constant reminder of the storm, and he couldn't shake the feeling he was falling over and over again.

Jasper sat up and took stock of the barn. His wagon of supplies had been wheeled into an open cow stall and inventoried. Broken timbers were stacked near the open end of the barn next to the shadow of his uncle's toolbox. Jasper's eyes fixed on the box. After a moment's hesitation, he slipped out of his makeshift bed and crept over to it.

As he lifted the tool trays out and onto the ground, each clink and clank halted his breathing as he listened for his uncle's snoring to change. Uncle Leo didn't stir. A strong wind hit the side of the barn. A chorus of creaks and groans sent Jasper shrinking into a ball as he braced for impact. But nothing fell. *I'm scared, Mom. I wish you were here.*

He lifted her diary from the bottom of the box and tried to imagine her voice. *Don't be ridiculous, Jasper. Leo would never let his family or his animals sleep in this barn if it weren't safe. Now get your butt to bed, or I'll give you something to be scared about.*

Uncle Leo's tools went back in the box one agonizing clink at a time. Jasper crept back to his makeshift bed and fell asleep, clutching her book to his chest.

The next morning, Jasper woke to the sound of a car engine rolling down the driveway. The morning light was pouring in through the open end of the barn. He was the only one still curled up on the floor. Everyone else was up and out. Panicked, he felt for his mother's diary under the straw.

A car door slammed.

"Christ Almighty," a hoarse voice said from the other side of the barn wall. "Everybody out there alright?"

"Hey, Wendell!" his uncle called from across the yard. "It sure is somethin', isn't it? Folks in town are sayin' it's the biggest storm on record. They counted more than five tornados touchin' down. All my life, I've never heard nothin' like it." His voice grew closer, and there was the sound of a hand clapping a shoulder. "Good to see you."

"I came to help out and to see if everybody . . . Is he—?"

"He's fine. Got knocked around a little, but he's fine. He's still lazin' about in there." A fist pounded the barn wall above Jasper's head. "Why don't you go get him?"

Jasper bolted up and found the book lodged in the straw under his own rear end.

Wendell appeared at the far end of the barn. "You in there, Son?"

"Yes, sir." Jasper tucked the diary into the back pocket of his overalls while making a show of dusting off the hay.

"Let me get a look at ya." The old man hobbled over to his ten-year-old with a wide grin. "I heard the storm parted your hair a bit."

"A bit." Jasper knew he'd never tell him how terrifying it had been. That sort of thing wasn't what men did.

"How long you get to wear that?" Wendell tapped the sling.

"About a week. It's not too bad."

Wendell's pale-blue eyes were glassy with tears that would not be let out. He patted him on the back instead. "We got our work cut out for us today, now don't we?"

"Yes, sir." Between rebuilding the cabin, tending to the animals, and cleaning up the yard, Jasper knew there would be precious little time to sit and read through his mother's handwriting. Or try to remember the sound of her voice.

"Well, quit your daydreamin', and let's get to it!"

The morning bled into the afternoon as they pieced the farm back together again. A couple of distant neighbors showed up around lunchtime with several slabs of beef to thank Uncle Leo and Wayne for their help butchering the cows. Aunt Velma grilled the steaks over an open fire, and they all sat on the floor of the barn for an aftermath feast.

As Jasper poked at his food, his eyes kept wandering to the faces of the two men that had come to help. They were both older, older than his uncle. He found himself wondering if either of them had kept a jug of giggle water up in their hayloft back when his mother was making her deliveries. Maybe they'd spent time up at Black River and had been friends with Hoyt too. *What other secrets were they hiding?*

"You alright, Son?" his father asked. "You've barely touched your steak."

"Sorry. I guess I'm just not . . ." Jasper searched for the right word and gave his father an apologetic shrug. Wendell just patted his knee, and the old man's trembling hand lifted another forkful to his mouth.

After Aunt Velma cleared the plates, Uncle Leo turned to the boys. "Jasper, I need you and Wayne to take the cart and tractor over to Jeddo. Pick up any decent-looking timbers you can find. Got it?"

"Yes, sir," they answered.

Ten minutes later, Wayne was driving the tractor up Harris Road, hauling his cousin in a cart behind him. The engine was too loud to talk over, which was fine with Jasper. He gazed out over the fallen trees toward Hoyt's farm on the other side of the horizon.

After a couple of hours of navigating down roads littered with branches and helping Wayne drag splintered wood onto the cart, the tractor finally turned up Jeddo toward Hoyt's farm. Jasper surveyed the surrounding fields, searching for the man who had ruined his mother. A wide swath of Hoyt's fields had been stripped down to the dirt, but his barn was still standing. "Stop!" Jasper called out.

Wayne cut the engine. "What?"

There weren't any usable pieces of lumber lying nearby, but Jasper didn't care. He jumped down off the cart. "I just want to see if he's alright."

Jasper trotted up the drive to the barn. He'd never talked to Hoyt, having only glimpsed his sagging face through windows and knotholes.

Now that he might have the chance, he had no idea what he'd say. A part of him worried he might just strangle the bastard to death. His feet slowed as he reached the door.

"Hello? Mr. Hoyt?" he called through the tightness in his throat and peeked inside. Nothing but the usual tools and implements lined the walls, but the ropes, crops, saddles, and pitchforks all looked like torture devices hanging in there. Jasper shuddered as he scanned the shadows of the dark barn. He could hear his mother whispering, *Lots of people been known to get hurt in haylofts, Jasper.*

"He in there?" Wayne trotted up beside his cousin and shouted, "Hey there! Mr. Hoyt? It's Wayne Williams. You need any help?"

No one answered.

Wayne let out a low whistle. "Shoot. I'd heard he'd slowed down a bit since his wife died, but man . . . There isn't a cow in here!"

The boys skirted around the side of the barn. Behind it, a fenced pasture stretched all the way down to the creek, separating Hoyt's farm from theirs. They'd run through it on their way to school more days than not and knew it well. It was empty.

The infamous bull, Nicodemus, snorted at them from his ragged holding pen.

"Hey, pal. Not so scary now, are you?" Wayne kicked at his fence. "Where's your papa?"

Nicodemus bellowed, then charged at them. Both boys jumped back despite the fencing.

"Easy there." Wayne chuckled and turned to Jasper. "See? I told you this was the meanest bull in the county."

The enormous black beast let out another snort and brandished his horns at them. He was a killer. Jasper's eyes traced the twenty-foot by twenty-foot pen abutting the pasture. *This is where she sat,* he thought. *This is where he made her watch.*

No one had ever explained to Jasper exactly how a heifer became a cow, or a girl became a mother for that matter, but he'd seen what goes on between goats in his uncle's barn. *We're not little girls anymore, Blue Bell.*

He had to shake off the image of his mother trapped inside the breeding pen with Hoyt. The weight of him pinning her down.

"You alright?" Wayne had seen him flinch.

"Hmm? Yeah. Fine."

"Don't look like he's here. We should be getting back." Wayne shrugged and headed back to the tractor. Jasper gave the pasture one last survey. Something moved over in the grass at the far end. *A hat? Was Hoyt out there mending a fence?*

Then it was gone. As he turned to leave, his eyes fell on the gate separating the bull's pen from the pasture. He glanced back at Wayne adjusting the logs on the cart, then gazed out over the field again.

"God help you, you son of a bitch," Jasper whispered. He leaned over and unlatched the gate.

CHAPTER 50

*The victim has been described as an addict
and a hustler. Would you say that's true?*

Jasper imagined Old Hoyt being chased by Nicodemus through the pasture the whole ride back to Uncle Leo's. The dirty bastard deserved to be gored, but he'd probably just hop the fence if he'd been out there at all. Still, picturing Hoyt scared shitless made Jasper feel just a little bit better. He deserved so much worse.

A car blew past them.

"Hey!" Jasper yelled after it. It was bad manners to pass a tractor that fast. But then it registered that it was the sheriff's cruiser slowing to a stop right in front of his uncle's farm.

Wayne turned to Jasper in the back. He was riding on top of a four-foot stack of boards and logs. "Whatdya think he wants?"

Jasper's mouth went dry. All he could think was that they had found his mother's body. He just shook his head.

Wayne eased their load down the sloped driveway, careful not to jostle loose the wood, while Jasper's eyes stayed locked on the sheriff's car. His uncle, his father, and the sheriff were nowhere to be seen.

Wayne hopped down and motioned him around to the back of the barn. They crept up to their usual spot and listened.

Uncle Leo was talking. "I'm sorry, Cal. I've got a house to rebuild today."

"I understand, Leo. You got your work cut out for you, but I still need to ask a few questions if you'll humor me. Have you seen any strange cars up or down the roads in the last two months?"

"Can't say I have."

"Any strange folks hangin' about? You hear of anybody odd stoppin' in at the Tally Ho or in town?"

"That's more a question for Clint Sharkey, don't ya think?" Uncle Leo sounded annoyed.

"I've talked to Clint. I'm just doin' my due diligence, Leo."

"Hang your due diligence, Cal. Now, what the hell is this all about?"

There was a sigh. Jasper squinted through a knot in the siding and could see the back of a tan hat shaking back and forth. "I tell ya, I never thought I'd see the day in St. Clair County . . . but storms like these are funny things."

"I don't see what's so funny about 'em," his uncle piped up. "This one damn near destroyed half the state."

"Yeah. And it kicked up all sorts stuff when it did."

Jasper braced himself. *They found her.*

"What stuff?" Uncle Leo asked.

"Jim Jenkins found a burlap sack in his back field this mornin'. We found another one in Harding's vegetable patch this afternoon."

"So?"

"So, we're sending them down to a lab in Detroit for analysis, but I can tell you those bags ain't filled with sugar."

"What are you sayin'?"

"I'm sayin' we're gonna need to check your fields, just like we're checkin' all the fields in the county."

"Fine. But what are you sayin', Cal?"

"I ain't sayin' nothin' about nothin' until the narcotics report comes back."

Jasper and Wayne turned to each other with the same question on their faces. *Narcotics?*

His aunt's voice calling from the driveway broke the silence that had fallen inside the barn. "Jasper? Wayne?"

The two boys scrambled away from their hiding spot, ran a wide circuit, and reappeared from behind the tractor. "Yes?"

"Oh, there you are! Jasper, honey, I need you to go walk the back fields and see what else there is. Wayne walk the front." Aunt Velma gave Jasper a worried smile. "Don't try to lift anything too heavy by yourself, you hear?"

"Yes'm," the boys answered. Jasper trotted to the other side of the barn to grab his wagon. The three men walked out to the drive. Jasper skirted around them as they were all shaking hands.

"It'll just take an hour or so," the sheriff was saying.

"Help yourself, Cal. You let us know if there's anything else we can do." Uncle Leo patted the man's shoulder, then headed back to the barn. His father gave the sheriff a nod and followed him.

Jasper kept his head down and pretended not to notice the policeman as he walked past. He recognized Sheriff Bradley's voice from that night at the Tally Ho. The man knew his mother and Big Bill and God knows what else. A second police car pulled into the driveway, and Jasper quickened his pace.

Random objects littered the ground—a shovel, a pitchfork driven over a foot into the ground, a tractor seat. He busied himself surveying the scarred rows of green sprouts in the barley field. He tried to focus on gathering what he could but felt himself drawn toward a stand of trees on the horizon that had somehow survived the storm.

The oaks and maples grew taller as he approached the patch of overgrown grass. Jasper stopped and looked over his shoulder. Sheriff

The Buried Book

Bradley and his man were a half mile away, walking rows of corn, searching for something.

The jolt he'd felt when he saw the police cruiser tremored in his gut. *They still haven't found her body.* He didn't know if he was relieved or disappointed.

The trees stood there waiting. Jasper hadn't visited the place since that night. He avoided it on purpose, taking convoluted routes through the fields to keep wide of his nightmares, but now his feet were drawn there.

Behind the trees, there was nothing left of his grandmother's house but a broken foundation. Charred stones stuck up out of the ground in a rectangular outline of what had once been. He gazed up at the spot where her window had looked out over the fields. Smoke had billowed out through the hole in the roof. He could smell it. Echoes of gunshots still hung in the trees. He reached up and touched the scar on his head. He hadn't fallen through the floorboards like they said.

Jasper sank down to his knees in front of a blackened stone.

"What happened?" he whispered, gripping the book in his pocket. "Were you there?"

"What brings you out here, son?" a voice said.

Jasper lurched up to see a man walking down the hill from the creek. It was Detective Russo.

CHAPTER 51

Did she have any enemies? Abusive boyfriends?

Jasper's mouth opened and shut, but no sound came out.

"I said, what brings you out here? Doesn't your uncle need you back at the house?" The detective cocked a sly grin. He wore a suit and a hat like a traveling salesman, but there was a gun at his hip.

"I—I was just . . . looking for stuff," Jasper stammered. His eyes darted about for a place to hide and came up empty. "I . . . my aunt asked me to go see what I could find from the storm."

The detective looked him up and down, amused at his consternation. "I didn't mean to startle you. Sheriff Bradley said it would be alright if I poked around. I'm looking for something too."

Jasper scanned the fields again for the sheriff and his deputy.

Detective Russo walked over to him and appraised the foundation of the old house. "It was quite a doozy of a storm, wasn't it? Blew half of St. Clair County off the map. Was this here blown away too?"

Jasper could tell he already knew the answer. "No, sir. It burned down."

"Really?" The detective raised his eyebrows. "When?"

Jasper shrugged the best he could with a busted shoulder. "I don't know. A year ago."

"How'd it burn down?"

He could feel the man's eyes drilling through him and turned away.

"What's wrong, son? It's not a hard question."

"Sorry, it's just that . . ." A lantern exploded in his head. "It was all my fault."

"Your fault?" The detective sounded surprised. "What happened?"

"I was snooping around in the old house, and I lit a lantern . . ." His mother had been holding it. He could see her plain as day, motioning him into her arms. Tears gathered at the thought, but he shook it away. It couldn't be right. "It, uh . . . and I knocked it over."

"Oh I see." The detective patted him on the shoulder. "That must've been very scary for a young boy—burning down a whole house. I bet your uncle was none too pleased."

Jasper blinked his eyes clear. "Yes, sir."

"Well, we all make mistakes, Jasper. The key is to learn from them." The detective squatted down on his haunches like they were about to discuss a football play. He was pretending to be his friend, but Jasper could tell he just wanted to get a closer look at him. "Now, you understand that lying to me would be a terrible mistake. Don't you, son?"

"Yes, sir." Jasper didn't like the way the man smiled at him. He took a step back.

"Not so fast." The detective grabbed his arm. "Who else was inside the house with you?"

"Sorry?" Jasper wanted to kick him in the groin and run. His eyes darted over the fields. The sheriff was nowhere in sight.

"You couldn't have been by yourself. You'd have only been, what? Seven years old?"

"I was nine," Jasper whispered. He'd always been small for his age, but he'd been old enough to know better. *It was my fault. I wasn't supposed to be there.*

"Right. So . . . who else was inside with you?"

"No one." Jasper could tell the man didn't believe him. He didn't believe it himself anymore.

"What were you doing in a house all by yourself?"

"I woke up early and . . ." He'd gone looking for his mother. Jasper searched for words that wouldn't betray her. She'd been hiding from Big Bill and Galatas and God knows who else. He risked a glance into the detective's hard eyes and quickly looked away. "I just got bored, I guess. I shouldn't have gone snooping."

"Bored, huh? You're lucky you didn't get yourself killed." It sounded like a threat.

"Yes, sir." Somewhere out there the sheriff was searching the fields. If he ran away screaming, maybe the detective would hesitate. He tensed his legs.

As if he could sense the boy's plan, the detective tightened his grip on his arm. "Where is your mother, Jasper?"

"What?" He tried to wrench his arm free, but it wouldn't budge.

"Where is she?"

"She's—she's gone."

"Where did she go?" Detective Russo demanded.

"I don't know, sir."

"You must know something, damn it. Where is she?"

She's dead! he wanted to scream. Instead, he just shook his head.

"I know this has been hard on you, kid, but you need to tell me what you know."

"I don't know *anything*!" Jasper cried, letting his arm go limp. "I'm just a kid. Nobody tells me anything."

"Damn it, Althea!" The detective let go of him and shook his head. "I'm sorry, kid. I hate to have to do this."

"Do what?" Jasper staggered several feet back. "Are you going to take me away? Is that why you're here?"

The detective sighed but didn't answer the question. "We were supposed to meet. She had something for me. Something very important. Do you know what I'm talking about?"

Jasper shook his head again.

"We had a deal. Then the next thing I know, one of my prime suspects blows up his car and she disappears like a goddamn ghost. We've been looking for her, high and low, for months. Damn it, she's been toying with me this whole time. We were so close to blowing the doors off this thing."

Jasper was hardly listening. His brain had ground to a halt.

"A lot of lives are going to be ruined if I don't find her, Jasper. A lot of lives. And now that this damn storm came through . . . I don't know if I can stop it. I need your help."

"What?" The man was obviously a lunatic. The trees were only ten feet away. Jasper took a step toward his escape route. "Why can't you just leave me alone?"

"You need to let me know if you see her. If you see or hear anything, I won't be far. Okay?" The detective dropped his voice to a gentler tone and smiled. "We don't want anything to happen to her. Do we?"

CHAPTER 52

If she had evidence of some sort of conspiracy, why wouldn't she go to the police?

The detective disappeared over the hill. Jasper watched until he was gone, then stumbled into the stand of trees. The man hadn't dragged him away to an orphanage or jail, but he could still feel his hand clenching his arm.

We don't want anything to happen to her, do we? The detective's warning repeated in his head. Jasper sank down with his back against a giant oak and cried.

She's gone, goddammit! And she's not coming back. File her under "Dead." His father had screamed it at the top of his lungs.

Jasper wiped his tears, then pulled the diary out of his pocket. *What does he want from me, Mom? Why did you have to die? I need you.*

He leafed through the book again, searching for any sign at all, forcing himself to read her last words again and again. *Anyone but you.* The last twenty pages were empty, but he searched them too.

"Jasper? What the hell are you doin' up here?" his uncle's voice boomed through the trees.

Jasper dropped the book. He jumped up and tried to block his uncle's view of it lying on the ground. "Sorry, I guess I just . . ."

"The rest of us are out workin' our tails off, and you're just sitting here on your duff? Didn't you hear your aunt callin'?" He could tell by the hard line of his face that Uncle Leo was in no mood for long explanations.

"Yes, sir. I'm sorry."

"Whatdya got there?" His uncle pointed to the ground behind his feet.

"No— nothin'. Just this uh . . . book. I was out doin' a sweep and found it right over there." Jasper pointed to a random spot in the field.

"Give it here." His uncle held out his hand, leaving Jasper no choice in the matter.

He picked the diary up off the ground and handed it to his uncle. "Why you standing there lookin' like somebody died? Git!"

Jasper knew he'd better run back to his wagon, but he hesitated for two seconds too long. His uncle grabbed him by the collar.

"You've been reading this nonsense?" he demanded, waving the open book in Jasper's face.

"Um . . ." Lying would only make it worse. "Yes, sir."

"Don't go believing a thing in here, ya hear me? She wasn't right in the head back then, making up all sorts of stories."

"What do you mean, not right in the head?" Jasper whispered.

"None of your goddamned business. That's what I mean. This book is not for you to read. I should've burned the thing months ago."

"But why did she—"

"Stop." His uncle held up a hand. "I don't want to hear another word about it. She's caused enough trouble for one lifetime. The last thing you need is to go snoopin' around in her mess. If you want answers, go read your Bible."

"But . . ." His uncle was going to burn it if he didn't say something. "They don't seem like lies! What happened to her?"

"I told you—"

"She's my mother!" Jasper shouted over him, not quite believing he was raising his voice to the man. "I need to know what happened to her."

"What do you want to know, huh?" he roared back. "You want to know how she went crazy and ran away from home? You want to know how she came back drunk and reeling, screaming a bunch of nonsense, and burned our house down? Or how she wrecked our family's reputation and my father hung himself? How my mother died of a broken heart? You want to know how she disappeared for ten years and we all thought she was dead or in prison? Is that the sort of thing you want to know, Jasper?"

The boy just stood there dumbstruck.

"Goddamn it!" his uncle shouted up at the sky. He swept a hand across his mouth as if to wipe away his last several words, and then he leaned down and grabbed Jasper by the chin. "Forget all that, Jasper. You're the best thing that miserable woman ever did. Don't mess that up for her. Just let it go. It's the only thing you can do to help her now. Understand?"

Jasper nodded but couldn't look his uncle in the eye. The man hated her, and maybe he was right. She'd left her own son to die on the farm she hated. She'd up and disappeared. Her father died because—

"Good. Now get yourself together and get your ass back to the house." Leo stormed off toward the barn with Althea's diary in his hand, leaving Jasper alone in the woods with black-and-white thoughts of his grandfather swinging from a noose.

Everything about her was a lie.

The only thing he knew for certain anymore was that she'd gotten mixed up with criminals like Big Bill and Galatas. *Who do you think ran the stills when making liquor was against the law?* Mrs. Babcock's voice asked him again. *Gangsters, killers, and thieves.* And she was one of them. The police were still after her.

But she's dead . . . isn't she?

The thought brought Jasper back to his feet. He scanned the trees and creek bed behind him for Detective Russo. Every shadow had eyes. The specter of his grandmother's house loomed behind the tall oaks, watching him.

I won't be far.

CHAPTER 53

Do you know much about law enforcement

on tribal lands?

The two sheriff's department cruisers were gone when Jasper dragged his half-empty wagon up the driveway. Uncle Leo and his father were up on the roof of the barn, pounding boards back into place. Wendell gave the boy a small wave as he approached, but his uncle kept on hammering nails as if he weren't there.

Aunt Velma was inside pulling together a makeshift kitchen in a cow stall when Jasper came through the door. "Well, there you are. You find anything good out there?"

"Not too much yet," Jasper mumbled. He'd forgotten all about his searching duties. "I still have a lot of looking to do. I—uh . . . Uncle Leo said you wanted to see me?"

She glanced up at him and stopped scrubbing the pot in her hand. "My goodness, Jasper! You look terrible. Is everything alright?"

His aunt had a way of seeing right through him, and he hated it. "I'm fine," he lied. "Did you want to see me about something?"

She read his eyes but decided not to probe deeper. "I need you and Wayne to take the cart into town. We're short on all sorts of supplies. Here's a list. Tell Calbry's to put it on our account."

Jasper took the scrap of paper from her hand and pretended to read, but all he could think about was the detective out in the fields and that terrible night he could only seem to remember in nightmares. His mother had been there. She had been holding the lamp. The more he thought about it, the more certain he became. He strained to see her face, the way it had looked. She had been smiling.

Wayne burst through the door. "Cart's all set. We ready to go? That the list?" He snatched it from Jasper's numb hand and gave it a quick read.

"And why don't you two swing by some of the neighbors' and see if anybody needs anything, alright? Just be home by sundown." Aunt Velma stopped washing dishes to kiss each of them on top of the head and wipe a stray tear. "Look at me gushin' over you two. Silly woman. I'm just so glad you boys are alright . . . Okay. Go on."

Wayne manned the driver's seat, and Jasper rode the rear axle as the tractor pulled down Harris toward Lakeshore. The older boy slowed the engine as they passed by the wreckage of Sheldon's farm, scanning the fields for the man.

"Shoot," his cousin said to himself. "I hope you made it out alright, Sheldon."

Jasper followed Wayne's gaze over the collapsed barn, but his mind wasn't on Sheldon. When the tractor slowed to a stop at Lakeshore, he said, "Would it be alright if we went and checked on the reservation. I'm—um . . . I'm worried about Dr. Whitebird."

Wayne glanced up the road toward Black River and then down toward town. "I'm not sure we've got the time."

"But Aunt Velma said to check on the neighbors, and I still owe the doctor for all his help," Jasper pleaded. It was the truth. He owed the man his life and the price of his mother's necklace. His eyes fell, thinking of her favorite piece of jewelry. He'd lost it that awful night. "Please, Wayne. I need to . . . I need to see if they're alright."

Wayne held his eyes for a moment and said, "Okay, Jas. We'll go see. But I don't think you're going to find what you're lookin' for."

The older boy turned the tractor north up Route 25 five miles. Jasper held on to the fender with his one good arm; the other rattled uncomfortably in its sling as Wayne cranked the engine into top gear.

The hidden narrow drive that led up the hill to the clinic had been laid bare by the storm. Trees and bushes were mowed down by a giant rake, but the signpost his mother had described in her diary that read "Door of Faith" was nowhere to be seen. Naked pines dotted the ridge as Wayne pulled the tractor up to where the clinic had once stood.

"Will ya look at that," Wayne whispered as they crested the hill and saw what was left. The roof and windows had been ripped from the cinder blocks. A tree had crushed the back corner of the building. Papers and broken glass littered the ground.

Jasper hopped off the axle. "Dr. Whitebird?" he called, running to the entrance. The door had been blown from its hinges, and he ran through the opening into a wreckage of roof rafters and tree limbs.

"Jasper! Get your butt back here!" Wayne called after him.

Jasper didn't listen. He pushed his way up and over broken timbers, through the waiting room to the back examination areas, banging his bad arm every few feet as he went. The back room where he'd spent several delirious nights had been flattened by an enormous tree trunk. "Dr. Whitebird?"

There was no answer but Wayne shouting from the doorway, "He's not here, dummy! Get out before something falls on you!"

Jasper turned back toward the entrance. Sun poured in through the collapsed sections of roof. He gazed up at a piece of sky framed in broken rafters. It was the same view from the attic of his grandmother's house. The sky had been pink that morning.

The sound of his cousin hollering at him outside snapped Jasper back to the present.

The walls of the clinic hallway had fallen over, giving him odd-angled glimpses into each examination room and a small filing closet full of crushed and upended cabinets. He climbed over the fallen wall to the piles of paper spilled onto the floor. The records mixed together with the different names scrawled across the top. He ripped through the sheets, searching for Althea Williams, Althea Leary, Thea. None of them were there.

Scattered under the papers were photographs of a girl. Her body was laid out on a table, naked and bruised. Dark marks and dried blood dotted her breasts and stomach. Crushed bones and dried blood distorted her face. Jasper picked up a picture with shaking fingers. Her dark-brown eyes stared back at him—dead.

Do you know who killed me?

"Hey!" Wayne's voice boomed behind him. "What the heck are you doing in here?"

Jasper dropped the photo and struggled to find his voice. "Nothing. I just thought, maybe . . ."

Wayne looked over his shoulder at the pictures. "Jesus Christ! Who the hell is that? We shouldn't be in here! C'mon!"

Wayne dragged Jasper out of the wreckage of the clinic. He was going to be sick. He doubled over at the knees.

"Shake it off, kid." Wayne slapped him on the back. "It wasn't her. It was just some girl . . . I don't know. We should just get out of here."

"No!" Jasper bolted up and took off running down the path he'd walked with Pati down to the game house. The trailers and campfires they'd passed months earlier were all gone. Most of the tiny houses had been flattened. Jasper stopped and surveyed the vacant sites.

"We ain't got time for this, Jas." Wayne marched up to where his cousin stood bewildered. "We gotta go."

"I have to keep looking," Jasper nearly shouted. "I have to—"

"Shh!" Wayne hissed and grabbed him by the bad arm, pulling him down to the ground.

"Ow!" Jasper yelped and pushed his cousin back.

"Quiet! Somebody's here."

Jasper followed Wayne's gaze to the horizon. Several hundred yards ahead of them, two cars were parked next to what had once been the game house. The barn had collapsed into scattered boards.

"I don't think they saw us," Wayne whispered.

"You don't think who saw us?"

"Those men out there." He pointed to two small figures emerging from the woods surrounding the flattened barn. One was carrying a large sack. He walked over to one of the cars and set it down in the trunk.

"I wonder if them's the same bags Sherriff Bradley was goin' on about," Wayne whispered. "Let's go see if we can get a closer look."

"Are you crazy?" Jasper hissed back. He could see even from a distance that they were white men, and he knew from Pati that white men on the reservation were a dangerous thing. "I thought you said we had to get back."

"Don't you want to help Sheriff Bradley get to the bottom of all this?" Wayne winked at him. "C'mon, Tonto! If we get caught, we'll just say we're looking for the doctor. It's the truth, ain't it? You got a busted arm and everything."

With that, Wayne pulled him into the trees.

CHAPTER 54

What can you tell me about drug trafficking
and prostitution at Black River?

The two boys crept up behind a fallen tree twenty yards from where the two men were arguing. Wayne squinted at their license plate numbers like a good deputy while Jasper listened.

"I don't know what else to tell you, Perry." The taller man in a tan suit held up his hands at the shorter man. "You have to get out."

"I appreciate your concerns, Charles." The shorter man rubbed his face for a moment.

Jasper recognized him from the roller rink. It was the same man who had talked with Not Lucy at the diner and ran the dairy where his mother worked.

"My whole life I've been told to get out," Perry Galatas said in his thick accent. "When I came to this country, I came with nothing. I worked thirty years to build this business for my family. Thirteen grandchildren I have. Every step of the way, someone tells me to get out. First the Irish, then the Italians, and now you. This is my home. I am not going anywhere."

"They're going to kill you, Perry. You owe too much."

"I have owed before." Galatas chuckled. "You and me. We get it back."

"How?" The tall man shook his head. He turned, and Jasper could see a gold star pinned to his lapel. "In case you didn't notice, forty sacks have been scattered across the damn state. The county sheriff has logged the evidence. I can't contain this!"

"Of course you can, Charles. I have much faith in you." Galatas patted him on the back. "Build a federal case against these wild peoples. They are trafficking in narcotics on this reservation and across state lines. It is your jurisdiction. Request all the evidence be returned to you. This is how it works. Yes?"

"It's a little more complicated than that, Perry."

"But it will make a famous case for you. The newspapers will love this story of our brave US marshal bringing these savages to justice." Galatas straightened the man's jacket and tie for him, brushing dust from his shoulders. "They've ruined our young people with these terrible drugs. And it's not just the Negroes that get addicted anymore. It is our own daughters. Don't you see? It is perfect."

The officer took a step back. "In case you haven't noticed, there aren't any savages left to arrest! They've been crossing the border for months. What did you think would happen when you cut off their supplies? I told you you'd go too far, and you did. I can't help you, Perry. At least now I can explain the desertion." He motioned to the wreckage left by the storm.

"Ah, you give up too easy." The short man waved a hand at him. "This chaos can help us both. Who is to say who lives here now in all this confusion? We can find more Indians. I will throw a big feast with booze and girls. They will be happy to come."

"It won't work, Perry. The sheriff's already contacted Detroit. You're under investigation and you know it."

"This is my worry, not yours. They have nothing on me. Not one scrap of paper. My lawyers will keep them busy for years . . . We need to stay focused. Our friends in Mexico deserve our best efforts to get their product back." Galatas gazed out at the farmland beyond the trees.

Jasper and Wayne hit the dirt.

"Think of these poor farmers, Charles. They have been through so much. They do not need sheriffs poking through their fields and their lives. I came from such a place. It is a hard life. Why should they suffer more? They have been forced to live all these years alongside these wild peoples. They deserve better. Bring them justice, Charles."

"Justice? Even Indians get a trial, Perry. And they'll be tried in a federal court. There aren't enough bribes in the world to manufacture the witnesses. How would we even link them to your friends in Mexico?"

Galatas shrugged. "You are the only witness that matters as far as these savages are concerned. Our brave federal marshal comes to break up this wild party of Indians during the investigation. They become violent as these peoples do. There is gunfire . . . You understand?"

The tall man shook his head. "What about her?"

Jasper sat up at this. Wayne grabbed his arm and pulled him back to the dirt.

"What about her? She's been taken care of."

"I never saw a body. Did you?"

"I trust my nephew. Poor William, may he rest." Galatas made the sign of the cross over his chest.

Poor William. Big Bill's sedan exploded into a fuel tank in Jasper's mind.

"Either way, it does not matter. No one would listen to such a woman. And if they did, we have all the leverage we need."

"I wish I shared your confidence. Russo's in town, you know."

"He has no jurisdiction here. This is not Detroit. I will take care of him."

The tall man sighed. "You need to take care of yourself, Perry. If this goes down wrong, I don't know you. Do you understand?"

"Ah, but I know you, Charles Andrew Duncan. I know where you live. I know where your kids go to school. I know how much of my money you've been hiding . . . You do not want to make an enemy of me. Now go. Find a way to get me back my heroin." With that, Galatas climbed into his Cadillac and cranked the engine.

Jasper turned to Wayne with alarm. *The tractor,* he mouthed. They had left it out in the open by the clinic. Wayne's eyes darted back the way they'd come, calculating whether he could make it back in time.

They didn't see the man crouched behind them until it was too late.

An enormous hand clamped over Jasper's mouth. Another knocked Wayne to the ground. A voice hissed, "Don't move."

CHAPTER 55

What can you tell me about Perry Galatas?

The side of Jasper's face pressed into the dirt as the weight of the man crushed his chest and wrenched his shoulder. He couldn't breathe. Wayne wrestled against the ground next to him, not budging the massive bulk pinning them down. They were helpless.

The sound of a car engine rumbled away. Several agonizing seconds passed until the second car drove off and their assailant finally released them.

Wayne sprang up and landed a wild punch right in the man's neck. Unfazed, their attacker just grabbed the boy's wrist and held him squirming like a hooked fish. "Easy there, coyote," the giant warned.

"Motega?" Jasper croaked, focusing his dazed eyes. "Is that you?"

The man glowered at Jasper. "Why are you here?"

"Uh, we just—I wanted to see if . . ."

"Do you know what you have done? This was my chance. And now it is gone."

"Your chance to do what?" Wayne wrenched his arm free and staggered back. There was a pistol tucked into the waistband of Motega's jeans.

"Galatas never comes here. He may never come here again. And now he's gone." Motega muttered something else in his own language and rose to his feet. "I moved your tractor to the other side of that hill. Go home, zhaagnaash. Go home and don't come back."

"Wait!" Jasper called after him. "Where is everyone? Where is Dr. Whitebird?"

"The people are free to go wherever they please. This is not a prison. Not anymore." Motega kept walking. "Black River was poisoned by that beast Galatas and his filth."

"What filth? What do you mean?"

Motega stopped at the top of the ridge. He gazed out through the woods over the fields of corn and barley lying to the west. The ordered squares of green and tan were scarred with shattered barns and upended tractors. He turned to Jasper and asked again, "Why did you come?"

Jasper could feel the tears building behind his eyes and blinked them away. "I—I don't know what she's done or why . . . I just need to find her."

Motega studied the foolish boy, standing there a full foot below his shoulder, and nodded as if he understood. "I once said those same words."

"You did?"

Motega didn't answer the question. "Dr. Whitebird worries you are too young. White children are not told the stories of your mothers and fathers. The dark stories. These are kept silent. The lies they tell instead become sacred." He glanced over Jasper's shoulder toward Wayne and added, "You are a very strange people."

"But I want to know the truth," Jasper protested. "No one will tell me."

"And what if you do not like this truth? What will you do then?" Motega studied him closely.

Jasper didn't have an answer. Horrifying pictures of a dead girl were still scattered on the floor of the clinic. His mother might've suffered a similar fate. The truth might be worse than his nightmares.

"Perhaps you are too young."

"No, I'm not!" he yelled. "I need to know where she went. I need to know why she left. I need to know if she's . . . if she's really dead. Not knowing is worse than anything you could tell me."

Motega studied both boys closely and pressed his mouth into a grim line. "Come with me."

They followed the Indian nearly a mile past the wreckage of the game house through the woods in silence. Wayne stole worried glances at Jasper the whole way, but the younger boy kept his eyes on the ground until they reached a clearing between the trees. The ground was dotted with mounds of earth. Sprays of wildflowers covered the uneven ground in purples and pinks.

Motega stopped beside a large tree where a makeshift wood cross stood in the ground. It was the only marker in the clearing. Jasper blinked at it with confusion for a moment until he realized. It was a grave.

His mother's necklace hung from the wood.

Jasper dropped to his knees and lifted the beaded pendant off the cross. The two boards tied together were weathered and gray. There was no name. Jasper felt himself falling through the sky again.

Mom?

Wayne's voice sounded far away. "Whose grave is this?"

Motega knelt down next to Jasper and put a hand on his back. "She was your sister."

The words barely registered as Jasper's stomach plummeted to the ground.

"She died last year," Motega continued. "She was only sixteen when they killed her."

"My—? Wait . . . What?" Jasper didn't have a sister. The grave marker didn't even have a name. "No. She couldn't be . . . She's not."

"She is."

"But if she's my sister, why is she here?"

Motega lowered his head. "Because she was my daughter."

Wayne plunked down next to a dumbstruck Jasper. "You and Aunt Althea?"

"Eya." The memory of a smile pulled at Motega's lips. "It was young love be . . . No one was pleased by this. My father would not permit us to marry. He said she had too many bad spirits, but it was because of her pale skin. She wasn't one of us. I should never have listened to him . . ."

"When the hell did this happen?" Wayne demanded on Jasper's behalf.

"Your mother was fifteen when she came to live with us. Your grandfather was furious with her. Her belly grew with child, but she had no husband. He threw her out. I found her bleeding in these woods. There were cuts here and here." Motega motioned to his wrist and his stomach.

Jasper stared at Motega's belly and remembered the scars he'd seen when he opened her bedroom door.

"Who was the father?" Wayne demanded.

"It was not me." Motega held up his hands in his own defense. "It is baataamo to make a mother so young. She had been taken by a white farmer. May he pay dearly for his crime."

Hoyt, Jasper thought. *It was that bastard Hoyt.*

"The baby died before it was born." Motega gazed over the mounds of dirt. "Dr. Whitebird said she was too wounded for its spirit to grow. My father said to turn her away. She was not our tribe. Even her own people did not want her. But I could not . . ."

"So what happened to her?" Wayne asked.

"Dr. Whitebird took her into his house to heal. We became friends. She grew up here, working odd jobs with no parents to watch over her . . . and then." Motega let out a heavy sigh. "I should have let her be. I thought I could make her happy. By the time our baby came, the bad spirits had taken their keep. She would not get out of bed. She would not eat. Dr. Whitebird did his best for her, but some wounds do not heal."

Jasper gazed at the cross and remembered the way his mother would look out the window sometimes like she had left the room.

"She would drink the firewater until she couldn't remember her name. She would run away, a frightened deer." Motega frowned and opened his hands as though she'd fallen through them. "There was never a place far enough to run to. She'd come back on her own sometimes. Sometimes I would find her. But she could never stay . . . She never forgave me."

"She never forgave you for what?" Wayne demanded, itching for a fight. "What did you do to her?"

"It is Manitonaaha law that a child belongs at the hearth of her father. Althea, she was twenty-two but still a wounded girl. She would get drunk and she'd . . . we couldn't let her be alone with the baby. My mother took Ayasha in as her own. My daughter needed a home, but Althea screamed that we had stolen her. She never forgave me or my family. And poor Ayasha . . ."

A faded memory fought its way to the front of Jasper's mind. He could hear the knock on the door again. *Who's there?*

"She came looking for her once," he whispered.

This made Motega stop talking.

"One night she knocked on our door. I was all alone . . ." Jasper remembered seeing her pleading brown eyes through the peephole. *Is your mother home?* "I didn't open the door. I told her that my mom was asleep, because I wasn't supposed to tell strangers my parents weren't home. She got so angry she started shouting and pounding the door to wake her up. I didn't know what to do. I hid under my bed until she went away. Mom found me sleeping there. She said it was just a bad dream."

"How many years ago was this?" Motega asked softly.

Jasper wiped a tear. "I don't know. I was really little, and I thought my mom was right. I thought it was just a dream."

He stared at the ground where his sister was buried. His mother could never seem to hug him for long. Her eyes were haunted by something. He thought of Hoyt's dark barn and hung his head.

"How'd she die?" Wayne motioned to the unmarked grave.

"It started the day she took her first drink and put that filth in her body. Then more filth. I should've seen it coming. I should've known. By the time I saw her sickness, she was already a slave to their drugs and to the white men that brought them here. In the end, she was . . ." Motega's jaw and fists tightened. "Galatas will pay the price of her head if our paths ever meet again."

The photos in the clinic flashed again. Dried blood. Broken bones. Jasper put his head in his hands. *Do you know who killed me?* The girl with the dark eyes in the picture outside Calbry's was his sister. His eyes fixed on the grave, and the world tilted beneath him.

"The Manitonaaha attacked the game house the night they dumped Ayasha at the clinic. We vowed to force the white men and their poisons off our lands." Motega lifted his shirt to show a collection of round scars on his torso that could only be the spray of a shotgun. "We failed. I woke up in the marshal's jail while Galatas burned the fields."

Wayne's eyes widened. "How'd you get out?"

"Althea. She paid my bail. She wanted to get a lawyer and bring Galatas to justice. She went to her police in Detroit. I tried to tell her there's only one justice, but she never listened to me."

Jasper remembered the smoke on the horizon the day they had driven down Route 25, the redness of her eyes, her shaking hands. "That's why she left."

Motega steadied Jasper's shoulder. "She did not want to leave you."

"Yes, she did," he whispered. "She was always leaving me . . . she never wanted me at all."

Motega shook his head. "She wanted you. After my mother took Ayasha, she disappeared into the dark alleys of the city. I thought I'd never see her again, that the streets would kill her. I had to turn away. But then, many years later, you came along. She wanted you and a family more than anything. More than firewater. More than money. More than me . . ." The man dropped his voice at those words. He glanced back up at Jasper and forced a smile. "You are her heart. You brought her back."

"He's right," Wayne piped in. "Pop says she didn't come back home until you were born."

"Then why didn't she tell me any of this? How could she let this happen? How could she work for Galatas?"

"Try to understand. Althea had no family of her own. Always she was looking. For a father. For a home. She was a lonely shadow, living in between, which made her very useful to bad men. Galatas was very kind to her. He coiled around her like a snake."

Jasper bit his lip at this, not sure he wanted to know more.

"He pulled her off the streets and promised her a real life. She could speak our language. She knew the elders. He used her to build his business here, gambling and smuggling. He said he would help us. After the profits from our stills dried up, our people were starving. It was supposed to bring us food." Motega motioned to the graves. "This is what it brought in the end."

Jasper hung his head in shame. "I'm so sorry."

"Do not blame yourself, Jasper. My father made this treaty with Galatas, not you, not your mother. We put his boot on our own necks when we took his money. We invited these bad spirits." Motega bowed his head and whispered something in his own language.

"But I didn't invite any of this! I just . . ." But a nagging voice in his head reminded him he had gone looking for her. In the silence that fell on the grave between them, he could hear her crying. He could feel the heat of his grandmother's house burning to the ground. He could see her in the lamplight smiling at him. And then—

Hot breath laughed in his ear. *Sorry, little champ. You're not invited to this party.* Jasper flinched.

"Hey, Jas? You alright?" Wayne nudged him.

Jasper whispered, "It was me. I killed her."

"No," Motega's voice boomed. "You did not kill anyone. I promise you."

"But the lamp . . . ," Jasper breathed. "I started the fire."

"It was an accident, Jas," Wayne protested. "Nobody blames you. You're just a kid."

Jasper shook his head. "It was me. I can't remember, but I know it was me."

"No. You saved her life . . . I am forever in your debt, ningozis."

Jasper gazed up at Motega, and the pain written over his face. He could see the man had loved her once and maybe still did. "Then tell me where she is."

CHAPTER 56

Why would federal officers protect
a known crime syndicate?

Jasper stared blankly at his plate all through dinner. No one sitting around the campfire seemed to notice. They were too busy balancing their own plates across their laps. They'd had no luck finding the kitchen table.

"Wendell, you look like you could use a beer," Uncle Leo announced from the other side of the fire. "Let's you and me go down and visit the tavern. Whatdya say?"

"I suppose buyin' a round is the least I could do." Wendell flashed a tired smile at Jasper and tousled his hair. "Thanks for lookin' after him, Leo. I don't know what I would've done . . ."

Jasper attempted to smile back but couldn't. He'd been hollowed out. Photographs of his dead sister scattered across his mind. He wished he'd never met Motega or seen the grave or found his mother's diary. Dr. Whitebird was right—he should have stayed up in his tree.

Wendell was still talking. "I'll call in and cancel work tomorrow. We need to get a start on that cabin."

The two men cleared their plates in short order and headed up the driveway.

An hour later, Jasper and Wayne piled up blankets and towels on the floor of their cow stall by candlelight. Neither of the boys spoke of what they'd seen or heard. Aunt Velma opened the stall door and kissed them both good night.

When she'd retired to her end of the barn, Wayne sat up and whispered, "What the heck did Motega mean when he said, 'Look inside yourself and you will find her?' What kind of answer was that?"

Jasper didn't say anything. He just stared up at the patchwork roof hanging over them, replaying everything the man had told him. *She gave me the necklace and asked me to bury it with Ayasha. She said she did not deserve it anymore. I'm sorry I cannot tell you where she went. Do not lose hope, my friend. There is a bond between you. You must look inside yourself, and you will find her.*

What if I can't? he'd asked on the verge of tears.

Then you are not ready.

Wayne eventually gave up on the conversation and rolled over. Jasper could tell by his breathing that he wasn't asleep, but his cousin let him be just the same. The shock of discovering a bastard cousin was enough scandal for Wayne to chew on for years. Jasper had sworn him to secrecy, but he could almost hear the wheels turning in the older boy's head.

The full moon shone in through a hole in the roof as he turned the words over and over in his mind. *Look inside yourself.* More riddles. Motega seemed to be saying he already knew the answer. Jasper racked his brain over and over, going through every clue and conversation he'd overheard.

But there was so much he didn't remember.

Jasper squeezed his eyes shut and tried. He tried to put himself back in his grandmother's house the night it burned down. His mother's face in the lamplight. The smell of the smoke. The black boots. Hands gripping his shoulders. The sound of her screaming while—

Jasper bolted upright, his heart racing.

Next to him, Wayne had started to snore. The barn was quiet except for the sounds of the cows chewing. And breathing. He could feel hot breath in his ear, a gruff laugh. He slapped it away with his hand, and his eyes circled the barn, searching for anything to block it out.

The children's Bible leaned against the wall next to him. Someone had found it in the yard and wiped away the mud, leaving a shadowy brown stain smeared across the smiling face of Baby Jesus. *Aunt Velma,* he figured. *Count your blessings, boys.*

But he didn't feel blessed. He felt haunted, and he couldn't bear to sit there in the dark with his thoughts. He wanted to hold her diary again, to hold her, but Uncle Leo had snatched it away. *If you want answers, go read your Bible.*

After a moment's hesitation, Jasper picked up the heavy book and slipped out of the stall. No one but the cows stirred as he crept to the open end of the barn. In the puddle of moonlight, muddy Baby Jesus beamed up at him.

He sat down and opened the cover, hoping against hope that he'd find something inside. A clue. A prayer. Anything. The pages were curled from sitting in the mud, but Aunt Velma's soup pot must've kept out the worst of the rain.

He turned to the first page and found a listing of chapters:

Chapter 1: In the Beginning . . .

Chapter 2: God's Garden

He scanned down the listings, searching for anything that might guide him to the right page. Maybe she'd given him the damn book for a reason, not just to taunt him with her jokes. *Everybody's a sinner, Jasper.*

There was no mention of mothers except the Virgin Mary. He turned the page and kept looking.

Chapter 22: Opening the Door of Faith

Jasper's eyes stopped at the words *Door of Faith* and read them again. It couldn't be a coincidence. He held his breath and began searching for the page where he hoped to find some piece of her. Kings and beggars and a choir of fat baby angels flew past as he flipped through sheet after sheet, looking for chapter 22.

Something that didn't belong flashed between the cherubs.

Jasper's hand halted mid-search, then backtracked one page at a time. After turning back ten, he was certain he'd imagined it, but he kept flipping through anyway until there it was. A strange piece of paper pasted over the commandments. It was a list of names and phone numbers.

"What the heck is that?" Wayne whispered from over his shoulder.

Jasper startled at the voice and slapped the book closed on his cousin's pointing finger.

"Take it easy." Wayne pushed it back open. "Look! The creamery's on here. So is Big Bill and his roller rink, see? Who is Perry Gal-a-toes?"

Jasper didn't answer. He read over the list of names and businesses. The roller rink, the dairy where his mother worked, even the diner where he'd eaten with Not Lucy were on the list. He scowled up at the moon. It wasn't an explanation, but it was something.

"Are there more?" Wayne took the book from his cousin and flipped through it.

Jasper barely noticed. All he could hear was the detective's voice. *She had something for me. Something very important. Do you know what I'm talking about?*

"There's a bunch of 'em." Wayne showed him another page.

It was a ledger sheet filled with dollar amounts and dates and names. Jasper snatched the book back from Wayne and found another sheet pasted in and then another.

"What is all this?"

Jasper just shook his head. One name kept showing up over and over again next to the smaller dollar amounts, *C. A. Duncan*.

Page after page, there was nothing but more figures. No instructions. No explanation. Nothing. Jasper flipped faster, growing more and more desperate. *I need more, Mom. What am I supposed to do with all this? Tell me!*

He reached the last page, ready to throw the book against the wall, but the sight of her handwriting stopped him. On the back cover, written in her scrawling pen were the words:

John Russo – Woodward 16221

Federal Investigation #58-MI-0906

"Is that the detective that came here?" Wayne asked too loudly.

"What on earth are you two doing over there?" Aunt Velma demanded from the other side of the barn. "Get back to bed."

"Yes, ma'am," they answered in unison.

Jasper closed the book, and both boys scrambled back to their stall. After a solid five minutes of silence, Wayne crawled over to Jasper's ear and whispered, "What are you going to do?"

Jasper didn't answer. He just stood up and grabbed his overalls.

"Where are you going?" Wayne hissed.

"I have to tell him."

"Tell who?" Wayne jumped up and swiped the book from his hands.

"My dad. I have to tell him." Jasper made a move to grab the book back from his cousin.

Wayne lifted the Bible high over his head where the smaller boy couldn't reach. "Tell him tomorrow, dummy. It can wait."

"No, it can't. She gave this to me. I have to help her!" Jasper kicked his cousin in the shin hard.

The book dropped to the dirt with a thunk.

"Now look what you did," Wayne muttered.

Aunt Velma came storming across the barn and threw back the stall door with a lantern in her hand. "What in God's green earth are you two monkeys arguing about at this hour? After all we've been through, can't we get some rest?" Her bare toe slammed into the book lying on the ground. "Ouch! Dammit!"

The boys jumped back as she stumbled forward. She snatched up the Bible and brandished it at them. "Sweet Lord! This is what you two are fighting over?"

Jasper panicked. "I'm sorry, Aunt Velma. Wayne wanted to borrow it, and I guess I just . . ."

She squinted at the cover in the yellow glow of the lantern. She shot Wayne a sideways glance, then turned her blazing eyes on Jasper in his overalls. "Why are you dressed? Going somewhere?"

"Uh. No." Jasper backed himself into the corner. "I was just . . ."

"You were just lyin' to me is what you were doin'. Why don't you try again? What is goin' on?" She tucked the book under her arm as a hostage. "Somebody better start talkin'."

"Jasper found somethin' in that book," Wayne blurted.

Jasper whacked him in the arm.

"What?" Wayne gave him a shove in return. "You did, didn't you?"

Aunt Velma frowned at her nephew. "What'd you find, honey?"

"I—I'm not sure." Jasper swallowed tears of frustration.

She gave him a hard look, then sat down and opened the cover. Jasper punched Wayne in the arm with all his might.

"Hey," he hissed back and showed the younger boy his fist. "She's family, ain't she? If you can't trust us, who can you trust, huh?"

"Jasper, honey? Do you recognize this handwriting?" Aunt Velma motioned him to her side.

He knew he was trapped now. "Uh . . . yes. It looks like my mother's. Some of it does anyway."

"These are accounting records for the dairy where she works, see the letterhead?" Aunt Velma pointed to the top of one of the ledger sheets. "Any idea why she'd put them in here?"

Jasper dropped his eyes to the dirt and told the truth. "No."

Aunt Velma picked his face up by the quivering chin. "You know I am gonna have to talk to your father about this."

"Talk to me about what?" Wendell asked from the other end of the barn. He walked over to the stall with Uncle Leo. His cheeks were rosy with alcohol. "Whatcha all doin' out of bed, Son?"

Jasper didn't answer.

"The boys were just showing me something they found." Aunt Velma stood up and motioned the men over to the book. "I think you're gonna want to see this, Wendell."

In the dull light of the lantern, Aunt Velma revealed his mother's secret. Jasper tried to breathe. This was what he'd wanted his father to see, but he couldn't shake the bad feeling in his gut as Wendell and Leo leafed through each piece of Galatas's accounting.

Uncle Leo let out a low whistle at the last page. "Federal investigation. Jeez, Althea. And there's that fellow Russo. What do you make of it, Wen?"

Wendell slammed the book shut and glanced from Jasper to Aunt Velma. "We should discuss this outside, Leo."

He handed the book to Velma, and the two men headed out the open end of the barn, with Jasper trailing behind them.

"Get back to bed, Son. Everything's going to be fine. Don't you worry." His father led him back to his bed and closed the stall door in Jasper's face.

He watched the men walk out to the tractor shed with his nose pressed between the slats.

Aunt Velma took his hand and pulled him away from the wall. She gave the boy a worried smile, and then her eyes dropped down to the Bible in her hands. After a moment's reflection, she set the book back down next to Jasper's pillow and said, "Well, boys. I'm dead tired . . . I'm going to turn in now, and I'm stuffin' cotton in my ears so you fools don't keep me up. Good night."

Jasper stood rooted to the spot, watching her walk back to her end of the barn.

Wayne gave him a gentle shove to the door. "Go, dummy! She's letting you go, so git. Before she changes her mind."

With that, Jasper slipped on his boots and was out of the barn running. He sprinted a wide circle around to the back side of the tractor shed where the men's voices leaked out into the night.

"He's a detective, Wendell. What do you want him to do?"

"I want him to leave my family alone, dammit! I told that son of a bitch to back off. I don't give a rat's ass about his investigation. It's none of our business. I lost my wife because of that bastard. Askin' her to take on a gangster like Galatas, pestering her at work. Back in Detroit, some poor family is still missin' their father tonight. They never did find a trace of that police sergeant except the blood in my damned bedroom. I'm not lettin' my family end up like that. We're not gonna call him about nothin'."

"What about that book? Looks like Althea went to quite a lot of trouble to hide them pages. There had to be a good reason. What should we do with it?"

"We ain't gonna do nothin' with it. I'm throwin' it in the fire. Althea never should've gone messin' with this stuff. Damn woman don't know what's good for her. If she'd have just taken care of Jasper and kept her nose out of it, none of this would've . . ."

Jasper didn't hear the rest. His feet took off running for the barn before his head could catch up.

CHAPTER 57

Charles Duncan was a respected US marshal.
Is there any evidence to support these claims?

Jasper raced into the cow stall and snatched the Bible off the ground.

Wayne sat up in his bed. "What are you doing?"

He just shook his head and ran back out before his cousin could stop him. He dashed up the driveway out onto Harris Road, clutching the book to his chest, eyes darting behind him. His father's truck would be starting up after him the minute the man realized what his son had done. The long ditch on the other side of Harris was littered with fallen branches that scraped at his arms as he climbed down from the road into its shadow.

He stopped to catch his breath. *Oh God, what am I doing?* His father and uncle would kill him, but he couldn't let them burn it. His foot sank down into the mud as he searched his head for options. There was no place on the farm to hide it. He supposed he could bury it, if he could find a dry spot.

"Jasper!" a voice hissed out on the road above him. "Where are you, dummy?"

Jasper debated whether or not to answer but finally decided he needed the help. "Down here."

Wayne climbed down into the ditch and found him there under the branches. "What the heck are you doin' out here? Pop and Uncle Wen are gonna be comin' in from the shed any second."

"I can't let him burn it, Wayne. He knows the truth, but he doesn't care."

"What are you talkin' about?"

"He doesn't care if they ever get Galatas. You heard Motega. They kill people. They killed Ayasha. They're plannin' something terrible. They're gonna shoot a bunch of Indians, and no one's gonna stop them!"

Wayne didn't speak for a moment, until he said, "That's probably why he wants to burn it, dummy. He don't want anyone killin' *you*. Ever think of that?"

"But somebody has to stop them. That's why she left me. That's what she was trying to do. She was trying to do something right."

"But this isn't right, Jas. You really think you can do anything to fix it? You think she'd want you to?"

"No. But someone has to. What about that detective? His number's on the back of the book."

"Where you gonna find a phone out here, huh?"

"There's a phone at the Tally Ho, isn't there?"

"Well, yeah. But Pop will feed us to the pigs if we go runnin' off like that."

Jasper regained his footing and stuffed the book down the back of his overalls. "You don't have to come. Just tell 'em I ran off again, alright? Say you saw me headin' back to where Grandma's house burned down."

"You're crazy!" But Wayne didn't try to stop him as he took off along the bottom of the ditch.

It was slow going up and over fallen trees, with his boots heavy with mud, but Jasper couldn't risk being seen. He kept his ears perked for the sound of his father's truck. He had no idea what he might tell the barkeep, Mr. Sharkey. He'd have to make something up about an emergency.

As he approached the end of Harris Road, a car's headlights blew past on Lakeshore. Jasper crouched in the shadow of the ditch until it was gone, then scrambled up into a small cluster of trees lining the field. The crops were too low to give much cover. He glanced back over his shoulder toward his uncle's farm. Harris Road was dark and quiet. The lit windows of the Tally Ho glowed a half mile away at the edge of the road. Jasper searched for the safest route through the open field. There was none. He would just have to run for it and hit the deck if he heard a car. *One, two . . .*

He took off running through the soft dirt with the heavy book banging against his back. His eyes stayed fixed on the windows, glancing back every ten strides at the road behind him. On the third look back, a pair of headlights appeared through the grove of trees lining the road.

Shit. He flattened himself to the ground and watched them inch up Harris toward him. The lights stopped moving two hundred yards from where he lay, and for a horrifying instant, Jasper was certain he'd been spotted. But they began to roll again and continued on toward Burtchville. The sedan wasn't familiar.

See any strange cars? Sheriff Bradley's voice repeated in his head.

Jasper stood back up on shaking legs. By now, his father would have discovered he'd gone. He could only hope that Wayne had pointed them soundly in the wrong direction and they were busy wandering the back fields and not climbing into his father's truck. He started running again.

The Tally Ho was empty except for one man slouched at the table near the window where Jasper peeked in. He was wearing a tan uniform. Jasper watched through the bug screen as the barkeep approached his table.

"Shouldn't you be gettin' home, Cal?"

"Just one more for the road, Clint. I've had one hell of a day." Jasper recognized the sheriff's voice.

"Won't Mrs. Bradley be missing you right about now?"

"You mind your bar. I'll mind my wife. One more and I'm gone."

"Comin' up," Clint agreed and grabbed the empty mug.

Next to the taps at the end of the bar sat a black telephone.

Jasper tried to work up the nerve to knock on the door. Sheriff Bradley knew his uncle and might drag him home by his ear, but he was the sheriff the federal marshal had been talking about. He'd found the bags of "product" Galatas wanted back. They were going to try to trick him into giving them back. Jasper sucked in a breath, knowing he had no choice. He had to talk to him, no matter the consequences. He headed around the back of the building to the door, but the sound of tires on gravel stopped him cold as another car pulled into the lot.

Jasper jumped behind the corner. The tavern door opened and closed.

"Evening, Clint. Evening, Cal. Mind if I join you?"

Jasper crawled back to his window. His eyes bulged as the same federal marshal who had been talking with Galatas at the reservation sat down next to the sheriff.

"Hey, Chuck," Sheriff Bradley said with a slur. "What brings you here at this hour?"

"Need a beer. Same as you."

The barkeep set down a mug in front of the marshal.

"Thanks." The marshal clinked the sheriff's mug with his own and took a swig. "So. You had any luck trackin' down more of that horse?"

Sheriff Bradley grabbed his mug and drained it in one go. He smacked the empty glass on the table. "Only found two sacks so far. We sent them down to Detroit, like I said."

"You will tell me if you find more, won't you, Cal?"

"It ain't exactly your jurisdiction, is it?"

"If it is what we think it is, this here's federal. And we don't want a bunch of strangers pokin' around disturbin' the peace, do we? Think of all the phone calls you'll get."

Sheriff Bradley nodded and stood to leave. "You're probably right. I gotta get home to the missus."

Marshal Duncan stood as well and held out his hand for a shake. "Good seein' you, Cal. Listen, I have uh . . . a little situation up at Black River. Do me a favor. If you get a call tonight, take your time answering the phone. Can you do that?"

The fog seemed to clear from Sheriff Bradley's eyes for a moment. "What are you sayin', Chuck?"

"I'm sayin' I need a little latitude tonight. I'm sure you understand."

"I'm not sure that I do."

"Course you do. We've given you a bit of latitude here or there up at the res . . ."

Sheriff Bradley held up an unsteady hand. "I don't know what the hell you're talkin' about."

Marshal Duncan pulled a small picture from his pocket and showed it to the sheriff. "Course you do. Remember her? A few months back?"

Squinting as the photograph went back in the pocket, Jasper could make out the ghostly pallor of a girl sprawled naked on a slab. It looked like one of the photos he'd seen at the clinic. "You understand what I'm sayin' now?"

The sheriff lowered his hand and voice to almost a whisper. "That there had nothin' to do with me."

"Sure it did, Cal. Wasn't it your cruiser that dumped her at the door of the clinic? Dr. Whitebird took copious notes, plenty of pictures too."

"But that was just protocol. She wasn't one of mine. She was just some junkie that got lost. I couldn't help her." His face was growing red.

"But you could help out a buddy, right? We've got a blood type on that friend of yours. He left evidence all over her. The file's real thick on this one."

"This is—this is bullshit, and you know it. You can't just come in here waving wild accusations." The sheriff was practically spitting in the marshal's face. He pushed past his chair with an awkward stutter toward the door.

"Fifteen minutes, Cal. That's all I'm askin'."

The sheriff waved his hand in disgust at the marshal and slammed open the door.

"You say hello to the wife for me now," Marshal Duncan called after him.

Once the sheriff had left, the marshal dropped a dollar on the table and abandoned his beer.

"Have a good evening, officer," Clint called from behind the bar and went back to washing mugs.

Jasper stayed under the window, staring wide into the empty field. The sound of a car engine turning over and tires on gravel barely registered. *Ayasha*, he thought. They were talking about her.

CHAPTER 58

Can you explain why the Detroit Police Department has no record of you or Detective Russo's alleged investigation?

"Evening. Can I help y—" The barkeep turned toward the door and stopped talking. He leaned over the counter. "What are you doin' here, son? Ain't it a bit late?"

"I—I need to use . . . I mean, excuse me, sir." Jasper steadied his shaking voice. "May I please use your telephone? It's an emergency."

"Boy, it's past eleven o'clock at night. You can't be calling anybody at this hour. Where's your folks?"

"They're um . . . our car broke down a ways back. We—uh—saw the lights on here. I'm supposed to try to call for help."

"You're gonna need Tony down in Burtchville. I'll ring him." Clint picked up the phone and started to dial.

Jasper's eyes circled the room, desperate for a way out of his disastrous lie. "Um . . . I'm supposed to call our mechanic in Detroit. I—uh—I have the number."

Clint stopped spinning the dial and glanced over at Jasper's stricken face. He hung up the phone. "Drop the act, kid. What are you doin' here?"

Jasper glanced at the door, debating whether or not to run, but he'd come this far. "My—my mother needs my help. I can't really explain, but please, sir, can I use your phone?"

Clint walked over and squatted down to get a look at him. "You're Althea's boy, ain't ya?"

Jasper bit his tongue.

"Althea's always been a friend. Can see her face all over yours. Your uncle know you're here?"

Jasper shook his head.

"Who you tryin' to call, kid?"

"A detective. From Detroit. I found something and . . . I just." Jasper didn't even know anymore, but she'd given the Bible to him. She had trusted him. It had to mean something. He couldn't let her down.

"I know who you mean." Clint grabbed the phone and dialed a number. "Pete? It's Clint over at the Tally . . . A bit slow. You? . . . Say, you still got a Detroit cop over there drinkin' up all your coffee? . . . That's the one. Could you send 'im on over. He'll know . . . Okay, see you Sunday."

He hung up the phone. "I don't know what your mom's got herself into, kid, but it's big. I've seen and heard a lot of strange stuff in my day, but nothin' like this. I hope you know what you're doin'."

Jasper really didn't. He stood there at the bar a moment feeling utterly lost until a thought came together. *Althea's always been a friend.* "Mr. Sharkey? Can I ask you somethin'?"

He lowered his gaze down from the window. "What?"

"When was the last time you saw her?"

Clint didn't speak at first. He just stood there weighing his words, the way a man who rarely speaks of anyone or anything does. He finally said, "I made a promise to your mother to keep that to myself. Some pretty bad people were lookin' for her."

"I'm not a bad person," Jasper whispered.

Clint smiled at him. "No. You're not, are you? It was at the end of last summer. She walked through that door pretty shook up. Said she'd left her car somewhere. Said these people were lookin' for her. Asked if I'd heard anything. I could tell somethin' about her wasn't right."

"Did she stay here?"

"Nope. She got herself cleaned up, had a few stiff drinks, then she took off."

"Where'd she go?"

"Wouldn't say. I offered to drive her somewhere, but she just waved me off. Said the only thing I could do was to never tell a soul I saw her . . . so I didn't."

A pair of headlights pulled up into the lot. The barkeep opened the door for Jasper and said, "I hope you find her, kid."

"Thanks," he whispered. A black sedan was waiting for him at the bottom of the stairs. Despite everything he'd just gone through, he felt an inexplicable urge to run the other way as the car window rolled down.

"Jasper!" the detective beamed brightly from behind the wheel. "I was hoping to hear from you. Get in."

Jasper couldn't believe he was climbing into the car of the very man who had chased him through the streets of Detroit. His stomach tightened as he sat down on the leather bench and closed the door, but Jasper didn't see any other way. He couldn't trust the sheriff or the marshal or even his own father.

"So what've you got for me, kid?" the detective asked as he pulled out of the parking lot.

Jasper eased the book out from the back of his pants and flipped it open. The detective glanced at a ledger page glued inside then back at the road. He was taking them north up Lakeshore. As they passed the turn to Harris Road, the knot in Jasper's stomach twisted. They weren't going back to the farm.

"So?" the detective said, unimpressed. "Is that all?"

"Well . . . no, there's a lot more pages like this one, and then there's this." Jasper turned to the sheet full of names and phone numbers.

The detective pulled the car to the side of the road and grabbed the book. He studied the list with a low whistle. "This is the entire Galatas network."

Jasper worked up the nerve to ask, "What's this all about?"

"Drugs, money, women," the detective muttered, not paying the boy much mind. He flipped through the accounting ledgers again. "I've been trying to nail Galatas for five years. Trafficking, racketeering, the works, but nobody will testify. I thought your mother would but . . ."

"Do you know where she is?" Jasper blurted out. "I have to find her."

"Kid, if I could find her, I wouldn't be here talkin' to you. I can't help you. Not with just this to go on." The detective tossed the book back onto Jasper's lap.

"But there's more," Jasper pleaded. "Something bad is going to happen. Tonight. Something really bad. I heard them talking. Marshal Duncan wants Sheriff Bradley to not answer the phone if it rings. Fifteen minutes, he said."

The detective flipped off the headlights, leaving only the moon to light his face as he glared down at the boy next to him. "You need to tell me everything you know, Jasper. The lives of innocent people depend on it. We don't want to let them down, do we?"

Jasper shook his head violently.

"So talk."

It was a relief to tell a grown-up all the things he'd witnessed that day. Galatas and Duncan in the woods, Motega, his dead sister, everything. The detective wrote down every word, raising his eyebrows from time to time at the revelation of his dead half-sister and especially at the implication that Duncan had some sort of picture he'd used to blackmail the sheriff.

"Very good, Jasper. That's very good. If I asked you to, could you show me where you saw Marshal Duncan and Galatas talking?"

"Yes, but—" He wanted to ask about his mother again. The detective cut him off.

"Why don't we go take a look?"

"Now?" The rotten feeling tightened its grip. "But it's late. My uncle and dad . . ."

"They would want you to do what's right, Jasper. I'm an officer of the law, and it's against the law to obstruct an investigation. You don't want to break the law, do you?"

He shook his head again, but his gut was telling him to get out of the car. It was the same feeling he'd had when that bus driver had walked toward him. He reached for the handle, but the detective was too quick and put the car back into gear.

The road up to Black River was hard to find in the dark. Jasper was almost too late in spotting it, but the detective slammed the brakes just in time, nearly driving the boy's forehead into the dash.

"Hold on, kid." The detective chuckled and pulled up the steep drive with his headlights off. He cut the engine behind the rubble of the clinic and ordered him out of the car. "Okay, Jasper. Lead the way."

His legs went numb as he led the man around the clinic and down the path toward the game house. *This isn't right,* he thought. *This is dangerous.* But he kept walking as if he could feel the detective's gun between his shoulder blades.

Halfway up the path, they heard voices. The detective crouched down, grabbed Jasper by the overall straps, and dragged him into the trees. Broken moonlight streamed through the branches, lighting their way as they inched closer to the sound.

"What do you mean it's not here!" a voice bellowed. "You make me come here in the middle of the night and you do not have it? This is lies. You have nothing."

"Have you found many bags?" a deep voice demanded. It was Motega. The detective halted Jasper behind a tree.

"We've just begun the search," Marshal Duncan piped in. "We'll find them."

"You won't find more than three. That is how many I left."

"What do you mean how many you left?"

"Let this man speak, Charles." It was Galatas talking.

The detective yanked Jasper's shoulder straps and pushed him forward to get a closer look. Every snap of a twig stopped his heart. They would hear them. They would find them and kill them.

His father was right. The detective didn't care.

"Do you see what is left?" Motega asked the men, motioning to the collapsed game house. "Do you see the trees? Do you see the ground?"

Jasper looked up as though Motega were commanding him. All the branches over his head still had their leaves. The fallen tree on the ground in front of him was covered in moss.

"What is it you are trying to say?" Galatas demanded.

Marshal Duncan surveyed the area, then slowly shook his head. "He's sayin' the twister didn't come through here. Shit. He's sayin' he tore down the game house himself along with the storeroom."

"Your men ran like scared children when the great winds came." Motega grinned at Galatas. "I did not."

"I see." Galatas nodded and went quiet for a moment. "Charles tells me you want us to leave Black River. This is right, yes? This we can do. You deliver what you stole, and we leave. Do we have a deal?"

"You do not honor deals. I have seen this. Besides, I already have what I want."

"I do not understand. What is it you have?"

"You." Motega pulled a knife from his waistband. "You are here."

"Charles?" Galatas took a step back. "I have no more time for these games. Will you please make this one talk?"

Marshal Duncan pulled his gun from his holster and pointed it at Motega.

Jasper lurched back only to have the detective clamp hands hard over his mouth and arms. He whispered in his ear, "Shh, kid. Galatas will burn for this. Just watch. Watch and remember it all for the jury."

The hot breath in his ear made his whole body recoil. *Stay down, boy. This isn't going to get any better for you.* Jasper shook his head and squeezed his eyes shut. He strained against the detective's grasp, and a pain shot up the arm held in by the sling. He was pinned.

Motega's voice did not waver. "I am not afraid of death, and I will not live without justice. Shoot me."

Jasper's eyes bulged open.

The marshal cocked his gun and glanced at Galatas.

The old man was the one smiling now. "First things first, Charles. We must have back what he stole. Shoot him in the foot. Shoot him until he talks."

Motega laughed. "You can bleed me all you want. I will die happy. Your Mexican friends will kill you for me. And they will kill you slow. My blood will be your blood. So shoot me."

The marshal fired a warning shot, and Jasper let out a muffled scream into the detective's palm and tried to kick free.

Galatas turned to Marshal Duncan. "Did you hear something?"

Marshal Duncan lowered his gun. "There's no one else here, Perry."

The detective wrestled Jasper to the ground in a crackle of leaves as Galatas called out into the trees. "Taki? Did you hear that?"

Detective Russo and Jasper froze. Heavy footsteps approached them from behind. The detective released Jasper and turned, but the sound of a pump shotgun loading a round stopped him. It was only then that Jasper noticed the gun in the detective's hand.

"Drop the piece, Russo," a low voice growled, and a dull thump hit the dirt by Jasper's feet. The voice called out, "I got something over here, boss."

"Let us see who you found."

"Move," the voice commanded.

"Just everybody stay calm," Detective Russo warned, but the authority had gone out of his voice. He grabbed Jasper by the overall straps and marched him out into the clearing. "This has nothing to do with either of us, Perry. I wasn't even here. Besides, I know we can work something out. I have friends over in Narcotics."

Jasper's eyes locked onto Motega. The man shot him a look of bewildered fury, then hung his head.

"Hello, John. It is so nice to see you again." Galatas smiled, then nodded his head at Taki.

The blast of the shotgun split the air. The ground crashed into Jasper's face as the man gripping his shoulder straps hit the dirt. Another blast of the gun drove a gurgling sigh through the detective's mouth.

A hand yanked Jasper up off the ground. Detective Russo didn't move.

"Jesus, Perry," a distant voice protested.

Galatas kept talking to the back of Russo's corpse, but Jasper could barely comprehend the muffled words through the blasts ringing in his ears. "Tell your Italian friends back in Detroit not to fuck with me. Now, Motega, you will show us where you've buried my product, or we will dig three graves tonight."

Motega answered in a voice too soft and defeated to hear.

Jasper was dragged through the woods, his mind beating its tiny wings against the bars of its cage. *Uncle Leo will never forgive me. When will they find out I've gone? The book is still in the detective's car. My mother will be furious I left it behind. I'm sorry, Mom.*

His captor kept a tight grip on the back of his neck even when they finally stopped moving. Jasper gazed down at his clothes, stained red with the detective's blood. *I'm so sorry.*

"So where is it?" Galatas demanded. Marshal Duncan trained his flashlight on Motega's grim face.

More muddled words were followed by the sounds of a shovel lifting dirt. *They're digging my grave.* Jasper's thoughts fluttered and fell. He felt himself falling too. There was no ground to catch him. *This is where they'll bury me.*

Then another voice, clear as a bell, cut through the buzzing in his ears.

"Evenin', gentlemen! Mind explaining what you're all up to out here?"

Jasper's eyes pulled back into focus. It was Sheriff Bradley coming up over the ridge with a deputy. He had a rifle in one hand and a light in the other. The man with him held a shotgun.

"Just tending to some tribal business. What are you doin' up here, Cal?" Marshal Duncan trained his flashlight onto the sheriff. "You're out of your jurisdiction."

"Well, beggin' your pardon, Chuck, but Black River ends about fifty feet up that hill. This here's St. Clair County, and I received an anonymous call an hour ago that we might find some more of them sacks around here. We heard gunshots. Mind explaining that?" The sheriff's light flitted between the marshal, Galatas, and Motega, and then fell on Jasper.

The man gripping his neck let go. The instant the sheriff's light lifted, the hands behind Jasper started fumbling with a shotgun. *He's reloading,* a voice whispered in his ear. *This is your only chance. Run.* Run!

Jasper took off blindly through the woods, stumbling and flailing through the dark. Cold air rushed past as leaves and twigs battered his face. He heard angry shouting behind him but couldn't register the voices. He just kept going, searching for the road. For help. For anybody.

A bloody scream tore through the woods somewhere behind him followed by gunshots.

He tripped over a log and went sprawling onto the ground. More shots rang out in the distance. Jasper scrambled into the shadow of a large tree and curled himself into a ball under a thicket of branches. He squeezed his eyes shut, praying to disappear. *Don't let them find me, Mom. Please don't let them find me.*

CHAPTER 59

*Do you expect us to believe you were
just an innocent bystander?*

Mom?

Jasper found himself back in his grandmother's house, standing at
the foot of the stairs into the loft above. He'd heard a voice. At least he
thought he had. *I'm dreaming,* he realized as he stared up at the pink
sky trapped between the broken rafters.

The only sound he could hear was the whistle of a distant bird
outside. Until a voice whispered, "Who's there?"

Jasper slowly climbed the stairs.

"Hello?" he whispered from the top step. The dark rectangle of
the dresser sat in the corner. Across from it were the two beds. A large
shadow sat on the edge of a mattress. He let out a startled yelp when
it moved.

"Jasper!" the voice gasped.

A yellow flame blazed up. He squinted in the sudden light.
"Mom?"

The shadow lowered the lamp so he could see its face. It was her. He grabbed the handrail to catch himself from falling down the stairs.

"What on earth are you doing here?" she hissed.

"I—I had a dream. A wolf was chasing me. I needed to find you," he stammered, still not believing his eyes. Her face blurred in his tears. "Is it really you?"

"Yes, baby. It's me. Come here." She smiled in the lamplight and held out her arms, beckoning him over, wanting to hold him.

He ran to her, nearly tripping on the warped floorboards. He'd never been so overwhelmed with emotions in his entire life. He couldn't even name them all.

She wrapped him in her arms. "Shh . . . It's okay, baby. Don't cry."

"I missed you," he sobbed. "I dreamed you were dead."

"Dead? Where did you get such a silly idea?"

His words smothered in her shoulder as he bawled about Ayasha and the detective getting shot and Galatas and the federal marshal and Motega. She didn't seem to understand any of it.

All she said was, "Shh! Shh! I missed you too, baby. I would never leave you all alone." After a few more incoherent minutes, she grabbed his shoulders and gently pushed him away. "You shouldn't be here. Where's your uncle?"

Jasper fought to regain his composure and remember. "I left . . . I had this dream, and I had to find you. They were still asleep."

"Well, they're not asleep now. You have to get back." She looked him hard in the eyes. "They can't know I'm here."

"Yes, ma'am." He nodded, but he couldn't bring himself to leave. Not yet. He wiped at his eyes. "Why? . . . Why are you here? Why did you leave?"

"I didn't leave. I just needed them to think I had. I had to protect you. I had to keep them away."

"Were you always here? In this house? At the clinic? Were you there?"

She bit her lips and nodded. "I came to visit you every chance I got, baby. I just couldn't let you or your uncle know. It's not safe."

"Big Bill said you only have two days until they're gonna do something terrible. Why? Why are they looking for you?"

Her eyes widened at the name. A deep frown creased her face, and her hands dug into his shoulders. For a moment, Jasper feared she'd hit him. "None of your damned business. Understand? You stay away from them. Don't you ever listen to one word they say—not about me, not about nothin'. They're liars, baby. They're killers . . . You have to stop asking questions."

He nodded and fought off another round of tears. He decided he didn't care if she hit him. "Are they going to kill you? Are you dead?"

"Not just yet," a deep voice answered from the top of the stairs.

His mother lurched up, grabbing Jasper by the arm, shoving him behind her back so he couldn't see. "Bill," she gasped. "I—I was coming to see you today. I was."

"Sure you were." Big Bill chuckled. "It's a bit too late for that. You're going to do exactly as I say, and maybe I'll let the kid go."

"Let him go now," she demanded, but Jasper could hear the panic in her voice. "He's got nothin' to do with this. He's just a boy."

"Don't worry, Thea. I kinda like the little fella. If it wasn't for him, I wouldn't have found this place." Big Bill walked over, grabbed Jasper by the wrist, and yanked him away from his mother. A gun was in his other hand. "I've been watching him for weeks."

A bolt of panic struck him. Bill had followed him, and he'd been too stupid to notice. *The stand of trees,* he realized, there were plenty of places to hide in the trees flanking the far side of the barn. He hadn't even bothered to look over his shoulder.

Big Bill picked up the oil lamp and winked at Jasper's mother. Bile flooded Jasper's stomach. Bill had seen the lamp burning in the windows out over the dark fields like a beacon.

"It's all kind of fitting when you think about it." Bill grinned. "You. Up here."

The blood drained from Althea's face.

"Just think. You'll get to finish what you started. I even brought a knife." He pulled a pocketknife out of his pants and tossed it onto the bed. The other hand kept the gun pressed to the back of Jasper's head.

"Stop it, Bill," she protested, but the fire had gone out of her voice.

"Don't worry, Thea. I'll be nice. See? I brought your favorite." He pulled a bottle of whiskey from his other pocket.

"I've stopped all that now," she whimpered.

"Sure you have." He tossed the bottle onto the bed. He pulled a small bag of powder out next and grinned. "Just like old times, huh?"

Tears began to run down her face. Jasper didn't understand what was happening, but he could see the terror in his mother's eyes. He had to do something. He thought of the bus driver.

Big Bill lowered the gun and grabbed the boy's arm. Without hesitating, Jasper reared up and took a hard kick at the man's nuts. His foot swung wide and landed on the man's thigh. Bill didn't even flinch.

"No, Jasper. Don't," his mother choked out and sobbed. "Leave him alone."

"Gotta love his spirit, don't ya?" He laughed, then smacked the boy soundly across the face. The room exploded into spots. Jasper hit the floor.

"Stay down, boy. This isn't going to get any better for you."

Jasper blinked his eyes clear and watched the man's black leather boots cross the floor over to the bed. His mother fell back onto the torn mattress with a squeak.

"Now, Thea. You're going to tell me everything you told that detective. Aren't you?"

"I didn't—" Her voice was cut short by a loud smack.

"Yes, you did. Now take your medicine . . ." An acrid-smelling smoke filled the air. "That's a good girl. I'm going to ask you again. What did you tell that cop about our business?"

"Nothing," she sobbed. "They took me in for questioning, but I didn't tell them anything, I sw—" Her voice was silenced by another slap.

"Where are the pages you took from our books, Thea? What were you plannin' to trade for them? Huh? Did you think your red-skinned boyfriend might get off easy? Did you think they might find the guy that did your girl?" The bed creaked as Bill plopped himself down next to her. "Ayasha tried this same shit, Thea, talkin' to cops about our business up at Black River, and look what happened to her."

"You son of a—" his mother screamed. Another hard slap rang out.

"You should've done your homework, Thea. No Detroit cop's gettin' anywhere up here. He's way out of his jurisdiction, and you're out of your fucking mind. You even check his credentials? He's on a goddamn payroll. The Italians bent him up years ago. There's no federal investigation. You'd have been better off getting on your knees for Marshal Duncan, but instead you chose to stab the only people that ever gave a rat's ass about you right in the back."

"Bill, I swear—"

"Shut up. You're only making this harder on yourself. How many more people gotta die over this, Thea? You already got one cop killed, stickin' his nose in this business. Right now it's just you and me, and I'm willing to let you go out on a high note. Shit, I've got a soft spot for ya. You don't want me to bring in the big boys, do you? They'll come up here and have a real nice party with you. And your boy. You know that. Right?"

The bed shook, and his mother let out a sob.

"Stop it!" Jasper shrieked and staggered to his feet in a daze. "Leave her alone!"

"Look who decided to join us." Bill brandished his yellow teeth in a wolfish grin. "Come here, Jasper. Come sit with Uncle Billy."

The man grabbed Jasper by the back of the neck and forced him down onto his knee. Jasper tried to wrench free, but the huge man held him tight against the barrel of his chest. His mother's face was swollen red on one side. Her eyes let out a silent scream.

"Leave him out of this, Bill," she pleaded. "It's got nothin' to do with him. I'll tell you what you want to know."

"I know you will, hon." He bounced Jasper on his knee. "He's real cute. Just like his daddy, right?"

"Stop it."

"Little Jasper. There's so much you don't know, isn't there? Do you want to know what Mommy here did for a living? How many men she wrapped those skinny legs around until she found one dumb enough to put a ring on her finger?"

Jasper fought to get his arms free but couldn't budge.

"Do you know who she works for?" Bill whispered in his ear, mocking his mother's voice. "Killers."

Jasper gaped up at the sky through the hole in the roof. A faraway voice told him it was getting lighter out, but it was drowned out by the sweaty laughter in his ear.

"Do you want to know how this place burned down, kid? She did it, you know. She got real hopped up one night and decided to come home to dear old Mom and Dad. Boy, the rumors flew back then that she'd gone crazy and tried to kill them all in their sleep.

That she'd tried to kill herself. The family called it an accident—a lit cigarette fallin' to the floor. But they found her poor daddy swinging from the rafters a few days later. It's amazing they didn't lock you up right then. Isn't it, baby? Shit, you've been lookin' for a way to die since I met you."

Jasper tried not to look at his mother. Her face had become grotesque as the room warped around him. He couldn't get his eyes to focus.

"Don't listen to him, baby. He's crazy," the pulsing face whimpered.

"No. She's the crazy one, Jasper. And after tonight, no one will ever doubt that."

"Let him go, Bill. This is between us, right? Just you and me. I'll tell you what you want to know." Her distorted face twisted into a smile as she took a long swig from the whiskey bottle.

"That's a good girl." He lifted Jasper from his lap and tousled his hair. "Sorry, little champ. You're not invited to this party."

The last thing Jasper heard before the pistol hit him in the head was his mother's voice. She was shrieking, *"No!"*

He came to, facedown on the floorboards. The worst noise he'd ever heard was coming from above him. It sounded like Hoyt's big boar Horace was in the room. He tried to lift his head, but a sharp pain in his skull sent it back to the floor. The room flashed white and purple.

Under the horrible noises, he could hear someone crying. It was his mother.

He pushed himself up to his knees, heaving his stomach into his throat at the sudden motion. Stomach acid dripped onto the floor. There was a puddle of blood where his head had landed. The room throbbed. A lumpy mass in the corner was thrashing about. A mess of arms and legs. Squinting in the yellow light, he could see a naked giant. It was moving violently.

Jasper gaped at it, paralyzed, unable to comprehend what he was seeing. His mother sobbed, and the room reeled around him. Somewhere in the distance, he could hear Sally screaming in the well. He pressed his hands to his ears and squeezed his eyes shut, hoping to disappear.

No.

He forced his hands back to the quaking floorboards. *I won't let her die.* The only light was the oil lamp on the floor. It seemed a million miles away. He couldn't feel his arms or legs but somehow willed them to move. *I won't let her die.* With his eyes fixed on the lamp, Jasper crawled toward it. He grabbed its steel handle and pulled himself to his feet.

It was as though he was watching himself from a perch on the ceiling as he silently approached the writhing beast. He swung the lamp with both hands like a baseball bat. It went crashing into the back of the monster's head with a hollow crack. Glass splintered into jagged shards as it shattered against its skull. Oil splattered over its back, and in the hanging instant before its hair caught fire, the beast stared dumbly into Jasper's eyes. But Jasper wasn't there. He was somewhere else, watching in terror. The shell of a boy just stared blankly as he raised the lamp up and whacked the beast again.

It let out a howl as the oil covering its torso lit. It rolled off Jasper's mother and fell to the ground, thrashing.

"Get out," his mother said in a hoarse whisper, pulling herself up off the bed. Her face was stained with blood and tears. She pushed Jasper toward the stairs. Her breasts swung freely just inches from his face. They were bruised. "Go. Get help."

She fell to her knees and began searching the floor. The burning giant lurched up, screaming. She scrambled back from the flames as it lunged for her. The bed caught fire.

"Get out, Jasper!" she shrieked. "Goddamn it! *Get out!*"

Jasper's thoughts were too slow to catch up to his feet. They carried him to the top of the stairs. *The gun.* He stopped. *She's looking for the gun.* He turned and scanned the smoking floorboards. In an instant, he saw it. On the floor by the bed. The growling demon fell to the ground again, rolling back and forth. All the hair on its enormous back was burning. His mother managed to skirt around it as the thing clawed for her ankles. The flames smothered under it as it tried to get up.

"The gun!" Jasper said in a weak voice. She didn't hear. He pointed to the place by the bed. "Mom, the gun."

She glared up at him, eyes blazing. *"Get out!"*

"The gun," he said again. This time she saw what he was pointing at.

"Thea!" the beast roared.

The flames had spread up the wall. The room clouded with smoke. Everything hazed over into a bad dream.

"Jasper!"

Her voice snapped him awake. She was by his side.

"Go get your uncle. Okay, baby?" She smiled at him reassuringly. "I'm alright. Now go."

Dazed, he pulled her necklace out from under his shirt and handed it to her as though it were important. "I took this from your room. I'm sorry."

She grabbed the necklace from him and patted his cheek. "It's okay, baby. You have to go now."

He nodded and headed down the steps in a trance.

"That's a good boy. I love you, baby," her voice whispered in his ear. He floated through the kitchen, wandering through the hazy cloud of the living room to the front door. *Smoke is good,* he thought sleepily. People would see it and know there was trouble. *Smoke signal.*

He stepped out onto the porch and straight into the chest of a giant Manitonaaha warrior. The man picked him up by the shoulders and stared him in the face. It was Motega. Jasper's head lolled on his neck as the man set him down and rushed into the house.

He watched himself fall back into the long grass. A giant black cloud of smoke darkened the morning sky. Yellow flames leapt up to the clouds, and the crackling sounds of his grandmother's house burning drowned out the unsteady rasp of his lungs. The echoes of a scream hung in the trees.

Somewhere far away came the crack of a gunshot. And then another.

Sally's dead, Jasper thought. Then he fell down the well.

CHAPTER 60

Where is this evidence of federal corruption?
Did it just up and walk away?

"Jasper?" A large hand shook him by the shoulder.

He jerked away from it with a scream. A blinding light shocked his eyes.

"Shh . . . it's alright, son." Sheriff Bradley crouched beside him. He set the flashlight on the ground. "You hurt?"

Jasper didn't answer. His eyes adjusted enough to see he was leaning up against a tree. *The woods, Galatas, Motega, the detective, the gunshots.* His whole body contracted.

"You sure gave us a scare. Let's get you up, son." The sheriff pulled him onto his feet. Jasper found himself searching the man's body for bullet holes.

"What happened?" he whispered.

"Don't you worry about that."

"Where's Galatas? And Duncan? Are they dead?"

"I'm afraid so, but don't fret over it. The world won't miss a man like Galatas or any of his associates. I can assure you. There isn't a judge in the country that wouldn't have sent those boys to the electric chair. I'm not gonna lose one wink of sleep over it. Neither should you."

"What about Motega? Is he—?"

"I don't know who you're talkin' about, son. Alls I know is that me and a couple deputies followed up on a report of some gunshots and came upon two gangsters digging up bags of narcotics. They'd shot a detective, a US marshal, and buried another police officer out here. As for them Indians, this don't concern them. They stay on their own land and keep to themselves. Lord knows they have their own troubles. I ain't seen one in ages. And neither have you. Understand?"

Jasper tried to nod.

"Now Deputy Sims is going to take you on home. We can't have young boys out wandering the woods, getting lost like this. Can we?"

Jasper struggled to find his footing as he processed all of it. He hadn't gotten lost, he'd—*the Bible!* "Sheriff?"

"Yes, son?"

"Go look in the detective's car. You'll find a book. A Bible. My mother hid some papers inside. About Galatas and the marshal."

The detective raised his eyebrows at this, then cracked a smile. "Your mother was a good woman, Jasper. Don't let anyone tell you any different."

The boy began shaking with tears.

A half hour later, Deputy Sims got out of the car. Out the side window, Jasper watched the officer survey the wreckage of his uncle's cabin and then knock on the side of the barn.

First Uncle Leo appeared and then Jasper's red-faced father. The deputy pointed toward the car and waved his hands in the air with a smile on his face. Uncle Leo nodded and shook the officer's hand while his father shot an unforgiving glare through the car window. Jasper just gazed back at him from behind the glass. It didn't matter if they beat him or whipped him or killed him for running off. He wouldn't feel a thing.

Deputy Sims walked back over to the car and opened Jasper's door, letting his merry voice pour into the backseat. ". . . lucky thing I was in the area. I'm just glad he's alright," he was saying over his shoulder. Then, loud enough for the men to hear, he added, "Now, Jasper, next time you want to go exploring, I want you to ask a parent's permission, understand?" He pulled Jasper out of the car by his good arm and said in a louder voice, "You stay out of trouble now, you hear?"

The deputy drove off, leaving Jasper standing in the driveway. He didn't hear his father coming.

"Do you have any idea what you've done? Worrying us all sick like that?" Wendell shook him by the shoulders, knocking his arm out of the sling. Jasper barely registered the pain. "I have half a mind to whip the skin off you! When are you going to learn, Son?"

"Easy, Wen. Take it easy. Look at him. His color. He don't look right. Christ, is that blood?"

Uncle Leo's face floated out of focus in front of him as the man knelt down. The closeness of him made Jasper's stomach recoil. *Don't touch me.*

"Jasper, look at me. What happened?"

"They're dead," Jasper told the blur.

"Who's dead?"

Jasper didn't answer. A pair of strong arms scooped him up and carried him back into the barn.

Jasper woke the next day on the floor of the cow stall. Wayne was nowhere in sight. For a flickering moment, he told himself it was a dream. Just a terrible dream. He turned to look at the children's Bible propped against the wall. It was gone.

Jasper balled himself up, but the minute he closed his eyes, Big Bill was standing over him. He sat up with a jolt.

Aunt Velma was cleaning plates and glasses out in the middle of the barn when he poked his head out. She set down a dish and rushed over to him. "Jasper, sweetie. Are you alright?" She scanned him head to toe and searched his eyes for permanent damage.

He was not all right.

"Your father had to get back to the city for work. He wanted me to tell you he'd be back Saturday."

"He hates me," Jasper whispered, remembering the red look in his father's eyes. He hated himself too. He'd done everything wrong. *If I hadn't gone looking for her—*

She grabbed his chin. "That's ridiculous. He's worried about you, that's all. He just wants to keep you safe. That's what a father does."

Jasper swallowed hard. "Where's Uncle Leo?"

"Out in the yard, I expect. And for the record, he doesn't hate you either. But Jasper," she said with a stern look, "I'm gonna be furious if you ever scare me like that again."

"Yes, ma'am. I'm sorry." He hung his head.

"Well, you better go and talk to him. Scoot!"

The scabbed-together barn was looking more like itself again. Boards and shingles had been nailed back into place, and the torn-open end was mended. Jasper walked through the rehung door to find Uncle Leo sifting through the scattered logs of their cabin.

"Hey, Jas!" Wayne trotted over to him and lowered his voice. "What the heck happened? Sheriff Bradley came by to check on you this morning. He said there was a shoot-out last night!"

"Wayne," Uncle Leo barked from what used to be the kitchen, "leave the kid alone. Go help your mother in the garden."

"Ah, do I have to?"

Uncle Leo shot him a look.

"Yes, sir."

Jasper caught his arm as he was leaving. "I'm sorry, Wayne. Did you catch hell for it?"

"A bit. But don't worry. I'll be sure to share some with you." Wayne gave him a stiff punch in the arm and then left.

"Jasper, son, follow me," Uncle Leo commanded.

"Yes, sir."

Uncle Leo led him back into the barn. Aunt Velma was nowhere to be seen. It was just the two of them, and Jasper figured the lashings were set to begin.

"I thought we had an agreement you and me that you wouldn't go lookin' for real-life trouble anymore."

"I'm sorry, sir. I just—" Jasper searched the ground for what he could say. There was nothing but the old rag rug on the ground where they had eaten dinner the night before. He should've listened to his father. He should've stayed in bed. "I just hope I can make it up to you."

"You're a good boy, Jasper, but you need to learn there are some things in this world that we can't fix. We just have to learn to live with them." The sympathetic bend in his uncle's eyebrows meant Sheriff Bradley had explained some things. The man reached into his pocket and handed him a small leather book. "Here. I believe this belongs to you."

Jasper's eyes widened as his uncle placed the book in his hands. It was his mother's diary.

"I'm sorry about your mother, Jasper . . . You know, when we were kids, she was like a firefly flittin' about the yard, full of spark. Man, she could make me laugh. And then one day . . ." His uncle lowered his eyes to the book and shook his head. "I don't know what really happened."

"I'm sorry, Uncle Leo," Jasper whispered, and he was. He was sorry about running off, the house burning down, his grandfather dying, his mother leaving him, everything he'd seen, and everything he'd done.

The book felt heavy with all her secrets. Or maybe they were just lies like his uncle said. It didn't matter anymore. They were his now. He hugged the book to his chest.

"The truth is a funny thing, Jasper. Sometimes you can only believe what you're willing to believe." He drew in a deep breath. "I will tell you one thing, though."

Jasper looked up at him.

"I never liked Arthur Hoyt. Your Grandpa Williams and him had a real falling-out, right before he . . . Right after Althea ran off. After we'd lost the house. Poor girl was only nineteen . . . Well, Hoyt tried to get our whole family thrown out of the church and run out of town. Times got real hard after that." Uncle Leo gave him a pained smile. "I guess I blamed her for it. For him dying. For everything . . ."

"It's not your fault," Jasper whispered.

"No. I should've listened. I should've tried . . ." His uncle's voice broke. He took a moment and cleared his throat. "My mother tried to get me to forgive her, you know, but she refused to rebuild the house. After a while she wouldn't even eat. It killed her, losing Althea and then Pops like that. I was just so angry. But there were rumors, you know. Shoot, there still *are* rumors about Hoyt and the girls he hires to do his housework. I just never believed anyone could ever . . ."

"What sort of rumors?"

Uncle Leo wiped a hand over his eyes. "I'm sorry, Jasper. I shouldn't be tellin' you all this. You're just a kid."

"No, I'm not," Jasper barked. He would never be a kid again. "What sort of rumors? I need to know."

"The sort you don't say out loud, son." Uncle Leo wanted to leave it at that.

"Did he hurt them?" Jasper already knew the answer but needed to hear it out loud. "Did he . . . do bad things to them?"

Uncle Leo's eyes fell to the book in Jasper's hands, and he said nothing.

"Why didn't anyone tell the police? The sheriff?"

"It's not that simple, Jasper. These sorts of things are kept quiet. For the sake of the girls. Proof is hard to come by. You can't go hang a man on nothin' but rumors. Your grandpa Williams tried to bring him to justice and nearly got us run out of town. Understand?"

Jasper shook his head. He did not understand at all. They didn't stop him. They'd let it happen.

"It hardly matters now anyway."

"How can you say it doesn't matter?" Jasper glared up at him with tears in his eyes.

"Because he's dead." His uncle paused to let the boy digest this. "I went over there to give him a piece of my mind this mornin'. I had half a mind to castrate 'im like a pig, but the good Lord took it out my hands."

"What do you mean? How?"

"It's up to the sheriff and the coroner to decide that, but it looked like a heart attack to me. He was lying facedown in the pasture. Looked like he'd been there a while. I only found him because Nicodemus was loose out there, circling the body. I thought the old bull had trampled a coyote or a wolf."

The air went out of Jasper's lungs.

"So you see?" Uncle Leo held up his hands. "This isn't for you or me to worry about anymore. We just gotta have faith, Jasper. God will sit in judgment now. Hoyt can't hide from it . . . None of us can."

Jasper felt the barn shrinking around him. He could feel his hand on the latch of the bull pen. He could see Nicodemus charging at Hoyt with the devil in his eyes.

"It's going to be okay, Jas." His uncle put a hand on his shoulder as though to keep his feet planted.

Jasper nodded, but none of it was okay. *We're all sinners, Jasper,* his mother's voice whispered in his ear. *Even you.*

"Just pray for his forgiveness and the strength to move on. That's all any of us can do."

Jasper bowed his head and tried. *Please, God. I didn't mean it . . .*

But when he closed his eyes, he could see Motega glaring down at him. Gripping him by the shoulders. Running inside the burning house. Dragging Big Bill to his car and sending it careening into a fuel tank. Carrying his battered mother to Dr. Whitebird. Taking his mother's necklace and laying it on the grave. *You saved her life . . . I am forever in your debt.*

"But it was all my fault," Jasper muttered to himself.

"You alright?" His uncle put a hand on his shoulder.

There is a bond between you. You must look inside yourself, and you will find her.

He looked up into his uncle's face and didn't see concern written in his eyes. He saw guilt.

He saw Dr. Whitebird sending word to his uncle that the boy and his mother were injured. Jasper lying there in a state of shock. His mother bleeding and crying. He could hear his uncle's muffled voice talking to the doctor, deciding what should be done. It wasn't Galatas, Marshal Duncan, Detective Russo, or Dr. Whitebird who took her away.

Jasper forced a weak smile. "Where did you take her?"

CHAPTER 61

Given your history, which you were generous enough
to share, I'm afraid you do not make
a credible witness.

"What?"

"Where did you take my mother?"

Uncle Leo held up a defending hand. "Listen. I only did what I thought was right."

Jasper's blood rose in disbelief. "What was right? What did you do?"

"If you could've seen her then at the clinic . . ." His uncle shook his head. "She'd come undone. Convinced people were trying to kill her . . . and you. The doctors said there was no way she could come home. Hysterical. Suicidal. Delusional. Paranoid. She was a danger to herself and to everyone around her. Even Wendell saw that eventually. We had to protect her from herself. We had to protect you. She'd become violent. It was like she was trying to claw out of her own skin. She'd tried to claw her way out the hospital. She injured an orderly."

Jasper drew in a tortured breath, trying not to imagine her tied to a bed. "But she wasn't crazy. I was there. I remember it now. They were trying to kill her."

"Another reason to keep her safe. Dammit, we did the best we could for her, Jasper. We did."

"You should've told me. I could've helped her."

"That's ridiculous. You're not a doctor. I couldn't let her drive you mad too. You deserve a chance to grow up without this burden. When you're a parent, Jasper, you'll understand. You have to make tough choices."

"You let me think she was dead!" Jasper screamed. He was beyond caring if he offended his uncle. He was done listening. He stormed across the barn, grabbed the castration knife from the wall, and brandished it at the man. "You did this. You have to tell them. You have to go and tell them the truth. She's not crazy . . ."

Leo held up both hands but took a step toward him. "It's not that simple, Jasper. She's not well. She's never been well. Not for years."

"She's not a broken cow you can shoot! She's my mother!" A cold calm settled over him as he realized screaming and carrying on would get him nothing. Jasper turned the knife on himself. "What if I'm just as crazy as she is, huh? Are you going to send me away too? You have to help her!"

"This has gone too far. Put the knife down, Jasper! Before you hurt yourself!" his uncle commanded.

"I am not afraid of death." They were Motega's words, but they were true. He wasn't afraid. A part of him welcomed it. One clean swipe and it would be over. The nightmare would stop. He pushed the blade into his skin and felt a small trickle run down his neck. "Promise me you'll tell them she's not crazy. *Promise me!*"

In two steps, Uncle Leo ripped the knife out of Jasper's hand and raised a fist. "That's enough, dammit!"

"Hit me. I don't care anymore." Jasper glared up into his uncle's eyes. "Just promise you'll do everything you can to bring her home. You owe it to me. You owe it to *her*."

Uncle Leo returned the knife to its proper place, then just stood there with his back to his nephew. After a solid minute he wiped his face and said, "Okay, Jasper, if I promise to try, will you stop? Will you stop runnin' off and tryin' to get yourself killed? Will you just give yourself a chance to grow up for God's sake?"

"Yes, sir." And Jasper did his best to mean it.

CHAPTER 62

All the suspects you've named are dead.
I'm sorry, but you'll have to find justice in that.
This case is closed.

Jasper's father pulled up to the barn on a Saturday morning in the late summer of 1954, as he did most Saturdays. Only this day, he stepped out of the truck dressed in a brown suit instead of his work clothes. Jasper puzzled at him through the window as he straightened his tie before walking through the door.

"Good morning, folks!"

"Well, don't you look nice, Wendell," Aunt Velma said from the stove. "You want some breakfast?"

"Nope. Can't stay today. I need to take Jasper back into the city with me." He turned to Jasper and winked. "Get on your school clothes, Son."

Jasper could tell by the twinkle in his eye something big was doing. The whole way back to Detroit, they hardly spoke. Aunt Velma insisted they take a breakfast plate, and they both munched on bacon as the cornfields rushed by. All his father would say was that he had a surprise for him. His smile was wide, but his eyes were nervous. Jasper decided to ignore the nagging feeling that something was off and stared out the window.

When his father turned off the highway ten miles sooner than usual, his curiosity got the best of him. "Where are we going?"

"You'll see."

Three minutes later, their truck pulled up a narrow driveway next to a small tract house. His father jumped out of the car and pounded on the hood. "We're here."

Jasper slowly climbed out and surveyed the street in confusion. It was lined with tiny houses nearly identical to the one in front of the truck. His mouth fell open with a question, but nothing came out. He just followed his father up the three steps to the front door. Wendell swung it open without knocking.

The front room was sparsely furnished, but Jasper recognized the yellow flowered couch and matching lamp. "What is this?" he asked, turning around in the room as more familiar objects appeared on the walls and shelves.

"Got a new place." His father beamed at him. "Been savin' up a few years. What do you think?"

"It's . . . nice." The smell of cookies baking wafted in from the kitchen. It was followed by the sound of dishes clinking in the sink. His throat tightened. "Dad? Who's here?"

The man's hands were shaking more than usual, but he forced a huge smile. "Go see."

Jasper's feet stayed rooted to the spot as a panic swelled inside him. His father had finally moved on. He'd given up on his mother and replaced her with someone else.

"Wipe that look off your face, boy. There's someone in there that would really like to see you." His father grabbed him by the shoulder and pushed him through the narrow dining room to the kitchen door.

With an unsteady hand, Wendell swung it open. "Look who's here, honey."

A woman with dark hair tied up in a bun stood at the sink with her back to them both. Her thick frame was covered in a plain blue dress. She stiffened and squeezed the counter before turning around.

At first he didn't recognize her, this strange woman who had come to take his mother's place. Her eyes were an empty blue that seemed to look right through him to the far wall. She held on to the edge of the counter with both hands as if to keep from falling.

Then he saw her. A spark of recognition lit up her face for an instant when their eyes finally met. In that hanging second, her chin trembled ever so slightly before her face fell slack again.

"Mom? Is that . . . you?" Jasper backed into the wall behind him. It was her. But it also wasn't. Her body had grown thick and soft. She was shorter, much shorter than she had ever looked before. Her hair was graying at the edges and seemed dead, like a wig. Her shoulders hung from her neck as though they'd given up.

"Jasper," she whispered. "My. You've gotten so big." Her voice was much slower than he remembered. Her mouth smiled but her eyes were drowning in tears.

"I told ya. Didn't I?" Wendell wrapped an arm around Jasper's shoulders and pulled him toward her. "They've been feedin' him real good up at the farm. Haven't they, Son?"

"Y—yes, sir." Jasper could feel the tremble in his father's hand.

His mother nodded and whispered, "Praise Jesus. Just look at you." But she couldn't seem to look at him at all. She turned back to the sink where the dishes were soaking.

"How 'bout them cookies, Althea? Think they might be done?" Wendell said in a voice reserved for small children.

The mother Jasper remembered would have snapped back that she didn't need a dullard like him telling her how to cook a damned batch of cookies. Instead, she said, "I think you might be right."

It was as though she were in some sort of trance as she grabbed the oven mitts and pulled a cookie sheet out of the oven.

"Smells great, honey," his father said with an overly enthusiastic smile. He nudged Jasper and motioned toward her expectantly.

"Sure does," Jasper chimed in a hair too loud.

Wendell hobbled over to the narrow Formica table in the corner and took a seat. "Jasper, go get us some plates and some milk."

"Yes, sir." He took quick stock of the cupboards and found three plates and glasses to set on the table.

His mother was standing at the electric oven, taking cookies off the sheet one at a time. Slow and steady. He opened the refrigerator and pulled out the milk, watching her. Once the cookies were off the sheet, she just stood there as though she were anchored to the stove. Jasper bit his lip hard enough to draw blood to keep his tears from spilling over. It wasn't her at all.

He pulled in a breath and walked over. She kept on staring at the stove. She still had the spatula in her hand. He took it from her gently and set it down on the counter. Her eyes stayed fixed on something far away that he couldn't see. From a locked room inside his head, he could hear the boy he used to be kicking and screaming at the horror of seeing her like this. Steeling himself, he wrapped his arm around her waist and rested his head against her shoulder.

"It's good to see you," he said softly. "It's good to have you home."

CHAPTER 63

The federal government thanks you
for your time, Mrs. Leary.

A week later, Jasper moved into the house on Clausen Street. He opened the door to his own private bedroom and placed his suitcase on the bed. It was the same bag his mother had packed for him two years earlier, only now it was filled with Wayne's hand-me-down overalls and work shirts and one good pair of pants. As he pulled each item out, the smells of the farm came with them. He pressed a shirt to his face, breathing in the hay and fresh-cut barley laced over the deeper aroma of sweat and August sunshine. It smelled like home.

He scanned the store-bought mattress, bureau, and empty bookcase and sank down onto the bed. He'd be able to go back and visit Wayne, Aunt Velma, and Uncle Leo whenever he wanted. His father promised.

Jasper glanced down at the suitcase next to him. He'd unpacked everything but a few books Miss Babcock had given him. *The First Book of Indians* sat on top, with its silly images of wild warriors screaming across the cover. He picked it up along with the others and placed them all on his empty shelf. He'd write Miss Babcock a letter after supper. He'd promised.

All that was left in the suitcase was his mother's necklace.

Your debt is paid, Ogichidaa. You have grown up well, Dr. Whitebird had said after they'd finished rebuilding the clinic. Jasper had spent every spare minute there, volunteering until the job was done. That day, Motega had put the beads in his hand. *Take this back for her. Tell her . . .* Then he just shook his head. The man didn't know what to tell her.

Jasper lifted the heavy beaded medallion off the bottom of his bag and held it in his palm. It had been his mother's favorite. Silent tears fell as he ran a finger over the beads. *Nimaamaa.* He missed her. He missed the woman who had not come back. The woman who wore red shoes and laughed too loud when she drank and cursed when she thought no one could hear.

With the necklace in his hand, he crept down the hall toward her room. She was sleeping. Every day she took a long nap in the afternoon while his father was out doing the shopping or at work. He could hear her snoring softly through the door and pushed it open.

She looked peaceful there on the bed, a pale-blue shadow of her old self. There were several pill bottles on the nightstand. He squinted at them for a moment, trying to read the labels. She still had to see her doctors twice a week, and Jasper wondered, cataloging the pills, if she would ever stop needing them.

He tiptoed past her to the jewelry box on her dresser. It was the same one he'd found spilled out all over the floor in the old apartment. Looking at it, he could see the way his parent's bedroom had been that day—ransacked and strewn with broken lamps and torn clothing. There had been blood on the wall—a policeman's blood. He glanced over at the blank plaster next to him, half expecting to see the stain, then back at her snoring on the bed. There was so much he'd never know or dare to ask.

Jasper pulled open the jewelry chest drawer where the beaded necklace had always lived, next to the flowering broaches and rhinestones she never wore. He placed it gently inside and gave it one last look before sliding the drawer closed. It squeaked.

"Jasper?" a muddled voice asked from the bed. "Jasper, is that you?"

"Sorry, Mom. I was just leaving," he whispered back and hurried to the door. The mother he knew would have killed him for trespassing.

"Don't go." She forced her eyes open for a second, but they rolled about in her head before falling shut again. "There's something . . . something I need to tell you."

He tentatively stepped back toward the bed where she lay. "What is it, Mom?"

"I'm just so . . . so sorry. If anything had happened to you . . ." Tears were leaking from her closed lids. Jumbled words fell from her mouth. "I can't let anything happen to you . . . Not you too. He almost killed you. You should never . . . Stay away from me, Jasper. I'm bad . . . I'm a bad moon . . . You should stay away."

"It's alright," Jasper whispered. "I'm fine. Everything is going to be fine now."

She shook her head and curled up into a ball. "Don't tell . . . don't tell Daddy about him, Jasper. He . . . can't know I did it. I did it . . . He'd never forgive me."

He frowned and scanned her contorted face. "Did what, Mom? What did you do?"

"It was me . . . the gun. It was me . . . I did it." She started to laugh through her tears. "You should have seen the look on his face. He couldn't believe it. When I pulled the trigger. He just couldn't believe it . . . that son of a bitch." She buried her head in the pillow and started sobbing.

Jasper sank down onto the bed. "It's okay. It's over. You did what you had to do. He was hurting you."

"How can you . . . stand me? Stay away . . . far away. I'm bad . . . so bad . . . They didn't believe me . . . No one will ever believe me," she wailed.

"Shh . . . I believe you. He was a bad man."

Her tears wouldn't slow down. "He'll never forgive me. Never, never, never . . ."

Jasper frowned unsure if she was talking about her husband or Grandpa Williams or—

The front door closed three rooms away. His father was home. There'd be hell to pay if he caught him riling her up like this. Jasper rubbed her back, trying to soothe her. "Shh . . . it's okay, Mom. I promise."

She kept crying in her pillow, shaking her head back and forth.

"Jasper?" his father called from the living room. "You home?"

"It's okay, Mom," he whispered in her ear. "He'll forgive you. He will."

She stopped shaking and fell silent.

"What the hell are you doin' in here?" his father hissed from the doorway.

Jasper jumped up from the bed. "She, uh—she was crying in her sleep. I just came to check on her."

His father shoved past him and put a hand on his mother's forehead. She let out a small whimper and started snoring again. After a full minute, he seemed satisfied and yanked Jasper by the arm out of her room. "You aren't supposed to be in there. The doctors said this is a very critical time right now for her recovery. Do you understand? She needs peace and quiet now."

"Yes, sir."

"Now, dammit, this is serious." He pointed a shaking finger at Jasper's nose. "She's been having trouble with these nightmares. She's been sayin' some real horrible things. Things you're not supposed to hear."

Jasper nodded.

"She say anything to you?"

"No, sir." Jasper looked him dead in the eye as he lied. "She didn't say a thing."

"Good." The old man nodded and then shuffled back to the front room to unload the groceries. Jasper watched him go and reminded himself that there had been a time when the man didn't even know how to find the grocery store. He was a gruff nurse, but he was doing all he could.

Jasper turned back to the closed bedroom door. He leaned his forehead against it and could hear her crying again. His mind rifled through all the things he'd wanted to tell her all the months she was gone, through all the things that she had missed. He picked the one that hurt the most to say, "I forgive you, Mom."

She went quiet on the other side of the door.

He kissed his hand and pressed it to the wood, praying his words would heal her. Praying she'd finally come home. His eyes filled up as he repeated it. "I forgive you. I'm okay. You're going to be okay too. Everything is going to be just fine. We're gonna be a family now. I promise. They can't hurt us anymore."

He didn't know if any of it was true, but it didn't matter. She deserved better than the truth. They both did.

CHAPTER 64

I hope you can put this all behind you and get well.
I'm sure your family misses you.

The following weekend, Uncle Leo came to check on his sister, then drove Jasper back to the farm for a visit. It was more of a home to Jasper than the new house, but none of it belonged to him anymore. It never did.

After lunch, he headed out to the back fields toward the faraway stand of trees, with his cousin Wayne trailing behind him.

"What we doin' out here?" Wayne finally asked when they'd reached the ring of charred stones marking the edges of the old farmhouse. Ashes and burnt shingles still dotted the overgrown yard.

Jasper didn't answer. He searched the ground between the trees until he found a large stick. He stepped over the foundation to the spot where the stairs had once led up to the attic. *Who's there?* He didn't bother to bat the whisper away as he began to dig.

After a minute of watching, Wayne picked up his own stick and helped his cousin pry up fieldstones and roots until they'd made a bucket-sized hole in the ground. Jasper pulled his mother's worn leather diary from its place in his pocket.

"Is that the book?" Wayne raised his eyebrows because he knew the answer.

Jasper ran his palm over the cracked leather. He'd carried it with him every day since his uncle had given it back. It had once held the answers to everything, to her. After a moment's hesitation, he placed it in the bottom of the hole and poured a handful of dirt and ashes over the cover. Then another.

When the hole had been firmly packed and healed to the point where no one would even know a book had been buried, Jasper put his hands back in his pockets and felt the empty space where it had been.

Wayne motioned to the tiny grave. "Should we say something?"

Jasper kept his eyes to the ground and shook his head.

"She gonna be alright, you think?"

There was no place for an honest answer, so Jasper gave his cousin a small nod. He didn't know if she would be all right. If she'd recover all the pieces of herself that mattered. If she'd ever laugh again. But she'd given him a smile that morning before he left. She'd touched his cheek and smiled, and for a moment her eyes looked as clear and blue as the sky after a storm. It reminded him of the morning after the tornado tore apart half the state, the way the sun cast a beautiful glow over the fallen trees and flattened houses and bloodied ground as though everything was right with the world.

All he could do was smile back.

ACKNOWLEDGMENTS

Jasper's story was inspired by my father's accounts of life on a dairy farm in 1950s Michigan. The voices of Leonard Williams and Wendell Leary were the voices I heard around the dinner table growing up. Thank you, Dad, for so graciously lending me pieces of your life. I hope this novel does your stories justice. It should be noted that the Tally Ho! joke will always be told better by my father.

Thank you to my husband for holding my hand through every twist and turn in this great adventure. You read each draft of this book from start to finish and never wavered in your support. I wouldn't be a writer if it weren't for your endless patience, advice, and love.

Thank you to my two sons for showing me the inner workings of a boy's mind. Watching you play and fight and grow up together brought Jasper and Wayne to life. Thanks, kiddos, for not burning the house down while Mommy was writing.

Thank you to my agent, Andrea Hurst, for finding a home for this story and guiding me through this next phase of my career. Thank you to Jodi Warshaw, Kjersi Egerdahl, Faith Black Ross, and all my friends at Lake Union and Thomas & Mercer for bringing *The Buried Book* into the world.

Finally, I'd like to thank my extended family, my friends, and my readers for your generous support. A book has no life or meaning without someone wonderful to open it.

AUTHOR'S NOTES

The Buried Book is a work of historical fiction, and as such it contains several true events and places that are used as the backdrop for a fictional story. The following is an index of factual events and places that give historical context to the novel:

Boggs Act—A federal law enacted in 1951 to increase prison sentences for trafficking and use of illicit drugs.

Burtchville, Michigan—A small community located north of Port Huron on the shore of Lake Huron.

Flint-Beecher Tornado—On Monday, June 8, 1953, several tornados touched down in central Michigan, resulting in a reported 116 fatalities, 844 injuries, and millions of dollars in damage.

Major Crimes Act of 1885—This legislation gave the United States federal government sole jurisdiction over major crimes committed on Native American lands and stripped tribes of much of their sovereignty and independence in law enforcement.

Prohibition—In January of 1920, Congress passed the Volstead Act to enforce the Eighteenth Amendment to the United States Constitution, prohibiting the sale and consumption of "intoxicating liquors" and beginning the Prohibition era. In December of 1933, the Twenty-First Amendment repealed the Eighteenth, ending Prohibition.

Prohibition on Indian Reservations—Congress passed a law in 1832 prohibiting alcohol sales and consumption on Indian reservations. This federal law was not repealed until 1953 when jurisdiction over alcohol was reverted back to the Native Americans; however, many reservations do not allow alcohol to this day.

Tally Ho—A roadside tavern on the outskirts of Burtchville.

The Buried Book depicts life in rural Michigan in the early 1950s. My research into this time period relied heavily on first-person interviews. I also visited the Museum of Western Reserve Farms & Equipment at Stone Garden Farm & Village (www.ohiofarmmuseum.com) to experience the feel of an outhouse, a one-room schoolhouse, and working with livestock. Several books gave me additional perspective on farming life, most notably the following:

Hoffbeck, Steven R. *Haymakers: A Chronicle of Five Farm Families (Minnesota)*. St. Paul: Minnesota Historical Society Press, 2000.

Peck, Robert Newton. *A Day No Pigs Would Die*. New York: Laurel-Leaf, 1972.

This novel includes characters from a fictional Native American tribe, the Manitonaaha, living on the fictional Black River Reservation. The language and customs used in the story were largely inspired by my research into Ojibwa tribes. Any errors or omissions are my own, and I sincerely apologize. This story is not intended to disparage or denigrate the vast cultural history or the traditions of any Native American. While the fictional Black River Reservation plays a role in illegal activities, including bootlegging liquor, drug smuggling, and gambling, throughout the story, it is not my intent to implicate any Native American in any wrongdoing. It is my intent to show how a fictional Native American tribe might fall victim to biased and unjust law enforcement and triumph over adversity in the end.

The difficult legal issues surrounding law enforcement on Native American lands are well documented. In my research, I read several works on this subject including the following:

Crane-Murdoch, Sierra. "On Indian Land, Criminals Can Get Away with Almost Anything." *The Atlantic*, February 22, 2013.

Bureau of Indian Affairs Law Enforcement Services. "Indian Law Enforcement History." Available at www.tribalinstitute.org/download/Indian%20Law%20Enforcement%20History.pdf. Accessed December 12, 2014.

Erdrich, Louise. *The Round House*. New York: Harper Perennial, 2012.

ABOUT THE AUTHOR

D.M. Pulley lives just outside Cleveland, Ohio, with her husband, two sons, and two dogs. She is a Professional Engineer who specializes in rehabbing historic structures as well as conducting forensic investigations of building failures. Pulley's structural survey of an abandoned building in Cleveland formed the basis for her debut novel, *The Dead Key*.